WASTED

RESOURCE

By

STEVEN PREECE

Bestselling author of AMONGST THE MARINES

ISBN 978 1 84914 095 9

This book was created from the author's imagination. Any
similarities with person's living or dead are purely coincidental.

About the author:

Steven Preece served in the Royal Marines from 1983 until 1990.
Since then he has forged a successful career in IT and currently
works as a Project Manager for a large corporate bank. He lives in
Hartlepool and is a black belt in Ninjutsu. This is his debut novel.

In memory of my brother, Michael and my father, James.

'You're always only ever a mere thought away!'

With thanks to my fellow author and mentor, Ray Watson.

'Your guidance has been invaluable'

Other books by this author:

Amongst The Marines

Always a Marine

PROLOGUE

Trained soldiers have a repertoire of fighting skills and specialist training that they use in dangerous and hostile situations. When they leave the armed forces, these skills are no longer of value to society and become a 'wasted resource.'

Some former service personnel experience problems when moving on from life in the military, such as homelessness, alcoholism, PTSD, depression and even misuse of their specialist military skills within organised crime and terrorist activities.

This story portrays some of those issues and the harsh reality of the adaptation to civvy-street of four former soldiers, with their specialist skills being used to the detriment of society, rather than to continue to protect it!

Chapter One

Moonlight pierced through an overcast sky, splaying shadows around the gloomy entrance of a derelict building in Liverpool. Gusts of wind were rattling the secured doors and blowing rain down onto several homeless people sheltering there.

Spike's stubbly face poked out from his tattered, wet sleeping bag. He was flushed and desperately in need of warmth. He hunched his broad shoulders and squeezed the material tightly around his neck, unintentionally forcing water to seep through onto his clothing. He rolled his eyes and gazed up at the damaged canopy overhanging the entrance to the building.

'It's going to be a long cold night,' he rasped to a frail old man lying next to him.

The man was weak and suffering from hypothermia. He frowned and nodded his head as the rain bounced off his face. He shook uncontrollably in the unforgiving cold and quietly closed his eyes. His body fell limp and his final breath dissipated into the freezing air, as his tormented spirit was set free.

It was an arduous life living on the streets amongst strangers. Keeping warm and dry was as tough a challenge as finding food, but ironically, alcohol was never too difficult to come-by. Spike had heard all kinds of reasons why people ended up living like this. Yet some preferred it, choosing to cut away from a normal everyday lifestyle.

He sighed heavily, tucking his head down out of the elements. Spike did not know the dead man and was unflustered by his death. It was a sight he had seen many times before when serving as a Royal Marine Commando during the second Gulf war in 2002. He was an Assault Engineer then, highly skilled and experienced in the handling and use of explosives. Two years after the war he had completed nine years service and chose to leave. Sadly, his move into civvy-street had not worked out for him. His once-muscular body was almost skeletal and his short, brown hair was shoulder length and matted with grease and dirt. His memory had deteriorated too, leaving him uncertain as to how he had ended up living this way.

His sleeping bag succumbed to the torrential rain, rendering it useless.

'Balls to this,' he said aloud. 'I am going to find somewhere warm to sleep tonight.'

He pushed his head up out of his partially unzipped bag and set eyes on a man dressed in a black padded jacket and woollen hat. He was rifling through the old man's clothing.

'Hey! Leave him alone. Take your hands out of his pockets now!' he snarled at the stranger, whilst struggling to get his arms free from the inside of his own soggy bag.

'Piss off and mind your own business!' the tall thief snarled, counting the money he held in his hand. 'He's dead. It's of no use to him.'

Spike struggled to free himself. 'Put it back you thieving bastard!' he growled.

'I said piss off and mind your own business!' The thief punched Spike hard in the face.

The blow made a heavy thudding noise; his nose crunching under the man's fist. Blood dripped from his nostrils into his mouth. He scrunched his face up and recoiled in fury. His fiery temper exploded as his arms finally tore free. Spike lunged at the thief but stumbled clumsily onto the floor with his feet still entangled in the bag.

The stranger made his exit turning and running off into the distance. He fiddled with his pocket, pushing some money inside and securing it.

Spike picked himself up and gave chase along a deserted road away from the suburb. He sprinted fast and was soon closing right behind him, struggling to maintain the pace. His lungs were almost bursting and a growing tightness in his diaphragm forced him to stop. He held his chest with both hands, gasping for air. He paced around with his hands on his hips, dressed in a green parka with a shoelace hanging down from his waist securing his soaked jeans. He could feel his heart pounding and concentrated on steadying his breathing. Blood continued to trickle down his face and dripped onto his black trainers. He gripped his bleeding nose and threw a clot down, landing on his shoe. He kicked out flicking it onto the nearby waste ground.

The blustery rain had eased and a damaged street light afforded improved visibility. Spike heard someone behind him and spun around. The thief lunged at him with a broken floorboard, but Spike slipped the blow and used the momentum gained to grab his adversary by the throat. The man twisted around, seized Spike's wrist and effortlessly threw him to the ground. Spike twisted free and expertly reversed the position to regain his feet. The man rolled forward breaking Spike's hold and equally found his footing in one fluid movement.

'Shit!' Spike gasped. 'Are you some sort of martial arts nut?'

The thief stood in a boxing stance, readying himself. He paused. 'No. I'm an ex-marine; mate and I know how to handle myself. If you want some more, come and get it.'

'No, wait!' Spike panted. 'I'm a marine too. I really am. I'm an ex Boot Neck the same as you?'

'Are you serious or is this just bullshit to get me to drop my guard?'

'I'm deadly serious, mate. My name's Spike. What's yours?"

'Bungy. My name is Bungy.'

Spike recognized the name from his service days. Bungy was a nickname given to marines who had a surname of Williams. The two men relaxed and moved closer. Spike held his hand out and they shook hands, lightly at first and then more sincere. Bungy then removed his hat and ran his fingers through his short, dark hair, brushing it across his forehead in a parting. A nearby street lamp allowed them to see they were of similar age, late twenties.

'Why did you steal the old man's money?' Spike asked, still seething about it.

'He was dead,' Bungy coughed, clearing his throat. 'The money was no good to him any more. I'm hungry. I haven't eaten anything for days. You know what it's like living on the streets. We have to scavenge to survive.'

'Yes, I suppose that's fair enough,' Spike conceded.

Rain started to teem down heavily again and a gusty wind made them shiver, mercilessly penetrating their saturated clothing.

'Come on Spike; let's find somewhere warm to sleep tonight. I'm bloody freezing. I feel like shit and my body is shaking with this damn rain and cold.'

'Okay, mate,' Spike answered. 'Have you got a sleeping bag?'

'Yes, it's in a doorway just a short distance from yours.'

'Okay, let's go and get them and shelter somewhere.'

Both men returned to the area where they had previously met and noticed that an ambulance had arrived. Its rotating blue light illuminated the doorway whilst the medical crew were busy lifting the corpse onto a stretcher. A police officer gave them a lift to a drop-in centre and wished them well.

'This is better than being outside in the cold all the time,' Bungy said, holding a hot soup.

'Bloody is,' Spike nodded. His cane chair creaking as he leaned back gazing at the bare light bulb suspended from the ceiling in the refuge. 'It's bizarre now, but after I left the marines I told myself that I would never willingly be cold again. Thinking about it now I feel like a hypocrite.'

'Which Commando Unit did you serve with, Spike?' Bungy asked, sticking to the common subject.

'42 Commando and I specialized in explosives as an Assault Engineer. What about you?'

Bungy's bushy eyebrows lifted. His sunken cheeks were glowing red, along with an angry looking scar spanning the width of his dimpled chin. He managed a smile.

'I was a Mountain Leader and worked mainly as a sniper during both Gulf wars. I killed more than my fair share of people. Many of them just fell like puppets with their strings cut.' His smile widened as his thoughts drifted off recalling how content he was with his life then. 'I wish I could turn the clock back. I absolutely loved being a marine.'

'Yes me too,' Spike beamed. 'I need a drink. How much money did you take from the old man's pockets?'

'I've got eighty pounds and twenty pence.'

'Bloody hell! The old codger told me he was broke!' Spike grinned. 'That'll buy us a few bottles of plonk to share.'

Bungy's face twisted and he shrugged his shoulders. 'No. Let's keep it and use it to get ourselves out of the gutter.'

'Why should we?' Spike sneered, his eyes widening in disapproval. He craved alcohol and pondered about purchasing some. His thoughts turned to the hot soup. Its warmth comforted him. I really need a drink, he thought. But maybe Bungy is right. Perhaps it would be good to get off the streets. I could get a good wash and a haircut too.

'Yes, okay,' he nodded. 'Let's buy a couple of beers and drink to it!'

Chapter Two

Beast had been working as a debt-collector for a number of years and this was just another one of the calls on his list that day. Generally, he took his profession seriously and worked hard at maintaining a huge, powerful physique that caused heads to turn when people caught sight of him. He was a callous, brutal man who would never hesitate to resort to violence when collecting for his employer. Prior to taking up this line of work, he had served in the Royal Marines for fifteen years, intentionally joining the elite fighting force to kill people. He saw active service in Cyprus, Northern Ireland and both gulf wars. Eventually, he opted to settle down from the conflicts and chose to specialize as a Physical Training Instructor (PTI). This was something he enjoyed, ensuring that the marines remained at a peak of physical fitness. After fulfilling his ambition, he had left to seek a new career in civvy-street.

'See you tonight babe,' he smiled lovingly, reaching over and brushing his wife's hair out of her eyes before pecking her on the cheek.

'Have a nice day,' she replied, waving to him as he climbed into his car and headed off for work.

On the way, he occasionally stopped every now and again, pulling into parking lay-bys' to check the scribbled directions. Eventually he arrived outside a remote house somewhere in the countryside. He stopped the car and applied the handbrake, making it creak loudly as he cranked it into the last notch. He briefly glanced at himself in the rear-view mirror, staring into his dark bulging eyes and combing his bushy moustache with his forefinger and thumb. He turned the car engine off, routinely killing his headlights prior to stepping outside.

It was a cold, dark morning and snowflakes were falling lightly from the overcast sky and settling on the ground. He pushed his hands inside the pockets of his black leather jacket and sniffed in a deep breath of cool fresh air. It was freezing so he briefly hunched his broad shoulders up towards his neck and pulled out a black woollen hat, tugging it down neatly over his baldhead. The fresh snow crunched under his feet, as he stepped away from the car and cautiously made his way up an overgrown garden path towards the house. He paused as he approached it.

It was an aged building, probably built before the Second World War. Its windows appeared to be the originals, single-glazed and framed in wood. A new paint job was long over-due; the existing was flaky with signs of decay.

Once he reached the house, he stopped opposite the entrance porch looking all around and searched for signs of human activity. There was no one visible so he banged hard with his fist several times on the solid wooden door. It rattled loosely under the forceful blows, echoing inside. He glanced around again and patiently waited for an answer.

Suddenly, somebody began to unlock the door from the inside. It creaked open and a short, stocky man cautiously peered around it. 'Hello can I help you?' he asked politely, whilst gingerly looking around beyond Beast before his eyes settled on his caller.

'Are you Mr. Paul Barclay?' Beast asked him with a fixed stare boring deep into his pupils.

'Yes I am. What do you want?' he retorted, stepping into full view.

Beast walked forward into the doorway and mercilessly grabbed him by the throat with one hand. He squeezed tightly on his windpipe, half choking him.

'You owe my boss five hundred quid and I want it now or else I'm going to break one or maybe even two of your debt-ridden limbs,' he growled in a threatening voice. 'Don't tell me you haven't got any money, because I haven't got any patience!' he continued.

Paul Barclay fought hard to pull Beast's hands from his throat but found that he was far too powerful for him. The colour started to drain from his face and his legs became weak and unsteady. For a moment, he felt that he was going to die. Beast released his grip, allowing him to cough and splutter desperately fighting hard to fill his depleted lungs with air.

'Can I give you a cheque?' he croaked, still trying to recover from his ordeal.

Beast viciously swung the back of his hand hard into his face, making him wince. The forceful blow made a loud smacking noise on impact and caused him to stumble backwards and onto the floor.

'Give me the money now,' Beast growled, looking down at him. He grabbed Paul tightly by his clothing, shaking him rigorously.

Paul was understandably terrified, his heart pounding like a forge-hammer immersing him in fear and causing him to urinate himself. The urine formed a dark patch on his pressed, cream trousers.

'Give me the money now!' Beast demanded again.

'Yes, yes, I'll get the money,' Paul cried, tears streaming down the cheeks of his worried face.

He pushed himself up from the floor and walked into an adjoining room, followed closely by the ruthless debt collector. He felt nervous and badly shaken and searched around in a sideboard drawer, pulling a small tin from it. His hand visibly trembled as he pushed it inside the container producing a bundle of fifty-pound notes from it, which he offered to Beast. 'There's six hundred pounds there,' he quivered holding the money out in his sweaty palm.

'Please take all of it and leave me alone. I don't want any more trouble.'

Beast snatched the cash from his hand and counted it. He brusquely nodded his head once to acknowledge the sum and stuffed the extra one hundred pounds into a separate pocket. He felt content. He had gotten what he'd come for and an extra bonus too. Then he turned away leaving through the open door without looking back. Outside, he casually jumped into his car, revved the engine a couple of times and drove away.

He drove for 15 miles or so and arrived at another remote location. This time he chose to park his car out of sight down a disused country lane and walked for a mile or so to another house to collect more debts. This was in accordance with instructions from his employer.

The sun was shining brightly as he got out of his car and the fallen snow had almost melted, apart from the odd patch here and there. Beast blew into his hands as he walked briskly, then rubbing them together keeping them warm. He stopped opposite a luxurious three-storey executive home, his keen eyes scanning the surroundings. It looked a year maybe two years old, at the most, with a keystone above the front door and a temple column either side of a protruding canopy.

As he walked up a red brick driveway, he noticed a net curtain move slightly and saw someone peering through the window towards him. He stopped at the door and pressed the doorbell, pausing for a minute or two to wait for an answer. The net curtain moved again and he initially pretended not to notice the person who was observing him. He squinted twisting his face up and decided to walk towards the window. The curtain slowly dropped to its original position. Beast tried his best to focus through the glass pane but the net curtain was too dense and obscured his view. He saw something move in the room behind it but could not be sure of whom or what it was. He turned and hurried back towards the front entrance, where without a second thought he forcibly kicked the door inwards. It crashed open slamming against a wall and shattering its frosted-glass pane all over the polished wooden floor. There was a short period of silence, after which he heard somebody moving around in the hallway. He stepped into the entrance and cautiously walked through to the interior. A Doberman Pincher came into view. It was barking wildly and bounding towards him at speed. It growled incessantly with saliva dripping from its snarling mouth. He tensed when it neared and breathed in deeply as he saw it leap into the air towards him. The hound gnashed its teeth intently and then opened its jaws wide to tear into the flesh of the intruder. Beast lashed out, punching the dog hard in the throat with a blow so lethal that it crushed its windpipe. Its head flopped to one side leading the way for its lifeless body to slump down with a thud on the glass littered floor.

'You bastard!' A man's voice called out from behind him. 'You've killed my dog.'

13

He turned around and saw a tall, skinny middle-aged man standing in the entrance hall opposite him. He was holding a double-barrelled shotgun that was pointing towards him.

'What do you want? Why have you killed my dog?' he asked, anxiously looking over the rim of his spectacles at the dead dog's carcass. 'I'm going to report you for cruelty.'

'I'm looking for someone called Perry Benshaw,' Beast replied with an angry expression. 'Are you Perry?'

'Yes I am. What do you want?' he sneered, feeling annoyed about the damage to his door and more importantly about the loss of his much-loved family pet.

'You owe my boss three grand and I've come to collect it.'

'You won't be collecting anything from me today,' Perry answered confidently. 'Because I'll blow you to kingdom come if I have to.'

'Have you got the balls to pull the trigger?' Beast asked appearing unflustered.

Perry stood firm with the shotgun. He kept it pointing menacingly towards his unwelcome visitor and carefully flicked off the safety catch. His hands were trembling slightly and sweat dripped down his furrowed brow. Suddenly, his eyes opened wide and he gulped fearfully after watching Beast put his mouth over the end of the two loaded barrels.

'Stop shaking and pull the fucking trigger,' Beast told him, his voice travelling down the length of the weapon.

'What?' Perry exclaimed feeling totally bemused with the situation.

'I said, pull the fucking trigger.'

'I..., I.....,' was all that Perry could say.

Beast moved his mouth off the end of the gun and ripped it out of Perry's grasp, surging forward and mercilessly hitting him hard in the face with the wooden butt.

Perry's screech rent the morning air. He fell backwards and down onto the floor. Blood dripped from his nose and he felt sick inside. He touched his nostrils with his fingers and stared at the thick red blood on them. Then he heard a click and looked up, fearing for his life.

Beast was standing over him, pointing the weapon at the middle of his forehead. 'You should have killed me you spineless bastard,' he snarled grinning. 'Now give me the three grand I've come for or I'm going to blow your stupid head off.'

Perry was petrified and could not stop himself from retching and trying not to be physically sick.

'I..., I haven't got any money,' he whimpered. 'Honestly I haven't. Please, please don't kill me.'

'Have you got a car? Have you got a bloody car?' Beast repeated after a short silence, pushing the double shotgun barrels hard against one of Perry's cheekbones.

Perry struggled to answer. He feared the worst and was in no doubt that this ruthless man would kill him.

'I....., I...., I.... yes I have a new BMW parked in the garage,' he eventually stammered. 'The keys, the keys are on the fireplace. Please, please take the car,' he pleaded, pointing towards a set of keys on top of an old oak fireplace.

'Fine,' Beast grinned contently, believing that the value of the car far exceeded the sum owed.

He pulled the shotgun away from Perry's face and broke the weapon open unloading both barrels. The live cartridges ejected and fell with a clatter onto the floor. He bent down and picked them up, pushing them inside one of his pockets. He placed the weapon against the wall and stamped on it heavily, damaging it before throwing it down away from Perry. He stepped past him and grabbed the car keys from the nearby fireplace. He was soon outside unlocking the garage door where he climbed into a red BMW, reversed it and drove off.

Perry let out a huge sigh of relief when he got up from the floor, straightening his damaged spectacles. He brushed himself down and looked into the distance seeing his car being driven away. I'm not worried about my BMW, he thought. I will report it stolen and will claim for it through my insurance policy.

Chapter Three

Barry sat gazing at an uninteresting programme on the television. It was early in the morning and leading up to the time that he routinely sets off for work. Uneasy rumbling noises danced around in his stomach and his diaphragm ached with indigestion. His discomfort was not caused by illness, but more so from drinking excessively the previous night.

There were never any half measures when he drank alcohol or when he did anything else for that matter. He drank for one reason only and that was to get drunk. He was an astute man, with short brown hair, a yellow complexion and a square chin. He was just over six-feet tall and powerfully built.

Although he'd been out of the marines for six years, he still managed to maintain a good level of physical fitness. He did this to keep his body weight down to an acceptable level rather than for any other reason. Deep down, he still missed the marine lifestyle immensely and in particular; he missed the comradeship that he once shared with his colleagues. He had served for twelve years, initially specializing as a Platoon Weapons expert and later as a fast-car driver working on covert operations. He had originally planned to spend the whole of his life in the marines, but his constant long periods of absence on tours of duty abroad put too much of a strain on his marriage. Eventually, his wife gave him an ultimatum that forced him to make a decision about his chosen career. It was either the marines or their relationship. Reluctantly, he left the marines for family reasons. His marriage was too important to him and he loved his wife, Diane very much.

Following his departure from the military, civilian life was rewarding. He worked as a shift manager in a local steel mill, supervising pipe production personnel. He found the job boring and mundane, but the lucrative salary made it tolerable. It was good enough to keep him and his wife in a nice cosy detached house with two expensive cars parked on the driveway.

Later that day after finishing work, he sat patiently waiting in a dentist's reception room casually browsing through some of the available magazines. There was nothing interesting to read in them, but he did find some pleasure in viewing the many pictures of scantily clad women.

'Mr. Broadhurst. Mr. Barry Broadhurst,' a young and attractive dental nurse called out, catching Barry's attention.

'That's me,' he smirked at the other customers, raising his hand.

He stood up from the chair he had been slouching in and casually followed the nurse, briefly eyeing her shapely buttocks as they entered the treatment room.

'Hello Mr. Broadhurst. How are you today?' a smartly dressed male dentist asked him.

'I'm fine thanks but I'm running late,' he responded abruptly, climbing onto the treatment chair. 'Can you be as quick as possible please?'

'What age are you Mr. Broadhurst?' the nurse asked eagerly wanting to complete a computer record with Barry's personal details on it.

'I'm thirty six but I thought I was going to turn thirty seven due to the excessive amount of time I've been sat in your waiting room. Can you be quick please, I'm already late.'

'Yes of course Mr. Broadhurst,' the dentist intervened. 'No problem.'

Barry continued to make himself comfortable in the chair and the dentist pressed a button to recline it. It was Friday afternoon and nearly five O'clock. The dentist felt pleased that his last customer of the day had asked him to hurry up. He too was running late and wanted to leave soon.

The nurse placed a plastic bib around Barry's neck, covering his upper half and shuffled a pair of plastic spectacles over his eyes. He stared at her, then at the light above him keeping his eyes fixed there instead of making constant eye contact. The Dentist began his work looking around inside his

18

patient's mouth with a small stainless steel mirror. His client's teeth were in good order and he was confident that he could quickly complete the routine hygiene treatment. His small Air Rotor whirred, grinding away the unwanted plaque from between Barry's teeth. At the same time, the nurse held an aspirator in his mouth.

Barry stared at the Dentist briefly, smelling his bad breath. It made the hairs on his nose tingle. He's the one who needs a bloody hygiene job, he thought, looking back towards the light.

Within a short space of time the bottom teeth were clear of plaque so the Dentist progressed to the top front teeth, feeling pleased with his speedy progress. Unfortunately, some of the plaque resisted the powerful spinning tool. 'This is awkward,' the dentist sighed and leaned more of his body weight onto the Air Rotor to try to loosen it. If I can only just get rid of this last piece of plaque, he thought. He increased the pressure. The tool ground heavily against the hard plaque and its motor groaned.

Barry felt uncomfortable during this process and became extremely tense, lying motionless in the chair. He knew it would all be over within a matter of minutes so he tried hard to relax until it was finished.

Just then, the Dentist's efforts met with success and he forced the reluctant plaque to give way. Contrary to his intentions, the pressure he had applied allowed the rotating instrument to continue on a downward spiral penetrating the surface of his helpless client's gum.

Barry winced as the tool viciously tore away at his gum and he could feel blood oozing out from the painful wound it had created. Excruciating pains began engulfing him thrashing around his head like bolts of lightning. He spontaneously reacted, snatching the Air Rotor from the dentist's hand and hurled it across the room. The trauma caused his mind to flash back to the conflict on the streets of Northern Ireland, where he saw himself on foot patrol down the infamous Falls Road and caught up in an ambush. There was unrelenting firepower raining down onto his position. It was coming from terrorist forces. His mind began to race amongst the chaos that ensued, as rounds began ripping into the bodies of his marine colleagues who were caught out in the open. Blood was everywhere. Both fear and adrenalin were screaming through his veins. It was either him or them. He had to act fast. 'Come on!' he screamed aloud, firing his weapon as the pain worsened. As far as Barry was concerned, a bullet had just ricocheted into his jaw inflicting the searing pain he was enduring. His military training took over and he reacted on impulse. 'Fucking die!' he bellowed with a twisted face and his tonsils vibrating. He saw a terrorist running close towards him, reaching for a bloodstained rifle on the ground. He lunged forward and grabbed the weapon hurling it away out of reach. He followed up by diving onto the terrorist, knocking him down onto the floor and forcefully holding him there. Sweat dripped profusely down his forehead and cheeks as he squeezed the trigger of his pistol to kill the man. Strangely, to his astonishment his finger moved through fresh air! He paused and blankly looked at his hand. It was empty! Why aren't they dying? He thought, staring at the people in front of him. He could feel the blood pouring from his mouth again, dripping down his chin onto his clothes. Barry focused on other oncoming terrorists who were just metres away. He had no weapon to return fire so the situation was grim. It was a close quarter battle now and things were getting desperate. 'Fucking die!' he yelled again, simultaneously grasping the man who had shot him, tightly by the throat. He sensed a growing submission from his opponent who was yielding and at his mercy. He had to act now and kill him and he needed to be quick about it too. His fingers sunk into the soft flesh of the terrorist's throat. He began squeezing it hard with all his might. He knew what it was like; he had done it so many times before. War is a dirty game. Barry had often stated this to his civilian friends, but it was doubtful that any of them really understood him.

'Please, no,' the petrified dentist croaked, fighting desperately to breathe.

A sudden rush of blood cleared the misguided thoughts in Barry's head. The dark memories of Northern Ireland were gone, allowing him to see the almost blue face of the helpless dentist crying beneath him.

'Shit, what have I done?' he gasped.

He relaxed his grip allowing the dentist to cough and splutter, tearfully breathing in big mouthfuls of air with saliva gurgling in his gaping mouth.

'Please can you leave us?' the young nurse cried, standing terrified and motionless against the surgery wall.

Barry paused again to gather his confused thoughts. He initially thought he had just imagined the nurse and the dentist, so he looked around for some cover to take him out of the line of fire. His vision cleared, allowing him to realise that he was not under attack as assumed. Everything became calm so he stood up and stared in disbelief at the dentist who was still trying hard to breathe. Shit! What's happened? He thought, removing the glasses and bib! What have I done?

'I'm so sorry,' the dentist said tearfully. 'I was rushing things. I didn't mean to hurt you.'

'I'm sorry too,' Barry said, staring emptily at the dentist and then at the young, petrified nurse, who was still braced against the wall. 'I'm really sorry. I don't know what came over me.'

A minute or so later, Barry paid his bill and walked away from the dental premises. He sucked the mouth wound that had now sealed itself and spat out the last piece of congealed blood. He was shaking his head in disbelief; unsettled about the flashback and his apparent lack of control. He stared at his hands with his palms facing him. They were damp with sweat.

Balls to this, he thought. I need a couple of beers to calm myself down. My head is throbbing like mad.

To fulfil his need, he headed straight for the nearest public house, just a mile or so away from where he lived. It was quiet inside when he arrived. The gloomy bar had only a few customers. This made little difference because he usually sat on his own anyway. He had decided some years before not to let anyone get too friendly with him. Generally, the calibre of friends he had found since leaving the marines were not the same as the ones with whom he had served. Those were irreplaceable colleagues, whom he trusted with his life.

He perched himself on a stool at the end of the bar, listening to the soft music that played in the background giving the place an air of tranquillity. He greedily gulped down his first couple of beers in as many minutes. He looked at his hands again, feeling settled because they had finally stopped sweating.

21

'You must be thirsty,' a young barmaid commented amiably, before passing him his fourth pint. 'Is it a woman that you're drowning your sorrows over?'

'No it isn't, love. It's the bloody dentist's chair.'

'That's similar I suppose,' she chortled. 'Sometimes a relationship can be like pulling teeth.'

Barry nodded and smiled at her. She turned around and started rearranging some beer glasses on the shelving arrangement behind the bar. She has a good figure, he thought, I could do some serious stuff with that. Mind you, she also has a face resembling a smacked arse! He grinned broadly staring at the empty tables, his mind drifting, pondering about his days in the military. He recalled the names of some of the men he had served with and thought about the hardships they had endured together.

'I'll give you a penny for your thoughts,' the barmaid said softly, running her hand through her short dark hair and then leaning over the bar to pass him a freshly pulled pint.

She smiled at him with interest in her eyes, pushing her breasts out so that they were protruding and visible through her partially fastened pink shirt.

'Huh what?' Barry muttered when his deep concentration was interrupted.

'It's time for last orders now. But seeing that everybody else has left, you can have another pint after this one if you want.'

'Thanks,' he slurred.

It was his sixth pint but the quantity did not really matter to him. Evidently, though the alcohol was taking its effect because the barmaid's face did not seem so unattractive anymore! 'Where's your boyfriend tonight? Is he taking you home?' He bluntly asked, staring into her piercing blue eyes.

'No he isn't,' she flirted, pleased that he had finally taken an interest in her. 'We live together, but he's working away from home at the moment. My name is Susan. What's yours?'

'Oh I see. It's Barry. My name's Barry.'

'You served in the Army didn't you? You're a very fit guy. I've seen you out running lots of times.'

'I was in the Marines sweetheart, not the Army.'

'Isn't it all the same thing?'

'No it isn't, but I suppose that's not important to me now.'

The barmaid fancied him and she felt fairly-certain that he was interested in her too. She had seen him peering at her as she moved around cleaning the empty tables, flaunting her self as she went.

'Are you married?' she asked, hoping he would say no.

'That depends.'

'On what?'

'On whether or not you like married men!'

She didn't answer. She walked back behind the bar and pulled him a final pint of beer, cashed up and closed the tills for the evening. She was excited and certain that he would say yes if she asked him to walk her home. It was a direct approach. She knew that, but he seemed to be the direct type anyway. It's now or never, she thought.

'Can you see your drink off please? I'm locking up now. It's very dark outside and I live in the same direction as you. Will you walk along with me? I'll certainly feel a lot safer.'

Barry drank the dregs of his last pint and looked at her over the rim of his empty glass. Susan was making it easy for him. Why not? He thought, Diane will never know!

They left the public house and walked hand in hand for a short distance along some quiet streets until they were close to Susan's home. The area was unmistakably a rough part of town. Smatterings of graffiti offended the surrounding walls and professionally painted murals covered the sides of terraced houses. Some of these buildings even had one or two windows boarded up with tin sheeting. They looked like slums but to the inhabitants it was nothing out of the ordinary.

They arrived at the house, stopped walking and spontaneously faced each other. Barry looked at her through glazed eyes and raised a smile. His body language more or less signalled her to move in for a passionate kiss, which she did fleetingly, pressing her body against his.

'Are you coming in for a coffee?' she asked.

'Yes, that would be nice,' he accepted.

They stepped in through a damaged entrance door, which had flimsy masking tape covering a crack that spanned the length of a small centred window. The living room was opposite, where a single lamp seated on a small coffee table dimly lit the cheap furnishings. A patterned carpet covered the floor and the surrounding wallpaper was off-white caused by years of cigarette smoke. The curtains were old and discoloured and the occupying furniture looked as if it was either very dated or possibly second hand. A dual bar electric fire also gave off some limited light, but produced very little heat to warm them after coming in from the cold night air.

Barry sat down and gladly accepted the hot cup of coffee that Susan poured from an already simmering coffee peculator. He took a couple of sips from it, but then began to feel uneasy because he could hear somebody else in the house moving around upstairs.

'I thought you said your boyfriend was working away?'

'He is. That's my parents who are upstairs. They're staying with me for a couple of days. Don't worry they won't come down. Honestly they won't,' she finished and kissed him passionately once again.

'Susan? Susan?' an elderly man shouted down the stairs. 'Who's that with you?'

'It's just a friend dad. That's all,' she tactfully responded.

'It's getting late, Susan. Is he leaving soon?'

'Yes dad, in a short while.'

'Do you want to have sex with me?' she whispered excitedly in Barry's ear, unconcerned about her parents being close-by.

Barry nodded, although he wasn't really sure if this was what he wanted. Susan keenly locked onto him with another warm wet kiss and started fumbling with the button on his dark blue jeans.

'Susan has he gone yet?' the old man shouted down again.

She unwillingly withdrew from kissing Barry, sighing and rolling her eyes desperately hoping he would not lose interest in her.

'Yes dad he's gone,' she lied, hoping that he would believe her. Her fingers were crossed and she strongly wanted her father to be quiet and to go back to bed.

'That's good Susan,' he retorted in a more gentle tone. 'Bring the bucket up; your mother wants a shit!'

Barry fought hard to control his laughter at the man's extreme bluntness. He held a nearby cushion over his mouth to console himself whilst Susan raced into the kitchen. She reappeared seconds later rushing upstairs with a plastic bucket in her hand that was half-full of water. He cupped his hands over his face and exhaled, running them down his cheeks. What the hell am I doing here? He thought, fuck this I'm going home.

Outside he sucked in a deep breath of cold air and laughed aloud to himself, briskly walking away with the vision of Susan and the bucket tickling his broad sense of humour.

'Hi darling,' Diane smiled with a warm glow on her pretty face, as Barry entered through the front door of their home.

'Hi, Diane. It's been one of those days again!'

'What do you mean?' she asked curiously, pulling her short skirt down over her shapely, tanned legs.

'I've had a busting headache all day and the loud clanging noise of steel being manufactured nearly pierced my ear drums through my ear defenders. And please don't ask about my appointment at the dentist!'

'Don't kid your self Barry,' Diane raised her eyebrows. 'It's not work at all. It's the excessive amount of booze you keep drinking. You use anything and everything as an excuse to drink beer and you blame everything else when you suffer the after effects of it.'

'No I don't,' he grimaced knowing she was right. 'It is the noise at work. Anyway, its not as if I'm an overweight fat bastard because of the booze is it?'

'You're pissed again and you're late,' she frowned. 'I've put your meal in the bin.'

'Sorry sweetheart,' he said softly, wisely opting to back down rather than starting an argument that he could not possibly win. 'It won't happen again. I promise you,' he slurred, staggering off to bed.

Diane shook her head and stared aimlessly at the television. She loved her husband immensely but he did have some terrible habits that she found hard to tolerate.

The following morning was Saturday and Barry rose early. He grinned at Diane as she lay half-asleep in bed and flexed his six-pack stomach muscles. He washed in the bathroom prior to pulling on his tracksuit and heading downstairs into the garage for one of his regular keep-fit sessions. He switched on the light and then his CD player, playing the kind of music that was popular during the days of his military career. He always did this. It reminded him of some of the very best days of his life. His punch bag, which hung down from the rafters, thudded repeatedly under the heavy blows he threw at it using both hands and feet. He maintained this form of work out for at least twenty minutes, using it to sweat the residual effects of the beer out of his system. Next, he moved onto pumping the weights on his small multi-gym methodically moving through a series of different exercises, ensuring all muscle groups were being pushed to their limit. He felt good inside. His fitness training was his way of releasing tension and coping with life's ups and downs.

Afterwards, he took a cold shower and changed his clothes; sitting down at the breakfast table to eat a delicious cooked breakfast that Diane had prepared.

'Judith, from next door, has invited us for a meal and a few beers tomorrow night Barry, and I've accepted the invitation. Is that okay with you?' she asked.

'No it bloody isn't,' he grumbled. 'I'm not sitting there watching her pathetic excuse of a husband staring at you all night. He's a dickhead.'

'Come now dear, he doesn't do that,' she said carefully trying to convince Barry otherwise.

'He bloody does. John's eyes are all over you. His wife is an ugly fat boiler and I'm absolutely certain that he's got his eye on you.'

'Don't be silly, darling. He doesn't, he hasn't,' she insisted, reaching for a cup of tea and casually walking through into the living room to watch the television.

Barry exhaled deeply. He felt bemused and continued to eat what was left of his meal. He grabbed a four-pack of beer and sat down in the living room next to Diane, where he quenched his thirst. His idle thoughts drifted towards John next door. He did not like him and only tolerated him because their wives were good friends. I hate that little shit-bag, he thought. If he goes anywhere near my wife I'm going to beat him to a pulp.

Several weeks later, whilst Barry was at work, Diane was tending their back garden. It was a nice warm day and the flowerbeds were badly in need of weeding. She wore a low cut tee shirt that allowed a breeze to blow over her protruding breasts, and a small pair of sports shorts that clung tightly to her buttocks. She knelt down, using a sponge-mat to protect her knees from being scratched by the small stones in the soil.

John, from next door, was also routinely tending his garden. He had taken the day off work to complete the never-ending job-list that his wife had left for him, whilst she was out shopping for the day with her sister. The warm, humid weather caused sweat to trickle down his forehead so he stood up from the flowerbeds and wiped his brow with a clean handkerchief pulled from his pocket. He browsed across the top of the garden fence and noticed Diane tending her flowers; focusing on her shapely buttocks.

Wow, he thought, running one of his hands through his short black hair. I would chop my left leg off and fry my eyeballs in butter to get into her knickers. He grinned broadly to himself and walked towards the fence, resting his arms on it whilst continuing to enjoy the exciting view.

'Hi, Diane,' he called out, eagerly hoping to get her to turn around so that he could get a good look of the rest of her.

Diane recognized his voice and stood up to say hello to her neighbour. 'Hi, John,' she smiled. 'It's really hot today, isn't it?'

'It certainly is,' he replied with a high level of interest. His bulging eyes stared hungrily at her ample breasts and sexual fantasies began racing around inside his mind.

Diane continued to smile at him. She knew that he fancied her, although sensibly she would never admit this to Barry. She often saw him eyeing her body whenever he had the chance to do so. It made her feel good and boosted her confidence about looking attractive. On this occasion, she sensed his excitement and decided to flirt and tease him for a while. 'It's far too humid for garden work, John. I'm sorry I can't make too much idle chatter with you. I'm going to chill out for a while and make the most of this hot weather.'

John raised a half smile and disappointingly waited for her to leave and go back indoors. However, his eyes nearly popped out of their sockets when he saw her casually pull her tight-fitting tee shirt off exposing a low cut bra and lightly tanned body. He looked on, eyeing her breasts as she angled a close-by deck chair so that it faced the beaming sun. She sat down on it and closed her eyes. John stood motionless and at the same time speechless. He had always got on well with Diane and was somewhat flabbergasted with what he was seeing right now. His mind began to race with more sexual fantasies. Is this a come-on signal? He thought. Am I supposed to walk away? Her husband is some sort of former commando or something like that. So what? I think she is stunning. I'm going to try my luck with her.

28

'Diane, do you fancy a cool beer?' he asked, eagerly hoping she would say yes.

'What, oh sorry John, I didn't realize you were still there,' she lied, knowing he was lustfully staring. 'What a nice gesture,' she smiled. 'Yes please, I'd love a cool beer right now.'

John did not need telling twice. He hurried into his house and grabbed some beer cans from the fridge. Excitement engulfed him as he rushed back to the fence where he stopped and pulled the ring tabs from two cans.

'Here suck on this,' he gestured cheekily, passing one to Diane who had stood up next to the fence.

'Thank you, I will,' she replied, looking as interested in the situation as he was.

The two of them talked for a while. They initially discussed the pleasantries of gardening, but after drinking a little more the conversation became more personal about their partners and even their intimate sex lives.

'Have you got any more beer?' Diane asked, holding an empty can up and shaking it.

'No. Unfortunately, I'm afraid I haven't,' John frowned and then raised his bushy eyebrows. He looked down at the ground discontented, believing that the conversation and rare chance opportunity meeting were about to end.

Contrary to expectation, Diane paused for a short while, before pushing one of her fingers into the air indicating that she had thought of a solution to the problem.

'Not to worry, John, I've got plenty of cans in my fridge. Do you fancy a couple more?'

He looked up, surprised and nodded. 'Yes, yes. I would love a couple more. I really would,' he assured her.

'Well you'll have to come inside my house to get them.' 'They're on the top shelf of my fridge-freezer and I know I won't be able to reach them.'

'But…, but what if your husband comes home? He'll get the wrong idea.'

Diane gave a reassuring grin. 'Barry isn't due home for three or four hours yet. He'll never know.'

John could not believe his ears and suddenly developed the speed and agility of a highly tuned athlete, swinging himself swiftly over the fence and into the garden on the other side.

Meanwhile, back at the steel mill sweat streamed down Barry's face. It was hot and the constant clanging of steel pipes gave him a migraine. Normally he would just ignore it, but the unrelenting heat made it worse, much worse. Bugger this for a game of soldiers, he thought. I'm going home early today. I'm going to have a shower, a meal and an early night in bed. With this mindset, he walked out of the noisy steel mill and removed his safety hat. Even more sweat dripped down his face so he pulled a handkerchief from his pocket and wiped it across his forehead.

'I'm having half a day today boss,' he shouted across to his to his manager, through an open office window. 'My head is banging and I feel lousy.'

The manager shrugged his shoulders and nodded his head acknowledging that he approved and had no objections.

Barry headed for the company car park, where he climbed into his car and stared at his reflection in the rear view mirror. He mopped some more sweat from his brow. I hate this job, he thought. I wish I was back in the marines. I was much happier then. He switched on the engine and pushed the gear stick into first gear. It clunked into place allowing him to accelerate and begin the short journey home.

'Cheers, Babe.' John gestured, chinking beer glasses with Diane in the spacious kitchen of her home.

Both of them were tipsy, feeling comfortably relaxed conversing together. Normally their interchange of words would not be so intimate, but the alcohol continued to remove any inhibitions between them.

'I've always fancied you, you know Diane. I really have. I think you're absolutely gorgeous,' John told her, hoping she would reciprocate.

Diane smiled, blinking her eyelashes in response to his flattery. It was very rare that Barry paid her such meaningful compliments. She had never really thought of anybody else except Barry in this way. Why not, she thought. Barry will never know if I have just one secret fling.

'Do you really fancy me, John?' she asked seriously, gazing into his overly keen eyes.

John moved in, embracing her with a heavy lustful kiss. Their tongues began darting in and out of each other's mouth and their hands caressed each other's body. He started to fondle her breasts and easily unfastened her bra, which fell to the floor as they continued to kiss. His hands gradually moved to her skimpy shorts; but suddenly she stopped him.

'Let's go upstairs,' she whispered softly, pointing towards the adjacent stairway.

Her words were music to John's ears and he could hardly contain himself. Both of them started to climb the stairs removing items of their clothing on the way up. They walked into the main bedroom where they embraced in yet another wet kiss. John started tugging at Diane's clothes again and slowly removed her underwear easing them down to the top of her feet. He was highly aroused at this point, like a teenager having his first sexual experience.

At that moment, Diane's conscience gave her a deep feeling of guilt about her intended adulterous actions. Thoughts of how much she loved her husband raced around in her mind. What am I doing? She thought. I don't really want to do this. I love my husband. This is silly. It really isn't worth it. She disengaged from kissing John, stepped back and quickly put on her underwear.

'No, no, John. I don't want to do this,' she insisted. 'I really don't. I've been silly. I haven't thought about this. I've had too much to drink.'

31

'Don't be silly, you know you want to do it. Come on,' John insisted. She knows she wants it, he thought, moving closer and tugging at her underwear again.

'No get off me,' she demanded, pushing his hands away from her. 'I love my husband. I'm not doing this. I'm not, I won't,' she cried, with tears beginning to drip down her flushed cheeks.

John felt dejected. Diane's body was at the ends of his fingertips. This was something he had fantasized about for years. He did not want to stop, not even if it meant forcing her to have sex with him. She wouldn't dare say anything to Barry. After all, how could she possibly explain this situation to him?

Smack! John's hand made hard contact with Diane's cheek.

'Nooo!' she screamed aloud, pleading with him. 'Please no.'

John was not listening. There was only one thing on his mind and he was fully intent on getting it. No matter what!

'No!' Diane screamed again, after John smacked her hard in the face a second time trying to persuade her to stop struggling.

The powerful blow knocked her backwards and down onto the neatly made bed, where he tore forcefully at her knickers ripping them from her body and tossing them aside.

Barry pulled up onto the driveway, parking his car in front of his garage door. He paused for a second, cupping his hands over his face. His headache throbbed incessantly. At least I'm home now, he thought. I'll get Diane to run the bath and put the kettle on. He turned the key and the front door lock clicked open. He pushed it inwards and stepped inside. Almost immediately, he noticed the discarded clothing scattered around the foot of the stairs. Something is going on here, he thought suspiciously, suddenly feeling a deep dread. He looked down the hallway and into the kitchen where he could see the empty beer cans. He glanced at them briefly, following the trail of scattered clothing leading up stairs. What the hell is going on here? His mind raced hoping he had misinterpreted the situation; but also knowing he had stumbled upon something he did not want to believe.

'Please no, I don't want to,' Diane pleaded tearfully. 'No. Please don't, John. I don't want to do it. Please don't do this.'

Barry sensed his wife was in danger and quickened his pace without calling out. He reached the top of the stairs and could see through the half-open door. He saw John holding Diane down on the bed with one hand and fumbling with his own underwear with the other.

'Bastard! Fucking bastard!' he snarled, slamming the door wide open and surging inside.

He lunged straight at John, grabbing a hand-full of his hair and dragged him backwards down onto the floor and away from his terrified wife.

'No!' was all that John could scream as he helplessly slumped down.

Barry's rage erupted. He repeatedly kicked John hard in the face with his steel toecap boots, battering his nose and lips. Deep red blood splattered onto the cream pile carpet and several teeth smashed loose from his open mouth. Barry was unforgiving and continued to beat him, kicking him hard in the bollocks.

'No please stop, Barry it was my fault,' Diane cried, hoping to stop her husband before he killed John. 'It was my fault. I led him on. I led him on,' she told him and hoped he would cease the onslaught.

Barry instantly stopped his attack and stood back panting heavily. He looked at his wife in disbelief and with an expression of hurt and betrayal.

'What do you mean you led him on? He was raping you. I saw him with my own eyes. He was, wasn't he?' he snapped, anxiously hoping Diane would agree. His grimace changed to a look of bewilderment whilst John pulled his clothes back on.

'I led him on, but I changed my mind at the last moment. It's my fault. I'm so sorry Barry. I am so sorry.' Fresh tears streamed down her bruised face. She began replacing the clothing over her naked body. Half of her clothing had been scattered around the stairs so she pulled clean garments from an open drawer.

John continued to pull his clothes on, with blood dripping from his nose and mouth, staining them. His face and body were battered; but his fear of a further assault gave him the energy to pick himself up to make a quick exit.

Barry looked at him with hate-filled eyes watching him limp towards the door. Instinctively, he lashed out again kicking him hard in the crease of his buttocks.

John winced, raising his arms to protect his face as he fell headfirst down the stairs. He groaned again, coming to a sudden halt at the foot of the stairwell. His face ached from carpet burns and blood curdled in his throat so he spat the remnants of his broken teeth out onto the floor. Quickly, he pushed himself up and staggered out through the door slamming it closed behind him.

For several seconds there was an almost complete silence inside the house, except for an analogue clock ticking on a bedside cabinet. Barry sat simmering, motionless and aimlessly staring at his wife who looked ridden with guilt.

'I didn't do anything Barry,' she said, breaking the silence between them. 'I thought about it but then changed my mind. I love you too much. It's the truth, please believe me,' she begged. 'It will never happen again. It was a stupid, thoughtless mistake.'

Barry rubbed his hands over the stubble on his cheeks. He was deeply hurt and too angry to answer. He closed his eyes and shook his head, quietly leaving the room.

A couple of weeks passed, during which time Barry had seen no sign of John or his wife. He found himself coming home early from work unannounced to check on Diane. He couldn't help it. The recent events remained at the forefront of his thoughts. His anger lingered too. So much so, that he put together a stealthy plan to take his retribution. To execute this, he obtained two kilos of illegal drugs from an indirectly known supplier. He was not a user of drugs; that never appealed to him. He knew about the dealer's existence from his wife's gossiping friends. The package cost him a serious amount of money, which he willingly withdrew from his savings. He did not care about the cost. If his plan worked, it would be worth every penny.

One dark Friday night whilst Diane was out shopping, he watched through an upstairs window as John and his wife routinely left their house for the evening. When they were gone, he donned a black tracksuit, woollen hat, gloves and a pair of black training shoes. He checked his clothing making sure there were no loose pieces that could become snagged on something. He grabbed the drugs package and pushed it inside his top, zipping it up and gazing out through the window again. Dense clouds shrouded the full moon. This pleased him.

Outside, he crept around quietly climbing over a sturdy wooden fence leading in to his neighbour's garden. He was aware that John's house had an active burglar alarm. He had previously been given the combination to the keypad when they were still friends, during a time when they were away on holiday. However, that was ages ago and he hoped that the alarm code had not been changed. Entering the house would be easy for him. He knew that John kept a spare key under the dustbin. He did this because he had once lost his keys and had to break in. This proved costly, having to hire an expensive locksmith and consequently displeasing his wife.

Barry removed a glove and leaned against the bin lifting it up. He searched the area underneath with his bare hand. After a couple of seconds he met with success, feeling and hearing the key scrape across the concrete floor. He smiled contently.

A bright external house light illuminated the garden. It came from the home on the other side of John's house. It was a neighbour letting his dog out to do its business. The dog ran around the neighbour's garden barking wildly in Barry's direction. It poked its head through the fence towards him growling and baring its teeth.

Barry kept hold of the key, slowly easing the bin back down onto the ground and carefully moved down behind a garden bush. Its leaves made a light brushing sound as he sat down on the floor twisting his face with disappointment. His plan was in danger of failing.

'Come here boy, what are you growling at?' the neighbour said to his dog.

He shone a torch light over the fence and around the bushes, holding the beam next to where Barry was hiding. He concentrated hard and thought he saw something move whilst the dog continued to growl.

Barry had not anticipated the possibility of compromise. It posed a grave risk of being identified. He decided that he would have to kill the dog and assault the neighbour if they came into the garden

Out of the blue and purely by coincidence, a cat ran at great speed from underneath another bush. The dog went berserk and his owner shone his torch on the creature, watching it leap over a fence at the end of the garden and away out of sight. The dog chose not to pursue the cat. Instead, it refocused on Barry growling and barking in his direction.

'Come here boy. It's just a cat,' said the neighbour.

His torch light went out and he dragged the dog away by its collar and back indoors. Then the external house light was extinguished.

Barry waited for several minutes before he broke from cover, proceeding with his plan pushing the key into the door lock. He knew he had approximately thirty seconds to tap in the correct key code before the alarm burst into action alerting the neighbours. He turned the key and opened the door, slipping inside and closing it behind him. The zone alarm started to bleep quietly with its red neon lights flashing. He moved further inside, found the keypad and carefully tapped in the number.

'Shit,' he whispered nervously. The code he had used failed to stop the triggered countdown. He gasped frantically wracking his brains. He was sure he had used the correct code. He tried again, then again, but still without success. He clenched one of his glove-covered fists and twisted his face with frustration believing his plan was about fail.

The bleeping sound started to intensify as the device neared the time limit that would trigger the main alarm and blue flashing light outside.

Barry paused for several seconds during which time he felt like ripping it from the wall. That would trigger the tamper alarm though. He knew this so he stood motionless staring at it. He

36

cupped his hands over his face and reluctantly accepted defeat, turning towards the door to make his exit. Bollocks, he thought, turning back to the keypad for one last try. He tapped in the default numbers normally used as a standard factory reset code. One, two, three and four. The alarm stopped dead and he breathed a huge sigh of relief. His heart was pounding heavily with anxiety but he knew he had done it. Thank fuck for that, he thought. He pulled the drugs package from inside his clothing and headed upstairs. The steps creaked under his weight as he ascended, being careful not to be seen through any of the windows.

Outside, he could hear people talking and walking past unawares going about their business.

From the landing, he entered the master bedroom. He located a set of wooden-drawers next to a king-size double bed, opened the top drawer and peered inside. It was full to the brim with female underwear. Perfect, he thought. This is almost as close to his wife's gusset as he was to Diane's!

'Revenge is sweet, John,' he whispered, placing the package inside and closed the drawer.

He briefly scanned a couple of wedding photographs that hung on the painted walls and headed back down stairs.

A couple of minutes later he had reset the alarm, locked the door and placed the key back into its original place. Temporarily, his shadow stood out against the moonlight, the earlier dense clouds having dispersed. It did not matter though. The main part of his well-planned mission had been successfully executed. He moved into the shadows where the garden trees' foliage hid him from view, shuffling back over the garden fence. His feet landed softly on his flowerbed, just as he heard John and his wife returning home early and deactivating their alarm. He felt satisfied and amused with himself, content that his undetected act of vengeance would soon come to fruition. He re-entered his own home, making a quick change of clothes prior to leaving and walking to a nearby shopping precinct. His intention now was to complete the final phase. He planned to use a payphone to make an anonymous call, informing the police about the drugs. That way the call would not be traceable back to him. He entered the phone box opposite the shops, picked up the receiver and dialled the number for the local police station.

'Hello, is that the police?' he asked, disguising his voice.

'One moment please, sir,' a woman replied. 'I'll just try to connect you to the required service.'

'Hello is that the police?' he asked again.

'Yes it is, sir. How can we help you?'

'I want to report a known drug dealer. His name is John and he lives in number four Belk Street. I'm sorry I don't know his surname,' he tactfully lied, trying not to sound too knowledgeable.

'May I ask how you came by this information, sir?'

'Yes, he's been trying to sell cocaine to my daughter. This was about an hour ago.'

'Okay, sir. We'll check it out. Please could I take some personal details from you, sir?'

'No. I'm sorry, Officer. I want to remain anonymous. I'm sure you understand.'

'Yes of course, sir,' the officer responded and Barry replaced the handset.

After the call, he plucked a handkerchief from his pocket and wiped down the telephone receiver and number pad, looking outside to ensure no one was watching him. He then left, nipping into an adjacent off-license where he bought himself an expensive bottle of cognac to celebrate. Moments later, he calmly ambled back towards his home where he noticed a police car parked outside John's house. Its blue lights were flashing, alerting neighbours who curiously peered out beyond their curtains. 'That was bloody quick,' he mumbled, glancing discreetly inside the car to see the occupants. There was nobody visible. He looked around and noticed that John's front door was damaged, probably from being forced open. He could hear Judith shouting her objections at the police officers as they continued to search the premises. Barry was satisfied with the disruption caused next door, believing his plan to have worked with precision. He entered his own home and locked the door behind him. Diane was still out. She must have gone back to her mother's house for a cup of tea after shopping, he thought. He made his way into the kitchen and pulled a brandy glass from one of the cupboards. Then he reached inside the fridge for some ice cubes. They chinked inside the glass and he poured himself a drink. Normally he would add a mixer such as lemonade or coke, but this time the celebratory occasion called for something stronger. Once his glass was full, he took a couple of sips wetting his pallet. Then he extinguished the light and opened the door leading to the back garden. Outside, he sat down on the step facing his neighbour's house. He couldn't be seen by anybody; thick bushes that bordered that particular part of the garden hid him from view. He remained motionless and silent, sipping his brandy and listening with interest to the commotion next door.

'It's a plant. It's a bloody plant. I've been set up,' John shouted at the two police officers who were escorting him in handcuffs to the waiting patrol car.

One of them held a brown package in his hands, whilst the other roughly pushed John inside the rear of the vehicle and slammed the door behind him.

For an unknown reason they had not arrested Judith, but Barry was not too concerned about that. He just sat enjoying his drink and giggling to himself until the police car sped off into the distance.

The next morning, Barry sat eating his breakfast with Diane. He had a slight hangover and almost felt like he had dreamt about the events of the previous evening. That was until Diane spoke to him.

'One of my friends called me on the telephone this morning and told me that John from next door has been arrested for supplying hard drugs,' she told him.

'Supplying what?' Barry answered, trying to sound surprised.

'Hard drugs!'

'He's a tosser,' Barry snarled. 'Its scum like him who pollutes our society. I hope he gets ten years for it.'

39

'Yes I hope so too,' Diane replied, expressing how she felt about people who peddled drugs. 'The rumour is; he will get ten years. I would never have guessed that him and Judith were that type of people. There's nothing as strange as folk is there?'

Barry didn't comment. He just sat quietly enjoying his hearty breakfast!

Chapter Four

Spike's forefinger and thumb repeatedly brushed across the smooth surface of his black bow tie, whilst loud disco music thumped away in the background. Bungy and himself were working as security men, dressed immaculately in black tuxedos on the entrance doors of a local nightclub.

Things had been positive over recent months. They were looking more civilized, healthier and kempt. They resided in a two-bedroom apartment, paid for by working in a food warehouse during the day and in the nightclub most nights.

Spike initially found it difficult to wean himself away from his alcohol addiction, but their busy work schedule and Bungy's support helped him to overcome this.

'One moment please, sir,' Bungy said politely to a punter. 'I just need to carry out a routine body search.'

He began frisking a spiky haired young man who appeared overly keen to get into the club with his friends.

The door security attendants were not searching everyone. That would make an easy job difficult. Instead, they chose to search people at random. In particular, they searched for weapons but often-found drugs too, ejecting the carrier without question.

'Why are you searching me?' the young man asked. 'Why didn't you search those other people who walked in before me?'

'There's nothing to worry about, mate.' Bungy smiled, trying to reassure him. 'It's just a routine random search, nothing more.'

The man's growing frustration attracted Spike's attention. He cautiously watched him whilst his colleague completed the search.

'You didn't frisk his groin area,' he commented, practically insisting he should.

'My bollocks mate!' the man exclaimed, grinning and rolling his eyes. 'Are you gay or what?'

Bungy acknowledged his friend's observation by bluntly rubbing his hand around the man's crotch.   Almost immediately, he felt a small square shaped object and positively nodded towards Spike signalling he had found something.

Spike knew the drill, without hesitation he swiftly pushed the queuing punters back outside the entrance door and locked it shut.

'Okay, okay, you've found my stash,' the young man conceded, holding his hands up.   'Just leave me alone and I'll leave quietly.'

Spike surged towards him, punching him hard in the stomach.   The powerful blow winded him, forcing him to bend at the waist gasping for air.   He focused on the exit door desperately wanting to make a break for it, but there was no way out.   Spike struck him again causing the box of narcotics to fall down his trouser leg and onto the floor.

'That's for calling me gay, you piece of shit,' he snapped.

Bungy grabbed hold on the man's clothing pushing him through an adjacent swing door, which slammed hard against a wall.   He kept pushing him, forcing him out through a side entrance into a deserted street.

'Go away, piss off,' he snarled, swiping the back of his hand inches away from his face.

'Please give me my stash back,' the man pleaded.   'I haven't caused any trouble.   I just want what's mine.'

There was no response and the loud bang made by the door slamming shut echoed loudly in the dark empty street around him.

Spike picked up the small box and studied it briefly, placing it into a half-full container labelled 'Drug Store'. They routinely did this, storing their confiscated items to handover to the authorities.

Later, the nightclub manager checked the container and decided to call the police, asking them to make a collection.

A tall middle-aged police officer arrived. He stepped in through the entrance door, removing his peak cap and tucking it under his arm. He had short-cropped hair, a straight back and faded scars on his chin and forehead. His face seemed strangely familiar to Spike who concentrated hard trying to place him.

'Do I know you from somewhere?' the police officer asked, looking just as curious.

'You probably recognise his ugly mug from the TV show called Crime Watch,' Bungy cut in. 'Spike is an honest man but has a guilt ridden-face.'

'Spike. Spike,' the officer repeated, the name triggering his memory. 'Bloody hell mate! It's been a long time. Its great to see you,' he continued and shook Spike firmly by the hand.

'Where do you know me from? Spike asked curiously, wondering if the police officer had locked him up at some point.

The officer smiled warmly, conveying the impression that he was familiar with him in an amiable way. Spike was unsure and began to feel uneasy about the situation.

'Spike, it's me, mate, Dave Watson. We were marines together. We were in the same troop and we fought side by side in the gulf war. I have got the right guy haven't I?'

'Err yes I believe I do recognize you,' Spike replied unconvincingly. 'I'm sorry. My memory is little vague.'

'My nick-name back then was Spot. Spot Watson. It's great to see you, Spike. You once saved my life. Do you remember?'

Bungy relaxed, grinning broadly after hearing these words. He introduced himself to Dave and shook his hand.

Spike's clouded memories started to return, but remained unclear. He thought he recognised Dave from his time in the marines but was uncertain.

'Err......yes....., Spot Watson,' he stammered. 'I remember you, mate. You were a top guy.'

'So were you, Spike,' Dave said. 'You saved my life. I got shot in the shoulder and you broke from cover and dragged me to safety out of the line-of-fire.'

Spike's eyebrows raised and his hair rode back on his scalp. His memories were rather distant in relation to the gulf war. His time on the streets and the alcohol abuse over the past couple of years had eroded them. He glanced idly at Bungy who was eagerly waiting for his response.

The three men talked affably for a while until Dave received a call on his radio; instructing him to attend an incident elsewhere.

Bungy handed him the drugs container, which he grabbed by a hanging handle. 'It's been a pleasure to meet you, Dave,' he said courteously offering a handshake.

Dave shook his hand for a second time but was more interested in saying goodbye to his former colleague. He placed his hat back onto his head, taking a moment to ensure it was straight. Then he stepped closer to Spike.

'I owe you a big favour, Spike,' he grinned, meaningfully shaking his hand and then hugging him. 'I owe you my life mate. I'll always remember that.'

'Don't mention it, Dave', Spike chirped. 'You would have done the same for me. Just get the beers in next time I see you.'

'That will be a pleasure,' he waved, walking outside to his patrol car and driving away at speed.

When he was gone, Bungy turned towards Spike who had a distant look in his eyes. 'You can't remember him can you?' he said, certain that Spike would agree with him.

'No I can't. I can vaguely remember his face but that's all. Some things about my service days are clear in my mind and others are sort of fuzzy.'

'Not to worry, mate,' Bungy sympathized. 'Even if you can't recall everything, that guy certainly remembers you.'

Spike gave a vacant look, unable to find the words to reply. He shrugged his shoulders and nodded.

Minutes later, the music had ceased and the ceiling lights were being extinguished. The two men were handed their pay packets from the manager, bidding him goodnight and leaving via the side door.

Outside, the street was empty - probably because it was off the main thoroughfare. They walked briskly, their footsteps echoing up amongst the fire escapes of neighbouring businesses.

For no particular reason, Bungy felt uneasy and could feel the hairs standing up on the back of his neck. He exchanged a glance with Spike who also looked uncomfortable. They stopped walking, the echoing ceased and they turned around. To their astonishment, they saw the young spiky haired man. He was standing close-by, holding a small calibre handgun and pointing it towards them. He aimed the weapon at Bungy first and then at Spike, fluctuating between the two of them.

'Where's my stash? I want my stash now,' he demanded.

Nobody spoke. The two men were focusing on the gun and the area around their assailant, making certain that nobody was with him.

'We haven't got your stuff,' Spike informed him. 'We had to take it from you and hand it over to the police. That's what we get paid for.'

'I want my stash now or I want all your money. Give me it now,' he hollered waving the gun around menacingly.

Their eyes were fixed on the weapon and its owner, watching his hand shaking as beads of sweat glinted on his forehead. He wiped them away with the back of his hand.

Spike launched himself forward, grabbing a hold of both the gun and the young man's hand. His momentum and body weight took the adversary by surprise, knocking him down with a heavy thud. As he hit the ground, his head banged on a cobblestone causing him to drop the weapon. It clattered on the uneven ground and settled close to Spike.

The man cried out in pain, blood oozing from a gash on the back of his head. He scrambled to his feet, leaving the weapon and sprinted off down the empty thoroughfare amongst the shadows. His echoing footsteps faded until he eventually vanished out of sight.

Neither of the two friends gave chase, they just watched him running away before Bungy assisted Spike back up onto his feet.

'Talk about reacting on impulse,' Bungy said. 'What type of gun is it?'

'It's a nine millimetre Browning pistol, the same as they issued us with in the military.'

'Yes I recognize it now. Is it a fake?'

Spike pointed the cocked weapon into the air and pulled the trigger. A round thundered from its barrel and a deafening BANG echoed repeatedly off the surrounding buildings.

'Come on, put that thing away and let's get out of here before someone comes to investigate the noise,' Bungy urged and they hurried off towards their car.

Elsewhere, Barry's life had gone from one extreme to another. Following a short-term jail sentence, his troubled neighbours had moved away and his wife was eternally sorry for her actions. His attitude towards her had dramatically changed and a tense atmosphere prevailed. That was inescapable. He still worked at the steel mill but hated being there. He had become dull and subdued, often avoiding conversation with his workmates. He had become such a miserable person that his colleagues began to resent his sullen presence.

The steelworks canteen was bustling and Barry was sitting alone eating his lunch at the end of a row of tables. His mind was

46

completely engrossed pondering about his time in the marines. He recalled his basic training and the relentless physical and mental demands of the course. The failure rate was high and only a select few actually made the grade. The majority of those who fell by the wayside, either suffered injury or had found the requirements to be beyond their reach. Barry did find some aspects very challenging, but as the weeks went by, he excelled in his quest to earn the coveted Green Beret. Eventually, he made it through and was a Royal Marine Commando. His passing-out-parade was one of the greatest days of his life; often remaining at the forefront of his memories.

'Hey you; miserable bastard! Pass me the pepper now,' a rough looking man bellowed across the canteen towards him. 'I said pass the fucking pepper now!' he growled again after a short pause.

Other seated customers put their heads down fearfully, looking the other away.

Barry sat grinning, thinking about an amusing social antic, years ago in Plymouth.

The fiery-man was a heavily built supervisor. He had a skinhead and tattooed arms and was dressed in blue overalls. He had a bad reputation for causing trouble and liked to keep it intact by throwing his weight around every so often, threatening people. His remarks were beginning to attract everyone's attention. He was pleased about this; knowing that people were scared of him. It made him feel good.

The silence and apparent ignorance from the man at the end of the row of tables infuriated him. He glared at him, annoyed that he had ignored his bold words and was seemingly smiling about them. He was becoming increasingly agitated and believed that he needed to do something to save face in front of the crowd. He decided to teach the man a lesson that he would never forget.

'Hey you fuck dust!' he snarled, gritting his teeth and stomping towards Barry who remained deep in thought.

The supervisor's cheeks were glowing red with anger. 'When I say pass the pepper; you pass me the fucking pepper!' he snapped once more, moving to grab his victim.

At this point, Barry broke from his daydream. He saw a man coming towards him reaching out in a threatening manner. He swiftly jumped up to defend himself, raising his clenched fists and striking hard onto the back of one of the outstretched hands. The timely blow caused the assailant to stumble forwards, losing his balance. Barry struck again thumping the man hard in the face with his fist. The blow made a crunching noise when it contacted his exposed jaw, smashing him down into the empty chairs that clattered around him.

The room fell silent and Barry stepped back to allow the supervisor to push himself up on his feet. Blood trickled down from his cut lips and he stared angrily towards Barry, spitting some of it out onto the floor in front of him. The air was filled with tension and nobody spoke. The two men stood glaring deep into each other's eyes like animals, neither of them breaking from the stare.

'I don't know what your problem is mate,' Barry panted, but if you want a war I'll give you one.'

'No, no,' the supervisor replied, shaking his head.

He wiped the blood from his mouth with the back of his hand and pulled a handkerchief from his pocket to absorb it.

'I don't want to fight with you,' he said with a deflated ego. 'I've made a mistake. I thought you were somebody else.'

Barry held his fearsome glare. He knew better than to let his guard down. His years of experience, gained amongst some of the toughest soldiers in the world had taught him that.

The injured and subdued supervisor broke from the confrontation and put his head down, turning away defeated and slowly walking out of the adjacent exit. He did not look back and the door slammed shut behind him.

Barry sat down at the table and casually finished his meal. Nobody said anything to him and just spoke amongst themselves in whispers. The majority seemed secretly pleased about the outcome of the fracas, believing the result to be long over due.

Later that day, Barry returned home where he saw Diane sifting through a pile of mail in the kitchen. She turned to him with a heavy frown.

'I've got a letter from a debt collection company,' she sighed. If you don't pay the finance on my car they're going to repossess it.'

'I don't care,' he sneered, gritting his teeth and calmly popped the cork from a bottle of red wine. He poured himself a glass.

Outside, in the darkness, the rain gently tapped on the windowpanes and a mild wind scattered fallen leaves around the garden. A single headlight shone its beam on the house. It came from an approaching motorbike, whose mysterious rider stopped on the tarmac road cautiously scrutinising the area. His well-tuned engine purred quietly, ticking over. There was nobody else around. Nothing stirred except the elements.

Beast unzipped his black-leather jacket, reached inside and pulled out a piece of paper. He unfolded it, checking the address and confirming it was the house he was looking at. It was correct and the additional instructions described the bad debtor, Mr. Broadhurst as being aggressive. He grinned amused and buzzed with excitement. He was no stranger to hard men. In fact, he enjoyed it when they put up some heated resistance. It made his job more challenging, giving a rush of adrenalin. He steered his bike up onto the driveway and turned the engine off, kicking the stand down before climbing off the seat. He removed his helmet and gloves and placed them inside a bulky fibreglass box attached to the rear of the bike. He pulled out a plastic groin protector, normally used by cricket players, pushing it down his trousers and over his genitals. It was standard practice for him when he expected trouble from the bad debtors. The groin area was often the place where some people would strike first, expecting him to crumple. He took several moments readying himself by shrugging and loosening his shoulders, like a boxer preparing for a fight. His gnarled knuckles wrapped hard on the house door causing it to rattle and shudder. The forceful thumps echoed around inside the passageway.

Barry jumped up from his seat startled, almost spilling his wine. He immediately put down his glass and rushed to an under-stairs cupboard, where he grabbed a baseball bat to use as a weapon. It must be that supervisor, he thought. He must be coming back for some more trouble. Well, this time, I'm going to knock his bloody teeth out. He strode towards the door and cautiously opened it, holding the bat poised at the ready behind his back.

'Are you Mr Broadhurst?' Beast asked, as several dead leaves blew inside the unlit porch.

Barry squinted studying the man's features. He was not the supervisor as he had initially thought. Maybe he is some-how connected to him, he wondered. Oddly, he thought he recognised his face but the lack of light did not help to place him. He glanced around outside beyond the caller, just to be certain there was no backup waiting in shadows.

'Yes I am,' he replied, preparing himself to strike out with his weapon.

Beast paused. Mr Broadhurst looked vaguely familiar.

'Fucking have some,' Barry hollered, lunging at him and swinging the wooden bat.

Beast dropped down ducking to avoid the incoming blow. Luckily, it narrowly missed his exposed skull, allowing him to launch his counter attack punching the debtor hard in the stomach. The blow was forceful and on target, winding Barry. He winced and stumbled forwards outside and down onto the wet grass in the garden. Beast dropped down on top of him pinning him to the floor with his knees.

'You owe my employer some money, Mr Broadhurst,' he informed him.

Barry struggled to get up, remaining suppressed. He was defeated and vulnerable and he knew it.

'I only goffered the supervisor because he attacked me,' he grimaced, fighting hard to breathe.

'What did you say, Mr Broadhurst?' Beast asked, unsure if he had misheard the comments.

'I said I goffered him because he attacked me.'

Beast was intrigued. He had no idea who the man was referring to, but recognised the word goffered as a slang word used by the marines. It meant to punch someone.

Who is this Mr. Broadhurst, he frowned? He looked at the baseball bat, still held in the hand that he had pinned to the floor. He grabbed it and threw it into the darkness. Curiosity was getting the better of him and he strongly wanted to have a closer look. Quite bizarrely, he was certain that he recognized his voice.

'Are you a boot neck?' he asked, fully expecting a definite yes.

'I'm an ex-boot neck,' Barry replied, breathing freely because he was no longer winded.

Could this possibly be Baz Broadhurst? Beast wondered, believing it to be a long-shot but hoping he was right.

Barry raised his head up from the floor and started grinning and nodding his head. 'Get your knee out of my back you fat bastard,' he laughed, having placed the voice of his previously unwelcome visitor.

'Yes it's me, Beast. It's Baz Broadhurst,' he panted.

Beast's eyes opened wide and a broad grin covered his wind-chilled face as he realised it was his former colleague whom he had pinned to the floor. He was pleased about the unexpected turn of events, but felt a little silly too because of the situation. Slowly, he eased off the hold and helped Barry back up onto his feet.

'Fuck me, Baz, you've changed a bit since the last time I saw you,' he exclaimed. 'I can't believe it's you, mate.'

'Of course I've changed. I'm six years older. You haven't altered. You're still a big ugly bastard, even in the dark,' he chortled.

During their military careers, they had been good friends experiencing hardships and conflict as well as fun and laughter. Six years on, they were overjoyed with being reunited, ironically in the strangest of circumstances. They hugged one another and patted each other on the back like long-lost brothers.

'So.., are you going to beat me up then fatty?' Barry asked, continuing with the sarcasm.

51

They laughed loudly. Barry had always referred to Beast as a fat bastard during their service days, which was always taken in jest. That was the reference that cemented the positive authentication of Barry's identity. Barry's nickname as a marine was Baz and both men had served side by side in the Arctic and Northern Ireland.

'No I'm not going to pummel you, Baz,' Beast smirked. 'I suggest you get us both a couple of cold beers from your fridge to cool my temper.'

'Yes of course, fatty. I'll do that. Let's go inside.'

'Hello, Mrs Broadhurst. Nice to meet you,' Beast gestured politely, setting eyes on Diane in the doorway.

'Don't speak to her, she's a fucking hussy,' Barry told him. 'She was trying to have it away with our neighbour.'

'I hope you've sorted it,' Beast grunted, contemplating paying the neighbour an unpleasant visit.

'Yes I've sorted it. He did a short spell in jail before him and his plug-ugly wife moved house.'

Beast did not pursue an explanation. He settled knowing the problem had been resolved. He blanked Diane and made himself comfortable on a chair in the spacious living room. If Baz said she was a tart then she was a tart and that was final.

'Here get this down your neck, mate,' Barry smirked, pulling a ring top from a can of beer.

The men sat together drinking ale and using the time to reflect on the past six years. It had been a long time and they had plenty of catching up to do.

In the background, Diane packed some cosmetics into her handbag and quietly left, heading for her mother's house out of the way.

'I'm not going to have a job when I leave here Baz, as I obviously won't be collecting the outstanding debt from you,' Beast shrugged.

'That's not a problem. It was purely because of the neighbour circumstances why I hadn't paid the finance on Diane's car. I've got the cash here.'

Beast took the role of money and stuffed it inside his coat pocket without counting it. Already, he was deciding that he no longer wanted to do this job anymore. It was something he had been contemplating for quite some time. Afterwards, he planned to hand the cash over to his manager, making this his final house call.

'Baz, I'm going home now. I'm wrapping this debt collection lark. I'm sick of it anyway. Is there any chance of getting a job with you?' he smirked raising his eyebrows. He looked sincere and sounded convincing so Barry took his words seriously.

'Leave it with me and I'll sort something out,' he assured him, following him to the doorway where he stepped out into the darkness. 'Take it easy on the roads mate. I hope you've passed your test on that thing,' Barry joked, but was in fact reminding him to be careful - especially after the amount of beer he had consumed.

'I'm always careful,' Beast replied, looking unperturbed whilst climbing onto his bike.

He pulled on his gloves and helmet, switched on the engine and calmly rode off through the rain, waving as he disappeared into the night.

Several miles away, Spike and Bungy were driving home after working at the nightclub. The roads were deserted and the rain had ceased. A dense fog engulfed the highway, consuming trees, buildings and open land.

'It's like pea soup out here.' Spike squinted, slowing the car and dropping it into a lower gear.

'Yes it is,' Bungy agreed. 'The visibility is terrible. We'll have to be careful. Do you think we should pull over for a while to wait and see if it clears?"

'That's a good idea,' Spike nodded, briefly taking his eyes of the road. 'I can't see a bloody thing; it's dangerous.'

Suddenly, there was a loud BANG. The car jolted heavily, bumping up onto what felt like a collision with a pavement.

'Shit!' Spike shouted loudly, fighting hard to keep the shuddering vehicle under control and to bring it to a halt.

Bushes crumpled under the path of the car and thorns tore at the paintwork. They hung on tightly for a while longer, until their vehicle finally stopped. The dense fog outside reduced visibility to a mere few feet.

'Shit,' Spike repeated. 'I think we're in a field.'

'No, we're not,' Bungy disagreed.

'We are; we've driven into a field.'

'No we haven't. We've run onto a big roundabout. I saw the sign several yards back just before we hit the curb.'

'Well we're shafted now,' Spike sighed. 'One of the front tyres blew out on impact. Even after we fit the spare tyre, we won't get far in this weather.'

'So we'll just have to stay here until it clears,' Bungy accepted. 'Our old sleeping bags are in the boot. I kept them for a rainy day. Don't worry they're clean. I washed them.'

Both men conceded that it would be sensible to spend the night in the car. They changed the damaged tyre and retrieved the sleeping bags, climbing inside them on the back seat. The suspension creaked as they moved around to make themselves comfortable.

'How did you end up living on the streets, Bungy?' Spiked asked, pulling his bedding in tightly around his neck.

'It's a long story but we've got a bit of time on our hands tonight so I'll tell you. I served in the Marines for twelve years from nineteen-ninety until two-thousand-and-two. I saw action in both gulf wars, Northern Ireland and the Arctic. I absolutely loved my job but left the marines believing I was ready for a change of career. Unfortunately, civvy-street wasn't my forte. I did think about joining up again but I ended up living rough on the streets, choosing to stay there. Don't ask me why I chose this path in my life, I just did. What about you?'

Spike paused and exhaled, rubbing his hand over his clean-shaven chin. His face twisted a little as he searched for his answer.

'I remember being in the Royal Marines for nine years. I served in Northern Ireland and fought in the second gulf war before I too left to seek a new career. I have very vague memories after that and have no idea how I ended up living on the streets.'

A faint sound of a motorbike engine could be heard nearing from the opposite direction. It was Beast. He was relentlessly trying to focus on the way ahead through the fog. The highway was deserted but the risk of collision remained possible because he rode in the middle of the road to avoid colliding with the pavement. He began to wish he had asked Barry if he could have spent the night at his house. He had wanted to stop a number of times but it seemed pointless with nowhere to shelter or secure his bike. Consequently, he slowed his speed to around twenty miles per hour. It was still a big risk and far too dangerous to go any faster. Without expectation, the bike leapt up into the air after striking the curb of the barely-visible roundabout. He tumbled forwards over the handlebars and clear of the screaming bike falling down with a heavy thud on to sodden grass. The bike came to an abrupt halt in some bushes with its engine spluttering to a fast throb. Next to it, Beast's body lay motionless in the fog.

'Shit, did you hear that?' Spike said, looking at Bungy who evidently had. 'It sounded like a motor bike crashing onto the roundabout just like we did. One of those thuds must have been the rider hitting the ground.'

Bungy made no effort to respond and was already out of his sleeping bag and climbing out from the car. Visibility in the dark and dense fog remained poor so he instinctively started to feel around near the ground with his feet, hoping that he could find the rider. Spike followed him but stumbled down half way out of the car with his feet snagged in something.

'Oh shit!' he cursed, spitting out a mouthful of wet grass.

'Are you okay?' Bungy called out.

'Yes, I must have got my feet caught in my sleeping bag. And before you say it, yes I know it's becoming a habit of mine.'

He freed his feet and climbed clear of the vehicle before making his way towards Bungy. During their search, they found the bike. That was easy; the constant ticking of its engine led them straight to it. Bungy dragged it out of the bushes; located the ignition key and switched the engine off. They listened for any other sound of movement, hoping to get some indication of where to look next.

'I can hear someone groaning,' Spike said. 'It sounds close-by.'

'Here!' Bungy indicated raising his voice. 'He's over here.' He could feel the rider's helmet with his hands and then his body. It was slowly becoming visible through the patchy fog, which was starting to clear.

Soon their vision was no longer impaired and they could see Beast, who was unconscious and still. He was lying face down so they carefully turned him over onto his back. He was breathing but seemingly knocked out cold. They knew it was not a recommended practice to remove a motorcyclist's headgear after an accident, but they wanted to check for head or facial injuries. The rest of his body seemed intact so they carefully removed his helmet. Beast groaned again but remained in an unconscious state.

'At least he's alive,' Spike chirped.

'Yes, thank God for that,' Bungy grinned. 'He's a big ugly bastard and the last person on earth I would want to give the kiss of life to!'

The fog had partially dispersed and the increasing morning light shone around them as they observed the rider more closely.

'Look he's wearing the marines' corps badge on his jacket. He's an ex-boot neck, one of us,' Spike said; certain he was right and also excited about it.

'Yeah it looks like it,' Bungy nodded. 'Do you know him?'

'No, I'd have remembered his big ugly mug. He's got a face like a bulldog chewing a wasp,' Spike joked. 'Let's try and revive him.'

'Okay, but if you remember rightly; you only ever wake a Serviceman by his feet because he might jump up and kick your head in!'

'Yes I remember. Here goes,' Spike laughed holding and shaking the stranger's boots.

Beast opened his eyes. His head ached and he felt confused and disorientated. He stared up at the sky, opened his mouth and breathed in a deep breath of fresh air.

'Who are you two?' he asked, wondering where he was.

'We're ex-boot necks, mate,' Spike answered, pointing at Bungy and himself. 'Are you a former or serving marine? We saw your badge!'

Beast scrunched his face up squinting and rubbing his eyes with his gloved hands. He looked back up towards the sky and listened to the bird's whistling in the background before refocusing on the two strangers above him.

'Am I dead? Or is this a dream?' he asked, uncertain of the response he would receive.

Bungy and Spike laughed aloud and helped him up onto his feet. They held onto his arms whilst checking him over for any undiscovered injuries. He was unhurt, apparently just suffering minor concussion.

'Where are my wheels?' he asked, wanting to see if his bike was damaged. 'Are they still in one piece?'

Bungy weaved the bike onto its stand and tapped it with his hand. 'Your bike looks okay to me mate, apart from a minor dent on the fuel tank and some scratches on the paintwork.'

Beast climbed on board keeping one foot either side on the floor. He turned the ignition key, which immediately started the engine. He revved it a couple of times and then switched it off, satisfied and pushed it back onto its stand.

'Did you mention something about boot necks or did I imagine it?' he asked them.

'We saw your badge,' Spike repeated. 'We're both former boot necks.' 'Are you a boot neck?'

'I'm an ex-boot neck the same as you.'

The men talked about their experiences in the marines for a while and found that although they did not know each other, they had certainly chewed some of the same dirt. Beast told them he had specialised as a physical training instructor (PTI) and mentioned his earlier visit to collect debts at Barry's house.

'Is that Baz Broadhurst, the P.W.?' (Platoon Weapons - a weapons specialist). Bungy queried.

'Yes that's him. He also spent some time working as a covert operations car driver.'

'I know him. He wasn't a mate of mine but we did serve together. We served in the Arctic during the cold war.'

The three of them conversed for a while longer until Beast eventually decided it was time to go their separate ways. He suggested they should meet up for a social evening some time later and both men keenly accepted.

'I'll telephone Baz and tell him what we're planning so we can arrange something,' Beast said. 'I'm certain he'll be up for it.'

They exchanged contact details, scribbling them down on pieces of paper and then headed off.

Several days later, Beast called Bungy on his mobile telling him that he was arranging a reunion. He also confirmed that Baz was keen to join them too, which pleased Bungy. They agreed to organize the event in Plymouth; choosing the location because it was somewhere they had all been familiar with at some point in their careers.

Chapter Five

"Next stop Plymouth." A voice sounded out across the slowing train's announcement system.

'We're here,' Bungy chortled towards Spike, who was opposite him with his chin resting on top of his hands leaning on the table between them.

The expression on his face remained blank and he just nodded his head once to acknowledge his friend's observation. He sat trying hard to recall the last time he had been to Plymouth. Strangely, he felt as if he had been there a number of times since leaving the marines but no matter how hard he tried, he could not remember.

'I'll give you a penny for your thoughts, mate?' Bungy said softly, containing his growing excitement and breaking Spike's concentration.

'That's the problem. I can't remember much after I left the marines,' Spike told him.

'Don't worry about it, mate. Let's just have a good run ashore.' (A marine term for a night on the town)

The train's brakes screeched loudly under the carriages, bringing them to a halt. The men stood up, collected their baggage and disembarked out onto the platform. Spike took a couple of deep breaths and started to cough after inhaling some of the exhaust fumes that belched out from the train's diesel engine.

'Oh bollocks,' Bungy hollered, sounding unhappy about something.

'What's the matter with you?' Spiked asked curiously, coughing a few more times into a soft tissue handkerchief.

Bungy wrinkled his forehead with a look of worry. Whatever the problem was, it looked serious!

'I've just stood in some sloppy dog shit!' he snapped flinging his hand in the air.

His sudden outburst made Spike laugh and was just the formula needed to cheer him up. His laughter continued as he watched Bungy scraping his foot along the floor, desperately trying to remove the dog dirt from the sole of his shoe.

A short taxi ride later they checked into a guesthouse, showered and headed into the city centre. The agreed rendezvous was a pub called, The Phoenix, located off the city's busy Union-Street. Baz and Beast had already arrived and were waiting inside to greet their friends.

The four of them sat together for a while drinking beer and spinning yarns about their military service, recalling encounters from challenging and dangerous experiences. This was something the marines referred to as telling dits or swinging the lamp. After a couple of hours of raucous laughter, their conversation turned to their lives after they had been de-mobbed. Three of them agreed that they weren't very happy with their lives in civvy-street in comparison with their days in the marines. Spike, of course; could not recall what he had been up to, apart from living rough on the streets.

During the evening, they moved from pub to pub. Some of these places were old haunts, which had been refurbished and turned into posh wine-bars. The nightlife was busy in Plymouth; so busy that it was difficult to be served at the bar without fierce competition. Because of this, they opted to go to a quieter venue where they would have more space and the ability to hold a conversation without loud background music.

Twenty minutes later, they sat together in a quiet back street pub. It was far away from the bustling Union-Street atmosphere and much easier going when it came to buying a round of drinks.

'Is this a sign of us getting old or what?' Bungy referred to the preference of a more sedate atmosphere.

'No, it's a sign of being sensible,' Beast piped up. 'We're not as young and wild as we used to be, but that doesn't mean we're old men.'

'Yeah you're right,' Baz added. 'I'm older and wiser these days, but I'm middle aged not old aged. I'm still full of hell when somebody pisses me off and I can still produce the goods in a fight if I have to.'

At that moment, someone turned the volume up on the pub's stereo system and a popular rock and roll record thumped out of the hi-fi speakers attached to the walls. They were opposite a small wooden dance floor. Baz grinned, jumping up onto his feet nonchalantly walking across the room towards two attractive middle-aged women.

'Would you like to dance, babe?' he asked one of them, beaming with confidence.

She initially looked surprised at the invitation, but nodded her head to grant his request. As she stood up, she smiled at her friend who was shyly hiding behind her half-full beer glass. She took hold of the hand offered to her, fully expecting Baz to escort her like a true gent. Contrary to this and to her surprise he bent forward at the waist and put his arms around her upper legs, hoisting her upwards and over onto his shoulder. He ran onto the dance floor where he started to swing her around his neck like a rag doll. Her long black hair spilled over her pretty face and she held on tightly to him and her skirt. When the music ended, he carefully placed her down onto her feet bowing towards her. Sweat was pouring from his brow and he panted for breath. The woman unbelievably enjoyed the experience and laughed loudly, tidying her ruffled hair. It was not the first time that this had happened to her, but it was the first time in a good number of years. She curtsied contently towards Baz, walking away to re-join her friend who was patiently holding onto their handbags waiting to leave.

'I might see you later,' she smiled at Baz, hinting that she liked him.

He beamed a content smile nodding and waving to her. Then he sat down amongst his friends, taking deep breaths to steady his breathing.

'Look, you're breathing heavy like a hoax telephone caller or even a rapist!' Bungy joked.

'Yes but like I said, I'm middle-aged not old aged and I'm still fairly fit too. Plus I can still pull the dolly birds.'

'Evidently,' Bungy grinned, just as another lively record sounded out from the jukebox.

Instantly, he jumped up onto his feet and started running around the pub pretending to bounce and skilfully move a make-believe basketball on the floor and around his body. Other customers looked on and laughed as he sped past them jumping on and off the empty chairs and across the tables. When the record finished he stopped and simulated kicking the ball like a goalkeeper, away and far into the distance. Then he sat back down with his friends where he wiped the sweat from his cheeks and guzzled his beer.

'Yeah, I'm still full of beans too,' he chortled and gurgled a mouth full of ale.

'I didn't realise you were so talented with a ball,' Baz winked.

Bungy wasn't listening. He broke from their conversation and decided to try his luck at getting off with a loose girl.

'Hi babe,' he waved at a middle-aged woman who was standing with another female. 'Can I buy you a drink?'

'Yes why not?' she answered cheerfully. 'Can you get my friend one too?

'Yes no problem.'

He went to the bar to order the drinks and returned a few minutes later. He handed them to the girls, searching his mind for the best chat up lines he could use to try to impress them.

'So what do you guys do for a living?' One of the girls asked him.

'Urm, we're Lighthouse Keepers.'

'Lighthouse Keepers!' she exclaimed, wondering if he was pulling her leg.

'Yes, Lighthouse Keepers. I polish the bulbs and those guys do the rest.'

'What do you mean?'

Bungy pointed to each of his friends in turn. 'Well, he cleans the mirrors, he washes the windows and that big ugly gorilla with the muscles is our Chef.'

'You mean you're boot necks,' one of girls said and the three of them burst into laughter.

Several metres away, Beast was leaning forward on his chair, taking charge of the conversation between them. He was slurring as he spoke, but his speech was clear enough for his friends to understand.

'Listen men. We're all back here in Plymouth reminiscing about the days when we served as marines. That was a long time ago now, but we're all still fit and active middle-aged men.'

'Where is this leading?' Spike interjected, unsure of the point that Beast was trying to make.

'Well, we were all once highly skilled elite soldiers.'

'Yes and....' Baz questioned, looking a little lost with the conversation.

'Wait a minute,' Beast grunted, getting up and walking over to Bungy who was still working hard trying to impress the two women.

'Bungy, we've got an important conversation going on here.'

'So?' he shrugged, not wanting to be distracted from the interested females.

'So, get rid of the two gronks.' (A marine nickname for an ugly woman.) Beast snapped pointing at the girls who frowned at his derogatory remark.

Bungy was hesitant, but succumbed to the request when Spike and Baz also insisted he joined them. A couple of minutes

63

later, the two women were gone and the men all sat down together with a fresh round of drinks.

'This had better be bloody good,' Bungy frowned, more than a little disappointed with his friend's harsh behaviour.

Beast had their undivided attention and this time was adamant that he would get his point across. 'Right, as I was saying earlier. Once we were elite Royal Marine Commandos and were highly skilled soldiers.'

'You mean we're ex-marines now,' Spike interrupted. 'Tell us something new.'

'No wait. Let's hear what he has to say,' Baz insisted.

'During our time in the marines we all trained in various roles, gaining specialist skills in addition to our soldiering abilities,' Beast continued. 'Baz was a P.W. (Platoon Weapons specialist) and a covert operations fast car driver. Bungy was a Mountain Leader and a reputed Sniper. Spike was an Assault Engineer (Explosives Specialist) and I was a Physical Training Instructor (PTI).'

For a number of seconds there was a complete silence amongst them. They looked somewhat confused about the point being made and listened with focused curiosity.

'Basically men, we have a lot of specialist skills that are not being utilized and could in my opinion, have the potential to be put to better use. We are what could be termed as a wasted resource.'

'Yes and...? Baz shrugged, repeating his earlier half-finished question.

'We're all missing the buzz, the challenges, hardships and the excitement of being marines. We have all expressed unhappiness with our lives since leaving the Corps. I assume you will all agree that we have some very useful skills between us. So why don't we put them to good use to pull a bank job or something like that.'

'What a pile of crap,' Bungy chirped, still reeling because the two women had left. 'You're making us sound like the A Team that used to be on the TV.'

'I'm very serious about this,' Beast insisted, hoping his idea was being taken seriously. 'In reality, once skilled soldiers leave the armed forces their specialist skills go to waste. Yet the world would probably be a much safer place if these skills were redeployed and pitted against terrorists, drug pushers and organised crime. Unfortunately they aren't. However, if we utilize these skills ourselves then we could soon be very rich men.'

'That would be breaking the law,' Spike pointed out, simultaneously contemplating the proposition. 'Oh what the hell, I'm up for it,' he added. 'But, it will take a lot of planning.'

'Me too I'm in,' Bungy nodded, losing his annoyance about the women.

'Well I don't want to be left out,' Baz chipped in. 'But let's make it one good job so that we can reduce the risk of going to jail, and preferably retire abroad.'

Each of them expressed their full commitment by making a toast to it; agreeing to carry out some form of heist. They talked collectively putting together some high-level preparation ideas. Beast said that he would formulate a fitness programme to get them back to a reasonable level of physical fitness. Baz said he knew of an undisturbed IRA weapons and explosives cache that they could raid. This was apparently located in the hills of South Armagh in Northern Ireland.

They all raised their glasses again and drank a final toast to enforce their willingness to put the group together. There was an air of excitement amongst them. It was the type of buzz they felt when they faced difficult and trying situations together during their service careers.

'Spike! Spike!' a young woman's voice hollered across the half-crowded bar. Her words interrupted the short-lived celebration. 'Spike! Spike! Spike!' she repeatedly cried out.

The men looked up, setting eyes on an attractive woman with long blonde hair, who was staring at Spike with a shocked expression. She ran towards him and started to cry, throwing her arms around him and cuddling him like a long lost friend. Spike was puzzled and did not reciprocate. He vaguely recognized her soft voice but could not place her pretty and tearful face.

'Spike! Spike! Spike! I thought I'd lost you,' she sorrowfully repeated, still hanging tightly onto him.

'Is this some gronk he used to know?' Bungy asked, feeling certain it was.

'No it isn't,' another strange female butted in. 'She's his wife.'

Everybody fell silent! The woman hugging Spike introduced herself as Lindsay and went on to explain that her husband had suffered a serious head injury shortly after leaving the marines. She told them that he had been unwell for a long period and was feared dead after disappearing from a hospital ward.

'I can see you're still having problems with amnesia,' she said, releasing her hold on Spike. 'Please look at these.'

She rummaged through her handbag, pulling a number of family photographs from it and showing them to Spike and his friends. There was no doubt about it. It was definitely him. Lindsay pulled several more photographs out and handed them to Spike who appeared totally shocked, speechless and unsure of how he should deal with the currently unexplainable situation.

'These are our two children, Paul and David,' she told him. 'They really miss you. When you disappeared you broke their hearts and mine too.'

Spike found it hard to recollect this part of his life. His mind reeled with confusion as he repeatedly flicked through the photographs.

'Will you come home with me,' she tearfully asked.

He stared at her, then at his friends and then at the photographs. Its definitely me, he thought. Maybe I was this person before I lived on the streets. He agreed to go home with her to see their children. At least then, he could be optimistic about piecing his life back together after leaving the marines. Even so,

66

he felt afraid about walking into the unknown and about the anxiety; he must have caused his family. If indeed, it was his family!

Lindsay took him by the hand and held on tightly as they walked out of the bar together. Spike bade his friends' goodnight and discreetly told them he still wanted to honour his agreement and that he would be in touch with them later.

Bungy started reeling again about not getting off with one of the two loose women, earlier. He set eyes on Lindsay's friend and moved his attention towards her. She was a petite woman with long brown hair, firm looking breasts and a nice, shapely figure. At first he thought about trying his best chat up lines on her, but the beer he had consumed brought out his mischievous side. Instead, he decided to give her some abuse, just to see if she had the sense of humour to handle it.

'So what do they call a good looking babe like you then?' he asked her.

'Amanda,' she responded with interest. 'Are you going to buy me a drink?'

'That depends.'

'On what?'

'Whether or not you look at the toilet paper after you've wiped your shitty arse on it.'

'Don't try to flatter me,' she smirked, showing she could handle his foul comments.

Bungy kissed her on the cheek, inviting her to sit down at a spare table opposite Beast and Bungy. He was impressed with her quick wit, so he went to the bar and bought her and his two remaining friends a drink. When he returned he discreetly winked at his colleagues, indicating he was comfortable in the company of his female friend. He put his arm around Amanda's shoulders, grinning and whispering in her ear.

'I'd walk a million miles over broken glass on my hands and knees to smell the exhaust fumes of the wagon carrying your sweaty knickers to the cleaners.'

Amanda laughed hysterically, before embracing him in a wet tongue-lashing kiss. Baz and Beast ignored the two love-birds. They sat talking about old times, recalling names of former colleagues and characters in their military days.

A short while later, Bungy walked over to bid his friends goodnight. He put his hand up level with his cheek and whispered to them tactfully so that Amanda could not hear.

'I'm off guys, I've pulled. I'm going to give this honey some ex-commando dagger. I'm going shag the arse off her,' he sniggered, turning and walking away out of the exit door with Amanda.

The men grinned at him and at each other, nodding to acknowledge that he was leaving. They were secretly pleased that they were making tracks. They wanted the privacy so that they could discuss the fundamentals and high level planning for a future operation. Beast bought another round of beers and the two of them drank late into the night.

Chapter Six

Paul and David were overjoyed when they saw their father, as he unceremoniously entered their home with their mother. The two six-year old twins jumped up from the arms of their teenage baby-sitter and ran towards him, hugging him tightly with tears of joy streaming down their faces. They didn't know why he had left them two years ago, but that didn't matter now. They were just glad he was home with them again.

Spike reciprocated by hugging his children, but showed no emotion at their reunion; struggling to remember them. Lindsay watched his expressionless face and felt feint with the events of the evening. She sat down and cupped her hands over her eyes, sobbing heavily. Her child minder looked on without saying anything. She had only known Lindsay for the last year or so, but did have a good idea who the visitor was. She had seen him on the many photographs that littered the walls.

Spike sat down on one of the easy chairs next to Lindsay. He did not acknowledge the presence of the child minder. He just looked blankly at Lindsay and the children. He sat back, idly glancing around the walls of the sitting room with raised eyebrows, recognizing himself in some of the many photographs that hung there. One of the pictures had been taken outside a small church on their wedding day, when he was still in the marines. He was dressed in his blues uniform with his medals glinting in the sunlight. Strangely, this home appeared unfamiliar to him and he wondered if they had lived somewhere else previously. He tactfully chose not to pose this question to Lindsay, for fear of upsetting her further. Instead, he casually walked around the house and looked inside all the rooms to see if he could recognize something that would help to trigger his memory. The children followed him everywhere and were keen not to let him move out of their sight.

Lindsay bade goodnight to her child minder and switched on the kettle to make Spike and herself a cup of tea. She had mixed feelings for her husband who had strangely reappeared after a long-term unexplainable absence. Her emotions remained at the forefront of her mind, with tears intermittently streaming down her cheeks. It was more out of relief than anger, because she truly had thought she had lost him forever. The whole experience had been a stressful and traumatic time for her. At one stage, things got so difficult that she even contemplated committing suicide. Eventually, she struggled through this state of mind, because of her love for their children.

Prior to his disappearance, Spike had suffered a severe head injury after being involved in a serious car crash. The tragic accident had happened only two weeks after he had left the marines. Sadly, his younger sister had been a passenger in the car and had unfortunately lost her life.

Lindsay knew Spike was still confused with the events of the evening - so she showed him several photograph albums to try to jog his memory. He smiled and nodded his head every now and then trying to convince Lindsey and himself that he could remember all of them but truthfully, he could not.

That night, for the first time in over two years, Lindsay slept soundly. She felt content and secure now that her husband was safe and back with her and the children.

However, Spike lay wide-awake beside her staring around the room in the darkness. He was tired and a little tipsy too, but he still found it hard to drift off to sleep. The house was strange to him. So was the woman who claimed to be his wife and the mother of his children. Could it be possible that she was married to someone else who strongly resembles me? he thought. Maybe this is some kind of big mix up. Maybe it's just a bad dream and I'll wake up soon.

Even so, there was no doubt that the photographs showed him in the marines. He vaguely recognized all of them, except the one when he had apparently got married to Lindsay. He wondered if that was another marine or possibly even his twin brother. If he had one! That would certainly explain things, although he couldn't remember if he had any brothers or sisters. Then again, maybe she was right; maybe he had lost his memory. It would certainly explain his lack of recall. He hoped a little more time would allow his memory to return. We will see, he thought, feeling a little happier, turning onto his side and finally dozing off to sleep.

Spike dreamt about a military operation that he took part in during the gulf war. It was a familiar dream he had experienced repeatedly during the times he had been sleeping rough on the streets. Several loud explosions thundered into the sky in the distance, as allied forces targeted and bombed key electrical power installations deep inside Iraq's city of Basra. It was night time and the distant activity was irrelevant to Spike's objective. He was attached to the Special Boat Squadron (SBS). They were special-forces and the cream of the cream amongst the world's elite fighting soldiers. He busied himself carefully attaching explosives to the lower beams of a bridge that the Iraqis' used as a main supply route. The insulated plastic explosives were strapped tightly to the woodwork, twelve inches above the icy cold water line. Thankfully, Spike's body wasn't wet. He had climbed through the beams with the explosives packed inside a bergen strapped to his back. He was understandably a little nervous as he carefully eased his way across the structure. He wasn't alone. Another Assault Engineer nicknamed Smudger accompanied him. The two of them were only a minute or so away from finishing their work. Suddenly, Smudger fell silently backwards splashing into the cold running water. He was dead and had been killed by a single bullet propelled from a lone Iraqi sniper's rifle. Spike was terrified and at the same time defenceless. He had seen his colleague's deadly fate, just a few moments ago and was nervously struggling to make his way back across to the safety of the riverbank. He could almost feel the presence of the sniper homing in with his sights poised on his head.

Deep in the undergrowth a marine sniper searched frantically for the opposing sniper, whom he knew would be lining up his next shot on the vulnerable Assault Engineer. The image-intensifying sights outlined the well-camouflaged body of the enemy. The marine sniper squeezed on his trigger firing one single shot, recoiling. An instant later, the opposing marksman slumped dead to the ground.

Spike moved nervously unaware of this and eventually dropped from the bridge ducking into the undergrowth on the other side of the river. He felt a deep sadness for Smudger, but he was gone now. That was the ultimate reality of the job. They perceived death as an acceptable risk or even a destiny for some. He knew that, but it didn't make life any easier. Being a soldier was not just about death. It was also about survival, fitness and comradeship,

71

as well as enduring hardships and life threatening situations together. Spike's thoughts rushed back to Smudger's twisted face. In despair, he screamed out into the night.

'NNNNNNNNOOOOOOOOOO!'

'Spike. Spike, wake up you're still having those nightmares,' Lindsay called out, holding tightly onto his hand.

'Uh what?' he murmured opening his eyes. 'Oh I'm sorry it was a bad dream.'

'You were having those dreams before you disappeared. You should go and see a doctor, somebody who can help you.'

'No, Lindsay. I'm okay. I haven't had one of those dreams for a long time now.

Something must have triggered it. Maybe it was something I saw when I looked through the photographs last night."

'I don't know. I'm just glad you're back home again,' she smiled affectionately and kissed him on the forehead.

A while later, she got out of bed and went down stairs to make them some breakfast.

Spike rose a few minutes later, but not before the children ran inside the room to make sure their father was still there.

'Daddy, Daddy,' they called out to him, jumping onto the bed and hugging him tightly.

He grinned amiably. It felt good to be made so welcome.

During breakfast, they sat around the kitchen table and Lindsay chose to tell Spike more about his accident and the unfortunate death of his sister. She also told him about their lives together before it all happened, about her fears for his life whilst he was in hospital and the despair she experienced after he had disappeared. As she spoke, she could not help but notice the blank look of perplexity on his face. It alerted her to the fact that he was still having problems remembering things. At this point, she couldn't help herself. She felt compelled to ask him what he had done with his time after he had mysteriously disappeared.

72

'Where did you go when you left the hospital?' she questioned.

'I don't remember ever being in hospital,' Spike answered truthfully.

'Where have you lived for the past two years?'

'I've been living rough on the streets. I can't remember how or even when I got there. Eventually I met Bungy and we moved into a flat together and took on a couple of jobs in a warehouse and in a nightclub working as security men.'

Lindsay was eager. Her compulsion to know the answer to the next question on her mind was overpowering. 'Is there another woman in your life?' she fearfully asked, almost expecting her husband to say yes.

'I don't think so,' he told her, trying hard to recollect a woman on the streets.

His unsure response deeply annoyed Lindsay and made her feel disconcerted and angry towards him. He's got another woman, she thought, practically convincing herself that he had been unfaithful.

'You've got another woman haven't you? Haven't you?' she snapped, lunging forward and slapping Spike hard across the face.

'Ouch. What the hell did you do that for?' he yelled and grabbed tight hold of her wrists.

'Why didn't you come home? Why didn't you bloody come home?' she cried with a flushed face and tearful eyes.

Spike did not answer. He couldn't. His mind was blank. The children began to cry, upset by their parents' aggressive argument. Spike released his grip on Lindsay, allowing her to console their children. He stood up leaving his unfinished meal and headed into the bathroom to wash and dress.

'I'm going out for a walk,' he said, combing his hair. 'My head is bursting and I need to gather my thoughts.'

Lindsey just nodded to acknowledge his intentions. She dared not speak. Deep inside, she was hurting and fearful that he may choose to disappear again.

Outside, Spike drew in several sharp breaths of fresh morning air. He took a good look at the street house and also at the street signpost. He needed to be sure he could find the house again after he had returned from his walk. Rain started to fall from a cloudy sky and it trickled down his clean-shaven face. He wasn't bothered about getting wet. He was used to it. He recognized most of the surrounding area, probably from when he served in the marines. He ambled along a series of streets towards an area called Stonehouse. There was a Royal Marines' barracks there, logically named Stonehouse Barracks. On his way there, he walked down Union Street smiling to himself. The place held so many memories for him that remained clear in his mind. This was where he had socialized with his friends during his spare time at weekends and after tours abroad, including the war in the Gulf. Quite often, they would go into town in fancy dress. It was a fun way of letting off steam, along with excessive boozing.

Half way along the street, he stopped for a while and sat down on an empty wooden-bench. He looked up and down the busy area and along the adjacent streets that were in view. He could remember the fun, the banter and the odd scrap he had experienced here. It was strange to him, because he could clearly remember this but not his life after the marines, with the exception of living rough on the streets! He felt like he'd been doing that for an eternity until recently.

A convoy of military vehicles thundered past him. Their dense exhaust fumes billowing out through rattling exhaust pipes. Royal Marines drove them. That was obvious, because they were wearing their coveted green berets. Spike watched the vehicles with interest until they disappeared out of sight. Then he stood up and made his way towards the barracks knowing the vehicles would be heading there.

The large off-white building came into view. Its high, green, metal perimeter railings were still the same as previous except for a new lick of paint. A Union Jack flag housed high up on a flagpole flapped rhythmically in the mild wind. He felt good inside. It was almost as if he was still serving there and had just popped outside for a newspaper. He casually stood on the pavement on the opposite side of the road from the stone archway that led inside of the barracks. A lone marine sentry, armed with an SA80 assault rifle, stood guarding the entrance gate. Spike took a particular interest in his attire and especially his green beret. Winning that took a lot of blood, sweat and tears, he thought. It was worth it.

His presence caught the marine sentry's attention. He was vigilant about the strange suspicious looking man, observing him from the other side of the road. He spoke a few words into a small radio strapped to his combat jacket, remaining focused on Spike.

'Are you looking for someone?' he shouted aloud across the street, deeming it necessary to challenge the man.

Spike's face lit up. He recalled the many times he had stood guard at this gate and the odd occasion when he too had to challenge someone who looked suspicious. He laughed aloud and nonchalantly walked across the road towards the marine.

'Are you looking for someone?' the sentry repeated.

Spike didn't reply and stopped just a couple of feet away from him, with the light rain dripping down his face. For no particular reason, he chose to joke with the sentry. Why not? he thought; people used to do it to me!

'Hi there marine, is that a cabbage on your head?' he smirked, facetiously referring to the marine's beret.

The sentry's facial expression remained serious, looking displeased about being insulted.

'Are you looking for someone?' he asked again, but this time in a raised voice.

His abrupt manner irritated Spike. He felt it would be unfair to vent his frustration on the marine and decided to continue taunting him. 'I've got a gun in my pocket and I'm going to shoot some bastard with it,' he scoffed tapping the under arm area of his coat.

The sentry reacted on impulse when Spike neared, grabbing a tight hold of his jacket. He pushed him down onto the ground and was joined by two other armed guards who came running out of the nearby guardroom.

'Stay down on the floor,' the sentry shouted, pointing his rifle at the back of Spike's head.

Spike was taken by surprise. Everything happened so fast and it never occurred to him that this would happen. He thought the sentry would laugh and joke with him; just like he used to.

'It's alright mate I'm an ex-marine,' he said, face down but consciously nervous that a loaded rifle was being pointed at him.

'Stay down and don't move,' the sentry hollered, as passers-by, innocently going about their business, looked on in disbelief.

The other two men moved quickly, searching Spike's clothing for concealed weapons. One of them put his hand on Spike's wallet, so he naturally reacted by pulling it back towards himself. The marines deemed this a threatening move and swiftly struck him on the back of the head with a rifle butt. Spike's mouth fell open and the pain caused by the blow engulfed him, temporarily paralyzing him and rendering him helpless. They handcuffed his hands behind his back, dragged him up onto his feet and through the entrance archway into the guardroom.

The inside was small and brightly painted. It had a reception counter used to greet visitors. It was almost the same as when he had served. They pushed him through an opening in the counter and into a small prison cell, slamming the steel door shut behind him. There was an echo for a couple of seconds; then a bunch of keys rattled in the lock.

Spike stood motionless, staring blankly at the clean, cream walls. He shook his head rigorously from side to side in astonishment of the events that had occurred in the past few minutes. He sighed, sitting down on a striped mattress placed on top of a single metal- bed frame. He slouched back against the cold brick wall and stared mutely at the white ceiling, aimlessly occupying himself with counting the screws that held a light fitting in place.

A bunch of keys rattled in the cell door lock again and the steel door creaked open. A tall, broadly built marine with a thick walrus moustache walked in. He was dressed in combat uniform and Spike noticed that he had three stripes on his right sleeve indicating he was the duty Sergeant. He towered over Spike and looked down at him.

'Who are you and what the hell are you playing at telling the main gate sentry that you've got a gun when you clearly haven't?' the sergeant asked abruptly. 'Do you realise how serious this is? You could have been killed.'

Spike eased himself up. 'I.., ouch.' he squirmed, feeling the effects of his swollen sore head.

'What's your name?' the sergeant continued, unlocking the handcuffs.

'Its Spike Millard, I'm an ex-boot neck. I left the corps a couple of years ago. Ouch my bloody head hurts. He didn't have to hit me with the bloody rifle butt, did he?'

'Hit you, Spike,' the Sergeant snapped, wide-eyed. 'You're lucky he didn't bloody shoot you!'

The sergeant took all of Spike's personal details, including his former service number and date of discharge and left the cell. He closed the door shut but didn't lock it. Inside the guardroom, his voice echoed as he made a couple of telephone calls to authenticate the details he had been given. The Records Officer on the other end of the telephone confirmed Spike's identity and instructed the sergeant to check for a distinguishing mark that was tattooed on Spike's bottom.

When he returned to the cell, he felt a little silly. Almost, seemingly part of some pathetic joke that had gone drastically wrong. 'I've been told I can confirm your identity by a couple of tattoos that you've got on your buttocks, sir,' he said, looking embarrassed.

'Yes, I'll drop my trousers, bend over for you and look for the golden rivet on the floor,' Spike grinned, unbuckling his trousers.

The sergeant ignored the supposedly humorous comments and nodded his head after Spike exposed a tattoo of a single eye on both of his cheeks.

'I like to keep an eye out for any bastard who tries to shoot me in the arse,' he joked.

'Okay, okay four eyes.' the Sergeant retorted. 'Come and get yourself a cup of tea and you can go home.'

The marine who had struck Spike in the head with his rifle butt came into the guardroom and apologized to him. There were no hard feelings between the two men and they shook hands to close the matter amiably. Spike sat comfortably amongst the marines for a while sipping his drink and exchanging war stories. Eventually he shook their hands and bade them goodbye.

Outside the barracks, he paused and took one last look at the historical building. The place held so many great memories for him, so he absorbed the view before heading back towards Lindsay's house.

The rain had ceased and he focused his thoughts on Lindsay and her children, ambling along with his hands in his pockets. He tried hard to recall any memory of them, but still had absolutely no recollection whatsoever. He concluded that he couldn't possibly live with this family and pretend to be somebody else. Why should he? His conscience wouldn't let him. Nor did he want to for that matter. Why would he? He would explain this to Lindsay face-to-face when he got back to her house. Then he intended to leave and meet up with his friends again. Yes that's what I'm going to do, he thought.

When Spike arrived back at the house, he found Lindsay sitting distraught at the kitchen table. Her eyes were reddened by the many tears shed since he left. Paul and David were crying too, trying hard to console her.

'Christopher.' Thank god you've come back.' she said to him. 'We thought we'd lost you again.'

'Daddy, daddy we've missed you,' the children added, holding onto his clothing.

Spike's face dropped and his mouth fell slightly open. His mind was empty of thoughts and he was initially unsure of what to do.

'Look, I can't do this,' he insisted. 'I'm not Christopher. I'm not your husband and I'm not the father of these children.'

'Christopher, please don't say that,' Lindsay choked. 'You still aren't very well. You've had a memory relapse. We can get professional help for you. Yes, we can do that,' she assured him.

'No, no,' he replied shaking his head. 'You're the one who needs help. I can't pretend to be somebody else. It doesn't feel morally right. It's not morally right. You've got me mixed up with somebody else who looks like me.'

'Christopher. No I haven't. It's your memory. The car accident's caused this. Please understand that,' she pleaded and gently took hold of his hand.

'Get off,' Spike snapped, coldly pulling his hand away. 'Look here, my name is Spike. It's not Christopher.'

'Daddy, please don't leave us again,' Paul sobbed, still clutching onto his father's clothing along with David.

'Bollocks to this,' Spike exclaimed angrily. 'I've had enough of this crap. I'm getting out of here.'

He turned and headed towards the front door, coldly pushing the children away from him as he went.

'No please. Please don't go. Please don't leave us again,' Lindsay pleaded reaching out with both arms to hug him.

Spike pushed her hands away and rushed out of the house, running off along the deserted street outside and hurriedly out of sight. As he ran, he could hear Lindsay and the children desperately calling after him. He ignored their pleas and felt relieved to have gotten himself out of this strange situation.

Chapter Seven

'Is my friend still here? Spike asked the Landlady at the guesthouse where Bungy and himself had checked into.

'No I'm afraid he's not,' she answered mildly. 'Two other gentlemen came to meet him a short while ago and they all left together. He's paid your bill and has taken your things with him. They said they were going to the train station. They haven't been gone long.'

Spike did not stop to hear her last sentence and was already rushing away from the doorstep, off towards Plymouth's train-station.

'Hey, big nuts. Are you looking for us?' Bungy shouted through an open cafeteria window where he was sitting with Beast and Baz.

Spike smiled and waved, feeling very relieved that he had managed to locate his friends without too much hassle. He pushed the swing door open and entered inside the busy premises, where he joined a small queue to purchase a fresh cup of coffee for himself and the others.

His three friends were understandably a little surprised to see him and wondered why he had returned after being reunited with his family.

'What are you doing here?' Baz asked him.

The same question was on the tip of the tongues of Bungy and Beast's too.

'What do you mean?' he shrugged, holding his hands out with the palms up.

He appeared bemused with the question and gave the impression that he deemed it irrelevant.

'Have you come to say goodbye to us?' Bungy asked him.

'No I haven't. There's no reason to say goodbye. I'm going wherever you lot are going.'

'But, what about your wife and family?' Beast asked, visibly concerned about their welfare.

'They aren't my family,' Spike replied convincingly. 'That woman was drunk and was spouting crap.'

'Did you shag her?' Bungy asked cheekily.

'Yeah, but when I got to the vinegar strokes I pulled my penis out and wiped it on the blankets,' he quipped, making the difficult subject humorous.

Everybody started to laugh and rolled around holding their ribs. Each of them shook Spike's hand in turn and welcomed him back into their present company with no further questions posed. They laughed and joked together for a while longer, prior to informing Spike that they were heading off to Beast's house for a number of weeks.

Once there, Beast would use his PTI (Physical Training Instructor) skills to get them back into good physical shape. Then they planned to collect some small arms from a hidden IRA weapons cache, located at South Armagh in Northern Ireland, utilizing them to pull some sort of bank or pay roll robbery.

Beast's house was situated in the sticks on the outskirts of Liverpool. It was very private where he lived, with his home set in its own grounds. This seclusion proved beneficial. There were no issues with nosey, interfering neighbours, the closest being over a mile away.

The men travelled second class on the train and then jumped into Beast's car on arrival at Liverpool. It was parked in a hotel car park just a short distance away from the station. They drove for twenty minutes or so, up the East Lancashire Road and down a country lane near Knowsley Safari Park. Eventually they approached an old Victorian house visible through an edging of surrounding conifers.

'Wow, this is a nice pad, mate,' Baz exclaimed when they drove beyond the wrought iron gates. 'This debt collecting game must pay well.'

'It does,' Beast retorted. 'But I've got a mortgage to pay and I'm out of work now. Remember?'

'Oh yes. I forgot about that,' Baz nodded, suddenly recalling that Beast had quit his job after being sent to collect debts from him.

The car came to a halt and everybody stepped outside, viewing the building's stone clad brickwork and freshly painted window frames with lead flashings crisscrossing the glass panes.

Beast showed the men around his abode and introduced them to his wife, who later packed some of her belongings into a suitcase and left to stay with her mother for a while. She didn't mind doing this. If her husband told her he had some business to tend to, she just packed her things and never asked questions - past experience had taught her that it was best not to.

The men were shown to the rooms they would be sleeping in for the duration of their stay. Baz felt privileged with unexpectedly getting one to himself. Nobody disagreed with this decision. They were told it was allocated to reflect his former rank and the number of years he had served in the Corps. Bungy and Spike would have to share a room, but this was okay as it contained two single beds.

'I hope you don't have any homosexual tendencies,' Spike joked. 'I don't want to see you trying to shag me when I'm asleep!'

'Careful,' Bungy warned him. 'If I find that you don't sleep with one eye open I might just shoot you right in the arse. Yes, in the rusty bullet hole!' Bungy humorously responded, referring to the fact that he was a former sniper.

Once they had settled in, the four of them talked idly amongst themselves for a while, before moving their focus towards Beast when he asked for their attention.

'Okay guys, listen in. I guess its time to go back to basics. Before we plan any form of heist or operation together, if you want to call it that. I need to get you lot into some form of decent physical shape. Fitness you may remember was always paramount when we served in the Corps. It's still paramount. There will be no room for any slackers.'

They looked around at one another nodding their heads, mutually agreeing that this would be imperative. For a while, the initial emphasis would be on physical fitness. The rules were set and there was to be no straying off with loose women or drinking alcohol. They were to treat the situation in the same professional manner that they had adopted when serving in the military on active tours of duty. It was the best and most professional way to conduct this.

Beast had actively played the part of the spokesperson of the group up until now and even though it was assumed that he would take the lead role, he boldly confirmed this by saying that he would be the one giving the orders from now on. Additionally he appointed Baz to act as his second in command. Nobody disagreed with his announcement, maybe because it seemed the most logical choice of leadership.

Although Beast was comfortable in monetary terms, everybody wanted to contribute some funds to pay for their food and upkeep, which they did. They also wanted to purchase some physical training kit such as training shoes, socks, shorts and tee shirts; instead of running around inappropriately in jeans and pullovers. Baz was tasked with buying the kit. He took everybody's measurements and nipped out to a sports store.

Later; and in contrast to the no alcohol agreement they decided to drink some ale together. It would be one last time before the commencement of their physical training routine, which was scheduled to start the following day. After trying their newly acquired training kit on, they settled on easy chairs in the living room drinking excessive amounts of wine and beer. They laughed and joked between themselves, playing cards around a table and spinning yarns about hair-raising experiences. It was enjoyable to reminisce. They felt a sense of pride and belonging amongst themselves, allowing them to begin bonding their friendships together as a team.

'Come on you idle git. It's time to get up,' Bungy said to Spike early the following morning, shaking him by the feet.

Spike sucked his lips and opened his eyes, rubbing them with his fingers. He squinted and concentrated hard trying to make out the time on a close-by ticking clock.

'Bloody hell mate,' he yawned. 'It's only five to six. It's still the middle of the night. Have you pissed the bed or something?'

Bungy grinned broadly. 'Come on you idle git,' he repeated. 'The others will be up shortly.'

They were all awake by 6 a.m. and queued up to use the bathroom, filling the air with a strong smell of alcohol and bad wind. Afterwards, they dressed in their newly acquired sports kit.

Beast was already waiting patiently on his driveway when they made their way outside. It was a mild and cloudless day. There was no wind blowing and the red sun was just starting to rise in the distance. The men stood in a line facing towards him and waited for their first instruction.

'Good morning men,' Beast piped up. 'Has anybody got any injuries that they want to inform me about before we start training?'

Baz thrust one of his hands sharply into the air and he cocked his leg, breaking wind heavily. 'Yes I have a medical issue. My head aches from all that booze we drank last night and my arse stinks.'

'Me too,' Bungy added. 'I'm still under the influence and his arse stinks.'

'Okay, let's get this show on the road,' Beast chuckled. 'I've planned a five mile run that we can all do together. I need to assess what level of fitness you're all at. And Baz, you're right mate, your arse does stink!'

The four of them set off jogging down a remote country lane running in pairs, side by side with their training shoes lightly thudding as they hit the ground in step together. They covered the first couple of miles with very little difficulty and held their heads high, admiring the scenic view around them and sucking in huge refreshing breaths of the cool morning air. The hills started to get steeper but Beast purposely ensured the steady running pace remained constant. Gradually, both Spike and Bungy began gasping heavily, fighting hard to inhale as much oxygen as possible to satisfy the demands of their labouring lungs. Even so, the pace remained the same and Beast offered them words of encouragement.

'Come on lads, let's keep this together. We're all boot necks aren't we?' He began calling out the pace in tandem with their left feet hitting the floor together. 'One up, two, three, four. One up, two three, four.'

'Yeah come on lads lets keep it together,' added Baz, sounding positive and at the same time realising that his years of maintaining a good level of physical fitness were proving worthwhile.

Even though they suffered, Bungy and Spike ignored the stress placed on their lungs and tired legs and pressed onto the four mile marker. They were aware of this, because Beast called out.

'That's four miles completed. There's one mile to go.'

'Shit,' Bungy gasped; his pace gradually faltering as his stomach knotted with a searing bout of cramps.

He began to wretch uncontrollably. Vomit poured from his gaping mouth and splashed down onto the floor. Spike almost mirrored this action when he too began to wretch. Beast smirked to himself and slowed the pace right down to a mild jog. He wanted to ensure that he kept them all together and that nobody stopped or fell behind.

'Come on men, keep it together,' he encouraged them. 'Breathe in deeply. In through the nose and out through the mouth.'

Both Bungy and Spike responded positively to the instruction, which helped them to control their erratic and almost desperate breathing patterns. The slowed pace remained constant for a while, until Beast felt everybody was ready to push a little harder towards the finishing line.

'One…, Two…, Three…, Four,' he shouted aloud, helping everybody to stay in step. 'One…, Two…, Three…, Four.'

The steady pace quickened and their breathing continued to labour. Even so, the group stayed firmly together and ran as one body of men. When they neared the end of the five miles stretch Beast gave them an instruction to slow to a brisk walking pace, which they did. Eventually, they came to a halt and stood with their feet together and their hands on their hips. They were sucking in mouthfuls of air with steam evaporating into the atmosphere from their fatigued, sweating bodies

'Breathe in.....and out.   Breathe in.....and out,' Beast instructed.

He had planned this first run as a test, allowing him to assess the men's level of fitness or the lack of it for that matter. On reflection, it was quite evident that they had a lot of work to do to improve their physical ability. Yet Beast was quietly pleased with the outcome. He had expected one of them to give up on the way, especially after they had started throwing up.

When they got back to his house, he made a couple of telephone calls and informed the group that he had managed to get them some work. This would allow them to continue to contribute towards their upkeep during their stay. It was not the best of jobs filling trolleys with food orders from warehouse shelves, but it paid enough money to meet their needs and was also an indirect way of continuing to build on their fitness.

The first week together was repetitive and went like clockwork. Beast woke them at 6 a.m. and they ran the same five-mile stretch, sometimes alternating the route and running the opposite way to prevent boredom. At the finish they would briefly discuss their physical performance, before showering and heading off to work. On an evening, they took it in turn to cook some high protein food and to wash the pots, prior to settling down to watch the television. At 10:30 p.m. they all retired to bed. Their bodies ached from head to toe as muscles they had not used for a while or had forgotten they had, reminded them of their existence.

During the second and third weeks, Beast progressively increased the intensity of their training. He lengthened the distance they were running from five miles to eight and introduced one hour of circuit training with weights at the end of it. It was hard going, but they were all in the right frame of mind now, able to push themselves to their physical limit. By the end of the fourth week, their level of fitness and endurance began to rise sharply and with it came an air of confidence amongst them.

Chapter Eight

A small cobble boat chugged quietly down the river Mersey towards the open sea. It was a calm day and the vessel swayed gently from side to side as it progressed on its way. Baz had chartered the boat with its course set for Dundrum Bay in County Down on the South East coast of Northern Ireland.

Bungy had never really been a big fan of sea travel. The swaying boat caused his stomach to lift and churn as the swell of the open sea roughened. He held his stomach with both hands and sucked in several deep breaths. Suddenly, he heaved forward with his mouth wide open. The contents of his stomach spewed into the seawater.

'Get a grip of yourself you soft git,' Baz laughed. 'You're an ex-marine, mate. You're supposed to be used to the bloody sea. Anyway, this throwing up business is becoming a bit of a habit of yours, isn't it?"

Bungy wasn't listening and continued to cough and splutter. Beast and Spike smirked at each other, after Baz slapped Bungy on the back a couple of times and passed him a bottle of water. He drank it down in one go, sitting down and burping loudly.

'I feel terrible,' he croaked with watery eyes and flushed cheeks.

'You look like shit,' Beast laughed, nodding his head.

'I feel like shit. The last time I felt like this was on-board H.M.S. Intrepid off the coast of Norway. The sea was RAF.'

'Royal Air Force,' Spike frowned, baffled by the term.

'No I said RAF; rough as fuck,' Bungy sniggered.

Everybody laughed, except Baz. He was preoccupied with thoughts about getting from the quay at Dundrum Bay to the location of the hidden weapons cache.

'I hope it's still there,' he said under his breath to Beast, but not loud enough for the others to hear. 'I hope no one has somehow stumbled on it and that the IRA haven't decommissioned it.'

'Look into the far distance. I can see land,' Spike hollered, pointing ahead of the boat to inform the others that their destination was in sight.

Baz's diaphragm fluttered as he cogitated about his active service some years previous in Northern Ireland. He remembered an occasion when his section of marines had returned from a three-day patrol in the hills of South Armagh. Back then, the inclement weather had been abysmal to say the least and the going was exceptionally tough. It would have been an understatement to say that the men were exhausted and extremely hungry as they hurriedly scrambled back inside the safe perimeter fence of their barracks.

'Corporal Broadhurst. It's good to see you and your section back in one piece,' Baz's troop officer gestured. 'You look tired.'

'We are tired sir. The weather has been crap and we had a live contact to contend with. We were engaged in an exchange of fire with an active terrorist cell.'

'Did you kill or capture any of them?'

'No sir, we didn't. The firefight went on for about fifteen minutes. They made a tactful withdrawal, getting away in an unmarked van.

'Oh well, not to worry, Broadhurst. I need you and your men to go out on a vehicle patrol within one hour. So get yourself a quick shower and a bite to eat and report back here pronto.'

'No sir, I won't be doing that. We won't be doing that,' Baz shrugged defiantly.

89

'Don't give me this rubbish Broadhurst, get your shit together man and report back here in one hour or I'll have you charged for insubordination.'

'But sir, we've been out in the field for three days. We're knackered and we're entitled to some rest.'

'Back here in one hour and that's an order,' the officer warned and stormed off into a nearby building.

The other marines in Baz's section frowned towards the officer and then disappointingly towards Baz. They did not look to blame him for the officer's order. Instead, they were waiting for his instructions. At that point, their Sergeant Major casually walked towards them. He had a warm smile on his face and was pleased to see that they had made it back in one piece following the radio reports about the live contact.

'Good to see you, Baz? he chirped rubbing his chin. 'You lot must be knackered. I heard about the firefight. Go and get yourselves cleaned up and get some rest. You've earned it.'

'We are knackered sir, but the troop officer has told us we have to go straight back out on a vehicle patrol in one hour.'

'What?' he gasped in disbelief.

'Out on a vehicle patrol, sir!'

'Ignore the order its absurd.' he shook his head. 'You men need some rest. It's against SOPs (Standard Operational Procedures) to send you straight back out on patrol.'

'But sir....'

'I said ignore it. I'll have a word with the troop officer. Now go and get some rest,' he finished and walked away.

Baz and his men felt relieved as they made their weapons safe and entered into the accommodation block. Their fatigued bodies ached from head to toe, their legs felt like they weighed a tonne and their feet were sore with blisters.

Meanwhile, the Sergeant Major detailed another section of men to carry out the task, despatching them out on the vehicle patrol and satisfying the needs of the troop officer. Sadly, the following day, Baz heard that the vehicle patrol had been caught in a terrorist ambush, resulting in all of the men being riddled with bullets and killed. He felt deeply sorry about the devastating news, but also quietly relieved that it was not his section's destiny.

'Pass me that rope beside you, Baz,' Beast asked, disturbing Barry's thoughts.

'Uh oh, yes will do mate,' he answered and passed the line.

Beast casually flicked a switch to turn off the idling engine and jumped from the boat with the rope onto a small wooden jetty where he secured the vessel.

'It's strange coming back here, Baz, isn't it?' Beast shrugged. 'Do you remember that vehicle patrol that got blown to pieces in an ambush, instead of us?'

'It's bizarre that you should mention that, mate. I was just thinking about that myself.'

'Never mind reminiscing,' Spike interrupted. 'We need to hire a van so we can drive to South Armagh.'

Half-an-hour later, Baz secured a deal leasing a minibus from a local car hire firm and the four men headed across the hills of South Armagh with Baz at the wheel. During the journey, the atmosphere fell silent. Those who had served in the past conflict in Northern Ireland were sat thinking about it.

Baz dropped the bus into a low gear as he started an ascent up a steep winding road. Its diesel engine laboured heavily, droning as he pressed the pedal to the floor. The weather outside was drizzly so he turned the windscreen wipers on, rubbing the condensation off the inside with his hand.

'I wish you lot would shut up,' he gestured, hoping to break the silence amongst them; but nobody answered. 'Can you see the plateau on top of that hill over there?' he went on, pointing towards the top of a steep tor in the distance. 'Beast, tell the men about that hill.'

'It's strange that you should say that, Baz.' Beast chirped up, helping to break the silence. 'I was going to mention it to you.'

91

'Well come on then guys. You two joined the marines long before I did, let's hear the story you are referring to,' Spike insisted.

'You tell the story, Baz,' Beast suggested. 'My memory is like a sieve these days.'

'Yes I'll do it,' Baz accepted; pleased about recalling one of their past military service experiences. 'In the mid nineteen-eighty's, me, Beast, another marine called Smudger and a Rupert (a marine term for an officer) were returning from a reconnaissance patrol in the field. We were absolutely knackered and the weather conditions were abysmal.

'Yeah so what's new?' Bungy remarked, rudely cutting in. 'I remember serving over here once and waiting in a hide for four days to shoot a known terrorist. The weather was crap then too.'

'No wait, don't interrupt. Let him tell you about this.' Beast insisted. 'It's worth listening to.'

They swapped idle glances and the odd sigh was breathed before they settled and focused their attention on Baz, listening with a half interest.

'The rain was tossing it down and the wind was blowing like a bastard,' Baz said. 'We were waiting at an LZ (Landing Zone) for a helicopter to pick us up. When the chopper came into sight, the Rupert took what he thought was a smoke grenade out of his combat jacket pocket. He pulled the pin out and threw it in front of us.'

'If it wasn't a smoke grenade, what was it?' Bungy asked inquisitively.

'It was a white phosphorus grenade and we all know that shit burns right through you like wild fire, if it hits you.'

'Bloody hell mate! Spike exclaimed. 'Did anyone get killed or seriously injured?'

'No, thankfully the wind was so strong that it blew the phosphorus away from us.'

'Shit, did you goffer the Rupert?'

'No I didn't, but Beast nearly throttled the fucking life out of him.'

Heads turned towards Beast who smirked and nodded his head a couple of times to acknowledge his actions.

'Right, we'll have to stop here and go the rest of the way on foot,' Baz told them, seconds before bringing the mini-bus to a halt at the end of a remote country lane.

He cranked the handbrake on and turned off the rattling diesel engine, turning the ignition key. They all climbed outside and Beast opened the back door.

'Here, grab one of these bags,' he said, throwing a sizeable holdall or a bergen at each of his colleagues to make ready to carry.

A light shower of rain continued to trickle down from the overcast sky bouncing raindrops off the men's waterproofs. They yomped (marine word for hike) steadily across a rugged terrain of steep winding hills, gauze bushes and boggy marshland.

'This gortex stuff is good kit,' Bungy grinned, referring to the waterproof material that his coat was made from.

'Yes its one hundred per cent waterproof,' Spike replied. 'Unlike the waterproofs we had in the marines some years ago. They were absorbent like wet tea bags.'

'Yeah, bleeding tea bags,' Bungy concurred. 'I was a coffee drinker myself,' he jested.

The group walked in a single line, along a steep winding path that ascended the side of a tor for about a mile. Beast led, followed closely by Baz, with Bungy and Spike bringing up the rear. Spike knew he needed to keep checking behind them, so that they could be sure they weren't being followed. He did this regularly and remained confident that there wasn't a single soul in sight.

'Don't we need a map?' Bungy shouted up the line towards Baz. 'How does Beast know where we are going? Are you sure you know where this weapons cache is?'

Baz looked down at the ground and shook his head. Then he reluctantly stopped for a short period to answer the questions and stop Bungy from moaning.

'Beast knows this territory like the back of his hand. He doesn't need a map. He knows exactly where the weapons cache is located because we stumbled on it together some years ago.'

'Why didn't you report it and confiscate the weapons?' Spike asked curiously.

'We followed an active member of the IRA here once and then covertly stalked him for a couple of days. He led us back to a house in Crossmaglen, where we set up an observation post in a neighbouring property. We were hoping he would lead us to more members of the IRA, but unfortunately he got killed by Loyalist terrorists.'

'How do you know if the weapons cache is still there?'

'We don't,' Beast cut in. 'We'll find out in a few minutes though because the location is down there.' He pointed to a small wooded area deep down in a valley below them.

Everybody paid attention and pressed on towards the area below with a renewed keenness. They stopped when they reached the trees and Beast pulled a flask of hot coffee from his bergen, pouring a cup full to share between them.

'Where did you get that from?' Bungy asked with an eager desire to know.

'He made it on the boat,' Baz told him. 'He's a switched on kiddie, isn't he?'

'Yes he is,' Spike piped up. 'Anybody would think he used to be a Royal Marine!'

The men smirked at Spike's humorous comments, taking shelter from the unrelenting rainfall under the leafy branches of the nearby trees. They huddled together in a group and stood talking amongst themselves sharing the hot drink. In turn, they took a sip from the cup and then passed it onto the next man. Beast poured a second cup and then another until it was all gone.

'So, where is this weapons cache?' Bungy inquired towards Baz, who was gazing into the empty flask to see if there was any coffee left. 'And how can you be sure you will be able to remember where it is?'

'You're standing on top of it,' Beast answered and pulled a small military style foldable shovel from the holdall he was carrying.

He pushed it into the earth near Bungy's feet and began to dig away at it. Before long, he had cleared a small area of grass and soil and started to scrape away at the earth below it. A clunking sound was heard when the shovel contacted something metal. Everybody looked on with an immediate high level of interest as Beast uncovered the surface of a rust covered door. He continued to remove the soil from it until it was all clear, leaving the door fully exposed.

'I bet it's full of water,' Spike commented, but at the same time hoping he was wrong.

'I bet it's not,' Baz confidently responded. 'This area is sheltered from the rain by the trees and the door has got rubber seals around it. 'Mind you!' he said, raising his index finger into the air to get everyone's attention. 'We'll need to be sure its not booby trapped!'

Beast pulled a short length of rope from his backpack and attached a small metal hook to the end of it. He clipped the hook over a handle on the door and instructed his friends to stand clear. They all moved back and cautiously crouched down close to the ground.

Beast tugged hard on the rope and the door steadily creaked open. There was a loud bang and Beast instantly released his grip, just before the metal booby-trapped door was blasted free from its hinges. The men held their hands tight over their heads and waited patiently for any debris to settle. After a couple of minutes, Baz jumped up and carefully made his way over to the opening.

'It looks clear. Wait here,' he instructed. 'I'll check inside.'

Baz steadily made his way in through the opening and down a short winding stairway. He used a mini pocket torch to see his way in the dark and shone it around a small chamber inside. The interior was literally a square room with smooth concrete walls littered with graffiti. Many different kinds of weapons and explosives were visible to him. They were stacked neatly on top of wooden tables and various bits of shelving that hung on the walls. Their luck was in. The cache appeared intact. Baz took his time. He needed to be certain that there were no more booby traps. One silly mistake now could cost him his life. After a while, he felt satisfied that it was safe and lit an oil lantern with some waterproof matches conveniently left beside it. The matches were easy to ignite with little effort. The dim light from the flickering lamp proved adequate and gave him a clear unrestricted view of an array of undisturbed weapons. He also observed the many spiders' webs that covered the equipment. Their presence pleased him, giving an assuring indication that no one else had been here for quite some time.

'Come inside guys. It is safe to enter. Come and see what uncle Baz has got for you,' he chuckled to his friends.

The men warily stepped inside the chamber and scanned the many types of weapons and explosives that lay neatly in front of them. Bungy naturally expressed an interest in a couple of sniper rifles.

'Fabulous. This is an M21 semi-automatic sniper rifle,' he said excitedly. 'It's magazine fed so you can get more shots off at speed. Although this can add recoil to the shot and may give away a sniper's position. 'Wow even better!' he exclaimed, picking up another rifle like an excited child with an opened Christmas present. 'This is an M40 single bolt action rifle. It has no recoil and truly is the type of weapon used by top snipers like me. It's also the standard weapon used by the yanks, the United States Marine Corp's snipers.' Bungy checked their functionality by repeatedly cocking the unloaded weapons. He broke them open and looked through their open barrels towards the flickering light. They appeared to be in good working order, probably due to the light coating of oil that somebody had once applied to their metal surfaces.

Elsewhere in the room, Spike sounded thrilled too. He was searching through the plentiful stocks of explosives, some of which had timing devices. 'Don't panic men!' he grinned placing some into his open rucksack. 'They're safe as houses until I arm them.'

Beast and Baz busied themselves with dismantling a number of semi-automatic rifles. This made it easier to stow them away inside their backpacks along with night vision goggles, pistols, Uzi machine guns, small anti-tank rockets, hand grenades and various types of ammunition.

Outside, in the drizzling rain; the men acted professionally by carrying out a series of weapons tests. Rat-a-tat-tat went a burst of machine gun fire after Baz squeezed lightly on the fully automatic Uzi machine gun trigger.

'Sheer music,' he grinned, satisfied that it was in fine working order.

'My turn,' Bungy chirped, wanting everybody's attention as he peered through the sight of an M21 sniper rifle. 'Approximately eight hundred meters away down in the valley below I can see a lone fox,' he called out, loud enough for everybody to hear.

'I can see it too,' Spike confirmed, eagerly looking through a pair of binoculars.

CRACK went the weapon as it discharged a single bullet.

'Target down,' Spike announced before Bungy fired another shot from the semi-automatic weapon.

'Hit,' Spike called out, still peering through the binoculars watching the fox's dead carcass shudder after the second bullet slammed mercilessly into its flesh.

Bungy casually put the weapon down and picked up an M40 rifle. He rubbed the sight lens with a piece of cloth and aligned it into the far distance. 'This is more my style,' he said, oozing with confidence. 'Fifteen hundred metres to the front at one O'clock. There's a small copse with a group of wild rabbits running around beneath it.'

'I can see them,' Spike acknowledged whilst the other men looked on.

'There's a lone rabbit moving to the right away from the copse. It has a white patch on its chest.'

'Yes I can see it,' Spike confirmed.

CRACK went the weapon as Bungy squeezed gently on the trigger, discharging a single round towards the target.

'Hit, target down,' Spike called out as Bungy pulled back the rifle's bolt-action mechanism and ejected the empty cartridge onto the ground. 'That was impressive.'

'That was easy,' Bungy grinned confidently, proceeding to dismantle the weapon so he could push it into his holdall.

Baz took the binoculars from Spike and peered through them. He nodded his head to further confirm the accuracy of Bungy's sniping. Personally, he was extremely impressed with the high level of shooting skills he had witnessed. He gave the thumbs up sign to Beast who also looked pleased with the demonstration. Baz moved his attention back to the rest of the kit that had been packed into the holdalls. He wanted to make certain that each weapon was fully loaded and made safe.

Meanwhile, Beast re-seated the damaged access door back onto its hinges over the entrance to the weapons cache. Its rubber-lined edges were dented to some extent so he did his best to seal it with plastic bags and clay. He completed the task by shovelling earth back over it and placing clumps of turf on the surface. It was a best endeavours attempt to try to conceal it from view again.

'That looks fine to me,' he said aloud; feeling satisfied with his handy work. 'You never know, we may need to come back here for more weapons in the future.'

The group were heavy laden on the way back. Yet they remained vigilant, as well as still managing to swap stories about various experiences using the same type of weapons. Some accounts were gruelling battle situations and others were humorous and side-splitting. The morale amongst the men was high. Even the unremitting pouring rain couldn't alter that.

'Hey Baz,' Beast piped up. 'We've blown a good number of people away over the years with these light machine guns, haven't we?'

'Yes we have, mate. Do you have any regrets about all those people we killed?'

'No, I don't. It was either them or us. They were our enemy. We did what we did because it was our job and we did what we did very well.'

'Hey, that sounds like philosophical wisdom,' Bungy interrupted. 'I remember when I was working as a sniper and chalked up a high kill ratio. A priest asked me if I believed in God and I told him that I did, but I also believed that some one was going to die very shortly after I cocked my weapon.'

'That's ice cold,' Beast remarked with an unconcerned expression.

'That sounds highly amusing coming from you, big guy!' Baz smirked. 'You once told me that you joined the marines to kill people and when you did you were cold too.'

'Yes that's me, cold on the outside and warm on the in.'

'So, what job have you got in mind for us, Beast,' Spike asked, whilst admiring the feel of the weapon he was carrying.

Beast briefly paused in thought. Although he was keen to pull off some kind of heist or bank robbery, he had absolutely no idea about what their target could possibly be. He instantly felt insecure and unsure of what to say to his friends. Their preparations were complete, but any potential target was non-existent!

'Err, I'm working on a plan,' he lied tactfully, not wanting to disappoint the men. 'I can't share it with you yet, not until I've finalized a couple of things.'

The encouraging response gave Spike a sudden rush of adrenalin. The unknown dangers excited him. He felt eager and compelled to find out more specifically what Beast had planned for them.

'Is it a bank job? Is it a bank job?' he repeated with enthusiasm.

Beast looked rather bewildered and opted to give no response. He had no answers!

Baz sensed this and quickly came to his aid to kill the sudden silence amongst them. 'Beast is waiting for me to collate some information prior to finalizing our plans. He needs this before we can share them with you. Be patient. It'll be worth the wait.'

Beast breathed a deep sigh of relief. The last thing he needed right now was for the men to lose faith in him. That wouldn't bode well with the commitment, effort and preparations the group had made so far.

'Anyway, Spike, we don't want to tell you yet in case you get scared,' he said, hoping humour would alleviate the situation.

Spike grinned and stuck his tongue out. 'The only thing I'm scared of mate, is me. For a moment there, I was beginning to think you hadn't planned our heist at all. I guess we'll find out sooner or later what it is.'

'How do you keep a psychopath in suspense?' Baz asked.

Spike shook his head and shrugged his shoulders. He had no idea about a possible answer to the out-of-context question.

'We'll tell you later!' he quipped.

The group burst into a bout of laughter and suddenly the atmosphere amongst them became warm and amiable again. Baz's experience and ability to produce humour in the face of adversity and difficult situations had once again proved fruitful.

'There's the van,' Bungy called out as it came into view a short distance away. 'Let's get this stuff inside and out of sight.'

Spirits were high during the journey back to Dundrum Bay. Luckily, there had been no real issues so far. Their quest to find the weapons cache and to bring the arms and explosives back to the boat had gone without incident.

In spite of this, unforseen circumstances were about to unfold that would make things a little more complicated as they boarded the boat and prepared to set sail.

'Good afternoon gentlemen,' a uniformed man said politely, removing his peak cap and preparing himself to speak more openly to the group of men.

Everyone immediately became alert. They looked at the man, who had short-cropped hair and was quite evidently an Irish Police Officer. He appeared calm and relaxed, so they tried to reciprocate in the same manner. However, they remained uneasy, knowing this situation had potential to turn into a disaster for them.

'Are you from these parts?' the policeman asked curiously, whilst scratching his head. 'I don't recognize your boat.'

Bungy fiddled with the noose that secured the boat to the jetty. He took his time. He knew that getting away by sea, would be virtually impossible if they were rumbled.

'We're on a day trip out from Liverpool,' he smiled warmly. 'We came over to sample some of the true Irish Guinness instead of the second rate piss they serve in England.'

'I like Guinness too,' the police officer replied, warming towards the strangers. 'It puts hairs on your chest.'

The officer stepped off the jetty and onto the boat causing the vessel to rock gently under his weight as he landed with both feet on the wooden deck. Immediately the men were tense. They had secured the weapons inside the cupboards onboard prior to the police officer's arrival, but wondered what he was doing here and more importantly, what he was looking for.

Spike went unnoticed as he lifted one of his hands and slowly reached into an inside coat pocket. He paused for a couple of seconds when he saw Beast looking at him. He was shaking his head with disapproval, probably to deter him from taking whatever action he was thinking of. Spike nodded to assure his friend that his intended action was the right thing to do. He smirked as his hand touched the electronic device he was searching for.

Out of the blue; there was a sound of an explosion far off in the distance. Everybody including the police officer stopped what they were doing and looked up towards the direction that it came from.

'Bloody hell!' the policeman gasped. 'You lads had better set sail and get out of here. I'm going back to my car to call for some back up and then I'm going to check out that explosion. It may well be terrorist activity.'

'Your job sounds dangerous, officer. Please be careful,' Baz said convincingly before the officer turned away and jumped from the boat and back onto the jetty.

The policeman reported the explosion on his car radio and waved goodbye to the men after Bungy untied the mooring rope and climbed on-board with the others. The officer waved one last time, watching the boat slip away from the shore and out towards the open sea.

'Phew that was close,' Bungy sighed with relief.

'Yes I know,' Spike agreed. 'I left a remote controlled explosive device up on the side of the hill next to the van hire place. It was a precautionary measure.'

Beast looked overly pleased about the precaution. He grabbed Spike's hand and shook it firmly with a meaningful grasp.

'I'm sorry Spike, mate,' he said sincerely. 'I thought you were reaching for a pistol. I thought it would be best to bind and gag the policeman if we were compromised, rather than kill him. I am truly sorry though. I underestimated your professionalism.'

'It's not a problem,' Spike assured him. 'It's all in a days work.'

Later in the evening, they arrived back in Liverpool under the cover of darkness. They moored the boat beside a jetty; prior to looking around to be certain they were not under the watchful eye of any surveillance cameras. Once they were satisfied, they collected all the weapons and explosives and loaded them into the boot of their car, heading back to Beast's house.

On arrival, Beast made everyone a hot meal and a cup of tea. Shortly after, he told them he was tired and had decided to retire to bed early. In contrast, he wasn't really fatigued. His conscience was irritating him and he needed to be alone for a while. He had to think quickly about the heist he was supposed to be planning. Otherwise, he would inevitably let everybody down.

Chapter Nine

Beast sat pondering in his bedroom. He felt miserable and gazed emptily at the wide-screen television with the volume turned down low. He was agitated and stood up, pacing up and down and gazing out of the window. How the hell am I going to tell the men that there is no payroll job that we can pull together? He thought. How am I going to tell them that it is all bullshit and I've been wasting their time? The chair he slouched in creaked under his huge powerful frame, when he leaned back reaching for a half-empty bottle of whiskey. He felt torn with guilt, looking vacantly at the label and unscrewing the top off the bottle. He raised it to his lips gulping down two successive mouthfuls and swilling a third around his mouth. He stopped for a moment, coughed and spluttered. His eyes watered so he wiped the tears away with the palm of his hand and then took another swig. He sighed and sunk deeper into his chair to focus on the television. He picked up the remote control, flicking aimlessly through the channels until eventually he settled on a news channel and waited for it to start.

The late news immediately caught his attention. His ears pricked up like a wolf. The newsreader reported that the police from a location in the south of England had recovered a vast sum of stolen money. The amount was estimated to be in the region of sixty million pounds sterling and had been smuggled into the U.K. from a bank in Iraq. The bank had been raided during the war there some years previous. The police were aware of the smuggling operation when it happened and were also aware of the location of the hidden money. They had waited patiently to catch all the criminals who would eventually return to collect it. The money was stored in heavily armoured security vans. It was the ideal cover to conceal the operation. Well almost! Unfortunately, the identical vans had attracted suspicion following an anonymous tip off. The criminals where known to have concealed the vans inside a disused tunnel on an old railway embankment. They had sealed the entrance with neatly laid brickwork, planning to return two years later to collect their haul. When the collection day finally came, the police were ready for them. Their operation was a complete success ending in the result they had been patiently waiting for.

Beast sat transfixed to the television with wide-open eyes. He listened to the newsreader as he closed out by reporting that the money had been secured at an Air Force base under armed military guard. Beast was familiar with the location of the base. He had attended a couple of training courses there during his service days. The stolen money would apparently remain there for a short while until it could be safely moved to a more secure location. Beast greedily swilled the remnants of the whiskey bottle with a look of exultant glee on his face. That's out target, he thought. That's our bloody target.

A short while later, the day's series of events and the half bottle of whiskey took their toll on him and he drifted off into a much-needed deep sleep.

'Wakey, wakey sleepy head. It's time to get up,' Baz said, after pushing Beast's bedroom door open the following morning.

'Uh, what? Oh, I woke earlier. I must have dozed off again. Oh, my head is bloody killing me,' he grimaced, holding his throbbing head between his hands.

'Are we going for a run this morning or what?'

'No we're not. We're ready to pull the job now.'

'What job? There is no job, is there?' Baz shrugged and sighed.

'Oh yes there is mate,' Beast assured him, looking seriously at Baz to ensure he realized he meant what he said.

As they spoke, a newspaper dropped through the letterbox. He didn't normally have one delivered but had telephoned the nearest newsagents earlier, to agree a small fee to have a one-off delivery made. Beast jumped out of bed, pulled his underpants on and raced towards the door to collect the paper. He grabbed it and frantically flicked through the pages before tapping one of them repeatedly with his index finger.

'Look! Police swoop on Sixty Million Gang.'

Baz was initially puzzled and unsure of what Beast was trying to tell him. He took the newspaper from his friend and began to read the report about the recovery of the stolen money and where it was being guarded. After scanning the page and absorbing the information, he broke into a warm smile. He started nodding and exchanged a prolonged glance with Beast.

'Yes. You beauty. That's our target,' Baz beamed with enthusiasm. 'Let's get the lads together and discuss this. We need to formulate a plan.'

Before they all got together, Beast read the newspaper article several more times and sat alone for a while, thinking about a strategy and the finer details of how they could make it work. He wanted to be clear about how they would approach and execute this, prior to discussing it with the others.

An hour later, he assembled the men in the spacious kitchen where they were all sat on wooden stools facing towards him. A sizeable white board housed on a stand with wheels was pushed into view. He pulled a black marker pen from a clip on the side of it and drew three separate boxes, which he then labelled with RAF Northolt/Target (Money), RAF Brize Norton (Helo) and Final Rendezvous (Hotel). He cleared his throat and casually winked at Baz, who passed him a glass of water.

'Right men, we've come a long way since we all met up again some months ago. I now believe we are finally ready to put our skills to use by pulling of one of the UK's biggest ever heists.'

Nobody responded to his statement and there was silence around the room. Yet all of them gave their undivided attention to what he had to say.

'Have any of you watched the news this morning, featuring the report about the security vans being captured?'

They all made brief eye contact with him, nodding and looking at each other to confirm they had.

'The money you saw being recovered on TV by the joint military and police operation was smuggled in from Iraq after the second gulf war. The smuggling operation was thwarted and the money has since been transferred to a single security van at RAF

105

Northolt. Apparently, it will remain there for a short period of time until the police can find a more secure home for it.'

'Is it really sixty million quid?' Spike asked, wondering if the vast sum had been blown out of proportion by the media.

'It is,' Baz affirmed. 'It's in all the newspapers as well as being on the national news. We can now tell you that this is our target so we will need to carry out a reconnaissance mission tonight to collate more information. We need to act quickly too, before they move the money.'

'Quickly!' Bungy gasped.

'Yes very quickly,' Beast added. 'We'll be leaving later today and expect to return sometime during the early hours of tomorrow morning.'

'What happens if something goes wrong and we get caught?' Bungy asked.

'Then it's all over. If we fall at the first hurdle then our belief in being highly skilled former elite soldiers is worthless.' He turned towards Baz. 'How are your driving skills these days? Are they still shit hot?'

'Yeah, red hot,' he grinned, knowing that Beast knew what he was capable of.

'Good. I know just the place we can steal a decent fast car from. Bungy, I'll need you to bring a couple of ghillie suits (snipers camouflage suits), for you and Spike and also some close observation equipment.

'Great, I always wanted to be a sniper,' Spike joked. 'Can I bring some explosives too?'

'No. Those skills won't be needed yet.'

Baz sat motionless pondering and rubbing his fingers across his clean-shaven chin. 'Wait a minute; let's do this the right way,' he suggested. 'I've just remembered the seven golden P's. Prior, preparation and planning, prevents piss poor performance. Yes, there's logic there. Let's use the NATO sequence of orders to plan our mission properly. After all, it was the way we were taught,' he shrugged with the palms of his hands held out in front of him.

'Okay,' Beast agreed. 'They've changed a little over the years, but I'll use the ones I was taught back in the nineteen nineties. You lot can take a break for a short while whilst I prepare.'

He spent the next fifteen minutes or so writing on the white board, whilst his colleagues shared some biscuits and poured themselves a cup of tea.

Soon afterwards, the men sat quietly together focusing on Beast again, waiting for him to explain their mission to them in detail. He turned towards them.

'Okay men, this is it,' he said, tapping the white board lightly with a short piece of bamboo cane.

Nobody moved or detracted their attention from him, so he continued.

'Ground. The ground we will be covering for an initial surveillance operation will be as follows: Baz and I will check out the location at RAF Northolt, where the money is being held. We need to confirm the size and type of van or vans it is being secured in, as well as the number and type of guards who are safeguarding it. Bungy, Spike, you two will head for RAF Brize Norton, where I want you to find a helicopter we can steal.'

'Wait a minute,' Bungy frowned. 'I was a mountain leader and a sniper not a bloody helicopter pilot.'

'No worries,' Baz replied confidently. 'I know you know RAF Brize Norton quite well because you did your parachute training course there.'

'Yes that's true, but that still doesn't mean I can fly helicopters, does it?'

'Its not you he's referring to, Bungy. It's me,' Spike said, pointing to himself and tapping his finger on his chest.

Bungy twisted his face and rubbed the palm of his hand up and down the side of his left cheek. 'But you're an Assault Engineer, an explosives expert,' he said.

'Yes he is,' Baz agreed. 'But he was also trained as a helicopter pilot and served with 3 Commando Brigade, Air Squadron for a while.'

'Situation; enemy forces,' Beast continued with his sequence of orders. 'No doubt both the money and the helicopters will be heavily guarded. Therefore, common sense tells us that we will need to create some form of diversion when we put our plan into action. Of course, this will be after the initial surveillance operation.'

'Great,' Spike chirped. 'Looks like I will get to use some explosives after all.'

'Mission,' Beast went on; turning to the boxes, he had previously drawn on the board behind him. 'Our mission is firstly to carry out a simultaneous covert reconnaissance operation at both RAF Northolt and RAF Brize Norton. This is to allow us to collate information about base security and the van or vans holding the money. Additionally we need to check for the availability of a suitable helicopter. Remembering of course, without the helicopter our mission is a non starter, so it is imperative that this objective is achieved successfully.'

'What if there are no helicopters available?' Spike asked.

'It's an air training base. Helicopters are always available,' Bungy asserted.

'Once we have collated the information we need,' Beast interjected, bringing their attention back towards him-self. 'Our objective is firstly to steal the helicopter and then to use it to help us to steal the sixty million haul. Execution;' Bungy, Spike, you two will steal the helicopter from RAF Brize Norton and will fly to a deserted farmhouse in Beckley on the outskirts of Oxford, where you will await further instructions. I'll give you a map and a grid reference of its location after this meeting. I'm quite familiar with the place and have used it a few times to store hot vehicles for clients of mine. When you get there, you will find a large magnet inside the barn that I want you to hook onto the winch of the helicopter. It's from a scrap-yard and needs electricity to work, so you'll need to hook it up to the power supply. Once Baz and I have found out where they are moving the money to, we will inform you. At this point, we will use a fast car to slow down the traffic behind the security van and will throw a stinger across the road in front of it to blow the tyres out. This will allow you to drop the magnet onto the roof of the van and to pull it up off the road and fly away with it.

'What if the magnet isn't strong enough?' Bungy asked.

'Please be optimistic. The magnet will be strong enough. It's more important that you get a big enough helicopter to allow you to lift the security van; and one with a winch too.'

'How are you going to slow the traffic down behind it and then blow the tyres out with a stinger in front of it?' Spike asked, believing the idea to be disjointed.

'Don't worry, leave that to us. Baz will achieve this by using the fast car we're going to acquire. Once you've secured the van we need you to take it somewhere remote, where you can offload the guards who will probably be seated inside. Hopefully nobody will get killed! Has anybody got any more questions?'

'Yes, yes,' Bungy answered, eagerly raising his hand into the air. Where are we going to hide the money?'

'I have a number of suitable locations in mind, but we're going to have to cuff it, depending on where we make the hit. If we're successful up to this point, then I'll make a decision on the spot.'

'How are we going to take care of any escort vehicles? There's bound to be some, there may even be another helicopter working as an aerial escort.'

'Yes that's true. We hope to take out any escort vehicles with the stingers, but may also need your sniper skills to give us some accurate firepower from the air. The same applies to any aerial escorts, if indeed there are any.'

'That isn't going to be easy. I'll be shooting at a moving target from a moving helicopter.'

'Yes I know, but your reputation as a sniper precedes you my friend. If anybody can do this, you can.'

'Yes okay,' he agreed with confidence.

'Service support;' Beast continued. 'Evidently, between us we have all the required skills to complete the mission. However, a little bit of luck never goes astray. Baz and I will operate from the fast car with stingers and small arms. Spike and Bungy will operate from the helicopter with Spike as the pilot. Bungy will have a sniper weapon and a couple of rocket launchers. Not forgetting of course, the electric magnet. You will also have small arms available to you, plastic explosives, some cutting equipment and tear gas to clear the guards out of the security van. We'll both have a radio, so we'll need to agree and set the correct frequency to enable two way communications.'

'Why don't we use mobile phones,' Spike asked.

'I did think about that, but there's more chance of conversations being picked up via mobile phones and there's also a risk of weak signal coverage areas. A lack of communication would have a detrimental impact on the operation. Is everybody clear so far?'

Each man nodded to acknowledge his understanding.

'Command and signals. I will continue to act as the number one in charge and will have total control over co-ordinating the whole operation. We will use our radio's to keep in contact and to ensure we all know what and when, everything is happening. Our call sign will be Green Leader. Bungy, your call sign will be Zulu one. Gentlemen any more questions?'

Nobody answered.

'Okay let's complete the surveillance operation and on conclusion we'll meet up at a Travel Lodge, situated near Southall. It's just off the M4 motorway. I'll show you it on the map. Don't worry; the two double rooms I have booked are under assumed names of Smith and Jones.'

'That's so imaginative!' One of them commented facetiously.

'Try and get back there for around 7 a.m. tomorrow morning,' Beast concluded.

Later that day, the four men split up into their respective two man teams. They collected and checked their equipment and tested their radio frequency setting, prior to heading off in their cars to commence the surveillance operations.

Spike and Bungy drove past the main gate of RAF Brize Norton. There was an armed soldier guarding the entrance to the base, probably from the RAF Regiment. He looked alert and watched them as they disappeared into the distance.

'How are we going to get inside the perimeter fence?' Spike asked.

'We'll approach the base from the West near the airfield. It's fairly remote down there. We'll cut a hole in the fence and crawl through it. Once we're inside, we'll set up an O.P. (Observation Post) and use our night vision glasses to suss out where the choppers are.'

'Sounds like a plan,' Spike retorted with a hint of friendly humour.

'Yes a cunning plan,' Bungy grinned and pulled off the highway onto a deserted off-road dirt track, where he stopped the car. 'We'll hang loose here for a while until last light and then make our way to the perimeter fence.'

Spike looked around. They had parked in a sizeable clearance, but the surrounding tree line hid the area from view of the road.

'This looks like a good place to hide the car, Bungy. Have you been here before?'

'Yes, I was here during my parachute training course. I used to bring some of the RAF women here to shag them in the back of my car.'

'That sounds good. What type of chat up lines did you use? How would you like to see the soles of your feet in my wing mirrors?'

111

'No. I used to ask them if they knew the difference between a man's penis and a car's gear stick. If they said no, I used to invite them out for a drive!'

'Yeah, cool, I like it. I bet they were like turtles?'

'What do you mean?'

'When they ended up on their backs they were shagged.'

Both men burst into laughter and Bungy gave Spike a friendly pat on the back.

When the sun finally set, they climbed out of the car and donned ghillie suits. Military snipers commonly used these to help them to break up the outline of their bodies, allowing them to blend into the natural surroundings. Spike grabbed a bulky backpack that was loaded with equipment and slung it over his shoulder, pulling the straps in tight. Bungy pulled a piece of camouflage netting over Spike's bergan for him, prior to pulling a larger net out of a sack and spreading it over the car to break up its outline.

'From here on, we'll use hand signals only,' Bungy said, rubbing camouflage cream across his cheeks and forehead with his fingers. 'We'll leave the radio behind for the time being. It'll be more relevant during phase two.'

Spike agreed and the two men set off across a cornfield towards the base, which was approximately half a mile away. The preceding fields were thick with growth and provided excellent cover. When the perimeter fence came into sight, they stopped and scanned its length using night vision goggles to check for guards and more importantly for guard dogs. The coast was clear, so Bungy pulled some wire cutters from Spike's backpack and an electric cable tester to check that the fence was not electrified. Fortunately it wasn't, so he quickly cut a small hole in it, big enough for both of them to crawl through. Once inside, he tactfully fastened the fence back together to hide the hole.

Spike squinted as Bungy replaced the wire cutters and cable tester back inside his backpack and continued to search around looking for something. He wondered what his friend was looking for.

Bungy grunted a couple of times, sounding satisfied that he had found what he was seeking. He pulled two rancid meaty bones from a plastic bag and briefly placed them under Spike's nose. Spike pulled his head away gasping, because the smell of them was disgusting and nearly made him throw up. Yet he remained silent because he knew Bungy was waving them in front of him to alert him of their intended purpose, which was to act as alternative bait to them-selves, if they happened to be pursued by guard dogs. Bungy moved slowly and cautiously through the undergrowth to place the bones a good fifty metres or so away from the hole in the fence. He was applying the principles of why things are seen, as taught in basic training. Fast movements could attract the naked eye of a sentry, whereas slow movements had more chance of remaining undetected. The principles of why things are seen are, shine, shape, silhouette, surface, spacing and movement. In addition, if guard dogs did chase them, he wanted their handlers to only see the dogs moving towards the bones. Instead of Spike and himself, who would hopefully be evading capture out of sight. He signalled Spike by waving his hand, telling him to scurry with him towards a small copse across the runway on the other side of the silent airfield. It was situated opposite a brick built aircraft hanger and would give excellent cover to set up an observation post. The grass in the area preceding the tarmac runway offered no camouflage because it was too short. Therefore, only the pitch-darkness gave them cover from view, as they stayed low to the ground, swiftly moving towards the copse.

Without warning, just as they were about to step onto the runway, the airfield lights came on and flood lit the whole area around them. Immediately their approach was in danger of being compromised. They reacted tactfully, easing themselves down onto their bellies in the grass, hoping their ghillie suits would prove sufficient. They lay still and listened with their weapons poised for the expectant sound of approaching guards or dogs. Instead, they breathed a sigh of relief when the thundering noise of a Chinook helicopter's engines and dual rotating blades filled the air. It was descending down towards a landing zone next to the aircraft hanger. They watched it land, moments before the building's mechanical hanger doors began to open.

The airfield's lights mainly lit up the runway area, rather than the surrounding fields, whereas the hanger's lights clearly exposed its interior. The men looked on as the chopper taxied inside. Once it was through the doorway, the motorized doors drew shut and the airfield lights extinguished. Darkness engulfed them as they lay still, patiently waiting for twenty minutes or so to get their eyes used to the dark again. When they were ready, they carefully made their way across the airfield and into the cover of the copse.

Meanwhile, Beast and Baz had parked in a long stay car park at Luton Airport. They purchased two parking tickets from a ticket machine, placing one on the dashboard below the windscreen and locking the door. They walked around the half-full car park and viewed the many vehicles there. It was a good idea of Beast's to steal a car from here, as it wouldn't be reported stolen until the owner had returned from holiday.

'That one,' Baz said, pointing towards a sporty-silver BMW. 'They'll go up to one hundred and fifty miles an hour. No problem'

'You'll get a speeding ticket,' Beast joked, pulling a bunch of keys from his pocket.

'What about the alarm?' Baz asked, feeling certain it had one.

'Don't worry. If one of these keys fits in the lock, it won't go off.'

'If,' Bungy exclaimed.

'Yes, if. Don't panic. I know what I'm doing. I spent a couple of years working as a locksmith, shortly after I left the Corps.'

Beast tried three different keys in the door lock, whilst Baz tried to be inconspicuous acting as a look out. None of them worked so he pulled another bunch from his pocket and tried a few more. The result was the same.

'Where are you going?' Baz asked when Beast started walking back towards their car without explanation.

'I won't be a minute,' he answered calmly.

Soon after, he returned carrying a pack containing some equipment. He was also holding a light green tennis-ball in his

114

hand. He pierced a small hole in it with one of his keys and placed it over the surface of the door lock. Baz looked on intrigued, as he hit the ball forcefully with his hand, forcing the air inside it to expel into the centralized door locks, freely popping them open.

'Anything else just isn't tennis,' he wittingly chuckled, casually climbing inside the vehicle where he hot-wired the engine's starting mechanism.

A grin of amusement covered Baz's face when he hurried back to their car to collect a couple of kitbags. On his return, he slung them onto the back seat before slamming the rear door shut. He opened the front passenger door and climbed into the vehicle beside Beast who was gently revving the engine. They drove off, stopping opposite a ticket machine that controlled the exit barrier.

Beast pulled a second parking ticket from his pocket and pushed it into slot. 'Great,' he smirked at Baz. 'It's only five pounds. The owner must have left it a mere hour or so before we arrived.'

He fed a small amount of money into the machine and pressed a button, triggering the barrier release mechanism. It opened, allowing them to drive off towards RAF Northolt.

Back at the airfield, Spike and Bungy continued to observe the routine operations of the hanger for a while, during which time the doors opened up intermittently. They did not need their night vision goggles for this. The lights inside the hanger lit up the interior like a fairground's illuminations. There were several helicopters to choose from, but Spike was keen to make a Chinook their target. He had once used one of these to lift an armoured tank and was sure it would best suit their needs. Each time the doors opened, they collated more information, such as were there any armed guards in the vicinity, how many helicopters were available, what type they were, refuelling operations, where the door controls were located etc. In addition to this, they checked for other entrances that they could use to sneak into the building.

After a couple of hours, they were satisfied that they had seen enough and that the hanger contained what they needed. They stealthily withdrew, making their way back across the airfield towards the hole. As they reached it, they could hear the sound of dogs barking in the distance.

Bungy's stomach churned with dread as he frantically raked around inside his jacket for his night vision goggles. He slipped them on and looked towards the sound of the barking.

'Shit, we've been sussed,' he whispered, pointing towards the close-by fence to signal to Spike to make a run for it.

Spike was already in motion and sprinted towards the fence ahead of Bungy, as the snarling dogs came bounding in their direction. They squeezed through the hole one at a time, taking care not to trap their ghillie suits in the wire. On the other side, they dropped down low amongst some bushes and remained still. Bungy pulled out a sharp, jagged knife from a holster that he had clipped onto his trouser belt. He would probably have to kill the dogs. He knew that. Just then, the two pursuing guard dogs stopped still in their tracks. They were a mere few metres away. They went quiet and started to sniff the ground around them, following the heavy scent given off by the rancid bones. One of them grabbed a hold of a bone and began tearing at the meat on it. The other dog wanted a piece of it too, so both dogs started fighting over it. Eventually, two security guards came into view and were keen to take control of the dogs. They were unaware of the nearby presence of the two intruders!

'Get the leash on them,' one of them shouted. 'Quickly before some one sees us, or we'll both end up in serious trouble.'

Bungy and Spike looked on from the undergrowth as the two unsuspecting guards dragged the fiercely growling dogs apart and led them off, back in the direction they originally came from.

The former marines' eye balled each other and sighed with relief, prior to sealing the hole and heading back to their car.

'It looks like you're not the only one who uses this spot to shag women,' Spike whispered, pointing to another car that was parked several metres away from theirs.

The unfamiliar vehicle had its engine switched off and its windows were steaming up with condensation. The car rocked gently from side to side as a couple copulated on the back seat. The female was moaning with pleasure. The men understandably resisted the temptation to have a look through the window to see who it was. They knew, professionally it wouldn't be a good idea.

Instead, they removed their ghillie suits and the camouflage netting from their car, stowing them away in the boot. It did not matter that the occupants of the other car would hear their engine start. They were too preoccupied to care!

Elsewhere, Baz and Beast parked the stolen BMW in a tree-lined lay-by, situated several hundred metres from the entrance to the RAF Northolt base. They opened one of their kit bags and pulled out two combat jackets and matching pairs of camouflage trousers. They dressed in them and pulled woollen balaclavas over their heads. Baz passed Beast one of the two nine-millimetre browning pistols he was holding and both of them secured their weapon inside a holster, fastened to their waist belt.

'How's your climbing skills these days, Baz?' Beast asked in a subdued voice.

'They're as rusty as hell, mate. The only things I've climbed over the past few years are the bloody walls in the steel works and my garden fence.'

'No problem,' Beast retorted. Let's go.'

They cautiously made their way across a couple of fields, tactfully remaining alert and using the natural heavy foliage as cover. Soon after, they stopped beneath some trees at the edge of a field that overlooked the base's main entrance, across the other side of a scarcely busy main road. Beast pointed upwards into the branches of a tree above them. He believed it to be an advantageous position to use as an observation post, allowing them to see beyond the perimeter of the base.

'I'll never manage to climb up there. Not in a month of Sundays,' Baz whispered; dismayed with his own lack of confidence.

'There's a rope in the kit bag,' Beast informed him. 'I can use it to pull you up there. Then we can both see what's going on inside the base. You know what they say mate, two pairs of eyes are better than one. Give me a couple of minutes and I'll haul you up with this,' Beast continued, waving a coiled rope that he pulled from his kit bag. He slung it around his neck and shoulder and checked it was secure. Then he climbed up the tree branches and into the darkness above.

117

Baz patiently waited. He could hear the rustling of leaves with the branches occasionally shuddering under Beast's weight. The sound was feint though and not enough to attract any attention from the security forces across the road. His mind drifted for a while, casting his memory back to his days in the military. He never faltered with climbing anything back then or with anything else for that matter.

Beast let down the rope next to him and he watched it loosely swinging around from side to side in the darkness. He grabbed hold of it with both hands and looked up to try to make out where his colleague was. He couldn't see him, but he could see a huge heavy branch that the rope appeared to be hanging from. He estimated that it must be around thirty feet high.

Surely, he is not expecting to pull me all the way up there, he thought with a degree of negativity. He'll never succeed. I'm far too heavy for him.

He felt the rope being tugged upwards and grabbed a better hold on it with his hands, knees and feet. He was half expecting Beast to take the weight and then shout something like, you are too heavy you fat bastard. Nevertheless, to his astonishment he slowly started to ascend. The movement was continuous and he wondered if his friend had rigged up some sort of pulley system. Then Beast came into view, passing him on the other end of the rope on his way down to the ground. Baz grinned, realizing that Beast was heavier than he was and was using himself and the heavy branch above as a pulley system. Soon he was at the top and found himself clambering amongst the branches wanting to pull him-self up onto a firm part. He felt around in the darkness with his hands and feet, making a sturdy foothold before sitting down and making him-self comfortable. In the mean time, Beast had made short work of climbing back up and was sitting beside him within a matter of minutes. Together they looked out towards the well-lit entrance to the base. Their view was good, but soon became more enhanced when Beast produced a pair of binoculars from inside his jacket.

The base's floodlights lit up the inside of the perimeter and allowed them to locate the heavily armoured security van that contained the money. It was parked in the middle of an open square, well away from the cover of the surrounding buildings.

'I thought you said there were two security vans,' Baz said, wondering where the second van was.

'There were two vans initially, but they were used by the crooks. I did explain during the briefing that the money was transferred to a single security van and it would appear that my information was correct.'

'Oh yes,' Baz agreed. 'I'd forgotten about that. You can tell there's a lot of cash in there; because of the number of soldiers they've got guarding it.'

Both men looked on. There were armed soldiers everywhere, probably from the RAF Regiment as assumed. They were situated inside, on top and all around the buildings that gave any access to the van.

'Oh fuck, fuck!' Beast sighed in a whisper, strongly expressing his disappointment. 'We'll never get inside the perimeter without being spotted. They'll easily see us and cut us to pieces before we get anywhere near the damn van.'

'Yes, I believe you're right,' Baz agreed. 'What else could we do?'

'We can't do anything else, mate. We'll have to abort the operation.'

Baz thought he heard something rustling in the trees about fifty metres away to their right. 'Shush,' he whispered, putting his finger to his lips and then pointing in the direction of the noise.

Unfortunately, it was too dark amongst the dense trees and no matter how hard they tried, they could not see a thing. The rustling continued.

'It could be a squirrel,' Baz said.

'Give me two minutes,' Beast replied, climbing back down the tree and pulling something from his kit bag. 'Here put these on,' he said when he retuned, passing Baz a set of night-vision goggles.

He also donned a pair and looked through the darkness towards the now still, but viewable trees. Both of them acknowledged they could see two other men, who were preoccupied observing the RAF base too.

'It looks like we've got competition,' Baz murmured, feeling excited about it.

Beast placed his hand on Baz's shoulder and patted him lightly. 'It doesn't matter now. The van is too heavily guarded to get anywhere near it or even near anyone whose even going to be talking about it. If they, who-ever they are, want to die trying, then that's fine by me; but for us it's a non-starter.'

'Yes, you're right. Fuck it, let's get out of here.'

Both men were disappointed that their operation was thwarted, even if it was thought impossible to achieve before it had even begun! They weren't used to giving up so easily. Realistically though, common sense and experience told them it was the right thing to do.

Back at the car, they removed their camouflage clothing and put their casual clothes back on. For a while neither of them spoke as they drove off into the night, passing the RAF base without even glancing at it. Baz eventually broke the silence.

'What are we going to tell Bungy and Spike when we get back? We're supposed to be very experienced men who they trust to come up with the goods. Telling them we've failed is going to sound a bit of a bastard.'

'Yes I know,' Beast replied disheartened. 'Let's face it. It was never going to be on a plate for us was it? Hey look,' he said, pointing at a public house that came into view.

It was late, but the many people who sat casually drinking beer at the tables outside, made it evident that the place was still open for business. Beast slowed the car down and pulled up into the half-full car park.

'What are you doing?' Baz asked curiously.

'My head is in pieces, mate. I need a beer.'

'Yeah, good idea,' Baz concurred, still feeling deflated. 'Me too.'

120

They parked the car and stepped out into the well-lit car park. The front of the pub was busy with customers and so was the interior as the two men stepped inside. Beast raised his hand and checked his watch.

'It's nearly 3 O'clock in the morning and they still seem to be serving beer, he said with raised eye brows. 'Maybe it's someone's private party and they've organised a late bar?'

'Can I order a couple of beers please?' Baz asked a middle-aged barman - half expecting to be turned away.

'Yes of course you can, sir. We're always open. We have a special license because the military personnel in the nearby RAF. base work shifts. Those guys are working hard to protect our country. They need a drink, you know.'

'They're bloody train-spotters you mean!' Baz scoffed facetiously under his breath, expressing disappointment that similar privileges were never afforded to him and his colleagues.

'Sorry, sir,' the barman responded abruptly, bemused at the remark.

'Uh, oh, he means rightly so,' Beast quickly intervened. 'These boys need a break after a hard days work.'

'Yes a break,' the barman smiled affably, placing two cool beers onto the bar in front of them.

Even though it was busy inside, the atmosphere was calm and relaxed. There were plenty of military women available too, who would have normally been a target of amusement for the two men. However, their deflated egos this evening had numbed their usual desire for the female species. Instead, they sat together at a vacant table drowning their sorrows and hoping to think of an easy way to break the bad news to their friends.

Baz sat with his left elbow on the table resting his chin on his hand. He raised his beer glass with the other, drinking half of it down. 'What are we going to say to Bungy and Spike?' He asked, repeating an earlier question.

Beast shrugged his shoulders and scrunched his face. He had no idea what they could possibly say and believed that they needed more time to think about it.

At that moment, a grim looking middle-aged man with greasy, grey hair started a conversation on an adjacent table. 'How am I going to pay my bills?' he moaned, expressing his worries to his friend. 'They've terminated my contract.'

'Don't worry, Frank. Just drink your beer and forget about them,' his friend advised. 'The military are a law unto themselves.'

Frank sat simmering with a red angry expression on his flushed face. He was fifty-five years old and had worked as a civilian van driver at the RAF base for the past ten years. It was only an hour or so ago at the end of his shift when the Ministry Of Defence had decided to terminate his contract with them. The cessation of employment came unexpectedly and had been announced at short notice. With it, they used a petty excuse that the transport funds were over budget, resulting in immediate job cuts.

Unbeknown to Frank, the real reason for his termination was in the interests of national security relating to the vast sum of money. The M.O.D. had assessed their risks and had decided to remove any potential vulnerability afforded by non-service personnel. It was a necessary preventative measure, avoiding the possibility of a bribed civilian driver who could compromise their transportation operation.

'If it wasn't for that damn stolen money I would still be there. I have a mortgage to pay and credit card bills. It's just not fair,' Frank protested. 'They shouldn't be allowed to do this.'

'Listen,' Baz whispered; nudging Beast who was already eavesdropping with wide-open eyes and his ears pinned back intently.

'They're going to use two vans now and will transport the money in just one of them,' Frank explained to his friend. 'One of the vans is just a decoy you know.'

The words were music to Beast's ears and he sat back smiling towards Baz, who was grinning too. Frank's openness and loose tongue reminded him of listening posts. Years before, he had used them to obtain intelligence from suspected Irish terrorists sitting unassumingly in public houses in Northern Ireland. The terrorists would sometimes divulge random bits of information between themselves, which the under cover operatives would overhear. The term then and evidently now was, loose lips sink ships.

'The two vans are going to take different routes. The one carrying the money is going to a bank vault in Aylesbury,' Frank continued. 'They're going to set off at 6 a.m. tomorrow morning and travel via the A40 and A413. The decoy van is going to leave first and head for the High Wycombe RAF base along the M40.'

'Whatever,' his friend responded uninterested.

The elated expression on Beast's face said it all. The impossible had suddenly become possible, because Frank's loose lips had given him enough information to reignite their intention to steal the money. Albeit, with a modified plan of execution. Equally as important, it had given them both a much-welcomed way out of having to disappoint their friends with news of failure!

'Alleluia!' Baz whispered cheerfully giving the thumbs up, as they left the pub car park and continued towards the Travel Lodge at Southall.

Chapter Ten

Back in the undergrowth, opposite RAF Northolt, Mikel and Lukic looked on towards the base entrance, through night vision goggles. They were illegal immigrants from Kurdistan, both having lengthy criminal records that would probably shock even the most hardened criminals. They were ruthless people who would viciously kill anybody who got in their way.

Normally they dealt in hard drugs, supplying mainly to pushers rather than selling directly to the punters. Their business proved more fruitful this way because the pushers always came up with the money in cash. Also, it dramatically reduced the risk of being caught by the police. Away from that line of work, the possibility of stealing sixty million pounds in one go seemed a lot more attractive than making a living by feeding the habit of low-life drug addicts.

Previously they had left their home country when the police had detected their antics and issued warrants for their immediate arrest. Getting into the U.K. was easy for them. They had hitchhiked across Europe via freight lorries and then scaled twenty-foot high fences, sneaking into the channel tunnel under the cover of darkness. When they entered the tunnel, they found their way into a small service tunnel that ran parallel with two main tunnels that were used by trains. Maintenance workers used the service tunnel infrequently. They rode through it on pedal bikes or in small motor vehicles to carry out essential maintenance work. The thirty-one mile passage was a long slog, but using this route meant that the fast moving trains in the other tunnels would not compromise their safety.

The journey proved tiresome and their footsteps echoed lightly around the concrete walls. Fortunately, there were small spotlights hanging down from the high ceiling above, adequately lighting the way for them. Every so often, they could hear the trains in the adjacent tunnels running in both directions. The noise they made was so loud at times that they had to cover their ears with their hands, until they had passed.

A good way into the tunnel they could hear the sound of a vehicle approaching. They glanced at each other and looked ahead towards the sound, unable to see anything due to the moderate decline of the passage preventing vision in the far distance. The sound was gradually intensifying so they cautiously looked for somewhere to hide to avoid being discovered.

The service tunnel had small entrance doors situated every one thousand metres or so, on both sides of the underground passageway. These led into the adjoining train tunnels. Their design purpose was to allow maintenance workers to gain access to the train tunnels, but train passengers could also use them as escape routes in the event of an emergency.

The echo of the approaching vehicle continued to get louder, so the two men started to run frantically into each doorway where they pulled hard on the steel doors to try to open them.

'It's locked,' Mikel sharply snapped, pulling hard on the door and kicking it.

'Fuck, so is this one,' Lukic replied from a doorway on the other side of the tunnel. His voice expressed immediate panic.

The increasing vibrations of the vehicle's whirring engine were being propelled into the distance towards them. Yet despite being several miles away and out of sight, it was seemingly closing fast.

'Come on. We need to hide,' Mikel said hastily.

They contemplated running back the way they had come to a previous doorway, but Lukic decided otherwise.

'No, let's run forward to the next door', he said. 'If we don't make it before the vehicle gets here we'll try and jump the occupants.'

'Okay,' Mikel agreed without question.

They ran quickly, panting heavily as they raced along. Eventually they reached a mid-point area in the tunnel that housed

125

two huge steel blast doors situated on both sides. A railway track ran underneath them. It was a crossover point. A designed safety feature to allow the running trains to change into the opposite tunnel in the event of an emergency. Lukic located an electrical junction box on the wall next to one of the blast doors. He gulped nervously and hesitated, but then pushed it hard because the oncoming car came into view. The button activated the automated door mechanism and the huge blast doors began to ease open. Lukic pressed the button again after the door had opened a few feet causing the mechanism to stop dead. It was just enough to allow them into the train tunnel and hopefully out of view of the approaching vehicle.

'Quick, go through here!' he prompted Mikel, who cautiously peered inside prior to entering into the darkness.

The approaching vehicle was only a hundred metres away, so Lukic made an impetuous dash behind his friend and together they moved further inside the cover of darkness.

A couple of minutes later, the two maintenance workers who were in the vehicle, stopped opposite the partially opened blast doors. The driver turned off the engine and they stepped out into the tunnel. One of them opened the car boot and grabbed a tin of paint and a brush. The other held a wire-brush in his hand. He used it to rub the rust away from the underneath of a corroding water-cooling pipe; that ran along the wall above their heads. Once he completed this task, his colleague applied a coat of paint to protect it from further corrosion.

Lukic and Mikel waited patiently in the darkness. Maybe we should sneak up on the occupants of the vehicle and kill them, Lukic thought. We could steal their vehicle instead of forever walking through this bloody tunnel. The going would be easier. He paused briefly, looking at Mikel who was having similar thoughts. Maybe the occupants are armed English border guards who had watched them enter the tunnel on a video camera. They could be searching for them to place them under arrest prior to deportation or imprisonment.

'No,' he whispered to Mikel, holding him lightly by the arm to persuade him not to approach the guards.

Unexpectedly, the vulgar sound of someone breaking wind echoed in the tunnel.

'Come on you dirty bastard,' one of the workers said. 'Let's finish this paint work before you shit yourself and we'll head back to the works canteen for some breakfast.'

'Hold on a second,' his colleague replied. 'This blast door has been left open. We'll have to close it before we go.'

Lukic and Mikel heard the men speak. Their fluency in English being good enough for them to realise that the two strangers were not armed guards as assumed. Lukic pulled a jagged rusting knife from the inside of his jacket. He had used it before on members of rival gangs back in his hometown. Now, he was going to use it again. He wanted the vehicle. Suddenly, one of the workers pressed the button on the electrical box and the door mechanism burst into life and started to close the doors. Lukic and Mikel saw them closing and instantly surged forward towards them. Surprisingly, they closed faster than they opened and echoed loudly around the tunnel when they slammed shut.

'NO,' Mikel screamed at the top of his voice, thumping hard on the door with his clenched fist. His voice echoed around the walls and up and down both directions of the tunnel.

'Did you hear somebody shout something there?' one of the workers asked his colleague.

'No. I think it was just an echo from the blast doors closing,' he grinned, releasing yet another burst of foul wind from his backside.

'You can cut that out,' his friend insisted. 'You should have a blast door in your underpants.'

'Yes I know. I desperately need a shit. I've got a turtle's head hanging out of my arsehole.'

They laughed together and climbed back into their vehicle, speeding off back in the direction they had come from.

Lukic and Mikel stood motionless in the pitch-darkness. They could hear a faint shuffling sound nearby. Lukic was leaning against the wall. He could feel some sort of switch, which he

127

flicked. A series of dim red wall lamps illuminated, producing very limited light.

'Is it a train?' Lukic asked, but a sudden sound of many rats squeaking answered his question for him.

The rats were moving in a dense pack towards the men. They were hungry and the meat from the two nervous humans would be enough to fill their rumbling bellies.

The men did not wait to be savaged and starting running in the opposite direction, hard and fast up the tunnel. Lukic tugged hard on the handle of the next exit door; desperate to move into the safety of the service tunnel. It was locked, so they continued to run along a steel gantry that ran parallel with the rail tracks towards the next one. Both of them gasped for air, hurrying along with sweat pouring down their panic-stricken faces. The sweat wasn't just created by the heat generated from their labouring bodies. It had a lot to do with their growing fear too.

'This one's open,' Lukic shouted, pulling the unlocked door ajar, seconds before two of the pursuing rats jumped onto his back whilst another sank its teeth deep into Mikel's leg.

Mikel screamed in pain, pushing his way through the doorway behind Lukic and back into the quiet service tunnel. He purposely slammed the door shut behind them and frantically fought hard to kill the rat that continued to cling onto the open wound it had created on his bleeding limb. He repeatedly punched it hard with a clenched fist until its razor sharp pincer teeth finally relented. He seized the opportunity, stamping on its head to finish it off. Its brains spilled out of its skull and it lay motionless on the floor in a small pool of thick red blood.

Lukic was also writhing around, trying desperately to get the two frenzied rodents off his body. One of them bit deep in to his hip, whilst the other concurrently bit into his scalp. He grabbed the one on his hip first and thrust his rusting knife deep inside its soft fury flesh. It let out a piercing squeal, falling down lifeless and onto its side. Mikel snatched the other rat from Lukic's head and slammed it down hard onto the floor, repeating his previous action until it burst open.

Back in the train tunnel, the other rats jumped and scratched at the closed door in an angry frenzy. Their efforts were futile because it was firmly locked shut.

Thankfully, the men's injuries were not too serious apart from a bit of blood that continued to drip from a minor flesh wound in Mikel's leg. He was by no means a stranger to applying first aid to this type of injury. He removed one of his socks, dabbing the wound with it before tying it around his leg like a bandage.

'I'm okay,' Mikel assured Lukic. 'Let's keep moving. We need to get as far away from those rats as possible.'

They hurried along through the tunnel; pressing hard to be sure they stayed ahead of the pack. On the way, they continued to check the exit doors as they reached them, making sure they were tightly shut!

A short distance ahead of them the two maintenance workers had stopped their vehicle. There was one more small maintenance job left on their list that they had planned to complete on their way back from the tunnels' mid crossover point.

'I don't think I'm going to be able to wait until we get back to have this crap,' one of them scoffed, squeezing his buttocks tight to stop a piece of oncoming excrement from exiting into his underpants. 'I'm bloody desperate. I'll nip into one of the train tunnels and curl it down in there.'

'You'd better be quick then,' his friend said. 'Or we'll both end up in the shit if somebody finds out.'

'If we work any overtime this week we could ask to get paid a time and a turd,' he joked in response, disappearing into one of the adjacent tunnels and closing the door shut behind him.

It was pitch-dark inside, but this did not deter the heavily built man who unbuttoned his trousers and pulled his pants down. He sighed with relief as his body's waste curled down onto the cold concrete floor near to the railway lines.

Meanwhile, the pursuing mass of frenzied rats moved stealthily towards him. The foul aroma of excrement filled their nostrils. They were excited and only moments away from overrunning their prey.

129

The maintenance worker finished his dump and paused after hearing a shuffling sound. He noticed that the floor seemed to be strangely moving around him. Maybe it is my eyes playing tricks on me, he thought.

The rats started to squeak hideously, surrounding him and moving in to launch their attack on him. They dived at the vulnerable human from all directions and sank their razor-sharp teeth deep into his exposed bare flesh. The worker desperately fought hard to pull his pants back up and at the same time, tried to run back to the exit door. He didn't scream; he was far too terrified to do that. His movement caused his legs to tangle in his loosely hanging trousers and he stumbled helplessly forwards and down onto the floor. His head cracked on the solid surface and the heaving mass of rats covered him, ravenously tearing away at his bleeding flesh. Less than one minute later, he was dead and the rodents continued to savage the bloodied flesh away from his corpse until their stomachs were full.

In the service tunnel, his colleague was starting to become impatient. They had long since finished the pipe maintenance job and he was waiting for his friend to finish doing his personal business. He glanced at his watch. His friend had been gone for over fifteen minutes. Maybe he has had an accident, he thought. He always seemed to take a long time when he visited the toilet and often joked that he was being paid during work time to take a crap. Their shift would be over soon though. I'll give him a shout to hurry him up, he thought impatiently and pushed the half-open steel door further inside the tunnel to create more light. He couldn't see clearly in the darkness, but he could hear some form of scuffling movement close-by.

'Hey shitty arse, have you finished yet?' he called out with a hint of sarcasm. 'I bet that's the best part of you gone.'

There was no answer and the sound of shuffling suddenly stopped. Initially the rats hesitated, waiting for him to come a little closer.

'Come on mate, stop messing around. We've been here ages,' he said, his voice echoing inside the tunnel. 'It smells rancid in here too. Maybe you should go to see a doctor.'

The dead silence continued.

Maybe he has fallen over; he thought and stepped further inside, reaching for a metallic pocket torch that he had clipped onto his trouser belt.

The steel entrance door continued to creak open until it reached a fulcrum point on its hinges, causing it to swing back the opposite way until it banged shut behind him. The worker was unphased by this and flicked the switch to turn his torchlight on. Its beam was powerful and he shone it around in the direction he had heard the sound.

'Come on, mate. We don't have time to start playing games like this,' he said.

With a gasp, his mouth fell open and his eyes bulged with disbelief when the beam revealed the furry mass of hissing rats. They stared hungrily at him from the area of his colleague's savaged corpse. Their eyes glistened in the artificial light. Fear instantly shot through his body along with an overwhelming dread that started churning in his stomach. He began to tremble and paused briefly, staring with deep shock at the almost fleshless state of his friend's body. The rats remained poised and still until the worker turned and ran for the exit door. His rapid movements alerted them and acted as the signal to make their move. The worker's hand touched the handle of the exit door, but it was too late. The savage rodents scurried onto him and started tearing at the exposed white flesh on his hands, face and neck. His grip on the door handle fell limp as one of the beasts sank its teeth into his windpipe, tearing it open. He desperately gasped for air and tried to scream; the sudden surge of blood in his throat only allowing him to gurgle. He took a step to the side and stumbled down onto the rats that massed everywhere, totally covering the cold concrete floor around him. This further excited the vermin; their victim relenting into a submission of death.

The feeding frenzy went on uninterrupted as they viciously tore away at his clothing, his flesh and internal organs. Afterwards, more of the pack moved in to claim their share of the fresh warm meat until there was very little left of their prey.

The exit door creaked ajar, allowing the outside light to beam into the immediate area. The rats became still; their eyes fixed intently on another unsuspecting human who was peering around in the darkness.

'I can't see anything in there. Its too dark,' Lukic said quietly to Mikel, who was standing in readiness to pounce on the maintenance workers from behind their unaccompanied vehicle.

The door creaked shut extinguishing the feint light. The pack of rats cautiously eased away from what was left of the second dead corpse. They did not intend to pursue their original prey now. Their bellies were too full for that!

'Look, the keys are still in the ignition,' Mikel said excitedly, pointing inside the vehicle and finding it a little difficult to believe their good fortune.

Without hesitation, they jumped inside and drove off heading towards the other side of the English Channel without being challenged. The going was easy from there. They were able to mix with other workers who had just finished their shift and queued to leave the tunnel area via rotating turnstiles. The gates opened with a mere push to exit, unlike on entrance when the turnstile clicked once to allow the pass-holder through. Outside, there were no police or customs personnel and the many workers eagerly headed for their cars and drove away.

Mikel and Lukic spoke excellent English, which was also the common language that they spoke between themselves. They came from different parts of Kurdistan. Mikel's native tongue was Kurdish, whereas Lukic's spoke Persian. Both had been taught the English Language at school as children.

Initially they found honest employment, working behind the bar of a public house in a small nearby town called Cheriton. The wages were poor but acceptable; their food and accommodation being included as part of the deal. After a few weeks, they became bored with the work and headed for the busy resort of Folkestone on the south coast. There, they violently forged a living amongst the low life drug traffickers who made money feeding the needs of habitual drug addicts. It was during this time that they too saw the news coverage about the money-laundering operation, deeming themselves capable of stealing it.

'The place is heavily guarded,' Lukic whispered as they looked on from amongst the trees opposite the entrance to RAF Northolt. 'There are armed soldiers everywhere.'

'Yes I can see that,' Mikel replied without concern. 'If we try to burst in there with all guns blazing we'll get shot to pieces. No amount of money is worth losing our lives for.'

'Are you saying it's too dangerous?'

'I'm saying it will be bloody suicide. The security van is too heavily guarded.'

Mikel did not like having to say this, nor did he like having to accept defeat at such an early stage. From what they had observed, the possibility of hijacking the security van and stealing the money looked virtually impossible.

'Come on. We can't sit here planning a suicide mission,' he sighed disheartened. 'Let's head back to Folkestone. The work is much easier there.'

Lukic had a bitter taste in his mouth when they climbed down from the trees. He hated defeat. It made him feel like a loser. Nevertheless, he too was also an advocate of common sense. His friend was right. There were far too many armed guards for them to try to overcome to steal the money. The inherent risks were too great and any such attempt would be fatal. He clunked his seat belt into place and turned the ignition key, starting the engine. He briefly looked towards Mikel and then glanced at himself in the rear view mirror. There was a complete silence between them as they pulled away and drove past the heavily guarded entrance to the RAF Base. They took one last look with sullen expressions, turning away and looking ahead.

'Hey look, that place is still open,' Mikel said, pointing to the well-lit public house that Beast and Baz had visited earlier. 'Let's go in there and buy a beer.'

'Yes, let's do that my friend,' Lukic replied, slowing the car and turning into the pub's car park.

Inside, the atmosphere was less lively than it was earlier. The background music from the jukebox had been turned down and most of the customers were starting to drink up and leave. Mikel and Lukic sat together at one of the many vacant tables and quietly sipped their beers.

Frank, the sacked van driver, was still inside talking to his friend within earshot of the two Kurds. He had been drinking heavily, starting with beer and then consuming a half bottle of whiskey that was sat empty on the table in front of him.

'I hate the bloody RAF and everything to do with that stupid sixty-million pounds worth of stolen money,' he slurred heavily, unknowingly catching the attention of Lukic and Mikel. 'I should be driving that security van tomorrow, not one of their drivers.'

'Yes I agree with you mate,' his half-interested friend answered. 'Look, I'll see you later. I'll have to go home now,' he finished, drinking the dregs of his pint and standing up.

He zipped up his jacket and patted Frank gently on the back a couple of times to console him, bidding him good night and leaving. He didn't really have to go home. Although he sympathized with Frank for losing his job, he was a little fed up with him constantly bending his ear about it.

'Do you want a drink my friend?' Lukic asked Frank, pointing to his half-empty whiskey glass and eagerly seizing this opportunity.

Frank was initially startled with the unexpected appearance of the two strangers. He had no idea anyone was sitting close-by. Nevertheless, he was pleased that they had offered to buy him a drink. Their amiable approach made him more receptive towards them and just as keen to vent his displeasure about his former employer.

'I don't want a drink thank you,' he answered. 'I've just lost my job you know.'

'What job was that my friend?' Lukic cut in; looking around gingerly to be sure no one else could hear him.

'I was employed as a van driver for the MOD.,' Frank continued. 'I was supposed to drive that security van from the RAF base. It was the one mentioned on the national news. Did you see it?'

Lukic nodded his head. 'Yes we saw it. Is there really sixty-million pounds in there?'

'Yes there is. Those bastards have fired me you know. They want to drive the van themselves. They're a bunch of bloody tossers. I hate them all.'

'Where is the van going? When is it leaving?' Mikel questioned ardently.

'The van is going to leave for the High Wycombe RAF base along the M40,' Frank responded spontaneously. 'They've sacked me you know. But I couldn't steal their money because....'

'When is the van leaving? When is the van leaving?' Mikel abruptly asked, interrupting Frank before he could finish his sentence.

Frank stared at Mikel through glazed eyes. He felt uneasy at the tone being used. Who are these people? he thought. They don't look or even sound English. Why are they asking so many questions? He suddenly became alert. His thoughts drifting to the many security lectures he had attended, teaching him not to divulge classified information. He wasn't bothered about the RAF. They had heartlessly terminated his employment. It was more so his personal pride at stake now. He refocused on the two men.

'When is the van leaving?' Mikel repeated with a growing level of agitation.

Frank did not answer. Instead, he tried to pull himself together and look in control of the situation. He purposely glanced at his watch. His vision was too blurred to read the time so he pretended he could see it.

'Is that the time?' he exclaimed. 'Sorry gents, I'll have to go. My wife is a serving police officer and will be arriving here any time now to give me a lift home,' he lied tactfully and stood up from the table. 'I'll see you another time.'

Mikel and Lukic were speechless as Frank brushed passed walking towards the exit door. He staggered and briefly looked back before disappearing out of sight.

'Shit!' Lukic exclaimed, frustrated and banging his clenched fists on the table. 'What are we going to do now? He didn't share the most crucial details. We know the day its being transported.

Its tomorrow, but we need to know what time the vehicle is leaving. We'll never get that information now.'

'Oh yes we will,' Mikel grinned reassuringly, pulling a sharp flick knife from his coat pocket and exposing the steel blade for Lukic to see. I'm going to prise it out of him with this.'

'You can't do that. His wife is coming to pick him up and she's a policewoman.'

'Yes and I'm Santa Claus. It was bullshit. Don't tell me you fell for it! Never mind that. You wait inside the car whilst I catch up with him.'

Frank was nervously hurrying along the deserted road. It was lit only by the moonlight. He hoped the two strangers had believed his reason for leaving. Personally, he thought he had sounded convincing. He chuckled to himself, oblivious to the fact that Mikel was closing in fast.

Initially Mikel was unsure which direction Frank had taken after leaving the public house. He looked both ways up and down the quiet country road. One way was long and straight and the other wound its way around a corner. If Frank had taken the straight road, Mikel felt certain that his shape would have been silhouetted against the open skyline. It had to be the other way. Yes he was sure.

Around the curve, Frank thought he heard footsteps coming from further down the road behind him. He was unfit and consequently panted heavily as he hastened his pace. Maybe it is my imagination, he thought, looking behind in the darkness. Maybe it is the sound of my heart pounding because I'm out of breath. He checked his pulse by pressing on the side of his neck with two fingers. He was taught this once during a first-aid course. It was racing and beating heavily, echoing in his ears. He held his breath......... Yes he was sure now, somebody was approaching. He was certain he could hear a faint sound of footsteps. He tried to focus in the middle distance, but the winding road with its heavy tree line obscured his view. He peered into the dense wooded area opposite. It was much darker in there. Perhaps a good place to hide, he thought and moved in amongst the trees. He didn't venture far. The ground was uneven and the darkness hindered his vision so he stopped and rested against a tree trunk.

Several minutes past and all was quiet. Time to make a move. It must be safe by now, he thought, opting to cautiously step away from his hiding place.

'Help!' he squirmed loudly, after someone pulled him backwards by a clump of his hair.

'Got you, you sneaky bastard,' Mikel snarled in his ear, pressing his knife blade against the bare skin on Frank's throat. 'What time is the security van leaving tomorrow?'

'I..., I Don't know,' Frank croaked. 'I made it all up. I'm not really a driver.'

'Don't bullshit me or I'll cut your throat. I heard you talking to your friend before you told us.'

'I'm telling the truth. Please let me go. I really don't know.'

Mikel pulled the knife away from Frank's throat. He was furious and did not believe him. On the other hand, Frank was feeling relieved that his assailant was backing off.

Frank let out an ear-piercing scream, after suddenly feeling a sharp numbing pain in his thigh. He reached down and squirmed, realising that Mikel was holding the knife with the blade stuck in his leg. Blood began to ooze out of the wound; tickling his skin as it steadily flowed down his thigh.

'Please don't hurt me anymore,' he pleaded with fear in his eyes. 'I don't want you to hurt me.'

'I'm not only going to hurt you my friend,' Mikel growled through gritted teeth. 'I'm going to fucking kill you if you don't give me the information I need.'

'I'll tell you everything, everything,' Frank cried, absolutely sure that his assailant meant what he said.

'Just tell me the time that the van will be leaving the base.'

Frank screamed again, as Mikel twisted the knife inside the bleeding wound.

'It's leaving at 6 a.m..., 6 a.m. tomorrow morning.'

'Thank you,' Mikel sneered coldly; his breath warming the inside of his victim's ear.

Frank was petrified and trembling with fear. He didn't want to die. He was going to tell his assailant everything, especially about the decoy van. That would be good information, which would surely please him. Yes that was the best thing to do. After all, the RAF were not important to him anymore. He certainly owed them no favours! He opened his mouth to offer the information, but inexplicably nothing came out. He fought hard to speak but started to choke with a sharp pain numbing his throat. He touched it with his fingers. To his horror, he felt a gaping hole with his neck cut wide-open.

'That's for telling me lies,' Mikel whispered bitterly to Frank as he began slipping away. He released the grip on his hair, allowing him to slump down onto the leaf-covered ground. Frank tried to focus but his heavy eyelids closed permanently shut.

Chapter Eleven

Knock, knock, knock, went the sound on the travel lodge guest-room door when the hotel receptionist tried to wake the occupants. There was no response. She tried again. Knock, knock, knock, but still no one answered. I bet they've had a late night and are lying in bed stinking of beer and still inebriated, she thought, pushing her master key card into the electronic door control system. The door lock clicked open allowing her to push the door ajar. She inhaled deeply through her nostrils, half-expecting to smell alcohol from the stale breaths of the occupants. This was the usual reason why people slept in late. Her assumption was wrong. She smelt nothing but fresh air wafting gently around the room expelled by the air conditioning system. She pushed the door further open and entered inside.

'Mr. and Mrs Smith its 2 p.m., I think you've overslept,' she said and watched the quilt cover being pulled down, exposing Beast's face.

He opened one eye and then the other seeing the smartly dressed woman looking at him.

'I think you've overslept sir, its 2 p.m.' she politely repeated. 'Would you like me to make you and your wife a nice cup of tea?'

'Err, no thanks,' Beast smirked, hoping that Baz would not raise his head from beneath the double bed quilt. We retired late last night and are feeling rather fatigued. Would I be asking too much for you to make that kind offer to Mr and Mrs Jones next door? They're very close friends of ours.'

'Yes of course sir. No problem,' she acknowledged and left the room, closing the door behind her.

'Just as well she didn't see you, you big ugly bastard,' Beast grinned at Baz, who was peering out from beneath the bedclothes. 'She would have suffered a heart attack.'

'She'll have a heart attack when she goes next door and sees those two big hairy arsed gorillas!,' Baz beamed, wiping the sleep from his eyes.

Knock, knock, knock, went the sound on the adjoining room. There was no response. The receptionist routinely tried again but there was still no response. Again, she used her master key card to unlock the door - pushing it open and stepping inside.

'Can I help you madam?' Spike grimaced from a chair by the window, wondering why the woman had knocked on the door and entered without invitation.

'Good afternoon Mr Jones. It's just after 2 p.m. I think you and your wife have overslept,' she said, innocently looking at the unexposed body that was lying beneath the bed quilt. 'Your friends Mr. and Mrs. Smith from next door requested that I inform you that you've overslept. Would you like me to make a nice cup of tea for you and your wife, sir?'

'That's not my wife,' Spike replied, momentarily thinking about the woman in Plymouth. 'I'm not married.'

Bungy lay grinning below the bed sheets scrunching his face and breaking wind loudly. The receptionist's face turned scarlet with immediate embarrassment and Spike smiled at her as Bungy let rip with another.

'I'm afraid she's got a sensitive tummy problem,' he grinned trying to contain himself. 'Unfortunately she kept it a secret until after we were engaged. It'll probably be best if you leave us to it. She'll probably follow through and shit herself if I don't wake her soon.'

Bungy again let out a blast of wind. 'Yes, yes I need the toilet,' he squeaked in a high-pitched voice trying to emulate a woman and sniggering beneath the bedclothes.

'Okay I'll leave you to it,' the woman responded with a straight face trying to look professional. 'You might want to open a window,' she tittered, turning away and closing the door shut behind her.

140

A short while later, the men washed and showered before packing their belongings and meeting up at the reception area where they paid their bills and booked out of the hotel.

'I know somewhere we can go to get something to eat,' Beast told everyone. 'You two follow us in your car,' he said to Spike and Bungy. 'There's a nice little café just a short ride away from here.'

'Do you think we'll manage to pull this job off successfully?' Bungy asked Spike after driving off.

'I don't know mate,' Spike shrugged. 'All I can say is that I'm getting a massive adrenalin buzz about the whole thing. It's really exciting me. I see it as being far better than living rough on the streets and a bit like being a boot neck again in a strange sort of way.'

'Yeah that's true, mate,' Bungy agreed. 'I had an indifference to life at one point when we first met, but now I have a purpose. I guess we all have.'

'The four of us make a good team, don't we?' Spike retorted. 'There's a serious amount of military skills and experience between us. It's a pity these skills can't be put to better use after people like us leave the military, instead of just going to waste.'

'That's a very valid point,' Bungy concurred. 'I think Beast or Baz mentioned that previously when we first met up in Plymouth. The skills just go to waste once we walk out of the barrack's gates for the last time, don't they?'

Spike nodded and pulled into the deserted car park adjacent to the BMW that their two friends were exiting.

The café was located in a rural area at the top of a steep hill. The view of the green valley below was breath-taking and was deservedly admired by the men as they walked across the tarmac car park and in through the café door. Inside it was quiet and scarce of people. An elderly woman came from behind a glass counter and warmly greeted her new customers, showing them to one of the many vacant tables.

'Good afternoon gentlemen, can I get you some drinks?' she politely asked.

'Yes please,' Beast answered. 'Can we have four strong coffees and four lots of steak and chips?'

'Yes of course. How would you like your steak?'

'Take the horns off and wipe its arse,' Baz chirped with his usual tone of sarcasm.

'I beg your pardon!' the old woman responded, innocently unsure of what she had just heard.

'He said medium rare for all of us please,' Beast grinned broadly, holding his rumbling stomach.

After finishing their lunch, each man paid his respective bill and they sat together on a bench outside overlooking the beautiful valley below.

'Gorgeous isn't it?' Baz reflected on the much-admired scenery. 'But I suppose we have more important things to think about at the moment.'

'Yes indeed,' Beast agreed. 'We need to finalize our plans and make some preparations for tomorrow. It's time to go to the deserted farmhouse in Beckley that I told you about. We'll cover all the important points there. We'll drive there via the A40 and A41 to Aylesbury. It'll give us an excellent opportunity to check the route that the security van will be taking after it leaves the RAF base. It'll also give you two a good indication of where to find it after you've successfully stolen the helicopter,' he pointed towards Spike and Bungy.

The distance from RAF Northolt, along the A40 to the start of the A413 was approximately 12 miles and then a further 20 miles to Aylesbury. Spike and Baz travelled as passengers between the two cars and made notes along the way. They recorded locations of all roundabouts, sets of traffic lights, steep hills and areas that they could potentially use as observation points. Eventually, they headed for the deserted farmhouse at Beckley on the outskirts of Oxford. Spike and Bungy were pleased they would be guided to its location prior to stealing the helicopter. Beast had made this decision back at the café, which reflected a change to their original plan. This way, there would be less chance of navigational errors later.

'These overgrown country lanes are like the ones near commando training centre, aren't they?' Spike said, referring to the place where they all did their basic training as marine recruits.

'Yes they are, mate,' Bungy acknowledged the comparison.

'Do you remember speed marching past the smelly farm?'

'Yes, I do. We called it that because it stank of cow shit?'

'It certainly did. I once threw up running past there. You could almost taste it.'

'Is it much further?' Baz asked Beast inside the BMW, whilst struggling to manoeuvre the stolen vehicle around a tight series of bends.

'We're nearly there, mate. We just need to drive up this track and around those trees up front. They provide good cover and conveniently hide the place from view from the road.'

The deserted farmhouse came into sight and the two cars slowed to a halt outside it. The old buff brick building was in good condition externally - with a grey-slated roof and steel security shutters locked shut over the down stairs doors and windows. A stone-built barn with heavy oak doors stood a few metres away from it. It too was firmly secured.

Beast stepped out of the car and temporarily disappeared amongst the dense trees behind the barn. He returned a short while later, waving a set of keys in his hand. The men stood patiently behind him as he unlocked the heavy shutters and removed them from their hinges, revealing new shiny white plastic window frames. Spike leaned against one of the windows with his hand pressed against his forehead blocking out the sunlight and trying to peer inside through the dense net curtains.

'Bloody hell, Beast!' he gasped. 'I thought you said this was a deserted farmhouse. The windows look new and the interior looks all modern and immaculately clean to me. Who owns this place?'

143

'I do,' Beast assured him, raising a half smile.

'But I thought you said this was a deserted farmhouse,' Bungy reiterated, airing confusion.

'It is deserted. Look,' Beast chortled and pointed to a sign inside the porch way. It read, Welcome to the Deserted Farmhouse. 'My auntie used to live here,' he continued. 'Her late husband deserted her several years before she passed away. Hence the referred name I use for it! She unexpectedly left the place to me in her will. Nobody else knows about it; not even my wife.'

Beast courteously showed his friends around. The interior was clean and tidy with the plush furniture being a mix of red wood mahogany and brown leather. Heavy glass chandeliers hung from the beamed wooden ceilings in each room. The modern décor being plush and elegant.

'It's rather posh here, Beast,' Baz said. 'Why don't you and your wife live here instead of Liverpool?'

'Like I said, my wife doesn't know about the place. I've always used it for my work. Nobody comes here except me. There's no postman, no milkman, nobody.'

'It must be worth a few bob,' Bungy added. 'Why don't you just sell this place? Surely it would make you a lot of cash.'

'Yes and if you own all this, why were you debt collecting for a living? Spike shrugged. 'And why are you now planning this robbery with us?' Spike shrugged.

'He wasn't debt collecting just for the money,' Baz cut in. 'Nor is he committed to pulling this robbery off just for the money. It's the buzz of excitement we all feel in dangerous situations. The comradeship and the fearless attitude we adopt on active service. Beast misses being a boot neck amongst boot necks the same as the rest of us. This is the closest any of us are ever going to come to that again. Albeit on the wrong side of the law I might add.'

'Thanks, Baz,' Beast said, grinning like a Cheshire cat. 'You know what they say about our brotherhood? Once a marine, always a marine!'

Everybody acknowledged their understanding, seemingly satisfied with the explanation. Part of them would always be a marine. None of them would ever want to change that.

Shortly after the guided tour, Beast switched the kettle on and made some tea. He invited his friends to sit down and cleared his throat to address the group.

'Okay men, it's 4 p.m. now and time to get down to business. Let's collect the weapons from the cars. We'll check them to ensure they're in good working order. Then we'll revisit the NATO sequence of orders to be sure we're all clear about our objectives.'

Each weapon was checked, cleaned and oiled. Watches were synchronized and the radio frequency was agreed and set. Beast didn't have any fresh food in the house, but he did have some military style ration packs that he kept stored there in case of emergencies. He collected a couple of these from a cupboard and rustled some food together, complete with a hot drink. After they'd dined he pinned a blank white sheet of paper to a kitchen wall notice board with some drawing pins and starting writing the key points on it.

'Right men, listen in!' he said aloud ensuring he got their undivided attention. 'It's time to brief you on the next phase of our operation. We touched on some points during the last briefing, but this one will be more specific.'

'Ground. The ground we will be covering will be as follows: Baz and I will start the operation close to RAF Northolt. We will travel along the A40 and then the A413, just a short distance behind the security van. We expect it to leave shortly after 0600 hours, tomorrow morning. Bungy, Spike, you two will fly from RAF Brize Norton and head for the A413 to a point just beyond Chalfont St. Peter, where the A40 terminates.

He paused for several seconds and looked at each of the men who were sitting in complete silence. Nobody asked any questions and all remained focused on him so he continued with his briefing.

'Situation; enemy forces. There are two security vans located at RAF Brize Norton. The first is scheduled to leave the base at 0600

145

hours. This vehicle is a decoy. The second van will leave a short while later and will head for Aylesbury via the A40 and A413. This one is our target. Logically we assume it will continue to be heavily guarded by armed soldiers, probably from the RAF Regiment. Any questions so far?'

Nobody responded, so he continued.

'Firstly, we need to steal a helicopter. This is a key requirement for the operation to succeed and without it; there really is no operation. The helicopter is located at RAF Brize Norton. There will be armed guards at that location too t I doubt they will be focused on guarding the helicopters.'

Bungy and Spike glanced at each other. Spike smirked confidently. Bungy looked uneasy.

'I hope you know how to fly these things,' Bungy said.

'The only thing I can't fly my friend, is a magic carpet,' Spike smirked and held his gaze until Bungy looked back at Beast.

'Mission,' Beast continued. 'Bungy and Spike must successfully steal a suitable fully fuelled helicopter from RAF Brize Norton and fly it to the remote field on the other side of this house. Simultaneously, Baz and I need to slow the traffic down on the A413 in preparation for hijacking the security van. Ultimately gentlemen, our mission is to steal sixty million pounds.'

'Say that figure a few more times. I like the sound of it,' Baz jested staring at the blank faces. 'Never mind, I'll say it. Sixty million, sixty million, sixty million. Okay that's better,' he tittered prior to looking back towards Beast.

'Execution; Bungy, Spike, you two will leave here at precisely 0400 hours, tomorrow morning and head for RAF Brize Norton to steal the helicopter. Yes, I know there is no contingency plan if this fails, but we'll cross that bridge if and when we come to it. Once you have acquired the helicopter you will fly back to this location, where you will attach a huge electric magnet to the winch and hook it up to the power supply. Then you will await further orders. I can't put a timing on this. We'll just have to cuff it and see how it goes. Remembering of course, that the security van we're going to hit begins its journey around or just after 0600 hours.

'You can't beat a bit of pressure,' Bungy sighed with concern. 'Hopefully all will go according to plan as you did say the mission is a non-starter without the chopper.'

The room fell silent and everyone paused with a degree of uncertainty.

'It's not going to be plain sailing; we all know that,' Beast rasped easing the tension. 'So undoubtedly some of the decisions I make will be spontaneous and unplanned. Baz and I will follow the target to the A413 where we expect to be in direct contact with the helicopter. We will use our car to slow the traffic down behind the security van. We plan to disable any escort vehicles with stingers. At this point, we need Bungy to take out the security guards by whatever means necessary so you can use the electro-magnet to winch the van into the air. Then you will take it to a remote location to remove any security guards from inside. If there are any! You will unload the money from the van and then fly it to another location to hide it.'

'What location?' Spike piped up.

'Do you remember the weapons cache location in South Armagh?' Baz asked.

'Yes what about it?'

'Well it's remained intact and totally untouched for over a decade. Nobody except us knows of its existence. This makes it an ideal place to hide the haul.

'But that's in the middle of nowhere,' Spike grimaced. 'It'll be difficult to ensure that nobody robs us.'

'That's true,' Beast intervened. 'But you can take countermeasures by booby trapping it with explosives. Logically, if we can't have the money then we'll make sure nobody else can either.'

'Okay I can work with that; but I'm a little concerned about Bungy killing the armed guards who will be escorting the vehicle,' Spike frowned rubbing his forehead. 'That will make us murderers as well as thieves.'

'There's a simple answer to that my friend,' Baz smirked.

'Which is?'

'Shoot them but don't shoot to kill.'

'This job is getting increasingly difficult by the minute,' Bungy sighed. 'I'm used to killing people not wounding them.'

'Yes, but your reputed level of sniping skills may solve this problem for us,' Beast replied. 'You can wound just as easily as slotting people.'

'Okay, but what about flying the helicopter across to South Armagh. That won't go unnoticed will it?'

'Oh yes it will,' Baz assured him. 'After the money has been loaded on to the helicopter you and Spike will paint the aircraft yellow.

'That's going to be a big job,' Spike said.

'There's a hefty barrel of yellow paint in the barn.' Beast informed them. 'You can brush it on with yard brushes. Don't worry about quality, just slap it on. Then it'll be the same colour as the Coast Guard's helicopters. No one will bat an eyelid in England or Ireland when that flies above them. Nor will it look like the helicopter that the military are looking for,' he concluded closing the point with everybody's approval.

'What if the magnet isn't strong enough?' Bungy queried.

'You asked that question last time we discussed this. Trust me; those things can lift armoured tanks if they need to,' Spike emphasized.

'Service support,' Beast continued. 'Remember men, we have all the required skills and professional ability to complete this mission successfully. Obviously, as always, a bit of luck here and there won't go amiss. Baz and I will operate from the fast car with stingers and small arms. Spike and Bungy will operate from the helicopter with Spike as the pilot. Bungy, you will use your most favourable sniper weapon to take out the guards or at least to wound them if necessary, although very probable. Oh, and Spike, you may need some plastic explosive to blow the security van doors in case you are unable to cut your way inside. You'll also need the dark yellow paint I mentioned.'

148

'Yes explosives, yes great,' Spike smirked.

'Command and signals;' Beast carried on. 'I am in charge of this operation and will have total control. We've already checked our weapons; set the frequencies for our radios and synchronized watches. Just as a reminder for you, our call sign will be Green Leader. Spike, Bungy, your call sign will be Zulu one. Men, that is all. Has anybody got any questions?'

Baz sat upright and thrust his hand into the air. 'Yes, if I get slotted can I have a decent funeral with full military honours? I want a Royal Marines' Band Bugler to play The Last Post, before they start shovelling dirt onto my coffin.'

He was sincere and serious about his request; everybody knew that.

'Yes of course, Baz,' Beast retorted and momentarily exchanged meaningful glances with all three men.

A period of silence followed, along with an air of mutual respect amongst the former elite soldiers ready to commence their dangerous operation.

'Okay men,' Beast piped up. 'It's early to bed for all of us tonight. We'll rise at 0200 hours tomorrow morning and start the operation at 0230 hours. Sleep well.'

Chapter Twelve

Bungy and Spike parked their car in the same remote location they'd used during their previous surveillance operation. Except this time, they planted an IED (improvised explosive device) inside it, along with a timing device to detonate it at 06:30 a.m. This would allow them enough time to return and defuse the bomb if they needed to make a quick getaway. Their preference was to use it to destroy their vehicle after they had successfully stolen the helicopter. Prior to priming the timing device they donned their ghillie suits, darkened their faces with cam cream and removed all their weapons and equipment from the car boot.

'Let's hope nobody decides to steal it,' Bungy joked.

'It'll be their last auto theft if they do mate,' Spike chuckled as he set the mechanism.

Between them, they had decided to use the same routine as before; going through the perimeter fence with as little kit as possible. Consequently, they had left most of their equipment back at the farmhouse. The items they chose to carry were Uzi machine guns, a few spare ammunition magazines, a couple of hand grenades and two pairs of night-vision goggles. Additionally, Spike took a small amount of semtex plastic explosive. He needed this to create some sort of diversion. When they reached the perimeter fence, they were pleased to find their previous patchwork had remained intact and undetected. Undoing the wires proved almost effortless and within minutes, they had breached the fence again. One at a time, they squeezed through the hole and assisted each other with untangling any parts of their ghillie suits that became snagged on loose ends. Spike checked his watch. It was 03:30 a.m. and the airfield and surrounding proximity was engulfed in darkness and very quiet. Nothing moved or stirred apart from the odd wild rabbit that casually hopped passed looking for its next meal.

'What are you doing?' Spike questioned when he saw Bungy searching inside his jacket for something.

Bungy did not answer and pulled a small plastic bag from one of his pockets. He opened it slightly and pushed it under Spike's nose revealing an unbearable smell of rancid meaty bones that danced around inside his nostrils.

'Oh my god! It stinks!' Spike whispered. 'Did I really need to give it a sniff test?'

Bungy just grinned and placed the bones several yards away from the hole in the fence just in case the guard dogs came prowling. Before long, the two men were peering through their night vision goggles tactfully scanning the area. They lay in the undergrowth beneath the cover of the copse foliage opposite the aircraft hanger. There was no movement or even the slightest sound of activity around the vicinity. They broke from cover, making their way to a side entrance door that they had noticed during their reconnaissance mission. It was unlocked so Spike peered inside whilst Bungy covered his rear. The way was clear so he used a hand-signal to inform Bungy to step inside behind him.

The inside of the hanger seemed as big as a football pitch with soft lighting provided by a string of red florescent lights that ran down the centre of its rafters.

There were three helicopters parked idly in the middle so the men approached with weapons poised airing on the side of caution. Fortunately, the aircraft were unattended.

The men's military training on aircraft recognition proved useful, because they were familiar with each type of model. There was a Sea King, a Lynx and a Chinook helicopter. The Lynx was out of scope for the operation because it was too small and had limited lifting ability. The Sea King was a good reliable type of chopper and possibly capable of lifting the security van as required. However, there would be no room for errors so the men scouted round the Chinook helicopter. It was the most difficult to fly and had a poor safety record, but it was the most powerful deeming it suitable for the operation.

At this point, they could have just opened the hanger doors and taxied out unopposed onto the quiet runway. Nevertheless, experience had taught them to proceed with caution. Undoubtedly, the sound of the hanger doors, suddenly opening would announce their presence and intentions to the armed soldiers in the Guardroom. The two of them cautiously walked the full length of the hanger towards another exit door on the other side. This door was also unlocked so Bungy pushed it ajar peering outside. All was quiet and his eyes settled on a well-lit office block in the distance. The word Guardroom, stood out from a sign attached to its wall, close to a large window and a double door entrance. Two soldiers were visible on the inside. They were sitting unawares, casually passing the long dark night away playing chess and drinking coffee.

Bungy and Spike tactfully stayed out of the light and moved with stealth amongst the shadows, close to the walls. A few metres away on the other side of the office block they saw another building. It was sign posted Armoury and was the ideal place to use to create a much-needed diversion. Bungy signalled with his hand to inform Spike that he would cover him whilst he looked for somewhere around this building to plant his explosives. Spike moved in and was soon leaning on a window ledge peering through a small window that had steel bars on the inside. He was fairly certain that the stack of ammunition boxes he could see piled on top of one another; were unopened. He thought about carefully breaking the glass, but then changed his mind because he would have no control over the amount of sound this would create. Nevertheless, the window ledge offered an ideal spot to place his explosives. It was a certainty that the imminent blast would affect the inside of the armoury, rather than the effects being contained by the outside wall. He removed his backpack and pulled out a metal container that housed the I.E.D. (improvised explosive device) made up of C4 explosives. He placed the bomb on to the window ledge and began to attach a timed-wire detonator complete with an electronic device.

As he was about to attach the detonator, an armed guard stepped outside of the guardroom. His movement alerted both men simultaneously. Spike could not clearly see the approaching guard from where he was standing so he looked towards Bungy, who was watching alertly from the shadows. His finger gently caressed the trigger of his Uzi machine gun.

The unsuspecting guard was a young, seventeen-year old soldier called Kevin. He had only been in the RAF Regiment for a short period and had passed out of basic training just a couple of weeks before. He didn't like night-time guard duties. They messed up his body clock. He was feeling a little disappointed because he had lost a game of chess and a stake of twenty pounds to his colleague. Following the game, he told his colleague that he needed some space and was making an unscheduled patrol around the airfield. This was a lie. He was really heading for the armoury where he occasionally caught a couple of hours sleep before day light broke. When he reached the building, he pulled a bunch of keys from his pocket and pushed one into the lock. It clunked as he turned the key and the door creaked inwards as he pushed it open and stepped inside. As usual, he opted not to switch the light on. That would be unwise and would potentially risk giving away his secret sleeping quarters. Instead, he closed the door behind him and bolted it shut.

Spike looked on through the window and watched Kevin as he pulled a sleeping bag out of a drawer, placed it onto the floor and climbed inside.

Bungy waited in anticipation for a few minutes, until he was sure that nobody else was approaching from the guardroom. His stomach was turning with dread so he crept towards Spike. The situation was grim and had all the traits of turning into a recipe for disaster - with the young soldier being oblivious to the fact that he was about to become an innocent victim of circumstance.

'What are we going to do?' Bungy anxiously whispered. 'Its 04:30 hours and we've got to get a move on. We'll have to kill this guy. He deserves it anyway. He's a careless tosser who isn't worthy of wearing his regiment's uniform.'

'No. I don't want to kill him,' Spike replied concerned. 'He's only a young kid. Yes, he needs a good kick up the arse, but he doesn't deserve to die like this. I've got another idea.'

He casually walked around to the armoury door and tapped lightly on it a couple of times. There was no response so he knocked again with a little more force than previous. Bungy stood several feet away shaking his head with disapproval of Spike's unorthodox approach.

'Uh,' Kevin murmured, waking from his sleep and opening his eyes.

Spike tapped on the door again.

Shit, Kevin thought, feeling acutely uneasy. I've been found out. I'll get into a lot of trouble for this. I know what I'll do. I'll tell the Guard Commander that I thought I heard a noise and came in to investigate. He jumped up out of the sleeping bag and pushed it into a corner. Then he grabbed his weapon before unbolting the door and nervously looked outside into the darkness. Almost instantaneously, he felt an almighty thump in his face, knocking him backwards and down onto the floor. Spike rushed inside quickly gagging the disorientated soldier with a cam scarf that he pulled from around his neck. Kevin was petrified and looked at the camouflaged face of his attacker with almost disbelief. His jaw throbbed in pain from the blow. Maybe it's a military exercise to test the security of the base, he thought. He had heard about these from a colleague, when the Royal Marines had targeted their base and carried out mock commando raids. He'd been told they were a rough lot. His aching face assured him of that.

'Get into this sleeping bag now,' Spike ordered and pushed the barrel of his Uzi under Kevin's chin.

'Okay, okay,' the young soldier winced. He nodded a couple of times too, fully intending to cooperate with the exercise. Then perhaps he would not be reported and put on a charge for going to sleep on guard duty.

Once he had climbed inside the sleeping bag, Spike zipped it up and pulled it over his head fastening several knots, partially sealing the top with a drawstring. He threw Kevin over his shoulder in a fire fighter's lift and casually stepped outside where Bungy remained watchful. Spike eased the sleeping bag down onto the ground so that he could put the final touches to his I.E.D. If the kid shouts out I will have to hurt him, he thought. Kevin didn't do this though. He had heard that they did not tolerate resistance from uncooperative captors if they offered resistance. Better safe than sorry, he thought.

Once the device was set, Spike picked the sleeping bag up again and walked amongst the shadows, back through the side entrance door and into the hanger. He placed Kevin down onto the floor and grabbed a tight hold of the sleeping bag near his head.

'If you make one false move before I tell you to, I'm going to slit your throat,' he whispered, gritting his teeth.

'I won't. I know its part of the exercise,' Kevin replied submissively.

Spike and Bungy hurried across to the other side of the hanger. Bungy pulled the Chinook door open and both men climbed inside. Spike jumped straight into the pilot's seat and started looking around and touching the controls, checking them.

'Bungy mate, why have you climbed in here? I need you to open the hanger doors?'

'Yes I know you do, but I want to be sure you know how to fly this thing.'

'Look!' Spike snapped sharply. 'Flying a helicopter isn't exactly straightforward, especially a Chinook. It's different to other choppers because it has two sets of rotor blades, which not only contra rotate but also mesh. This baby has around seven gear boxes which believe me, can be a recipe for hilarity or disaster.'

'It sounds complicated,' Bungy shrugged, still feeling a little unsure that his friend could actually fly this thing.

'Its only complicated if you don't understand it. The rotor blades provide lift through the application of pitch via the collective pitch lever. The power from the engine is increased as the lever is raised and decreased as it is lowered.'

'How do you control direction?' Bungy asked, still wanting to satisfy his genuine curiosity.

'Direction is controlled by the cyclic control. It operates through 360 Degrees. The yaw pedals control yawing which is created by the torque transference from the gearbox to the rotor head. There's loads more information on these things but the clock is ticking and we need to get it into the air.'

'Okay, okay,' Bungy grinned. 'You've baffled me with rocket science. Where are the ignition keys? How do you actually start the thing? Are you going to hotwire it like a car?'

'Aircraft don't have keys or even a gear lever. The system is set live by switching on the master battery.'

'The master what?' Bungy blurted out.

'Bungy for fuck sake knock the questions on the head. I don't have time to give lectures. Go and open the hanger doors before we get spotted.'

'What about the diversion?'

'It's about to blow,' Spike grinned excitedly holding up a mobile telephone in one of his hands and then dialling a number with the other.

Bungy's mind went blank as he stared emptily at the telephone. He couldn't recall any instructions to telephone anybody during their pre mission briefing.

'Who are you calling?' he asked, leaning half way out of the helicopter doorway.

'Bloody hell mate! God help you when you start sniping at people. I'm going to bombard you with loads of facetious questions before you ready yourself to pull the fucking trigger.'

'But who are you going to call?' Bungy reiterated.

'I'm not calling anyone, mate. I'm going to send a signal to the electronic receiver that I've attached to the explosives. It'll trigger the device and create our diversion. If you hear a loud bang, don't ask me what it was!' he said, hoping Bungy would stop questioning his specialist skills and just get on with the job.

'Okay, okay I'm on my way,' Bungy answered with a half smile, realizing how silly he had been by underestimating Spike and questioning him.

Spike made him-self comfortable and quickly regained his familiarity with the controls of the aircraft. He initially checked that all the switches were in the correct position and turned on the hydraulic fuel linkages before moving the speed select lever to the start gate. He watched from the cockpit as Bungy reached the hanger door's control box and waved his hand to signal that he was ready. He peered at the L.C.D. display on his mobile telephone. He had already dialled the number and just needed to press the go button to send the signal.

BOOOOOMMMMMMM, went a loud explosion as the I.E.D. exploded and ignited the ammunition boxes inside the armoury. A series of smaller explosions followed whilst Bungy flicked the switch on the control box engaging the automated mechanism to open the hanger.

Spike pressed the start button triggering the internal auxiliary power unit and the engine burst into life. It began to pick up speed progressively so he made a quick check of the temperature and pressure gauges and advanced the speed select lever. At the same time, he released the rotor brake and the rotors began to turn. Spike moved to start a second engine just as Bungy jumped into the helicopter beside him. He gave his colleague instructions to assist him with setting up the navigation aids and finally completing the start-up of the helicopter. More explosions continued from the area of the armoury at the other end of the hanger. Spike taxied the Chinook unopposed through the wide open doors. Once clear of the building he taxied onto the runway and increased the power of the engines, taking the helicopter up into the air.

The two of them exchanged smiles of contentment as they gained more height and distanced themselves from the air base far below. Spike checked his watch. It was 05:15 hours and the first part of their mission had been completed with great success.

The guards on the ground below could be seen operating a dated green goddess fire engine. They were working hard to extinguish the flames from the currently unexplained series of explosions.

'What are you doing?' Bungy asked as Spike pulled his mobile phone from his pocket again.

'Don't start with all the queries again! I'm going to trigger the explosive device that's sitting in our car. Now that we've got this far, there's no point waiting until 06:30 hours.'

Bungy agreed so Spike pressed the button sending the signal. In the far distance, the primed I.E.D. exploded and blew the vehicle into a display of flaming fragments.

'I'm sorry about all the questions earlier, Spike. I was just curious that's all.'

'No problems mate. I'll set a course for Beast's farmhouse as planned. We can collect the rest of our kit for the next phase of the operation and also hook the electric magnet up to the winch.'

Meanwhile, Baz and Beast were observing the entrance to RAF Northolt, from the same tree-lined location they had used during their previous visit. It was 05:45 hours and the morning sun was starting to rise in the east behind them.

'Can you see any activity?' Baz asked Beast, who was peering through a pair of binoculars.

'Yes I can. It seems like the civilian van driver was telling the truth. There are two security vans. There are also lots of armed soldiers guarding them.'

'It's just as we expected,' Baz signified, nodding his head. 'They're hardly going to move sixty-million pounds around the country without some level of assurance that no one is going to steal it. Are they?'

'That's true, Baz. However, we're a team of professionals with special skills and we mean business. That's for sure. Failure is not an option'

At this time, Lukic and Mikel were sitting patiently in their car just a couple of hundred metres away from the same RAF base entrance. They'd backed their vehicle off the main road, down a dirt track surrounded by trees that swayed gently in a mild breeze. Lukic tactfully chose this location strategically positioning themselves to allow good visibility of their target.

'There are two security vans and lots of guards,' said Lukic, peering through a small hand held telescope. 'Maybe they've split the money between the two vehicles. Or maybe there is double the amount of money than what was reported on the news.'

'Yes,' Mikel agreed. 'Or maybe one of the vans is a decoy.'

'Hmm,' Lukic frowned, thinking of the probability. 'If that's true, how will we know which one is the decoy?'

'The drunken van driver whose life I took said the security van leaves at 6 O'clock and will head for the M40. He never mentioned a decoy. If one of the vans is a decoy, I would guess that it would leave before or after 6 a.m. If they both leave together at six, I don't know what we will do. I wish I'd squeezed more information out of that weasel. Never mind, it's too late now,' Mikel sighed - twisting his face with disappointment.

'Excuse me chaps,' a strange male voice unexpectedly interjected through the half open car window. 'Can you tell me what you are doing here? This is my land. This is private land?'

'Erm,' was all that Mikel could say in response to the elderly man who had made an untimely appearance out of nowhere.

The short gaunt fellow was the farmer whose land bordered the RAF base. He'd seen countless numbers of people parking on his land over the years. Most often, they were young couples who used the track to park their cars and copulate. He always moved them on. This is his land and as far as he was concerned, none of them have any right to be here.

'I said this is private land,' he repeated with a tone of authority.

Mikel checked his watch. It was 05:50 a.m. and the security vehicle or vehicles, were scheduled to leave in ten minutes. He brushed his breast pocket earnestly with his hand, rubbing it against his flick knife.

'Can you tell me what you are doing parked on my land?' the farmer asked with growing impatience to get some answers.

Mikel did not respond. Instead, he pushed the door open and stepped outside next to the farmer. Before speaking to him, he cautiously looked around ensuring that no one else was going to turn up. There was nobody in sight.

'We are police officers,' he informed him. We are detectives, CID.'

'What are you doing here? This is private land!'

'We're on a special surveillance operation. I'm afraid I can't give you any more information than that. It's confidential.'

The old man paused, studying Mikel and his colleague. He also peered at their aged car and its registration number plate hoping he would be able to memorise it. The vehicle's poor condition and shabby internal appearance added to his growing suspicion. So did the men's pigeon English accents, which were peculiar to him. He felt almost certain that the two men were not whom or what they were claiming to be. He stepped back a couple of paces and pulled a sawn off shotgun from inside his green padded jacket. He raised it and pointed the barrel towards Mikel. 'You're lying!' he insinuated. 'I don't know who you are, but I am certain you're not policemen. Tell me who you are and what you're doing here trespassing on my land or I'll shoot both of you. I am within my rights you know.'

Lukic sat motionless inside the car. His mind was racing as he glanced at his wristwatch. He carefully pulled a nine-millimetre pistol from beneath his seat and cocked it. It would be easy to shoot the old man to end the situation but he knew that the sound of gunfire would alert the nearby soldiers at the base entrance. Mikel had similar thoughts, except he did not want the old man to fire his shotgun. Nor did he want to be shot either. Time was ticking away and he needed to end this quickly.

'I told you the truth my friend. We are policemen. We're from another country and are working with your police on a terrorist operation. I have identification. Would you like to see it?'

'Yes I would, but if you try any funny business I'll shoot you dead.'

Mikel smiled idly and casually reached inside his pocket for his flick knife, being aware that the old man's shotgun had not been cocked ready to fire. He grasped the knife and placed one of his fingers on the spring catch that would release the blade. He briefly looked to the left of the old man and behind him in a bid to distract him. It worked a treat because the old man looked away allowing him to produce the sharp knife. Mikel surged forward and mercilessly thrust the blade deep into the farmer's chest. Blood spurted out from the wound and the old man's face twisted as Mikel withdrew the knife and repeatedly stabbed him several times. He dropped his shotgun on the ground and tried in vain to call out for help. Lukic was already in motion, leaving the car and lunging forward. He struck the helpless man three times over the head with his pistol until he fell to the ground. The two of them continued to set about him violently like mad men. They repeatedly stabbed him and beat him with hard blows to his head and body. Blood saturated the old man's clothing and poured out of the many stab wounds Mikel had inflicted. Blood also spewed from the farmer's mouth. He shuddered and died.

'What time is it? What time is it?' Mikel asked repeatedly, whilst wiping the old man's blood from his hand and his knife using the corpse's clothing.

'It's six O'clock,' Lukic answered, eagerly looking through the telescopic sight towards the base. 'The first van is moving and there's an escort jeep in front of it with two soldiers inside. There is also another jeep behind the van at the tail end. It has another two soldiers inside it.

'What about the other van?'

'It's not moving. The first one is our target. I'm certain of it.'

The two men hurriedly dragged the corpse into some bushes. They covered it with leaves and brushwood in a somewhat sloppy attempt to conceal it. That was not a problem for them though as they deemed it unimportant. They moved quickly, jumping back into their car and pulled out onto the road just a couple of hundred metres behind the rear escort vehicle.

Back in the undergrowth opposite the RAF base, Beast and Baz were observing the first security van and its escort vehicles as they left the base to begin their journey to RAF High Wycombe.

'That's the decoy van out of the way,' Beast informed Baz. 'Let's hope our information is correct and that the second van is the one carrying the money.'

'Yes, but we won't know that until we rob the damn thing,' Baz grunted, hating the feeling that the supposed decoy van might not actually be the decoy. 'At least that reduces the number of armed guards we'll have to contend with.'

'I can see people boarding the second van now,' Beast said, peering through his binoculars. 'They're on the move. Its happening exactly like the civvie van driver informed us. It's time to make our move.'

He pulled a radio transmitter from his pocket and switched it on. 'Zulu One, Zulu One, this is Green Leader, over.' The radio crackled a few times, but there was no response. 'Zulu One, Zulu One, this is Green Leader, over,' he repeated.

'Green Leader, this is Zulu One, send over,' Spike's voice replied from the radio.

'Zulu One, send sitrep (situation report), send sitrep over.'

'Green Leader, our initial objective was completed successfully. We have hooked up the magnet and are awaiting further orders, over.'

'Zulu One, wait fifteen minutes and head for the road junction. I say again, wait fifteen minutes and head for the road junction, over.'

'Roger out,' Spike replied and the radio went silent.

During the conversation the two men exchanged limited information. However, they were unconcerned about potential eaves- droppers, as at this point there was no reason for anyone to be searching for them. The junction they were referring to was a location at Chalfont St. Peter, where the A40 runs into the A413.

Back at the farmhouse, Spike and Bungy busied themselves loading weapons into the helicopter. Bungy had opted to take his magazine fed M21 semi-automatic sniper rifle. He believed it would be more suitable for firing at a moving target than the M40 with its single bolt-action operation. He stripped the weapon down and lightly oiled its parts prior to reassembling it. Similarly, Spike was handling explosive devices, checking them over and carefully placing them in a rucksack.

'Bungy, give me a hand to load this paint onboard,' Spike said, cradling a large plastic container.'

Beast and Baz rushed back to their vehicle and closed on the security van and its escort vehicles. They tactfully remained a sensible distance away - staying in the streamline traffic to reduce the risk of looking suspicious. The time was 06:30 a.m. and the morning traffic was still light.

Spike's voice sounded out across the radio that Beast held in his hands, whilst Baz drove their vehicle.

'Green Leader, Green leader. This is Zulu One, over.'

'Zulu One, this is Green Leader, send over, send over,' Beast responded.

'Green Leader, we are airborne. We are airborne, over.'

'Zulu One, how long before you reach the junction, over?'

'About sixteen minutes, over.'

'Okay, we'll strike the target a couple of miles beyond the junction as planned.' There are two escort vehicles, one at the front and one at the rear of the security van. Did you receive that, over?'

'Received loud and clear, Green Leader,' Spike replied excitedly. Adrenalin was pumping thorough his veins. He was edgy but at the same time exhilarated, feeling a buzz similar to times when he worked on military operations.

'Good, let me know when you have an aerial view of the target, out,' Beast signed off the conversation.

Lukic and Mikel were closing fast on the other security van and its escorts. They were travelling at a steady sixty miles an hour along the M40. Mikel was driving the car, whilst Lukic busied himself removing the sunroof and making ready with two sixty-six millimetre anti-tank rockets and a couple of AK47 rifles that they had acquired illegally. Within a couple of minutes, he was organised after snapping a fresh magazine onto the second of the semi-automatic weapons.

'Okay, Mikel, I'm ready,' he said, placing the rifles onto the back passenger seat and taking hold of one of the rocket launchers. 'Let's do this.'

The military drivers in the security van and escort vehicles all noticed the average looking car when it pulled out to the outside

163

lane opposite them. They looked at the occupants indifferently as they drew level with the security van ahead of the rear escort vehicle. Their low-risk cargo of military ration packs was hardly worth stealing!

The driver of the rear escort vehicle caught the eye of one of the occupants of the car opposite them. He reciprocated by cheekily sticking his tongue out at them. He found the puzzled look on their concerned faces amusing and began acted childishly, pulling various faces.

Lukic stood up easing himself through the open sunroof. The military driver found this even more amusing and continued to pull hideous faces at them both. The driver of the security van watched the antics of the unscrupulous soldier behind him through his right wing mirror. He too was highly amused at the ongoing foolery and expected the passenger of the civilian car to retaliate by dropping his trousers and baring his buttocks, or something of that nature.

Suddenly, the escort driver's jaw dropped open and his eyes widened. He watched Lukic as he pulled one of the rocket launchers up through the sunroof and poised it ready over his shoulder. Without warning or hesitation, Lukic pressed the trigger and launched the rocket directly at the rear escort vehicle. He grinned gleefully, seeing the driver's face twist with panic before the rocket hit its target and blew the vehicle to pieces. Immediately, the motorway turned into carnage behind them. Cars began breaking hard to avoid the torn pieces of vehicle that were blown into their path. A series of car crashes resulted, causing a domino effect, blocking the road.

The guards in the other two vehicles fumbled nervously with their weapons. They hadn't bothered loading them or even routinely attaching their ammunition magazines. No one had thought about giving this order or even deeming it necessary before leaving the base. The guard in the front escort vehicle pulled a fully loaded magazine from one of his webbing pouches and snapped it onto his weapon. He cocked it to make it ready and pointed it out of the window towards their attackers.

'Shoot them, fucking shoot them,' his colleague screamed in panic, watching Lukic through his wing mirror as he readied another anti-tank weapon.

164

Whoosh! Went the second missile. It sped rapidly towards its target. BOOMING, on impact and blowing it to pieces before the armed soldier even managed to focus through the sight of his weapon.

Lukic grinned with satisfaction, changing his attention to the security van whose driver was struggling with the steering wheel, trying to keep the vehicle on the road. It swerved a couple of times to avoid the remnants of the burning vehicle in front of it. One of the tyres burst, forcing the driver to lose control. Crash, went the left hand side of the van as it hit a traffic barrier and toppled over onto its side, eventually coming to a standstill. A wake from the incident caused clouds of dust to fill the air around it, briefly obscuring it from view.

Lukic dropped down from the sunroof and into the passenger seat. He did this a mere instant before Mikel slammed his foot down hard onto the brake pedal, forcing their car to skid to an abrupt halt. Both men made eye contact and looked around assessing the situation behind them. There was no oncoming traffic in the immediate vicinity, due to the turmoil they had created moments ago. Nor were there any vehicles in view ahead of them. It was perfect, but the clock was ticking and they needed to finish the robbery as quickly as possible. Lukic grabbed one of the AK47 rifles and pushed the other one into Mikel's empty hands. They rushed out to the security van where the clouds of dust were beginning to settle.

The driver and his passenger were in deep shock and blood was trickling down their faces from wounds created by the collision with the barrier. They looked through the smashed windscreen and saw the two armed men who were coming towards them. They were both badly injured and defenceless so they raised their hands into the air for fear of being executed.

The sign of surrender meant nothing to the Kurds. They acted mercilessly by riddling the helpless soldiers with bullets and killing them instantly. Even after the men were dead, they fired another couple of short bursts into their dead corpses.

Mikel hurried towards the security van, looking all around to ensure they were still working unopposed. Lukic ran back to their car and collected a stihl-saw from inside the boot. He slung his weapon over his shoulder and climbed onto the van next to

Mikel. Once on top of the vehicle he placed his weapon down and yanked hard on the stihl-saw starter-cord, allowing the mechanical tool to burst into life. He pulled a pair of safety goggles from his pocket and put them over his eyes to protect them from any flying sparks. He pushed the rotating blade down into the metal bodywork that formed the side of the van. As expected, showers of sparks bounced off the van, which offered little resistance as the powerful cutting disc tore through it like a can opener. Within minutes, Lukic had cut a hole that was big enough to allow him to climb through. He switched off the saw and threw it away from the van. Mikel had been actively alert as a lookout but couldn't contain himself, pulling the loosely hanging tin sheet away and peered into the gaping hole. He saw the many boxes inside, smiled excitedly and jumped down amongst them. He grabbed one and opened it as Lukic anxiously looked on. Seconds later, he discarded it down onto the floor and looked up at his friend in disbelief of its contents.

'Fuck!' he screamed, suddenly realizing that this was the wrong van.

Lukic jumped down beside him and opened another couple of boxes, spilling their contents out onto the floor.

'This must have been a decoy. We're out of time. Let's move!' Lukic ordered, hearing the sound of wailing police sirens in the distance. They were not yet in view, but the two frustrated Kurds knew better than to hang around. They ran back to their vehicle and sped off. Their attempted robbery had been far from fruitful.

'That way!' Lukic ordered and pointed with urgency to a turn off at Junction 2, towards Beaconsfield on the A355. 'And put your foot down fast!'

Several miles away, Spike's voice sounded out over Beast's radio. 'Green Leader, Green Leader, this is Zulu One, this is Zulu One, over.'

'This is Green Leader, send, over,' Beast keenly responded.

'We have both you and the target in view,' Spike informed him. 'The traffic ahead is still fairly light, over.'

'We're pleased to hear it, over.'

166

'When do you want us to engage the target?'

'Not yet Zulu One. We've just passed Amersham and the road changes into a single carriageway soon. We're going to move ahead of the target in a few minutes time. Await further orders, out.'

He closed out his radio communication and nodded towards Baz who responded by pushing the gear stick into a higher gear and thrust his foot down on the accelerator. The high-performance car sped forward until it drew level with the convoy. Its exhaust fumes bellowing as it drove off into the distance.

Back in the helicopter, Bungy prepared his M21 sniper rifle. He clipped a magazine onto the weapon and cocked it. Next, he secured himself to the inside of the chopper with a harness and slid a side door open. A powerful down draft created by the aircraft's rotor blades hit him like a roundhouse kick in the face. He sat down on the floor with his legs resting outside on a metal bar that was fixed to the side of the helicopter. He focused through his telescopic sight and could clearly see the convoy below. He zoomed in on both pairs of guards who were sitting in the two escort vehicles. Initially, he lined up heads as if preparing to take a shot but then he looked ahead to see what was happening with the BMW.

Baz tactfully pulled in front of a large heavy goods vehicle, just at the point where the dual carriageway ended and the two lanes merged into one. He took his foot off the accelerator and eased it down onto the brake pedal to slow the car down. This caused the lorry behind him to brake heavily and dramatically reduce its speed. The lorry driver thought about trying to overtake the BMW but the heavy traffic, coming from the opposite direction deterred him. He felt angry towards the driver whose harsh braking action seemed unnecessary. He indicated his frustration by repeatedly sounding his horn. Albeit to no avail, because Baz continued to slow his vehicle down to almost ten miles an hour, causing a long tailback behind him.

Thoughts rushed through Bungy's mind about where he would shoot the escort vehicle guards without killing them. He repeatedly scanned their bodies through his weapon sight and moved from one soldier to the other, eventually settling his attention back towards his colleagues again. He saw the decelerating BMW come to a sudden halt and watched with interest as Beast jumped hurriedly out of the car. He was carrying something bulky in his hands so Bungy zoomed in on him to get a better view. He grinned when he saw that the object was a stinger device and watched Beast as he sprinted back down the side of the roadway towards the static security van.

The bemused lorry driver was becoming further agitated and impatient. He was a big grizzly man with broad shoulders and bulging biceps. His anger was at boiling point, so he stepped out of his vehicle to vent it by remonstrating with the driver of the BMW. Baz saw him approaching through his rear view mirror and stepped out of the car to greet him.

'What the bloody hell are you playing at?' The lorry driver screamed angrily with his fists clenched, wanting Baz to reciprocate so that he could thump him hard on the nose.

Baz remained calm and casually reached inside his coat pocket, producing his security pass from the steel mill. He swiftly flashed it in front of the angry driver's eyes and then placed it back inside his pocket.

'Look mate, we're MI6, Military Intelligence and we're on a covert operation here, trying to nail some armed terrorists. Now piss off back inside your vehicle before you get yourself into some serious trouble.'

The driver's anger instantly diffused. He squinted and paused in almost total disbelief of what he had just heard.

'I said piss off back inside your vehicle,' Baz reiterated and pointed towards the lorry.

The driver totally mellowed and felt embarrassed that he had interrupted something important. He thought about his vehicle's tax disc, which was out of date. He did not want the police to arrive and discover this so he quickly moved away and climbed back inside his cab, where he sat in silence.

Baz noticed Beast running back towards their car so he jumped inside and leaned over, pushing the passenger door open. Beast shuffled in beside him and slammed the door shut.

'Go, let's go!' he hollered eagerly.

Baz followed the instruction, pushing the car into gear and pulling away. He accelerated rapidly allowing them to distance themselves from the extensive queue of traffic.

'Did you do it?' he asked.

'Yes I did,' Beast nodded. 'The troops in the rear escort vehicle were too focused on the tail back of traffic to see what I was doing. I've released the stinger across the road in front of their tyres. They'll burst as soon as they drive over them.'

Soon, the front vehicles from the mass of traffic behind them started to move forward and pick up speed. The occupants of the rear escort vehicle watched as the lead escort vehicle and the security van drove forward. The driver paused, whilst the other soldier checked all around them using the vehicle's mirrors to ensure everything was okay. When he was satisfied, he positively nodded towards the driver and pointed forwards to signal him to pull away. The driver responded by pushing the vehicle into gear and stepping down gently on the accelerator.

Both front tyres hissed after passing over the sharp stinger spikes beneath them. Their vehicle shuddered erratically and came to an abrupt halt. The two soldiers were mystified with the situation so one of them jumped out to investigate. The traffic behind them began to queue again and some of motorists impatiently sounded their horns.

The investigating soldier sighed heavily and rubbed his forehead with the palm of his hand, puzzled about the appearance of a metal stinger lodged beneath their burst tyres. He realized that something was wrong and observed the rear of the security van in the distance as it disappeared over the brow of a hill.

'Quick! Pass me the radio,' he said to the other soldier with urgency.

The driver rolled his eyes and gave him a blank look. 'Who the hell are you going to call; bloody ghost busters?' he sneered sarcastically. 'We haven't got radio contact with anybody. I told you there was a problem with the radio before we set off and you told me not to worry about it.'

The soldier squinted, instantly regretting the rash decision he had made earlier when checking their equipment prior to

169

departure. He looked up at the sky and noticed the Chinook thrashing through the air until it too disappeared over the hill in the same direction as the remainder of the convoy.

'It's okay! It's okay!' he repeated. 'There's an aerial escort up there. Look, it's one of our Chinooks. There's no need to worry mate, let's walk to the next RAC call box. We'll get them to contact the base to organize a recovery.'

Spike manoeuvred the helicopter opposite the security van and its last remaining escort vehicle. The driver of the van saw the Chinook and smiled, admiring it. This was only for the blink of an eye, until he saw Bungy sitting in the doorway pointing his weapon at the escort vehicle.

'Zulu One, Zulu One, this is Green Leader, over,' Beast spoke into his radio.

'Green Leader, send over,' the radio crackled when Spike acknowledged the communication.

'Tell Bungy to take out the driver in the escort vehicle.'

'No, Beast, he's going to shoot their tyres out, more or less the same as you did with the rear escort vehicle,' Spike retorted.

'Okay, that's fine with me. Hey what's that music I can hear in the background?'

Spike started to laugh. 'It's Linkin Park, No More Sorrow. Why not?' He scoffed. 'They played Flight of the Val Kyrie in the Apocalypse Now film when they were stomping ass.'

'This part of the mission is all yours now, Spike,' Baz and I are about a mile a head. We want to avoid getting caught in any traffic build up, over.'

Bungy zeroed in on his target and squeezed the trigger. The sound of a single shot rang out resulting in one of the escort vehicle's tyres exploding.

'Contact, wait out,' Spike said across the radio, informing Green Leader that they had opened fire on the target.

The radio went quiet. Bungy zoomed in with his sight and watched as the escort vehicle swerved. The driver was desperately fighting to stay in control, trying to prevent it from leaving the road. Simultaneously, the driver of the security van reacted on impulse and slammed his brakes on hard to avoid crashing into the juddering vehicle. Both vehicles became still and a soldier in the escort vehicle climbed out to assess the situation. He gazed at the driver of the security van who was pointing at the marksman in the hovering helicopter.

'Sniper, sniper,' he bellowed repeatedly.

The soldier cocked his weapon and took aim at Bungy. It was too late, Bungy was already applying pressure to the M21's trigger once again. Another shot rang out and the soldier's weapon clattered to the ground as blood instantly oozed out from a shattered hand.

'Run! Fucking run!' the security van driver screamed as they jumped out of their vehicles. Don't worry about the money. They'll never land the helicopter here. Let's take cover in those bushes over there before they kill us.'

The vulnerable soldiers ran for cover in some bushes at the side of the road. Bungy watched them and then briefly looked back at the lengthy queue of traffic that was building up behind them. He jumped up stepping back inside the helicopter and hooked the huge magnet onto the winch. He pressed the relevant control buttons on a control panel and lowered the magnet down about thirty feet below the aircraft.

'Spike, steer over the top of the security van,' he instructed. 'We're ready to lift it out of here!'

Spike responded by hovering the Chinook over the top of the security vehicle until the magnet banged heavily onto its roof. Bungy pressed another button to activate it, allowing its powerful magnetic attraction to hold firmly against the van's steel roof. He picked his rifle up again and looked through the sight towards the soldiers who had taken cover. He observed one of them taking aim at him. He fired once again without hesitation and the soldier screamed with pain as a round ripped through one of his arms. His weapon fell to the ground, but he sensibly did not attempt to pick it up to try again. The soldiers knew they were clearly in the sights of the sniper and sensed that they would be shot if they made any further moves. They chose to lay flat on the floor with

171

their hands on top of their heads. There was a lot of money in the security van but it wasn't theirs and it was certainly not worth dying for.

Meanwhile, back amongst the queuing traffic, countless numbers of innocent drivers looked on in amazement as the helicopter rose into the air taking the security van with it. Some were fearful of what they saw. Others were flabbergasted!

'Green Leader, Green Leader, this is Zulu One. This is Zulu One, over,' Spike spoke excitedly into the radio.

'Zulu One, send over,' Beast responded.

'We have the cargo. I say again; we have the cargo.

'Did anyone get slotted? Over,' Beast asked, hoping that they hadn't.

'No, we had to wound a couple of them, but that's all. We're going to touch down a couple of miles away and check to see if there are any guards inside the vehicle before we unload the money. Over'

'Okay. Once you've finished, paint the helicopter yellow as planned and fly it to the weapons cache. Destroy the helicopter over there. It's only a matter of time before the authorities start looking for it, over.'

'I thought we were going to do that later, over?

'No we've made a change of plan. It'll be best to do it sooner rather than later, over.'

'How do you know we won't do a runner with all this cash? Over,' Spike smirked and patiently waited for a response.

'I know you won't do that. If we can trust each other with our lives, we can trust each other with other people's money,' Beast replied confidently, shaking his head. 'We'll see you back at my place sometime tomorrow. We're going to return this car to the airport now so from here onwards use your mobile phone if you want to get in touch with me, over.'

'Roger, out,' Spike responded and switched off the radio.

'Look over there,' Lukic urged Mikel, as they pulled up at a junction where the road joined the A413. 'I'll bet that's the other security van.'

They saw Beast speaking into a radio inside the BMW and observed the helicopter with its bulky cargo hanging below it. They watched eagerly as it flew away from them and across country. Immediately they were alert, realizing that whilst they had attacked the decoy van somebody else had hijacked the real one. There was no way they could track the helicopter so they logically chose to follow the BMW. They strongly suspected that its occupants were working as part of the robbery team and would be reunited with the huge sum of cash, somewhere along the line.

A short while later, in a remote cornfield, Spike carefully lowered the security van down onto the ground and Bungy released it from the magnet. It made a thumping sound when its wheels were reunited with the earth. Spike landed the aircraft a few yards away.

Bungy peered through his weapon sight to cover Spike, whilst he attached some plastic explosive to the van doors. Within seconds, it was done and Spike detonated the charge.

A relatively small explosion sounded out and emitted thick black smoke that clouded the air around it before dissipating. Bungy remained focused and looked on to see if there was any sign of movement. The smoke cleared and revealed that the doors had been blown. They hadn't detached; they just hung loosely ajar. Spike grabbed one of the doors and pulled it fully open without exposing himself to anybody who may be waiting inside.

'It's clear. There's no one inside it!' Bungy shouted and lowered his weapon.

Spike peered inside and cast his bulging eyes over a huge pile of money. It was stacked on pallets in bundles of fifty-pound notes with plastic cellophane neatly wrapped around them.

'Wow!' he gasped. 'This is the most money I have ever seen in my entire life. I feel like we've just won the Euro Millions lottery.'

'Let's unload it quickly, before anybody sees us,' Bungy said, choosing to contain his excitement. He turned and ran back to the helicopter to collect a thick roll of plastic bin-liners.

The two of them worked quickly. Spike loaded bundles of the money into the bin bags and Bungy ran back and forth to the helicopter, stacking them inside. This piece of work was physically demanding so they periodically changed roles. The unloading and reloading process was time consuming and took them nearly two hours before the last bag of money was secured inside. After the loading was completed, they set about painting the helicopter yellow as planned. Eventually, it did resemble a Coast Guard rescue aircraft. Before they left they agreed that there was still enough room to store the magnet onboard and winched it inside next to the money. They wanted to leave nothing behind.

Meanwhile, Baz and Beast drove back to Luton and returned the BMW to the airport car park. They felt pleased with themselves as they jumped back into their own car and casually drove out through the opening exit barrier. Unbeknown to them, they were being followed by the two Kurds who were now certain they were linked to the security van robbery.

Spike and Bungy enjoyed the flight across to Northern Ireland. They sat laughing and joking together and Spike gave Bungy a quick briefing on how to fly a Chinook helicopter. The robbery so far had been a great success, but it was more the underlying thrill of working together in dangerous situations that pleased them most.

'The operation was a piece of piss, wasn't it?' Spike said.

'Yes it was,' Bungy nodded. 'It's a shame we're using our military skills on the wrong side of the law though, isn't it?'

'Yes it is, but if we weren't working together on this, we'd probably be bored to death working in some dead-end job. Or living rough on the streets.'

'Yeah that's true, Spike. Anyway that reminds me; there's something I've been meaning to ask you for a while now."

'What's that?' Spike asked curiously.

'Do you remember that woman you went home with in Plymouth?'

'Yes I do. What about her?'

'She was your wife, wasn't she?'

'I'm not really sure,' Spike squinted. 'To be honest I couldn't recall knowing her or the children when I went back to her house. I wasn't sure if she had lost her husband and wanted me to fill his shoes. Maybe it's just a case of mistaken identity or a coincidence that I resemble someone else.'

'There are too many similarities to be a coincidence, mate. You should go back home you know. Those kids need their father.'

'I may go back to talk with her one of these days, just in case I have got some form of amnesia. What about you, Bungy? Have you got any family?'

'No I haven't. I was married for a couple of years but she left me. I think I was suffering from Post Traumatic Stress Syndrome. I was having nightmares all the time and was also fighting in my sleep. One day, out of the blue, she told me she'd had enough and filed for divorce. Since then I've had a few flings, but nothing serious. I guess once I ended up living rough on the streets I got lost for a while.'

'Yes me too,' Spike replied, gazing out of the window at the contours below. 'Look down there,' he pointed ahead of them. 'It's the location of the weapons cache.'

Spike tried to find a suitable area to land the Chinook, but his efforts proved futile, being restricted by the uneven ground and surrounding trees. Consequently, he hovered the aircraft on autopilot and slid open a side door.

'Give me a hand with this,' Bungy instructed, loading the money into an on-board cargo net.

They tirelessly worked at off loading it close to the weapons cache. Each time they lowered the net, Bungy went down with the load before being winched back up again. Once this task was complete, they flew the helicopter a short distance away where they landed it safely and switched the engines off. A while later, they headed back towards the money.

It was dusk before the two men had successfully transferred all the money inside the store. Spike completed the job by rigging a booby trap over the entrance doors, using semtex explosive. When he had finished he replaced the soil and roles of turf over the top to conceal it. As they walked back to the helicopter, they intermittently stopped and looked back through the darkness, hoping that no one would somehow stumble on their haul. They flew the Chinook a couple of miles away and landed it on a plateau, cutting the engines. Spike used the last of his stock of explosives, rigging them up to destroy it after taking cover behind some rocks. The resulting explosion lit up the night sky as a chain-reaction ignited the fuselage.

'Bloody hell, Spike! You don't do things by halves, mate!' Bungy blurted.

'And then it was gone,' Spike smirked with his ears ringing as an after effect of the thundering blasts.

'They won't recognize that from the air,' Bungy retorted, expressing his satisfaction. 'That's for sure.'

They hung around for a while until the flames died down, then they used a compass to navigate their way through the night towards Newry.

Once there, they hitch hiked to Dublin where they booked a ferry crossing over the Irish Sea to Liverpool. On the way, they caught up with some much-needed sleep waking shortly before docking. During the early hours of the morning, they began their lengthy train journey south towards Oxford

Chapter Thirteen

'How are we going to find out where the money is?' Mikel asked Lukic, who was busy looking through his telescopic lens. He was observing Beast's farmhouse from a tree-lined edge, located a couple of hundred metres away. They had followed the two men from the airport car park and had decided to keep the house under surveillance, hoping to finding out where the money was stashed.

'I don't know,' Lukic snapped, still reeling because their efforts of trying to rob the decoy van proved fruitless. 'Wait a minute. A taxi has just pulled up outside the house. Two men have stepped out of it. I bet you they were the men who were flying the helicopter. They've probably landed it somewhere else and hid the money.

'Are they carrying any bags?' Mikel keenly asked.

'Yes, but only small ones. They'll hardly be able to carry sixty million pounds inside them, will they? Like I said, they must have hid the haul somewhere else.'

'Yes,' Mikel agreed. 'We'll have to watch them for a while until they make a move to collect it. Hopefully, that won't be too long.'

'Hopefully,' Lukic reciprocated. 'But life is never that easy, is it? We'll try to kidnap one of them when they leave the house.'

'Yeah, that'll do the trick. I bet the one we capture cracks really easy.'

'I wouldn't be too sure about that, Mikel.'

'What do you mean?' he grunted.

'They seem to be well organised and have specialist skills, such as the ability to fly helicopters. I'm assuming they are probably former soldiers. Although, what kind of soldiers remains to be seen?'

'I'm not worried about that,' Mikel smirked, pulling his flick knife out and licking the blade. 'I'm ruthless with this, so I don't care who they are.'

Back at the Farmhouse, Beast greeted Spike and Bungy when they entered inside. 'It's good to see you made it back in one piece, men. How did it go?'

'It was a piece of cake,' Spike scoffed. 'The money is safely secured inside the weapons cache. I've booby trapped it, just to be sure that nobody else gets their grubby little mitts on it.'

Everybody started to hug each other and shook hands to celebrate the success of their operation.

'What about the chopper? Did you destroy it?' Beast asked, hoping they did.

'Yes, that's sorted too,' Bungy assured him. 'We blew it to pieces in accordance with our plan.'

'That's it then,' Baz grinned towards Beast. 'The operation is over. Are we going to drink some champagne to celebrate?'

'I wish!' Beast beamed. 'Unbelievably, I haven't got any readily available cash to buy any.'

'Fuck me!' Bungy gasped. 'Are you saying we've got sixty million lovely smackers stashed away and none of us can afford to buy some alcohol to celebrate?'

'Not quite, Baz,' Beast smirked, putting a finger in the air. 'Even though you think I'm not aware of it, I do know you've got four large bottles of scotch whiskey hidden in a box next to your bed.'

'How did you know that?' Baz asked curiously.

'Because I saw you sneak out of the travel lodge in Southall and nip down to the adjacent petrol station to buy the stuff.'

'How did you know it was whiskey?' Baz was humoured and curious too.

'I saw you hide the box in the boot of the BMW. Then you transferred it back to our car at the airport with a coat draped over the top. I couldn't really miss the stuff when I checked our kit inside the boot that morning.'

'Bloody hell, Beast! You should have been a detective. Okay you've got me,' Baz conceded, holding his hands up. 'Let's just say I was confident that we'd achieve our objective. There's one bottle for each of us.'

'Let's have an operational debrief first, before we start our celebrations,' Beast insisted and everybody pulled up a seat without protest.

The former marines sat together around a warm crackling log fire that radiated heat around them. Their celebratory mood was temporarily suppressed, whilst they discussed the different stages and decisions made during the operation. They reviewed the events and suggested ways of refining the methods used and lessons learned during their deployment. It was their military way of debriefing the success or failure of a mission, once it had been completed.

'Bungy,' Beast called out, seeking his attention. 'Your sniper skills were impressive. The accuracy was commendable. You did an absolutely excellent job without killing anybody.'

'Err yes,' Bungy answered and cleared his throat. 'It's not a habit of mine though. Generally, I like to think another one bites the dust every time I draw back the rifle's bolt action.'

'Beast has made a good point, Bungy,' Spike added. 'Your accuracy impressed the hell out of all of us.'

Bungy's cheeks flushed red and he felt innocently embarrassed. In the past, it had just been his job, usually without praise. Now his colleagues were commending his work, so he too chose to join in with courteously dishing out his own compliments.

'Well, Spike, mate. 'Maybe I can shoot a spider up the arse from a long distance away, but there's no way I could have flown the helicopter like you did.'

'Yeah, the music we played at the time was super cool too?' Spike smirked. 'I got a real buzz from it.'

'You two haven't seen him working with explosives,' Bungy continued. 'He's a flaming maestro.'

'Baz's driving skills were pretty cool too?' Beast added and patted his friend lightly on the back and then hugged him tightly.

'Yes, I drive people crazy. My wife for example,' Baz gestured, turning the compliment into humour. 'Whilst we're dishing the praises out lets not forget Beast. Not only did he plan the well-executed job, he also led the operation. Not forgetting of course, that he also got us all back into good physical shape.'

Baz slapped one of his thighs and stood up, heading upstairs to his bedroom to retrieve the box of whiskey. When he returned he gave one to each of his appreciative friends. Nobody asked for a glass to drink the spirit or even for a mixer drink to water it down. They just started proposing numerous toasts and swigging merrily from the bottles. This continued through lunchtime and into the early evening. Eventually, the men were heavily inebriated.

'I have a confession to make to you,' Beast slurred in a raised voice. Everybody gazed in his direction with a half interest in anything he had to say. 'There was a point when I thought I wouldn't be able to find us a payroll job to pull together. I was shitting myself and felt certain that I was going to let you all down.'

'Yeah of course you were!' Spike grinned. We believe you, mate!' He made a joke of Beast's comments, believing him to be pulling everybody's leg with his confession. The comments were literally taken with a pinch of salt and the group started laughing together.

'What about the next job?' Baz asked, looking around at each of his friends in turn. 'What are we going to do next? I haven't had this much fun in years.'

'There is no next job,' Beast frowned. 'We're millionaires now. We just need to lay low for a while and then we can take our split of the cash and go our separate ways.'

Instantly, the room fell silent. Nobody spoke for at least a minute. During this time, they exchanged blank looks with one another.

'It wasn't about the money,' Baz said, breaking the silence. 'It was the buzz of excitement we had. The same buzz we used to get when we served in the military together. No amount of money can buy that, can it?'

'Exactly,' Spike added. 'We need to start planning our next job together now, don't we? Come on lets do it. We can conquer the world together.'

'Wait a minute,' Beast interrupted, hoping to talk some sense into his friends. 'Sixty million pounds is a lot of money. I don't think we need any more.'

'I like the sound of that,' Baz cut in, ignoring Beast's comments. 'If we're all keen on continuing to work together as a team, why don't we utilize our skills on a different kind of target? Something that's a little more challenging.'

'Such as?' Bungy shrugged.

'Such as working as mercenaries in Angola or somewhere like that,' Baz continued, seemingly disinterested in the haul.

'That might not be a bad idea,' Bungy nodded. 'At least then I'll get to shoot people dead instead of just wounding them.'

'The mere thought of it excites me,' Baz added after gargling a mouthful of whiskey. 'What about you big guy? He asked Beast. 'Are you planning to lead a boring life as a retired millionaire or can you be talked into becoming seriously keen on this mercenary stuff?

'Okay,' Beast slurred. 'I'll make a proposal and we'll put it to a vote. We'll spend two days socializing together to celebrate our success and then we'll all go back to our homes for a while, until the heat from the robbery cools off. We can meet up later and decide if we still want to stay together as a team, or take our fair cut of the money and head for the hills.'

Each of them in turn agreed without any difference of opinion. They chinked their bottles together, making a final toast before swilling the dregs of their whiskey and retiring to bed.

Outside, it was getting dark and the two Kurds were becoming increasingly bored with spying on the unsuspecting robbers.

'The upstairs lights have been switched on and then extinguished,' Lukic said, peering through his telescopic sight. 'They must have gone to bed.'

'Are we going to break in after they've gone to sleep?'

'No, it's too risky. They'll probably be taking turns to keep watch.'

'Why don't we make our selves scarce? I'm freezing cold and piss wet through,' Mikel griped, shuffling his baseball cap from side to side. 'We could book a room in a bed and breakfast. I saw one in a village we drove passed. It's only a couple of miles away.'

'Yes,' Lukic agreed, folding his sight away. 'We'll do that. My joints are aching and I'm ready for a good nights rest too.'

Chapter Fourteen

The next day, the armed robbery was repeatedly screened on all television news stations. It also dominated the main headlines on the front pages of the national newspapers. One headline read, THE STOLEN MONEY IS STOLEN, and insinuated that it was possibly an inside job. The article reported that the authorities were unsure if the attempted robbery of the decoy security van and the real one were linked. However, the level of ruthless violence used during the attack on the decoy van indicated that there were questionable differences. This assumption was substantiated by the fact that the main robbery was carried out with military precision, during which it was arguably possible that there had been no deliberate intentions to kill anyone.

Later that morning, the body of the civilian RAF van driver was discovered beneath the trees where Mikel had murdered him. In addition, the missing farmer's body was found after being detected by sniffer dogs amongst some bushes close to the High Wycombe base entrance. The Scene of Crime Officers (S.O.C.O) combed the crime scenes looking for clues. On conclusion, they commented that they were shocked at the level of violence used to cause the two men to meet their deaths. They produced a report that reflected this and their resulting DNA evidence linked their murderers with the robbery carried out on the decoy van.

The authorities wasted no time in assembling a joint military and civilian police control-room at the RAF base.

'My gut feeling about the attempted robbery of the decoy van and the simultaneous robbery of the van carrying the money is that they weren't linked,' said Detective Sergeant Dave Watson; a former Royal Marine who had recently been promoted from the uniformed division. 'The two styles of approach were completely different. One was the work of ruthless murderers and the other I presume was the work of either serving or ex serving members of the armed forces. I have made these assumptions based on the information passed to us by eyewitnesses from both robbery crime scenes. Currently we assume that the assault on the decoy van was carried out by two foreign nationals. They were allegedly seen talking to the deceased, Frank Cotterill, in the White Horse public house during the early hours on the eve of the robbery. Frank, by the way, was a civilian driver who was initially tasked with driving one of the security vehicles. However, prior to the robbery he had been released from his duties for security reasons.'

The audience in attendance were a mixture of military and civilian police officers. They listened in silence and scribbled away on their note pads, as Dave explained the theories and facts of the crime.

'When and why was Frank Cotterill killed?' One of them asked, waving his hand in the air to seek Dave's attention.

'It has been estimated by the pathology autopsy that he was killed some time after leaving the public house, probably after being forced to provide information about the security vans. We can only assume that Frank tried to protect the interests of the transportation operation and purposely guided the two men towards the decoy van. His throat had been cut and his body was found in some nearby woods with multiple stab wounds.'

'What about the farmer?' another of the officers asked. 'Who killed him and why? Are the murders linked?' he finished, looking at Dave and waiting for an answer.

'The farmer, who incidentally was called Kenneth Ferill, was also killed by the same two guys who robbed the decoy van,' Dave explained. 'He was out walking on his land that morning, which coincidently borders the RAF High Wycombe base. The results from his pathology autopsy, estimates his time of death as being around the time when the first security van left the base at 6 a.m. Also, fresh tyre marks were found in the mud next to where the body was found.'

'How can we be sure the two robberies aren't linked?' somebody asked.

'At this stage of the investigation we can't be sure. We do know though, that the style of approach and execution of each robbery was noticeably different. The two men who tried to rob the decoy van were undoubtedly ruthless killers. The main robbery was coordinated with precision. It appears to have been carried out by a team of well-organised professionals, consisting of a helicopter pilot, a marksman or military sniper and a skilled car driver. There was also another accomplice who was observed by a civilian motorist, using a stinger to blow the rear escort vehicle's tyres out.'

'Why do you strongly believe they were either serving or ex serving military personnel?' a military policeman asked.

'How long have you served in the military?' Dave grimaced. His unexpected reciprocation startled the man, who initially paused to answer. 'Well,' Dave demanded, creating an air of unease.

'Err, six months,' he stammered, suddenly feeling nervous and conscious of the other police officers in the room.

'I thought as much,' Dave grunted. 'I served in the Royal Marines for seven years and I'll assure you; the main robbery carries all the hallmarks of a military style operation. They stole a Chinook helicopter from RAF Brize Norton without being compromised. They weren't misled by the decoy van; so I would assume they had previously carried out a surveillance operation. They used a stinger, similar to the type we used in Northern Ireland during the years of the troubles. One of them was a sniper whose marksmanship was outstanding. He wounded, but did not kill.'

'How do you know he didn't shoot to kill and missed his target?' the military policeman asked, trying to use the opportunity to raise his level of esteem.

'Bollocks,' Dave snapped - gritting his teeth. 'He was consistent. There was no way he could have missed every time. It's bloody obvious he had no intentions of killing anybody, isn't it? The use of the magnet was a piece of genius,' Dave continued. 'Finally, they executed the robbery with precision, accuracy and sheer professionalism. They're specialists. I'm certain about that. I'm not glorifying what they did. I'm just stating the facts of the case.'

'What about the helicopter?' a different officer chirped.

'What about it?' Dave asked.

'What did they do with it after the robbery?'

'We don't know? They may still have it. The security van was found abandoned and empty in a remote field several miles away. The forensic team have searched it with a fine tooth comb, but unfortunately have been unable to find anything.'

'Where do we start looking?' the military policeman asked.

'Okay,' Dave nodded looking around the audience. 'I guess it's time to talk about progressing the investigation. Before we do this, does anybody else have any questions?'

Nobody responded, so Dave casually walked across the room and pulled a white board out from a cupboard. Its thin wooden legs shuddered as he dragged it across the floor to the front of the room. The investigators looked on and observed the four colour photographs that were neatly pinned to it.

Dave cleared his throat. 'Unfortunately, we currently have no leads or in-depth information on the military team. However, from here onwards, we will refer to them as the Team.'

'Nice one, I like that,' the military policeman grinned facetiously. 'I bet the leader is called the brainy one.'

Dave ignored the silly remark. He was focusing on sharing the only lead he had with his investigation team, who listened with interest.

'Two of these photographs were taken from still shots of video camera footage, acquired from security cameras on the channel tunnel some time ago. The other two photographs were taken from a traffic surveillance camera on the M40 motorway, during the time of the attempted robbery of the decoy van. The two men you can see in the channel tunnel are the same two men on the M40 motorway. They are illegal immigrants from Kurdistan. We've checked them out and their credentials have shown that they are wanted men in their own country.'

'Wanted for what?' somebody asked.

'They're wanted for drug trafficking, robbery and murder. They are ruthless, mindless villains who should be approached with caution. I would like to add that two savaged bodies of maintenance workers were found around the time these photographs were taken. Although it is believed that their deaths may just be sheer coincidence, because their corpses had been viciously torn to pieces by wild rats.'

'But these men haven't got the stolen money, have they?' another investigator piped up.

'That's very true, but our superiors want some quick results to keep the media happy. I would like to think that these men are strongly disappointed about their failure and will still be keen to get their hands on the loot. If my hunch is right, they may have seen the media coverage and it is possible that they will pursue the team.'

'They might be out of the country by now,' an officer commented.

'Like I said, it's a hunch but it is also a possibility,' Dave affirmed, knowing that he was clutching at straws. 'Either way, we need to find them and mount a covert surveillance operation in the hope that they don't disappoint us.

Everybody gave a positive response and Dave felt satisfied with presenting the facts of the crime to the investigation team. Now he desperately needed to find the two Kurds and strongly hoped that his hunch was right, about them wanting to find the stolen money.

Chapter Fifteen

'I wish this bloody rain would stop,' Lukic griped. 'My clothes are piss wet through.'

'I'm fed up too, Lukic,' Mikel retorted. 'We've been sat amongst these trees for two days now.'

The two men had returned to re-establish their observation post next to Beast's farmhouse. This time they were better equipped with waterproof sleeping bags and a camouflaged flysheet to help keep them dry. At least that's what it said on the label! Their plan now was to wait for one of the security van robbers to leave the farmhouse, so that they could abduct him and question him about the location of the stolen money.

'Yes two bloody days, Mikel and these bastards haven't moved a muscle yet. This second hand military kit is supposed to be waterproof, but instead it acts like a sponge, absorbing water.'

'You're right,' Mikel agreed, rolling his eyes. 'All my stuff is soaking wet and my sleeping bag feels more like a wet gusset. Okay, fuck this for a game of soldiers. Let's go back to the car and get changed into dry clothing. We can park it somewhere near the end of the country lane that leads up to the farmhouse. We should still be able to watch the place from there without being sussed.'

Mikel took one last look through his binoculars, hoping to see some movement. There was none. So they began discarding most of their soaking wet equipment into the bushes and trundled off back towards their car.

Soon after, both men were feeling a lot more contented, making themselves comfortable in the front seats of their vehicle. They had changed into dry clothing and were peering out through the windscreen, watching the unrelenting rain as it bounced off the windows.

'This is better, Lukic,' Mikel sneezed into his hand.

'I agree, my friend. We should have done this in the beginning.'

They drove their car closer to the farmhouse - about three hundred metres away. They were undecided about where to park it, but eventually backed it off the road again, just inside the tree line. Fern bushes with broad leaves covered the front of the car, breaking up its outline and hiding it from view. It was perfect, so they settled and switched off the engine.

Meanwhile, back inside the farmhouse, Beast was sitting watching the morning news on television. It had been several days since the robbery and the main headlines had drifted from the hold-up to other worldwide pressing matters, such as the ongoing conflict in Iraq. This was not due to a shortage of investigative efforts on the side of the authorities, more so because they had very few leads to follow.

'Hey, Beast,' Baz grinned when he walked into the sitting room, dressed in his underclothes.

'What?' he yawned, without detracting his attention from flicking the channels on the remote-control.

'Who's cooking the breakfasts?'

'It looks like you've just volunteered your self, mate.'

'Huh, thanks very much,' Baz scoffed raising his eyebrows. 'I suppose it was kind of me to offer. Even, if I didn't!'

'I'll have a full fried breakfast, Bungy laughed, walking into the room sporting pyjamas and slippers. 'I feel as rough as guts after drinking that fire water last night.'

'Yes me too. I've got a head like a baby's pram. Full of crap and broken biscuits,' Spike added from behind him. 'I could eat a scabby horse right now. I'm ravenous.'

Baz brushed passed them and went into the kitchen, where he pulled the large fridge door open and scanned inside for bacon, eggs and tomatoes. Unfortunately, the food shelves were bare and his findings disappointed him. His stomach started to rumble.

'Shit, there's no food in the fridge,' he shouted aloud.

'You'll have to nip to the shop to get some,' Beast told him. 'There's one just a short journey away in Elsfield.'

'I've drawn the bloody short straw here,' Baz uttered, before quickly getting dressed and leaving via the front door with a set of car keys in his hand.

He climbed into Beast's car and drove off down the peaceful country road towards Elsfield. After a minute or so, he unknowingly drove past Mikel and Lukic who were eagerly watching him to see if he was alone.

'There's our man,' Lukic said, pointing at the car. 'Let's follow him and choose our moment to jump him.'

Mikel started the car engine and pulled out onto the road, heading off in pursuit of Baz. He was aware that he needed to avoid suspicion, so he drove at a steady speed and cautiously kept his distance.

Baz's stomach continued to rumble and he began to picture a full fried, English breakfast in his mind. He could almost taste it as the local general store came into view. He parked the car opposite the shop in a lay-by, pulling on the handbrake prior to stepping out and walking inside. He looked around and up and down the small isles, scanning the shelves for dairy and meat products. He reached for a loaf of bread, a dozen eggs, a good few rashes of bacon, some sausages, beans and a tin of chopped tomatoes. When he was satisfied, he placed them on the counter in front of a young female shopkeeper.

'Good morning, sir,' she smiled at him.

At that moment, Mikel and Lukic entered the store and cautiously looked around, instantly casting their eyes on Baz. His powerful stocky physique made them wary of him. Inevitably, he was not going to be easy to kidnap.

Baz noticed them staring and their eyes unintentionally met, creating an immediate level of tension. He wanted to turn and look away, but he found their direct glances annoying.

'Who are you two looking at?' he asked them. 'Do I know you from somewhere or do I owe you money?'

'No, no, we're not from around here,' Lukic calmly answered. 'We're just passing through. You look like someone we used to work with,' he lied tactfully.

Baz turned the other way and smiled at the shopkeeper who scanned his goods into the till and placed them inside two carrier bags.

'That'll be eight pounds and fifty pence please,' she politely told him.

Baz pulled a crisp ten-pound note from his wallet and handed it to her, grabbing the full shopping bags and walking out of the store.

The two Kurds followed close behind. They were ready. Their victim's hands were full, potentially aiding their attack on him. Baz looked up and down the relatively deserted road and trundled across it. He rolled his eyes in response to the continuance of rumbling acids in his stomach. Mikel and Lukic were just feet away. Both of them held onto a wooden baton, hidden inside their coat and were preparing to draw them. Suddenly, a voice called out.

'Excuse me. Excuse me, sir. You've forgotten your change,' the young female shopkeeper shouted.

Baz was nearing his car. He stopped and turned around, instantly noticing the closeness of the two approaching strangers. What do they want? He thought suspiciously.

Mikel and Lukic were startled by the young woman's unexpected appearance. They eased off their batons and broke the gaze of intent with Barry. To avoid suspicion they casually put their heads down and walked past him, climbing into their own vehicle. Baz briefly glanced at them as he made his was back across the road to collect his change. Their apparent lack of concern for him detracted his attention by the time he had reached the shopkeeper.

'Keep the change,' he smiled at her, as the two Kurds drove passed him. 'I appreciate your honesty.'

Minutes later, Baz was sitting inside his car and had started the short return journey back towards the farmhouse.

'Turn the car around, quickly,' Mikel insisted. 'The bastard is getting away.'

Lukic slammed the brakes on hard and the car screeched to an abrupt halt. There was no traffic around, so he quickly did a three-point turn and sped off in the opposite direction.

Baz was already speeding well ahead of them. His stomach continued to rumble and his mouth was watering as he thought about his cooked breakfast. He also took advantage of the lack of traffic and raced down the road breaking the legal speed limit. When he arrived at the house, he found his hungry colleagues sipping tea and patiently waiting for his return.

'Come on lads,' Baz grinned, raising the shopping bags into the air. 'Give me a hand with this lot before I eat it raw.'

Outside, Mikel and Lukic parked up amongst the fern bushes. They were disappointed about messing up the abduction. Lukic gritted his teeth and banged his fists on the dashboard. 'I can't believe we messed that up so badly,' he snarled.

'Neither can I,' Mikel frowned. 'Maybe we should have jumped him and ignored the shop keeper.'

'No that would have been too risky, Mikel. She would have reported us to the police.'

'Yes you're right about that. We'll have to be patient and hope we get another chance soon.'

Chapter Sixteen

'Well, lads my hangover has eased a little now,' Spike said gleefully. 'Why don't we go to Oxford for a run ashore?' (a marine term for a night on the town).

'Yes let's do that,' Bungy smirked. 'Let's go for a run ashore. My hangover has cleared too.'

Beast sat back in his chair with his hands clasped behind his head. He glanced meaningfully at his friends, one at a time. He looked concerned about something.

'What about you, Beast?' Spike prompted him. 'Are you and Baz up for one last night on the piss or what?'

'Look guys, I need to be honest with you,' Beast told them, immediately receiving their attention. 'Let's not forget we've just pulled one of the biggest security van robberies this country has ever seen. We need to split up and lay low for a while until the heat cools off. Otherwise we could all end up in prison.'

Spike's smile dropped and the room fell silent as everybody swapped blank looks and then looked back towards Beast.

'You can't be serious,' Spike said; his face twisted with disappointment. 'We don't have to split up, do we? What about the suggestion of us working together as mercenaries? You were keen about this earlier.'

Beast chose not to answer the latter question. 'I am serious,' he insisted. 'I've given this a lot more thought. I need to go back up north to spend some time with my wife. It would be best for us to go our separate ways for a couple of months or so. We can still keep in touch by telephone until we think its time to meet up again and split the money.'

'Come on Beast, you can't do this,' Spike pleaded. 'This has been the best time of my life since I left the marines. Can't we plan another heist together or something similar?'

'He's right men,' Baz unpretentiously intervened. 'We do need to lay low for a while and preferably not here and not together. Sixty million quid is a hell of a haul. I bet the whole world will want to know where it is and where we are too.'

Spike sat in silence for a while, running his fingers through his short brown hair, pondering over the comments made. He understood the implications.

'Okay,' Baz finally agreed. 'Let's have one final celebratory night out in Oxford like we suggested earlier. It could be our parting celebration or something like that. It sounds like a good idea to me,' he finished, looking towards Beast for his approval and half expecting him to agree.

Beast stared at each of them in turn again and lastly at Baz. 'Why not?' he endorsed. 'Yes why not?' he repeated.

'Love it, love iiiiiiitttttt,' Spike shouted excitedly. 'I've got another good idea too. Let's go out in fancy dress. Yes, let's go out dressed up as tarts.'

'We're supposed to be laying low guys,' Beast reminded them, concerned that they could end up drawing too much attention to them selves.

'People often go out dressed in fancy dress. We'll be okay,' Spike assured him. 'Come on lets get dressed up as tarts.'

'No we can't do that, because I haven't got any women's clothes here,' Beast sighed, already searching his mind for another theme. 'I've got it. Let's go out dressed as train spotters. I've got some long flasher macs in the cupboard and several sets of thick safety-glasses that will make us look the part.'

Beast mooched around in a cupboard, pulling the Macs and safety glasses from it and handed them out. Each man put them on and paraded up and down excitedly, like schoolchildren. They checked their attire using a mirror that hung in the hallway. Baz's coat fitted him perfectly, but Bungy and Spike's were a little on the large side so they rolled the sleeves up.

'We need note pads and pens to write the train numbers down,' Bungy said.

Beast poked a finger in the air, hurrying over to a sideboard and pulling four jotter pads and pens from it.

'Cameras, cameras, what about cameras?' Spike asked, racking his brain to think of things that a real train spotter would carry.

Beast scrunched his face and rubbed his chin. He had two expensive digital cameras in the house that they could use. Initially, he thought they were too expensive to risk breaking them. Then he smirked to himself, thinking about the massive amount of money that they had stashed in South Armagh.

'Yes cameras,' he piped up. 'I've only got two of those, so we'll have to share them.'

An air of excitement ran amongst them. They laughed together and shook each other's hands. They had not enjoyed a social evening out for quite some time, not since their night out in Plymouth when they first got together.

'What time is it?' Mikel asked in the car outside.

'It's 6:30 p.m.,' Lukic answered checking his watch. 'I'm getting sick of waiting around, are you? Wait, he hushed before Mikel could answer. 'There's a vehicle approaching. It's a cab.' He pointed towards a bright yellow taxi which drove passed them heading towards the farmhouse. They became curious.

'They must be going out on the town,' Mikel assumed.

'Why do you think that?' Lukic asked, scratching his head.

'Because they would have driven them selves if they were going somewhere else. They must be having a social night out together.'

'Oh I see. A celebration you mean.'

'Yes, that's exactly what I meant.'

Several minutes later, the taxi drove past them again heading in the opposite direction. All four of the former marines were passengers inside it and were bound for a pub in Oxford.

'Are we going to break into their house and search it, Lukic?' Mikel asked, believing it to be a good idea.

'No, I don't see any point in that. The money won't be there. It'll be wherever they've landed the helicopter. We'll stick to our original plan to try and kidnap one of them. This could be our ideal opportunity.'

Mikel nodded and started the car engine. He pushed the gear stick into first gear and drove off in pursuit of the taxi. He accelerated gradually, ensuring they stayed far enough behind not to be noticed.

The mood inside the taxi was jovial and many humorous jokes flowed between the men. Just then, Spike's nostrils twitched as they filled with a foul smell of bad wind.

'Bloody hell', he exclaimed. 'Which one of you big dirty bastards has let that one go?' He wound the window down desperately needing some fresh air. 'I bet you've got whopping great skid marks in your underpants and shit stains in the back of your collar.'

Nobody answered and everybody except the cab driver rolled around in hysterical fits of laughter. The driver frowned at the situation and felt absolutely disgusted at the foul behaviour inside his vehicle.

Soon after, the smell had dissipated and the car windows were closed, stopping the chilly night air from making everybody shudder with cold. The intermittent bouts of laughter ceased and Bungy had turned the car heater up higher to warm them through.

'Phew,' Spike frowned after inhaling yet another breath of foul air. It engulfed the inside of the cab again. 'For fucks sake,' he hollered and wound the window back down. 'I think one of you big hairy arsed gorillas has shit himself. Who ever dealt that smells like a dead corpse with rancid hemorrhoids.'

Again, everybody except the driver laughed about the smell and they wound down another couple of windows. The cab driver became incensed with anger and without warning; he slammed his foot down hard on the brakes, bringing the car to an abrupt halt.

'You are filthy pigs! Get out of my cab,' he screamed with disgust. 'Go on, get out now.'

The laughter immediately ceased and was followed by a short period of silence and an air of uncertainty. The cab driver was furious and reiterated his comments.

'Go on, get out now!' he snapped adamantly.

'Wait a minute, mate,' Beast said calmly, hoping to reason with him. 'You can't just throw us out because of a foul smell. It's not ethical.'

'Yes,' Baz added. 'It's probably the smell of the country outside.'

'More like the smell of one of you dirty gits inside,' Spike scoffed, causing them all to start smirking at one another.

Even Beast found it difficult to contain his amusement at the trivial matter, which was now in danger of being blown out of proportion.

'Get out, get out, get out,' the driver screamed again with an angry, reddened face.

'Why have they stopped?' Mikel asked as he drove past the static vehicle, trying to look inconspicuous.

The Kurds frowned at one another. They were puzzled as to why the cab had pulled-over for no apparent reason. It had stopped in the middle of nowhere! Mikel drove their vehicle several hundred metres further and pulled over into a lay-by. The area was darkened by a heavy tree line with branches that overhung the roof of the car. He stopped the engine and switched the headlights off.

'We'll wait here until they drive past us again,' Lukic told Mikel. 'We can still see the cab from here without drawing any attention to ourselves.'

Back in the taxi, Beast continued to plead with the driver. 'Please don't throw us out here. It's miles from anywhere and its freezing outside too. We're really sorry about the smell and we'll make it up to you by paying you double fare for your trouble.'

Beast's words were music to the driver's ears. The thought of double payment appeased him and settled his intense anger. The men waited in silence for his response and eventually he gave them an amiable smile.

'Okay,' he agreed. 'But any more of this foul farting business and you're all out. I don't care how much money you offer me.'

'That's fine, mate. It won't happen again,' Beast assured him and gave a quick wink towards his friends, who accepted the action as an acceptance of guilt!

'Quick, follow them and make sure you keep your distance,' Lukic said eagerly, as the taxi accelerated past them.

For the rest of the journey the air inside the cab remained fresh, warming from the air conditioning system. Beast sat in silence and occasionally glanced at the driver, who looked content. Even so, Beast was certain that another episode of nostril abuse would cancel out his attraction towards the extra cash!

Soon after, they reached their destination and the cab came to a halt outside a busy wine-bar. Beast paid the grateful driver his double fare as promised, whilst the other men climbed out of the rear doors.

'I'll get the first round of beers in,' Baz said as they walked towards the entrance door.

Several groups of people were standing and sitting around tables outside the premises. They were warming themselves beneath patio heaters, looking on with wide-open eyes at the appearance of the bizarrely dressed men.

'What on earth are you lot meant to be dressed up as, some kind of flashers?' a young man hollered as they trundled past.

'No we're train spotters,' Baz replied towards the crowd. 'Isn't that obvious?'

'Bloody hell! a young man gasped, referring to Beast's burly physique. 'Look at the size of him. I bet he's got muscles in his piss!'

Inside the bar, the former soldiers stood together, making short work of guzzling down their first beer to quench their thirsts. They looked around at the many female revellers and exchanged smiles with some of them. The women seemed amused with their chosen attire and especially their heavy framed spectacles. Some of them waved amiably towards the group, expressing their pleasure at seeing something out of the ordinary.

Bungy began pretending to spot trains that were pulling into platforms at a make believe train-station. He pulled out a notebook and started writing down serial numbers. Baz joined in the fun too. He began taking photographs of the ceiling, the walls and the floor. His camera flashed repeatedly.

A young woman grinned at Baz and gazed deep into his eyes. She was smartly dressed in loose fitting trousers and a low cut blouse that exposed her protruding breasts. She appeared to be very interested in him. Baz felt the same impulse and reciprocated with a smile. Their eyes continued to meet so Baz waved her over towards him.

'Did I hear one of you guys say you are dressed as train spotters?' she asked him.

'No we're doctors,' Baz replied, fibbing about the theme of their dress.

'You don't look like doctors. Say something medical to me?'

'How would you like some of Doctor Baz's internal spinal support?' Baz chuckled, whilst bluntly ogling her breasts.

His uncouth and direct approach was not to the young women's liking. She flared up at him in a tantrum. SLAP! went the sound of the her hand, making hard physical contact with his face. Then she stormed off looking visibly insulted, disgusted with the strange man's offensive behaviour. Baz just laughed aloud along with the rest of his friends, choosing to move into a less busy side-room. The room was small and cosy with several sets of wooden tables and chairs, sparingly spread around it. A crackling log fire burned away briskly inside a large old-fashioned fireplace. The men looked around admirably at the many elegant pictures of the countryside that littered the walls, before sitting down around one of the vacant tables.

Close behind them, Mikel and Lukic casually entered the side-room. They were carrying freshly poured beers and they sat down at an adjacent table. They initially tried not to appear obvious to the group they were stalking, but looked almost gob-smacked when they saw how they were dressed. They swapped a surprised look with each other, before peering over towards the men. The Kurds were desperate to kidnap one of them, but were currently unsure how they were going to achieve this.

'Who the fuck are you two looking at?' Bungy snarled at them. 'Do you fancy one of us or something? Or have we shagged your girlfriends?'

'Hey calm down numb nuts,' Beast quickly intervened, before either of the two Kurds.

'These two unscrupulous twats are staring at us,' Bungy ranted, strongly expressing his feelings.

'Gentlemen, gentlemen,' Lukic piped up with an amiable smile, hoping to defuse the situation. 'We don't mean to be rude. We're just looking at your clothes. We find your chosen attire to be most amusing. Are you dressed as rapists?'

'No,' Spike smirked. 'We sweat like rapists, but we're dressed as train-spotters. It's our spare time hobby.'

Mikel and Lukic felt a little uneasy about being confronted and nervously sipped their beers. They had hoped to sit unnoticed, which was now out of the question. They wondered how they could put the men at ease without compromising their underlying plan. Lukic chinked beer glasses with Mikel and winked at him. Then he turned towards the group.

'Do any of you gentlemen want an arm wrestle?' he asked, tactfully easing the air of tension between them.

200

'Yes we'll have some of that, mate,' Baz replied avidly, expressing his keenness to accept the challenge. Nevertheless, he remained reservedly curious about the strangers, feeling sure he had seem them somewhere before. Perhaps they are asylum seekers, he thought.

They cleared the table of glasses and beer mats and Baz sat at one end with his sleeve rolled up, preparing his arm in readiness for the challenge. Lukic grunted and raised his stiff shoulders to stretch them. He sat down opposite Baz and unclipped the sleeve of his jacket, rolling it up his arm.

'Where are you guys from?' Beast asked them, observing their foreign characteristics and brown tinted skin. 'Your not English are you?'

'No we're not my friend. We're from Kurdistan,' Mikel chirped up, before Lukic could respond. 'We're here on holiday.'

'Yes you look like holiday makers!' Beast replied in an unconvinced tone.

Baz and Lukic ignored the conversation between the two men and locked their eyes in a determined stare. They banged their elbows down on the table and clasped their hands tightly together. Baz momentarily released his grip and extended his fingers to get a better hold. Lukic was ready and signalled this by nodding his head towards his opponent, who grinned at him and pushed his spectacles onto the top of his head.

'Are you ready?' Beast asked, detracting his attention from Mikel. He positioned himself and his seat at the side of the table so that he faced the clasped hands.

Both of the men indicated that they were. Their smiles dropped away and each of them applied a little extra force against the other's hand. They shuffled their feet under the table, anchoring themselves and ensuring they had a firm foothold on the floor.

'Right, it's the best of three,' Beast informed them. 'If either of you lift your elbows off the table you will be disqualified. That's the only rule,' he grinned menacingly at each of them in turn.

'Come on Baz, whip his fucking arse,' Bungy shouted to encourage his friend to win the competition.

'Yeah smash his hand through the table,' Spike added, believing he should contribute some words of encouragement too.

Beast swilled the remaining three quarters of his beer down in one and gargled the last mouthful, before swallowing it. 'Begin on the count of three,' he advised them. 'One...., two....., three.'

Baz and Lukic swiftly applied more pressure against each other with equal strength. Yet neither of them tried to force the other's hand down. Instead, they began a tactful game of cat and mouse, each waiting for the other to apply all their strength to try to win the first fall. They stared deep into each other's eyes like wild animals, without expressing the underlying physical effort they were exerting.

Baz gripped a tight hold of the table leg with his other hand, holding firmly against the strong pressure that Lukic produced.

'Come on Lukic,' Mikel shouted, moments before Baz thrust all his energy into the hold and slammed his opponent's hand down hard onto the table.

'The first fall goes to Baz,' Beast shouted and slapped the palm of his own hand down with a thud on the table.

Mikel looked at his friend with disappointment and shook his head, because he strongly wanted him to win. He casually sat back in his chair, after Lukic sneaked him a reassuring wink; possibly hinting that he had purposely lost the first round.

'Get ready,' Beast prompted them.

Baz looked the other way, tapped the spectacles on the top of his head and grabbed a glass of whiskey that Bungy passed to him. He poured the spirit into his full pint of beer and drank it down in one. Then he turned his attention back towards Lukic.

Their hands locked tightly against each other once again. This time Baz felt overly confident. He smirked at his opponent and pushed his spectacles back down over his eyes.

'Take the strain,' Beast instructed.

They both applied more pressure with their knuckles whitening.

Baz leaned into the grip he had on Lukic and forced their hands halfway down onto Lukic's side. The Kurd puffed heavily and fought hard, digging deep to stop it falling any further. One corner of Baz's lip quivered as he sneered at his opponent. Then he pulled a cheeky face, sticking his tongue out and crossing his eyes. Lukic's expression remained unchanged, apart from his eyes, which remained fixed in a stare. He turned his head briefly, towards Mikel and winked at him again. Then he looked back at Baz, whose wide grin started to fall as he pushed against him with immense force. He began to relent and Baz gritted his teeth when his friends started shouting more words of encouragement.

'Come on Baz, fucking do him,' Bungy screamed. 'Do him,' he repeated.

Baz's whole body began to shudder. He strained as Lukic's burst of energy continued to force his hand down towards the table.

'NO!' he hollered as the back of his hand banged heavily on the dull wooden surface. He sighed deeply with disappointment and threw his spectacles down hard onto the floor in a fit of fiery temper that engulfed him.

'That's one fall each,' Beast told everybody, including the growing crowd of spectators. 'The next fall is the final and deciding fall'

'You're going down,' Baz sneered towards Lukic, who was busy grinning and sharing his joy with Mikel. There was no money at stake here, just his pride, but that meant everything to him!

'Are you ready men?' Beast asked, prompting the two participants to prepare for the final arm wrestle. 'This is it, the third and final round. Make ready.'

'Go on,' someone shouted enthusiastically from the on looking crowd. 'Let's see some grit and determination here.'

Other members of the crowd started shouting too. 'Go on, go on.'

Baz and Lukic stared determinedly at each other. The shouts from the crowd were making them more adamant to win. At this point, Lukic appeared to have totally forgotten about the intention of kidnapping one of the four men. He seemed too embroiled in the competition for that. Maybe it's part of an act and an underlying plan to lure the men into a false sense of security? Mikel thought, staring at Lukic from the opposite bustling table.

'Take the strain,' Beast called out, signalling the two men to lock hands for the last time, which they did.

They continued to bore deeply into each other's eyes, tensely psyching one another out and trying not to be the first to blink. They applied more strength into their holds, causing their hands to shake and their faces to shudder. Lukic leaned further into his grip, forcing Baz's arm to start to give way. It moved halfway down until he held it still, making a stance to fight back. Their hands repeatedly moved back and forth, each of them straining to try to get the other to relent. Sweat trickled slowly down Baz's brow as Lukic forced him over again. He gripped the table leg with his free hand and gritted his teeth to help him to channel all his strength into a reverse push.

'No,' Lukic screamed. His hand started to succumb to the overpowering force, which he could not stop.

Baz put everything into the motion, slamming the hand down heavily onto the wooden table. His temper roared and he practically crushed Lukic's hand with his grip. He rose to his feet and slapped the open palm of his other hand, hard into the face of his defeated opponent. The blow forced Lukic out of his chair and down onto the floor. The onlookers gasped with amazement and then roared with laughter after Lukic got up and scuttled out of the room. Mikel followed closely behind and never looked back.

'You didn't have to hit him,' Spike protested, feeling a little sorry for the man. 'He was a worthy opponent.'

'Hit him!' Baz snapped with hate-filled eyes. 'I wanted to fucking kill him.'

Spike shook his hand and grinned as the satisfied onlookers congratulated Baz by patting him on the back.

Outside in the shadows of the deserted street, the two Kurds reorganised themselves, focusing on their original intention of trying to kidnap one of the men.

'Let's wait in the car for a while,' Mikel suggested to Lukic, who was rubbing his sore cheek. 'We'll wait until they've consumed more beer or until they leave to go home. Then we'll make our move. Are you okay?'

'Yes I'm okay. That bastard didn't have to hit me. One way or another I will return the compliment. That's for sure!'

Back inside the smoke filled room, the interested crowd had fully dispersed and the former marines were sat casually drinking their beer. By this time, they were suitably inebriated. Most people would have been busy discussing the events of the evening, but predictability didn't apply to these guys. They sat laughing and joking, telling each other humorous stories about past social experiences from their military service days.

'I'm just going to siphon the python,' Spike said jokingly to inform his friends that he needed to visit the toilet. 'I'll just be a few minutes.'

His colleagues nodded and carried on talking together. Spike was visibly unsteady on his feet as he made his way into an adjacent corridor. Halfway down the hallway he paused and contemplated pulling an attractive painting from the wall to take home. 'No, not tonight,' he said under his breath and walked into the gents' toilet.

Meanwhile, Mikel and Lukic had grown impatient with waiting in the car and had re-entered the pub in time to see Spike entering the toilet before the door closed behind him.

The inside of the gents' toilet was in a bad state of repair. There were pieces missing from numerous blue and white tiles that covered the walls. The sound of water dripping, echoed around the room. It was coming from the inside of one of the sealed toilet cisterns. Spike sighed with relief as he released the growing pressure from his bladder, urinating into a urinal. He was unconcerned when he heard the door creak open behind him and didn't bother looking around to see who it was. He usually would but on this occasion, he just didn't bother. Instead, he automatically assumed that it was probably one of his friends. He breathed in deeply and shook the excess drips from the end of his penis, bending his knees slightly and breaking wind. He smirked as he pulled his zip up and turned around to see who was behind him.

CRACK, went the hard piece of wood that struck him hard on the side of his head. The resulting pain numbed and confused him. His knees gave way and he slumped down helplessly onto the floor, where he lost consciousness. Thick blood oozed out from a wound and formed a pool on the tiles.

'Quick, put the sack over him and let's get out of here before we are discovered, Lukic urged Mikel, who speedily busied himself with pushing a hessian sack over Spike's limp body. 'Quick,' he repeated.

They hurried out through the creaking door and along the corridor leading outside. Spike flopped around like a rag doll, slumped over Mikel's shoulder. Lukic walked several paces behind and watched out for anyone who might try to stop them. Their exit went unnoticed and Mikel carefully lowered their captive into the car boot, slamming it firmly shut behind him.

Chapter Seventeen

'Spike has been gone a long time,' Bungy said, showing concern for his friend's safety. 'I'll go and see if he's okay.'

'He has probably fallen asleep on one of the toilets,' Baz commented. 'Hopefully he hasn't shit himself in the process!'

'Aye,' Bungy grinned, rubbing the scar on his chin and leaping up out of his seat towards the gents' toilet.

The door squeaked open as he pushed it and peered around inside. At first, he thought about sneaking up on his sleepy friend and startling him; but the small pool of blood he noticed on the floor made him wary. He became immediately concerned for the well-being of his colleague. His eyes shifted from side to side, moving with a sense of urgency. He pushed each of the three toilet-cubicle doors open. All were empty. The sound of the doors banging shut on loaded springs echoed around him. He stood still and paused for thought. Only the sound of water dripping inside the toilet cisterns could be heard. He raced out past the door to search the adjoining rooms. It was late and the majority of people had left for the evening. The few that remained had been told to finish their drinks off and leave, by a weary barman.

Meanwhile, Spike groaned as he regained consciousness when the two men roughly dragged him out of the car boot. They cut the tied hessian sack off him and wrenched him up onto his feet.

'Stand up. Fucking stand up or I'll shoot you,' Lukic threatened, holding him by the arm and shaking him rigorously to bring him back to his senses.

Mikel grabbed his other arm and helped Lukic to tie his hands behind his back with a short length of rope. They pushed him through the doorway of an old derelict picture house.

The building had no windows and was disused, being built around the time of the second-world war. It was originally intended to become a cinema, but for some unknown reason it never opened.

One of the men pushed the heavy door shut behind them and thrust a bolt into place to lock it. The sound of the bolt action reverberated up and down the pitch-black corridor, as Lukic switched on a torch. The walls around them were old and chipped and the floor was covered with litter and rubble.

'Move now,' Lukic insisted, punching Spike hard in the middle of his back.

Spike grimaced and hurried his pace, wanting to hold his head because it throbbed incessantly. The blood from the scalp-wound had clotted and no longer dripped down the back of his neck. He was puzzled as to why the two men had abducted him. Maybe they wanted to blame him for Baz's violent actions, after he had abruptly ended the arm wrestling match, he wondered. Whatever the reason, he knew they meant business and sensibly thought it best to keep his mouth shut and to do as they say.

BANG, went the door at the end of the corridor, after it was kicked open by Mikel's size nine shoes. Spike was rigorously thrust inside and pushed down onto a wooden-chair with a rimmed backrest. Mikel moved around in the darkness shining his torch light. He opened a wooden box and pulled an oil lantern from it. He lit it with a lighter and hung it on a protruding hook, illuminating the room. He then grabbed some more rope and wrapped it around Spike's body, securing it to the chair. Spike winced as his bounds tightened and looked around the room. It was small and filthy, smelling strongly of stale urine. There was litter scattered all over the floor and the bare brick walls were covered in various styles and colours of graffiti.

Lukic dragged a wooden table across the room and pushed it in front of their captive. Then he pulled two chairs out of a dark corner and pushed one towards Mikel, who sat on it and focused on Spike.

'Where have you hid the money?' he questioned. 'Where's the money. Tell me where you have hidden it?'

Spike squinted with confusion and remained unfocused. His mind was still concentrating on the pain he could feel at the back of his head. Thankfully, the alcohol he had consumed during the evening helped to numb this, but it was still quite sore. His mind drifted off and back to his service days. He recalled a particular escape and evasion training exercise, when he had been captured. The purpose of the exercise was firstly to evade capture, then to be captured and to learn how to understand resistance to interrogation techniques. During this time, he was subjected to a number of different torture methods that were designed to give variable levels of pain and discomfort. The purpose was to make him succumb and disclose some information to his captors. At the time, their techniques were no match for his will power and he passed the course with flying colours. He smiled to himself as he thought about this.

'What are you grinning at? Do you think we are playing games here? Where's our fucking money?' Lukic screamed with his fists clenched. He surged forward and punched Spike hard in the face.

The forceful blow shook Spike badly, causing pain to shoot down through his jaw and into his upper back and neck.

'Where's our money?' Lukic repeated.

'What money?' Spike answered with true uncertainty. All he could think about was the arm wrestling event, for which he could not recall any bets or exchanges of cash taking place.

'I'm asking you about the money from the security van robbery,' Lukic said, wanting to be sure his captive hadn't misunderstood. 'Where is it? Tell me where it is or things will become very unpleasant for you?'

Spike remained silent. He just stared emptily at the two men opposite him. His mind began to drift again and he saw himself back in the marines. It was as if time had stood still. He had been captured and was being interrogated and pressed hard for information.

'Christopher Millard. Marine, PO43039E,' he answered, giving his name, rank and service number.

Lukic's face dropped. Initially with disbelief of the response. Suddenly he realized that his prisoner was a former Royal Marine Commando. He had heard of them. They were reputedly tough soldiers. He frowned towards Mikel, nodding his head to indicate that the interrogation techniques would need to be tougher. Much tougher!

'Where's the money?' he growled again. This time more aggressive than before and seemingly more determined to get an answer.

Spike still didn't reply. He was too tired from the after effects of the alcohol. He was also suffering mild concussion from the blow to his head. Its constant throbbing was taking its toll on him. He felt lethargic, distant and unconcerned about answering any questions or even paying attention to what his two interrogators were asking him. He fought to stay conscious and looked with blared vision towards Lukic, who was untying his hands from behind his back. He could hear the strange men screaming at him and felt them shaking his head by the hair. Their voices were becoming distant!

Just then, his eyes opened wide as he watched Mikel take a hold of his left hand and forcibly hold it still against the table. Lukic placed a jagged rusty nail between the bones on the back of his hand and whacked it with a mash hammer, pinning it to the table. Excruciating pain bolted through Spike's weak body. He screamed loudly and started to writhe around in agony. A second nail was driven through his bleeding hand, centimetres away from the first. He tried hard to pull the nails out with his other hand, but they were stuck fast. Blood was streaming out of the flesh wounds and dripping down onto the table and floor. Tears streamed down his face as he fought to stay conscious.

'Where have you hidden the money,' Lukic hollered with gritted teeth. 'Tell me now or I'm going to kill you.'

He thrust the barrel of a small calibre pistol deep into Spike's mouth. It past his tonsils and was pressed hard against the back of his throat. He began to choke on it, fighting hard to breathe passed the muzzle of the gun. This grim situation was far from any arduous training exercise he had ever undergone! These men were unforgiving and violently ruthless. They meant what they said. Inevitably, if he didn't cooperate with them they were going to kill him. He was sure about that now.

'Okay, okay,' he retorted and coughed up a clot of blood, moments after Lukic removed the gun-barrel from his mouth. 'Please pull the nails out of my hand and I'll give you the information you are seeking. Please remove them. I mean what I say,' he pleaded. His eyes appeared sorry and his voice a convincing tone.

'Let him loose. If he doesn't cooperate you can kill him,' Mikel grunted.

Lukic moved away into the dark shadows and began searching for something. After a minute or so of mooching around, he returned with a pair of pliers and used them to extract the nails. He pulled hard on the first nail, causing Spike to twist and turn in agony and then he quickly removed the second one with ease.

'Where's the money?' he snapped again, already wanting to hammer the nails back into the holes they were pulled from.

'It's in Northern Ireland,' Spike grumbled wearily, genuinely wanting his captors to cease inflicting torture.

'Whereabouts in Northern Ireland is it? You'll have to do better than that.'

'It's in South Armagh in the hills. We've hidden it in an abandoned weapons store.'

'How do we know you're telling the truth?' Mikel asked with deep interest. How will we find it?'

'I'll take you to it. I don't want to die. It's only money. It's not worth dying for.'

The Kurds nodded in agreement. One of them re-secured Spikes hands behind his back and tightened the rope around the chair's backrest. This made Spike feel a little more comfortable, amid this terrifying situation. That was until Lukic, punched him hard in the face. He struck him with the head of the mash hammer, held inside his clenched fist. It knocked him helplessly over rendering him unconscious.

'How do we know he's not telling us lies?' Mikel frowned. 'How will we know he isn't bullshitting?'

'We can't be sure,' Lukic said. 'He'll have to guide us there, so we'll see what happens. If he's lying we'll kill him and capture one of his colleagues.'

'Are we going to let him go if we get the money?'

'No, of course we're not,' Lukic smirked. 'Once we get our hands on the cash we'll kill him anyway. We'll have to do this, because he knows what we look like.'

'Why did you hit him so hard in the face like that? Mikel glared. There was no need!'

'I was returning the compliment for his friend, who hit me during our arm wrestling match. You're not going soft are you?'

Several hours later, Spike opened his eyes. His head, face and blood stained hand throbbed painfully. There was no sign of his captors and the room was silent. He tried to move but found he was still tied to the chair and was lying on his side on the floor. He spent a while trying to free his hands and to right himself, but his efforts proved fruitless. He lay still, gazing into the shadows of the room. His whole life seemed to flash before him. Strangely, he could clearly remember his wife, their wedding day and the birth of their two children. He missed them dearly. What the hell am I doing here? he thought. Why me? Why aren't I at home with my wife and children? He also recollected the time he had spent living rough on the streets. It all seemed such a long time ago now and pointless really. His family must have missed him terribly. His reflection of events made him feel guilty and selfish. The heavy blow he had received from Lukic had cleared his head and had somehow allowed his vague memory to clear. Without reason, the pain in his head worsened. The room started to spin and he slowly slipped back into a state of unconsciousness.

Back at the wine bar, Baz and the other members of the team sat with the landlord watching a replay of the outside CCTV recording. They observed the two familiar Kurds, carrying Spike's limp body out into the street and throwing him into the boot of their car. As they watched them drive away, they noted down the car registration number. They assumed they would need to track the vehicle down before they could rescue Spike.

'Why have they kidnapped him?' Beast asked with concern. 'Do you think it's because they got beat at arm wrestling and possibly because Baz thumped one of them?'

'Come on, Beast. You can't blame me,' Baz disagreed. 'They're probably going to get in touch with us with some sort of ransom demand.'

'No, wait a minute,' Bungy chirped up, suddenly feeling he had all the answers. 'It's not as simple as that.'

Before explaining further, he slipped the pub landlord a twenty-pound note and asked him to leave them alone for a while, which he did without question.

'What do you mean? It's not as simple as that!' Baz wanted to know.

'It has just occurred to me who those two foreigners really are,' Bungy resumed. During the time we carried out the robbery on the security van, somebody else attempted to rob the decoy van. It was mentioned on the news.'

'Yes, and......' Baz urged him to elaborate.

'I'll wager that those two men were the robbers. Apparently, they acted ruthlessly and killed all of the soldiers who were part of the convoy. They obviously came away empty-handed and are still hoping to get their hands on the money. They will most probably interrogate Spike, until they find out where it has been hidden.'

'Shit,' Baz exclaimed. 'You should have been a detective. These guys must be the people whom we noticed observing the entrance to the RAF base, around the same time as us. They'll kill Spike for sure. How the hell are we going to locate the car?'

'We can't,' Beast commented. 'There isn't enough time. We must assume they'll break Spike and will use him to lead them to the money. We'll need to go back to Northern Ireland ahead of them and quickly too.'

'Were there any more helicopters available at the Brize Norton base?' Baz asked Bungy.

213

'Yes. There were a couple of others,' he answered.

'Well, we've done it once so we can do it again. We'll have to go back there and steal another one and then fly across the water to South Armagh within the next couple of days,' Beast said, already thinking strategically.

'Sounds like a plan,' Baz grinned, sold on the idea. 'Let's head back to the farmhouse and sleep the ale off. We'll rise early tomorrow morning and put some sort of action plan together.'

They all agreed this course of action and left the bar, jumping into a taxi and heading straight back to the farmhouse.

Chapter Eighteen

'Play the video again,' Detective Sergeant, Dave Watson requested for a fifth time. 'There's something familiar about the sniper's face.' He avidly studied the video footage that had been taken by a motorist using a mobile phone, during the robbery on the security van. The quality was poor and the sniper's face was blurred, but Dave felt almost certain he'd seen him somewhere before. 'The helicopter they used definitely fits the description of the Chinook that was stolen from Brize Norton,' he said. 'The timings coincide too and I'm a non believer in sheer coincidence.'

'Yes,' Brett nodded, running his hand through his wavy hair. He was a fellow detective who had been assigned to work with Dave on this case. Dave was the lead detective with Brett acting as his understudy. 'However, the chopper has not been seen since. So we need to assume it's been hidden somewhere, so that it can be used again later,' he added.

'That's true,' Dave agreed. 'It's just like I said previously, these guys definitely have specialist military skills of the highest level. One of them is a helicopter pilot, one of them is a sniper and one or more of them are explosives experts. They're not your average run of the mill criminals.'

'Explosive experts!' Brett gasped, unsure of Dave's assumption.

'Yes, they used explosives when they stole the helicopter from Brize Norton.'

'Ah yes, of course they did. Sorry I'd forgotten about that. Weren't you in the Royal Marines some years ago?'

Dave did not answer the question, but strangely, it chugged away in his subconscious mind. Eventually, it triggered something from his past.

'Wait a minute......! That face! It's just come back to me. Yes I was in the marines and I'm almost sure that sniper was too.'

'Did you serve with him?' Brett questioned, tapping his pencil on his notebook.

'No I didn't. I think he may be the guy whom I met in a Liverpool nightclub some time before I got promoted. He was working with a former colleague of mine. Let's break for lunch now. I need to make some telephone enquiries.'

During his lunch break, Dave made a telephone call to the Liverpool nightclub he had been referring to earlier. He paused for thought, then picked up the telephone receiver and dialled the number. Even though he had not yet made the call, he felt almost certain that his hunch was going to be right.

'Hello, Paradox night club,' a male voice answered.

'Hello, my name is Detective Sergeant Watson from the Oxfordshire police. Can I speak to the manager please?'

'This is the manager speaking.'

'Oh hello Jon. Sorry I should have recognised your voice. It's Dave Watson speaking. I used to call round to your club some months back, when I was based in Liverpool. I was the police officer who carried out the routine narcotics checks.'

'Yes of course, Dave. I remember you. I thought it was you when you first spoke. I recognised your voice,' he said amiably. 'I'd heard that you'd moved house after being promoted.'

'Yes something like that,' Dave scoffed.

'What can I do for you, mate?'

'Does Spike and his friend still work for you?'

'Do you mean Spike and Bungy, the two former marines?'

'Yes, that's them, mate. Are they still working for you?'

'No, unfortunately they aren't. They left a couple of months ago. Shortly after, you moved on. They didn't give a reason for leaving. They just didn't turn up for work one night and we've never seen or heard of them since. Are they in some sort of trouble?'

'No, I'm just trying to trace them,' Dave tactfully lied. I served in the marines with one of them before I joined the police force. I'm planning a reunion with them.'

'That sounds good. Please pass my best regards onto them both when you meet up. Tell them the door to the Paradox nightclub is always open if they want their jobs back.'

'Yes I'll do that, Jon. Thanks anyway, mate. I think I know where they might have gone.' Dave had a glint in his eyes when he ended his telephone enquiry. His presumption was that Spike and Bungy were definitely part of the robbery team. He ambled back towards his office. He was staring down at the floor, trying hard to wrack his brains to recall Spike's surname. Inside his office, he rummaged through a filing cabinet, desperately hoping to find something.

'Yes,' he called out gleefully; kissing a photograph album like it was a long lost relative.

The album was covered in dust and fastened closed with a Velcro strap. He pulled it free and flipped it open. He paused at the first photograph of himself. It was taken during his passing-out parade, after completing basic training. Happy days, he thought. Then he moved through the pages, browsing through the many photographs of former marine colleagues.

'That's it,' he eventually said aloud and simultaneously tapped his fingers on a troop photograph with listed names, including Spike's surname. 'It's C. Millard. Chris Millard if I remember rightly.'

Later that day, Dave boarded a train along with Brett and headed towards Plymouth. For a long while, he sat in silence and reminisced about his days in the marines and some of the great-times he had enjoyed with Spike. His mind drifted back to the battlefield in Iraq, during the Gulf war. His section was caught in the middle of a hostile fire-fight with an Iraqi special-forces patrol. Suddenly, he felt a deep pain in his shoulder. It was caused by a bullet, spat from an enemy soldier's semi-automatic rifle. It slammed deep into his flesh.

217

'I've been hit!' he bellowed.

The sheer force of the propelling round had knocked him backwards and down onto the floor, amid the turmoil of exchanges of rapid gunfire. He felt alone and watched helplessly as two of his fellow marines were shot dead. Both of them fell down with a heavy thud and lay motionless next to him. The air he breathed tasted of fear and he felt certain he too was about to die. He caught sight of an Iraqi soldier who was aiming his weapon at him. The soldier hesitated for no apparent reason; unknowingly because another marine had bolted from cover and shot him dead in his tracks! The Iraqi slumped down lifeless onto the floor. The brave marine grabbed a tight hold of Dave's clothing and hoisted him up and over his shoulder. More rounds reigned down from an enemy machine gun, bouncing around his feet as he darted into the cover of nearby trees. By this time, Dave had lost a lot of blood from his shoulder wound and had fallen into a state of unconsciousness. When he came too, he was lying in a hospital-bed with bandages wrapped around his upper body and a blood drip connected to his wrist. His vision was blared at first, but then he managed to focus on a marine dressed in uniform, standing by his bed. He was smiling broadly at him.

'Hi Spot, mate. Are you feeling any better?' Spike asked warmly, using the nickname Dave was known by.

'Spike, spike, was it you that saved me,' Spot whispered gratefully.

His colleague nodded a couple of times and continued to smile.

'How can I repay you for saving my life?' Dave carried on.

'That's easy, mate. Just get the beers in next time you see me.'

The two men grinned at each other, seconds before Spot started to lose consciousness and drifted off into a deep sleep.

'Dave. Dave, are you alright?' Brett asked.

He'd been watching his colleague sitting engrossed in deep thought. He had observed his facial expressions changing

218

from one look to another. 'We're pulling into Plymouth train-station now, Dave. Is everything okay?'

'Uh what? Oh yes Plymouth, great,' Dave responded, evidently distant. 'Yes I'm okay. I was just thinking about something.'

Dave looked to be in good spirits when they disembarked from the train. He had many fond memories of using this station in the past. For a fleeting moment, he even felt as if he had been cast back in time and was coming back from home leave.

'Where would you like to go to, gentlemen?' the driver of the black cab asked as they boarded.

'To Union Street, please,' Dave replied.

'Union Street!' Brett frowned, airing some confusion. 'I thought we were going to an address in Mutley Plain.'

'We are,' Dave assured him positively. 'Firstly though, I want to make a little detour. I used to frequent the pubs in Union Street some years ago and I want to see if things have changed much over the years. Don't worry; we've got plenty of time.'

A short while later, Dave instructed the driver to pull over opposite a street corner pub called The Prince Regent and asked him to wait for a period of time.

'Well some things have changed,' he said, looking at Brett who appeared bemused with the idea of pointlessly stopping off to look at some pubs. 'This pub is the Prince Regent, but we used to refer to it as the PR when I served in Plymouth as a boot neck.'

Brett raised his eyebrows, beaming a friendly smile. He falsely tried to look interested in Dave's former social life.

'That wine bar next door, used to be referred to as The Long Bar. A friend of mine used to work there as a bouncer.'

Brett smiled again and nodded!

'He was a Mountain Leader,' Dave continued. He was probably one of the toughest men I ever met in my whole life. I was talking to him once whilst he was working here. I'd bought him a beer and we stood together at the bar. A fight broke out

219

between four men. My friend politely excused himself from my company and literally floored the four of them with as many lethal punches. One for each of them!'

'He sounds like he was a tough man,' Brett said with a captured interest. 'I can tell you respected him.'

'Yes I did respect him. After he floored the four men, he grabbed hold of one of them and tucked him under one of his arms. He shuffled another one under his other arm and then grabbed the remaining two with his hands. It was amazing.'

'Wow!' Brett gasped. 'What did he do next?'

'He dragged them towards the rear exit door and flung them outside onto the concrete floor, before closing the door shut. Then he just came back towards me and started drinking his beer again, as if nothing had happened.'

'Wow!' Brett exclaimed again. 'What does this guy do for a living now? Is he a copper or a body guard or something like that?'

'No, he's not. He unfortunately suffered a fatal heart attack a couple of years ago and passed away. I was quite saddened at the news, but I guess that's life isn't it. I still think about him from time to time and treasure the memories of our friendship.'

'Is there anywhere else you want to see, before we go to the house in Mutley Plain?' Brett frowned, hoping Dave would take the hint that he wanted to leave.

This was understandable though. Dave was talking about people whom he knew nothing about or was even the slightest bit interested in, really.

'Yes okay I've seen enough,' Dave smirked. 'Lets get back into the cab and we'll go up to Mutley Plain to commence our enquiries.'

Soon after, the cab pulled up outside an address in the Mutley plain area of the city, where the two police officers climbed out into the street. Dave looked up and down the thoroughfare and along the row of terraced houses on both sides of the road. He observed their small gardens and variations of walls and fences.

Nothing of interest caught his attention so he leaned inside the cab and paid the driver.

'Shouldn't you have asked him to wait?' Brett asked, whilst tugging the creases out of his pinstriped suit. 'What if there's nobody at home?'

'Don't worry, Brett. The pubs in Union Street are only a short walk away. We could head down there and have a day on the ale if we draw a blank here.'

'You are joking aren't you?' Brett sneered.

'No I'm not,' Dave assured him. 'When I served as a marine we used to call Union Street the Strazzer. It's a great night out and anyway, we'll have to stay in the area until we obtain the information we are seeking.'

'Okay. You did say number thirty-four didn't you?' Brett checked as they walked up an over grown garden path towards a terraced house.

'Yes I did,' Dave nodded, knocking hard on the door of Spike's family home.

They waited for a minute or so, but there was no answer. Brett moved to one side of the house and tapped on the living room window. Again, there was no response after a short wait. That was until the partially open blinds moved slightly. The two men watched - fully expecting someone to appear. The blinds moved again and then again, but still nobody came into view. They were a little puzzled at first, but grinned at each other after a young boy peered out.

'Is your mum home?' Dave shouted and the young boy nodded. 'Can you ask her to open the door?'

The child nodded again, stepping away from the blinds and disappearing out of view.

They walked back towards the entrance, where they saw the shape of a woman approaching through the stained glass window. She began unlocking the door and opened it. Lindsay stepped into view. A gentle wind blew her long blonde hair across her face.

'Hello, can I help you?' she asked politely, brushing her flowing locks aside with her fingers.

'Good afternoon, madam. Are you Mrs Millard?' Dave asked.

'Yes, I am,' Lindsay acknowledged, curiously wondering who the two well-dressed callers were.

'My name is Dave Watson. I served in the marines with your husband some years ago.'

'He's not here,' Lindsay replied sharply. 'He went off some time ago to meet up with some other pesky former marine friends. Why don't you just go away and leave me alone?'

'No, no sorry,' Dave stammered, realising he needed to explain himself further before she slammed the door in their faces. 'We're police officers, ma'am. We're making enquires about a security van robbery and would like to ask Christopher some questions to assist with the investigation.'

Lindsay looked dumbstruck. She stared at them with a saddened look in her eyes.

'Is Christopher at home?' Brett asked.

'No he isn't. I've already told you, he's not here. I don't know where he is.'

'Can we come inside please ma'am?' Dave asked, waving his identification card at her until she focused on it.

'Err yes, please do,' she replied and opened the door further to allow them to enter.

The two young children, Paul and David, stood back against the wall when the strange men entered the living room. They ran behind the sofa and peered out with sorrowful eyes; listening to anything that these important looking men had to say about their daddy.

'Mrs Millard, I'm Detective Sergeant Dave Watson and my colleague is Detective Brett Mitchell. We're from the Oxfordshire Police Force,' Dave informed her, after they made themselves comfortable on two chairs. 'We're investigating a recent security van robbery which resulted in the theft of a huge sum of money. We have reason to believe that your husband may know something about this, and may be able to assist us with our enquiries. We're also investigating the murders of Frank Cotterill and Kenneth Ferill, which we believe may be linked with the robbery, although not directly linked to your husband at this point.'

Lindsay gulped at the mention of the murders. Her stomach turned with a heavy dread and she slouched back into the armchair.

'My husband isn't well,' she sobbed, deeply shocked at the allegations. 'He was involved in a serious car accident a couple of years ago. His sister was killed and he unfortunately suffered minor brain damage. Shortly afterwards, he disappeared from a hospital bed and we all thought he had taken his own life.'

Dave and Brett didn't interrupt as Lindsay explained about Spike. They just let her continue to speak and listened intently to what she had to say.

'He came back to Plymouth a short while ago with some former marine friends. At first I thought he'd run off with another woman, but he explained that he had ended up living rough on the streets somewhere. He only stayed here for one night, because he's still suffering from memory loss. He can't remember anything. Not even the children or myself,' she sniffed. 'It's horrible for us. I can't understand why he won't come home. We love him and miss him immensely.'

Tears were streaming down her face and the two children, who remained hidden behind the furniture, started to cry too.

Dave felt a deep sadness for his former colleague's family and was sorry to find that things had turned out the way they had. He reached inside his jacket pocket and pulled a handkerchief from it, passing it to Lindsay to wipe her eyes.

'Who were the other men who accompanied him?' he asked her. 'Did they tell you their names?'

'No. I only focused on my husband when I saw him in a pub near Union-Street. I don't know who they were. I wasn't introduced. Being honest, I can't even remember what they looked like. There were three of them. Christopher told me that they were

223

former marines when he came back home that night. That's all I can tell you. My husband is no murderer. I'm sure about that. He's poorly and is suffering from amnesia. He needs professional help.'

'Where's our daddy? Paul cried, poking his head out from behind the sofa. 'Why won't he come home to play with us? Doesn't he love us anymore?'

'Why won't he come home?' his brother sniffled. 'I want my daddy to come home. Please tell him to come home. Please,' he whimpered, rubbing the tears from his eyes with his fingers.

Dave could feel the sorrow and sensitivity expressed by the children. He had a lump in his throat and quickly exchanged a look with Brett, who also appeared emotionally moved. Dave inhaled deeply and sat back in the chair so that he could think about what to do next. He was certain that Spike was linked to the robbery, but also aware that his family were concerned about his welfare. They could do very little to assist with the investigation.

'Okay ma'am,' he said, choosing to end the enquiry. 'I have no further questions to ask you. If I hear any news about the whereabouts of your husband, I'll inform you straight away. Please can I ask you to give me a call in the event that you may hear from Christopher or any of his friends?'

Lindsay nodded tearfully and took the business card that Dave offered her. She walked to the doorway with the two men and bid them goodbye. She closed the door as soon as they left and slid down onto her knees. The palms of her hands covered her face and she sobbed heavily. The two children joined her and cuddled their mother to try to console her.

Dave and Brett briskly walked along the street outside and off into the distance. Initially, neither of them spoke, remaining locked in empathy.

'That was gut wrenching, wasn't it?' Dave said, after clearing his throat and breaking the silence. 'I don't think I could have stayed in there any longer. I really felt sorry for them.'

'Do you think he's one of the robbers?' Brett queried, choosing to change the subject quickly from Lindsay and the children. 'You said you thought the job was done with military precision, so a group of former marines would undoubtedly fit the bill. Wouldn't they?'

'Err, yes they would,' Dave answered after hesitating.

'Did you know Christopher very well when you served in the marines? Is he the type of guy to pull some sort of heist like this?'

'Yes I knew him very well,' Dave sighed. 'He was a first class marine who had my utmost respect. He once saved my life on the battlefield in Iraq. He may well be involved with the robbery. Maybe he's lost his marbles. I just don't know.'

'Wow!' Brett gasped. 'He saved your life in the heat of battle and now you have to find him, nick him and send him to jail. That can't be easy.'

'Life isn't easy,' Dave said truthfully. 'That was a long time ago now and you and I have a duty to perform. Okay....'

Brett raised his eyebrows and looked away. He saw the hurt look on his colleague's face and knew better than to discuss the matter further with him.

Chapter Nineteen

'It'll be dark in about thirty minutes,' Baz said. 'Let's check our equipment and finalize our plan of approach, before we make our assault on the aircraft hanger.'

The three men had parked down an off-road dirt track, located a short distance from the RAF Brize Norton base. Spike and Bungy had used the same location previously, when they stole the Chinook helicopter. Their burnt-out car and its fragmented framework had since been taken away. It had not been removed for forensic investigation purposes, nor had it been linked to the theft of the helicopter. A scrap merchant had salvaged it, after stumbling across it when he was using the place to copulate with somebody else's wife.

'What if they've tightened security? What if there are no helicopters left? Who's going to fly the thing?' Bungy wined. 'Spike was our skilled helicopter pilot, wasn't he?'

'Don't be pessimistic, mate,' Beast sighed. 'Be optimistic, for fucks sake. Baz has flown helicopters before too, you know.'

'Yes I have,' Baz assured him. 'I can't fly Chinooks like Spike did, because they're too intricate for me. So we'll have to hope we can find something smaller and a little less complex.'

Rain started to pour steadily down onto the car, drizzling down the windscreen. It was pitch-black outside now and time to put their plan into action.

'That's all we need. Bloody rain,' Bungy winced.

'Stop moaning, you miserable git. You're beginning to sound like an old fart,' Beast remarked. 'The rain will be useful to us. It will potentially help to persuade the RAF Regiment to cut their foot patrols short. Not guaranteed I know, but it does have potential. You know that, Bungy.'

'Yes, I know I do. Sorry for being a whining git.'

226

'You can't beat a good moan,' Baz grinned.

'Are we going to wear the ghillie suits?' Bungy asked as they pulled their weapons and equipment out of the boot of the car.

'Not this time, mate,' Beast said. 'We're sneaking in there with haste not stealth and if we're compromised, we'll blow the whole place and anybody who gets in our way to pieces.'

'Yeah,' Baz smiled. 'No more Mr. Nice Guy! For all we know, Spike may already be dead. So, if the shit hits the fan, its curtains for anybody who opposes us.'

The three of them worked together, pulling a camouflage-net over the car to break up its shape and hide it from view. The men checked their weapons and placed all the necessary equipment inside the pouches attached to their combat jackets. They each pulled black woollen balaclavas over their heads and faces and followed Bungy, who led the way through the wet undergrowth. The rain continued to drizzle, whilst they made their way to the same place where Bungy had previously cut a hole in the fence. On the way, the men moved cautiously through the long overgrown stems of grass. They pushed them aside as they went, clearing the way ahead. At the same time, each of them remained alert. They carefully looked around as they moved, in case any foot or vehicle patrols were to head their way.

'It's intact,' Bungy whispered, when he reached the part of the fence he was looking for.

Nobody answered. They just sunk down closer to the ground, remaining vigilant and maintaining all round observation. Bungy was now in familiar territory and started to undo the pieces of wire that held the mesh together. Seconds later, the men began to ease their way through the gap. Each of them gently pushing their weapon through ahead of them - making sure the fence did not snag the firing mechanism.

'Get down,' Baz whispered upon hearing the sound of a puppy-dog yelping close-by.

The other two men reacted, immediately laying low on the ground below the wet reeds of grass. A man's voice could be heard as he called after the dog.

'Mortar, mortar, come here boy,' Graham called out, flashing his torchlight in the direction of the men. 'Come here you stupid mutt. I've got a nice bone for you.'

Graham was a young soldier who worked as a dog-handler with the RAF Regiment. The small detachment of dog-handlers he belonged to, had been assigned to work at the base to strengthen the under resourced dog-section. The idea was to prevent a reoccurrence of someone breaking in and stealing the base's helicopters. Mortar was a young and inexperienced Alsatian, with whom Graham had been assigned to train and look after. It wasn't really a guard-dog yet, it was still too young and playful.

Earlier that evening, Graham had entered the guardroom with a couple of other soldiers, who wanted to cut their foot patrol short and shelter from the teaming rain. During this time, Mortar had been running around loose inside and had seized the opportunity to bolt outside, when the door opening presented itself. Because the dog was predominantly Graham's responsibility, the Guard Commander had tasked him with finding it before returning to the comfort of the warm guardroom. He was a fair and reasonable leader, who even promised to make him a hot cup of tea to drink on his return.

'Come here boy,' Graham shouted again.

He was a good forty-metres or so behind the dog and unawares that Beast was only a couple of metres away - clutching a rugged survival knife. The dog could smell him and stopped opposite, where it began to growl and bark repeatedly.

'Go away, shoo,' Beast whispered, waving his knife at the hound. 'Go away.'

Graham's torch beam was a short distance away and closing fast. He was waving it from side to side, close to locating the growling animal.

'Shoo go away,' Beast said again, desperately. 'Fuck off.'

Quite bizarrely, the dog stopped barking and ran off in the opposite direction, whimpering as it went. Graham was oblivious to the presence of the former commandos, who were expecting to be compromised. His certain death was a mere moment away. Mortar began barking wildly again, more or less beckoning

Graham to follow him. Suddenly, Graham heard some stems of grass rustling nearby. The faint noise frightened him and made the hairs stand up on the back of his neck. He paused briefly! As a young child, he had always been frightened of the dark and even now as a young adult, he still felt the same fear. It is probably just a fox or a wild rabbit, he thought. Nevertheless, to alleviate his trepidation he turned and ran hard and fast towards the sound of the barking dog. Reassuringly, that was also in the direction of the guardroom. His action of fearful retreat had inevitably saved his life. At one point, Baz was literally a whisker away from rising up and taking him down with his knife. Even so, the men were mutually pleased with the outcome. They were undoubtedly ready to kill, but innocent deaths would still be avoided where possible. Nobody moved for several minutes, whilst Baz observed Graham and his dog through his night vision goggles. They disappeared inside the floodlit guardroom in the distance.

'At least the dog understood the Queen's English,' Bungy jested.

'That was very fortunate,' Baz smirked. 'Because that young soldier was inches away from getting my survival knife shoved up his arse.'

Everybody grinned before continuing to move tactfully out from the cover of the shortening grass stems. They ran across the tarmac of the airfield and into the bushy copse area, opposite the aircraft hanger.

'This is a good spot,' Baz said after they took cover amongst the trees. 'It's perfect.'

They observed the deserted area of the aircraft hanger, scanning its full length and rooftop. They looked for any sign of movement or general activity.

'It looks derelict,' Baz whispered to Beast. 'I hope they haven't moved all the bloody choppers out. We'll be in the brown smelly stuff if they have! How are we going to get inside? The doors look locked to me?'

'It's not a problem,' Bungy cut in. 'There's a side-door that we used last time we entered the hanger. We can use that again. Let's hope it hasn't been alarmed or even booby trapped now.'

229

'There he goes again, looking on the bleak side of life,' Baz sighed, shaking his head. 'Think positive Bungy, for fucks sake.'

'Bungy is right, Baz,' Beast said. 'They might have got wise after the last visit and took precautions to prevent repetition. We'll have to be extra careful. If it was us who were guarding the place, I'm pretty sure we'd have wired it!'

'Yes, but that's us,' Baz shrugged.

'Come on, let's go,' Beast said, taking the lead. 'We haven't got much time. This drizzly rain is starting to ease up now, so the foot patrol may decide to come out to play again soon.'

They gripped their weapons tightly and hurried behind Beast towards the side door of the hanger.

Baz pulled a small infrared pocket torch from inside his jacket and used it to scan around the edges of the door. He checked for wires, whilst the other two men scanned the building for surveillance cameras. Nothing could be seen.

Beast cupped his hand around the door handle and gripped it tightly, turning it. Perhaps they have been complacent with tightening their security, he thought as he continued to turn the handle. We'll soon find out when I open this door. The door-latch released, allowing the door to creak open. He felt pleased when he peered inside through his night vision goggles. He saw two helicopters parked together. 'This is too easy,' he whispered. 'I hope it's not a fucking trap.'

Bungy and Baz looked around the outside of the hanger, half expecting someone to spring an ambush at any moment. They nimbly stepped backwards until they disappeared inside the hanger, behind Beast. The sound of the door closing echoed in the pitch-darkness. Both men paused for several seconds, hoping their eyes would quickly get used to the dark.

'Beast, are you standing close by?' Baz asked, knowing that Beast was wearing the night vision goggles.

'Yes, I'm only a few feet away.'

'Can you see anything?'

'Yes I can see you blind buggers, trying to focus in the dark!'

'Piss off you sarcastic bastard. I meant, are there any helicopters inside here?'

'See for your self,' Beast grinned, flicking a light-switch on the wall next to him.

The whole of the aircraft hanger lit up like a fairground's illuminations, exposing two helicopters in the middle of the hanger.

'Shit!' Bungy exclaimed. 'These lights dim red last time. They must have changed them. If someone sees the lights, we'll be in shit-street.'

'Don't worry, Bungy,' Beast grinned. 'The helicopter we're going to take is a Westland Wessex. Baz will have it out of here in no time. There's no point in fumbling around in the dark.'

'Bloody hell, Beast,' Baz said. 'Your helicopter recognition skills are worse than crap. That's not a Westland Wessex, mate. It's a mark seven Sea King. Look at the lower half of the frame. It has a dropped belly. The Westland Wessex doesn't.'

'Okay, so my helicopter recognition is a little rusty. Just get inside the thing and fly it out of here.'

'I will, but there are a number of checks that I need to make first. I need to be sure it has plenty of fuel. Then I need to re-familiarise myself with all the controls.'

Their subdued voices gently echoed around the hanger, but they remained relaxed about it.

'There's another chopper next to the Sea King,' Baz continued. 'It's a Lynx helicopter. It's not advisable to start the Sea King's rotors spinning this far inside the hanger, unless we have to. Let's use that fork lift to pull it clear of the Lynx.'

'There's plenty of room in here,' Beast smirked, looking around the hanger. 'I once played a game of football in one of these in Norway.'

He grabbed the towrope from the back of the forklift and hooked it up to the helicopter.

231

'Yes I know there's plenty of room,' Baz assured him. 'We're going to need it. The Sea King is only sixteen feet wide when folded, but when its blades are spread, they span sixty-two feet. So let's make good use of the space.'

The forklift engine fired up easily at the touch of a button and purred softly with Beast sat behind the wheel. Baz removed the wheel chocks and was soon sitting inside the helicopter. He released the handbrake and gave a thumbs-up signal to pull the aircraft forward. Beast drove the forklift, slowly taking up the slack on the rope. Then the helicopter started to edge forwards, until eventually it stood in a wide-open space. Baz waved at Beast to signal him to stop. The handbrake clicked several times and Beast jumped out. He unhooked the rope from the chopper and then drove the forklift clear to one side.

'Beast, there's another side-door at the bottom end of the hanger,' Baz said, after climbing down onto the ground. 'It's opposite the guardroom. I need you to guard that area in case we are compromised from there.'

'Okay, mate. No problem,' he retorted and speedily jogged across the length of the building.

At the far end, he climbed up onto a steel gantry and adopted a kneeling fire-position. The muzzle of his weapon pointed towards the entrance door.

'Bungy, I need you to open the hanger doors,' Baz said. 'They operate via a switch down there.' He pointed to a set of switches on the wall, adjacent to the huge sliding doors. 'Once they start opening they'll make a mega racket. Soldiers will come screaming from the guardroom, so please stand ready. Make sure the doors are wide open. It's going to be dangerous starting the Sea King and steering it out beyond the hanger-doors with the blades spinning.

'Yes I understand,' Bungy nodded. 'I know where the door opening switch is located. I used it last time I came here with Spike. Anyway, good luck with flying the chopper. Let me know when you're ready for me to open the doors,' he finished and put his thumb up.

232

'I won't need to,' Baz frowned. 'Once the engine fires up and the blades start rotating; press the door button!'

Bungy waved his hand and swiftly made his way towards the door mechanism switches. Once there, he looked through the sight of his weapon, checking the area where Beast was. He needed to be sure that he could zoom in on the side-entrance door to provide covering fire. He observed Beast, who was high up on the steel gantry. He was busy hooking a rope over a steel bar and through a caribina that was housed in a harness around his waist. This would allow him to abseil down quickly, when he was ready to make his exit. Bungy smiled to himself, knowing that Beast must have found the equipment nearby.

Baz climbed back inside the helicopter and jumped into the pilot's seat, where he made himself comfortable. He was a little apprehensive at first. He felt a deep dread in his stomach, worried in case he experienced problems starting it. Initially, he spent several seconds rubbing his hands over the Collective Lever and the Cyclic Control sticks. They were located at the front of the overhead console. He touched the nipple like starter button on the end of the throttle. Then he felt the pedals with the soles of his feet. These would control the yawing of the helicopter. There were also lots of dials, buttons and knobs around him. He grunted something to himself as a form of self-assurance, expressing confidence that he could remember which ones to press. He paused once again and looked out of the window to his right.

Shit! I've forgotten about the power supply, he thought and stared at a Ground Power Unit (GPU) lying idly, several metres away. He jumped out and hooked the external power supply unit up to the A/C receptacle - on the front right side of the aircraft, below the pilot's window. Baz knew he needed one of his colleagues to help him pull power from the outside of the aircraft, so he signalled Bungy to come back to the chopper to help him. He leaned out of the window and gave him some instructions about making the unit live, before disappearing back inside.

Baz pressed the starter button for engine one, making the micro switches (micros) in the correct order, prior to releasing the button with a flick of his wrist. Next, he turned the generators on and pulled power from the external power source with Bungy's help. He flicked 3 switches on the overhead console and spread the rotor blades, which spread hydraulically. Once the blades were locked in flight position, he started engine two - increasing the power and releasing the rotor brake to engage the rotor. Soon the rotor was spinning at maximum capacity, so he set the first engine to idle and confidently made the switch from accessory drive to flight drive. He made a couple of more micro switches, to switch the operation and brought engine one backup to match engine two. This allowed both engines to turn the rotor and the helicopter was ready to move out of the hanger and fly. The sound of its engines thundered loudly around the inside of the building.

Bungy ran back to the area that housed the hanger door switches and waited. He turned his attention from the side-door towards the active helicopter. He could see Baz who was busy unplugging the GPU, before winching it off the ground and loading it into the helicopter through the sliding door. Baz climbed back inside the pilot's seat and started waving at him to signal him to open the hanger doors. He raised his thumb up into the air and the whooshing helicopter slowly moved towards him.

Bungy pushed the button that engaged the automated mechanism of the hanger's doors and they slowly started to open. The noise they created, coupled with sound of the helicopter engines, thundered around them and out into the darkness outside.

Suddenly, the hanger side-door sprung open and several armed soldiers burst inside. As anticipated, the noise had alerted them. They had previously been sitting idly in the guardroom, sheltering from the inclement weather. Running into this unexpected situation, filled them with nervous panic as they darted for cover behind a pile of wooden boxes. They moved out of view of the helicopter and took some time to get organised and assess the situation.

Without warning, Beast removed the safety catch from his Uzi machinegun and fired a small burst of nine-millimetre rounds towards them. The bullets slammed into the boxes that hid the men and ricocheted off the opposite walls. Two of the soldiers reacted by jumping out from cover for a fleeting moment and returning fire.

Bungy focused on the helicopter, ensuring it was able to exit the hanger unhindered. Then he looked across the spacious building towards the fire-fight. The chopper was ready now and he didn't want to leave without Beast, who had just fired another burst of bullets towards the opposing men. Suddenly, Bungy's stomach churned with dread, when he saw Beast fall down onto his back on the gantry.

He's been hit. His mind raced. They've fucking slotted him. He poised his weapon and looked vigilantly through his sight, ready to kill. A soldier came into view. He peered from behind the wooden boxes with his loaded weapon poised to engage any target that presented itself. Bungy's finger squeezed mildly against the trigger of his M21 rifle. He wanted to kill the opposition and avenge his dead or dying friend, who lay motionless on the steel-gantry above. There was no need to be benevolent any more. He had to be sure their mission continued on its course and that the soldiers could not prevent this. His finger squeezed a little more on the trigger. Subconsciously, he could recall some words that Beast had once said to him. We're not murderers, we're ex boot necks. We kill the people we have to kill, excluding friendly forces, who serve the needs of our great nation. Beast had uttered these words to him after a late night drinking session. They were causing him to hesitate. For this reason, he consciously released the pressure on the trigger and moved his weapon sight across to the area where Beast's body lay still. Unexpectedly, he observed Beast abseiling down from the gantry. He's alive, he thought. Shit! He's alive! Bungy felt instant elation. He was also relieved that he had not pulled the trigger, which would have resulted in a cold execution. He grinned to himself, laying down a number of warning shots in the soldiers' vicinity to keep them suppressed. He saw Beast who was close-by now. He was making haste, sprinting towards the helicopter.

There was a lull for a short period, during which one of the RAF soldiers peeked around the boxes again. Bungy saw him and forced him to duck back behind cover by intentionally firing a round into the boxes. Beast eventually reached the point where Bungy was standing. A wide grin covered his face.

'I thought they had slotted you,' Bungy told him. 'I thought you were dead.'

'No. They fired towards me, but they weren't even close. Believe it or not, mate, I actually slipped backwards on the gantry and stunned myself. Come on let's get in the chopper and get the hell out of here.'

Bungy moved with urgency behind Beast, joining Baz in the awaiting helicopter outside. He turned in the doorway and fired a couple of more shots. The rounds pinged loudly, ricocheting off the wall beyond the boxes where the soldiers were hiding. They remained pinned down, staying behind cover.

Inside the chopper, Baz looked over his shoulder ensuring everyone was onboard. Then he reached down to his left to take control of the Collective-Control-Lever and then the Cyclic-Control-stick; allowing him to finally make the helicopter airborne and scarce from the scene.

Chapter Twenty

'Uh,' Spike groaned, when he regained consciousness and opened his eyes. It was still dark and he found himself lying face down on a damp and bare wooden floor. He winced as he struggled to raise his head. His hands were still tied tightly behind his back, restraining him. His hair was matted with clotted blood and his head was throbbing. His left hand was aching too. The holes created by the nails had scabbed over and thankfully, he was still able to open and close it.

The small fishing vessel rolled gently from side-to-side on the calm waters of the Irish Sea. The kurds had stolen it earlier from a peaceful fishing port at Cardigan Bay. Now it was progressively making its way through the darkness towards Dundrum Bay in Northern Ireland. Mikel was confident of controlling and navigating the fishing boat. He had ample experience, gained when he had worked on a trawler with his father. That was until another fisherman stabbed his father to death during a disagreement about fish prices. Mikel was only a young teenager at that time, but took his revenge on his father's killer, some years later.

Mikel and Lukic sat together behind the steering wheel, inside the boat's cabin. They could see that Spike had regained consciousness and was trying to move around on the deck.

'There's not too long to go now before we arrive at our destination,' Lukic whispered to Mikel.

'Yes, but there is still a long way to go to get to the hidden weapons store he told us about,' Mikel replied under his breath, referring to Spike. 'We need to keep convincing him that we're going to let him live.'

'Yes I know,' Lukic grinned. 'But only until we get our hands on all that money.'

'Water, water. Please can I have a drink of water?' Spike pleaded, looking up at the cabin window. He remained lying on his belly and was frustratingly unable to change his position. His throat was sore and he could taste dried blood on his cut lips. He didn't feel sorry for himself. He just felt alone and weak, and realistically unsure about his future.

'Please can I have a drink of water?' he repeated with despair. 'Water, please.'

'Mikel, give the man a drink of water and something to eat?' Lukic said, pointing towards their captive without looking at him.

'Please, sit up,' Mikel said softly to Spike, prodding him with his hand and pushing him over onto his back.

Spike's face twisted as he rolled onto his front. His badly bruised body ached from head to toe and mentally he was drained. He'd roughed it for years on the streets and had experienced all kinds of hardships during his military career. Yet now, for the very first time in his life he felt broken and bewildered.

'Please, sit up,' Mikel said again, pulling him up into a sitting position.

He walked around behind Spike and knelt down, untying his hands from behind his back and then retying them in front of him.

'Here drink this,' he said, passing him a bottle of spring water.

'Ouch,' Spike squinted when he pushed the plastic bottle between his swollen lips. He was parched so he gulped the water greedily, spilling it down his chin and shirt.

Lukic came out of the cabin and gently grabbed hold of his arm, easing him up onto his feet. 'Look my friend,' he grinned amiably. 'We just want the money. If you lead us to it, we will let you go. It's as simple as that. Okay?'

'Yes,' Spike croaked, fully agreeing to lead them to the weapons cache after coming to terms with conceding. He was not a serving marine now. Nor was he fighting for queen and country or beside his comrades. He desperately wanted to stay alive, so that he could see his family again. Strangely, he could clearly recall his memories of them and he missed them terribly.

Mikel looked out towards the nearing shore line, where dawn was beginning to break and the bright shore lights started to dim in the distance. The fishing boat continued to rock gently on the calm morning tide, until Mikel cut the engine to allow the vessel to float along side a wooden jetty. There were a number of rubber fenders hanging there, suspended on short ropes. They creaked as they cushioned the jetty when the boat finally came to a halt against them. Lukic jumped off and onto dry land, where he secured the boat with ropes on the mooring guides.

Mikel held onto Spike as they jumped off the boat together and Lukic reached inside his jacket for his handgun, which he pointed towards Spike's face.

'We don't want to hurt you anymore,' he said quietly. 'We just want the money. Do you understand?'

Spike remained tight-lipped. He nodded to acknowledge his understanding and to reflect his intention of fully cooperating with them. He hoped they would let him go once they had got what they wanted. Then at least he would be able to be reunited with his wife and children. They were the only thing on his mind right now.

'Come on, lets go,' Lukic said, glaring at Spike. 'And no funny business or I'll shoot you dead.'

'Okay,' Spike said softly. He knew they could ill afford to kill him yet, if that was their underlying intention. He breathed in deeply and sighed, looking down at his bound wrists.

Their footsteps made a hollow thudding sound as they made their way from the jetty. They ascended a steep winding path on a hill that led to a main road. By this time, daylight had broken and the morning mist that covered the hills, started to dissipate. The immediate proximity was quiet and appeared almost uninhabited by people.

Unintentionally, spike stumbled forwards and onto the ground. He had been too preoccupied with his bounds to concentrate on where he was going.

239

'Get up, now,' Lukic snapped, kicking him hard on his thigh.

Spike grimaced and eased himself up onto his feet. He felt wide-awake now and looked around as he continued to walk up the path. He noticed the odd remote house scattered around the countryside in the distance. Thin lines of black smoke swayed gently from side-to-side, rising from chimneys. It was a picturesque view, oozing tranquillity.

At the top of the hill, the two Kurds chose to sit for a while. The steady climb proved tiresome, to a point where they had broken into a sweat and were out of breath. Contrary to this, Spike was unflustered. However, it didn't appear obvious because of his unkempt and badly bruised condition.

'How much further is it?' Mikel panted towards Spike.

'It's a good few miles yet and it's far too great a distance to walk. We'll need to steal a van or a lorry.'

'Why do we need a van or a lorry? Why don't we steal a car? Lukic sneered, sounding perplexed. 'I can see a couple of those dotted around here.'

'A car won't be big enough to put all the money in,' Spike assured him. 'There's absolutely loads of it. You won't get very much of it inside a car.'

The Kurds grinned at each other gleefully. They were excited with the mention of the vast amount of money, but also pleased that their captive seemed to be positively assisting them. Lukic lightly patted Spike on the back, like a puppy-dog. He reached inside his backpack and pulled a chunky pork pie from it.

'Here eat this, my friend,' he smiled. 'Enjoy, you've earned it.'

He handed the pie to Spike, who gladly accepted it. He hungrily chomped away at it, satisfying his growing hunger. At the roadside, Mikel tore the lining from inside his jacket and placed it over Spike's tied hands. He fastened it loosely to hide his bounds from view of any passers-by.

They made their way along a winding road and across a series of hills, following the directions given by Spike. On the way, they passed many more houses with cars parked outside of them. Their aching feet made the sight of them frustrating. There was still no sign of a van or a lorry.

'Why don't we steal two cars?' Mikel suggested, hoping that Lukic would agree.

'No,' Lukic snapped adamantly. 'There's a lot of money at stake here. I want all of it, not some of it. We'll keep going until we find something bigger. There must be a van around here somewhere.'

In the distance, they could hear the sound of a diesel engine motoring towards them. They turned towards it, looking back down the road. A sizeable white van was approaching. Its full load of furniture was causing it to struggle to get up the steep bank. Its engine laboured excessively.

The driver was a short tubby, middle-aged man called Martin. He was familiar with the route and routinely changed down to a lower gear, making a clunking sound in the cogs of the gearbox. Soon, the van neared the three men, who were standing together at the side of the road.

'What are we going to do?' Mikel asked anxiously.

Lukic turned towards Spike. He briefly glanced at the approaching van. 'Lie down on the floor, quickly,' he urged, pointing to the ground.

'What?' Spike frowned.

'Get on the fucking floor now or I'll shoot you dead,' Lukic threatened, aiming his concealed handgun at Spike's waist.

Spike's face dropped and he feared for his life. He nervously eased himself down onto the floor, where he lay still - looking up at the sky.

Martin was closer now. He saw the men at the side of the road and instantly noticed that one of them was lying motionless on the floor. One of them raised a white handkerchief in the air and began waving if from side-to-side. Martin felt compelled to

241

help. He was generally an amiable person, who would help anybody in their time of need. He was almost opposite when he dropped the gear stick into first gear, slowing his vehicle down to a halt.

'Yes, yes,' he uttered under his breath, leaning back and pulling on the handbrake. I wonder who the poor soul is, who has been injured? he thought. I hope I can help them to get him to a hospital. 'What's the problem, gentlemen?' Martin asked, switching off the engine and leaning out of the open window. 'Do you need some help?'

'Yes help us please,' Lukic pleaded in a distressed tone. 'Our friend has been seriously injured.'

'Yes of course I'll help you,' Martin replied sincerely, pulling off his cap and throwing it down on the seat next to him. He was no stranger to helping people who'd suffered injuries in the street or more usually in and around the work place. He was even an active member of a first aid organization too, whose invaluable medical-skills had been put to use many times before.

Prior to climbing out of the van, he opened the glove compartment and grabbed his first aid kit. He pushed the door open and gave the men a reassuring look, jumping out of the vehicle and hurrying towards Spike. His protruding belly wobbled over his loose fitting jeans, forcing the buttons to strain on his brown checked shirt.

Surprisingly, Spike started to get up off the floor unaided!

'Is this meant to be some sort of practical joke?' Martin frowned, unimpressed. 'He's not a real casualty. I said he's not a real casualty,' he repeated.

'No, he's not,' Lukic grinned, exposing his concealed handgun. 'But you are!'

Without warning, he squeezed the trigger and a loud bang sounded out. The bullet smashed mercilessly into Martin's chest, forcing him to crumple backwards and down onto the ground. Blood started spurting out of a crippling wound. He tried to stop the flow by cupping it tightly with both hands.

'Why?' he croaked, looking helplessly at Lukic. He was certain it had been a grave mistake and that the stranger had shot the wrong person. 'I've done nothing wrong. I stopped to help you.'

Copious amounts of dark red blood started swirling around the back of his throat, curdling and spilling out beyond his lips. It dripped down onto his chin and his clothing. He tried to speak again, but all he could do was to choke on the increasing flow of blood.

Lukic made no attempt to explain, nor did he even care for that matter. He just coldly fired another round into Martin's chest, killing him instantly. His victim's body rocked under the force of the bullet and then stayed motionless.

Spike's stomach churned. He looked on powerless at the merciless killing, deeming it unnecessary. It's not fair, he thought. The driver was a mere a caring soul who had tried to do nothing more than help them. These ruthless bastards are going to kill me too, once they get their hands on the money. I'm certain about that now.

'Grab a hold of his feet and help Mikel to throw him into the bushes,' Lukic instructed, pointing his handgun towards Spike. 'Quickly, before somebody comes.'

They lifted Martin's bloodied corpse by its hands and feet and swung it from side-to-side, releasing it into some bushes. The body made a dull thudding sound when it landed heavily amongst the roadside foliage. The leafy branches of a bush sprung up around it and totally concealed it from view.

Inside the van, Lukic turned the ignition key and started the engine. He revved it a couple of times and turned towards Spike, who was tied to a piece of furniture. 'You keep pointing in the direction we need to travel and I'll drive. Somewhere along the way, we'll dump this cargo to free up some space for our own use.'

Chapter Twenty-One

'Do you think it's the same team of former marines who have stolen both helicopters? Brett asked Dave, during their car journey towards RAF Brize Norton.

'I don't just think it's the same team,' Dave replied, taking his eyes off the road. 'I know it's them.'

'But why would they steal two helicopters? It doesn't make sense.'

'Are you serious? You're supposed to be a detective,' Dave sniggered.

'I am serious, Dave. Look at it this way. You used to be a marine and they used to be marines. You've all got one thing in common.'

'And what would that happen to be?' Dave scoffed, half expecting a stupid unrelated answer.

'You still act and think like marines. I don't and I truthfully have no idea why they stole a second helicopter.'

Dave stopped grinning and focused on the way ahead. He wondered if Brett had some substance with his observation. Perhaps he did still have that frame of mind. Perhaps deep inside him, that green light would always flicker away in the background and part of him would always be a marine. Undoubtedly, his years in the Corps were some of the best years of his life. Now though, he was a copper. He enjoyed his work as a detective, but it did not give him the same sense of pride and belonging that he had in the military. Nothing would ever replace that.

'Dave, you've drove passed the entrance to the RAF base,' Brett frowned. 'You appeared to be locked in deep thought there, mate. Were you thinking about the whole case, trying to piece it together?'

Dave ignored the question. He slowed the car to a halt and put his hazard lights on. Maybe Brett is right, he thought. Maybe we do have the same mind-set. Then he refocused on the subject matter and turned towards his colleague.

'I think they used the Chinook to steal and hide the money and I assume they later disposed of it or hid it somewhere. They've been thorough and careful not to leave too many clues. That makes me think they've taken the money somewhere remote, possibly to some place they're all familiar with. For some reason, they now need to get to that remote location quickly. This is possibly the reason for their need for a second helicopter. This may and probably does have something to do with the two foreigners, whom we believe murdered the civilian RAF driver and the farmer. Some how, we need to find out where they have gone and pursue them. I did mention this at the initial briefing.'

Brett slouched back into his seat. The missing pieces were starting to fall into place. Of course, he couldn't logically work it out like Dave did. Maybe I was right with my earlier theory, he thought. Dave was a marine once. That's why he thinks like them and understands them. That's how we'll probably manage to track them down and catch them too.

'We're police officers, C.I.D,' Dave said to the armed main gate sentry, when he pulled into the RAF base entrance. ' We've got a meeting with your Commanding Officer. Can you let him know we're here please?'

The sentry was alert and vigilant. He scrutinized the identity cards of both the detectives. Then he looked around and beneath their vehicle, as well as inside it. When he was satisfied, he announced their presence over a radio, opened the gate and waved them on.

Dave drove slowly inside the perimeter and looked all around, observing the layout of the base.

'Did you ever come here to do parachute training?' Brett asked curiously.

'No, I was issued one of those Irish parachutes. The one's that opened on impact!' Dave responded with his usual flare of sarcasm, cutting their conversation short.

He stopped the car and climbed outside to speak to the waiting Guard Commander. Following the introductions, Brett remained silent in the background. He let Dave take the lead, taking control and collating all kinds of information from everybody who was present.

'Could you show us around the aircraft hanger?' Dave asked.

'Yes of course I can,' the Guard Commander replied. 'I've been told to assist you as much as possible with your enquiries.'

'That's good to hear. Would it also be possible to assemble all the soldiers who tried to prevent the theft of the second helicopter, please?'

'Yes, no problem. Give me a few minutes and I'll sort that out too.'

After a while and a lot of discussion about the theft and apparent calmness of the specialist group, Dave seemed to be in awe of them. Particularly with the professional way, they had implemented the operation. Briefly, he even wished he was part of their team. He thought again, about the time when Spike had courageously saved his life. He often thought about this, but this time it was because he was puzzled as to why no one had described him. Why not, he wondered. He had already passed the point of being certain that Spike had a part in this. He knew he had the skills with explosives and the ability to fly helicopters. Yet the description of the Sea King helicopter pilot was vague. It wasn't even remotely like him. Something isn't right here, he thought. I feel almost positive that I know who most of the team are, but where's Spike? No one has mentioned him. Why have they stolen a second helicopter and where are the two illegal immigrants. There must be a connection somewhere. I'm almost certain of it.

'Is there any way of tracking the Sea King helicopter?' he asked one of the people present, when they entered the Guardroom.

'Err yes,' a short, grey-haired man answered from the back of the room. 'Years ago we only used to be able to track them if

246

they flew at a given altitude, but now some of the choppers have tracking devices.'

'I like the sound of that,' Dave smiled, instantly showing a strong interest in what the man had to say. 'Please enlighten me, sir.'

'There's not a great deal to tell you really, officer. 'I've worked in air traffic control for years now. We often used to lose track of the choppers in the air. To help resolve this issue, most of them now have inbuilt tracking devices.'

'Okay, that sounds logical,' Dave nodded. 'Was anybody killed during the theft of the chopper?' he asked the Guard Commander.

'No, officer,' he answered promptly. 'These guys were very professional in an elite sort of way. I feel sure they could have slotted all of our men if they had wanted to. For some reason they didn't seem to want to kill anyone.'

'Why do you say that?' Brett questioned. His expression reflected confusion.

'Because I've seen lots of active service in my time and I know sheer professionalism when I see it. These guys weren't just good, they were exceptional. Like I said, if they had wanted to kill our guys, I feel literally dead certain they would have.'

'Yes, so do I,' Dave smirked.

'What do you mean, officer?' the Air Flight Controller asked curiously.

'Sorry guys, just a hunch,' Dave responded and purposely killed the conversation. 'Okay, Mr Air Traffic Controller, can you tell me if the Chinook has one of these devices attached to it.'

'I'm afraid that's one of the few that hasn't.'

'Well, I hope you're going to tell me that the Sea King is one of those that do have a tracking device installed?'

'Yes. Yes it has,' he confirmed.

247

'Good, please lead us into your control-room to view the tracking system. Hopefully it will give us some form of indication as to where these people are heading.'

In the control-room, Dave and Brett stood beside the Air Traffic Controller as he switched on the tracking system. Within seconds, he tapped a moving object on the radar screen.

'Yes, that's the stolen Sea King Helicopter,' he said. 'The tracking device is working fine. They're crossing the Irish Sea, bound for Northern Ireland, it would appear. We've tried making radio contact with them, but they've switched off the communications equipment.'

Yes of course,' Dave uttered under his breath. 'They must have hid the money somewhere in Northern Ireland. The territory will be familiar to them and by the looks of that flight-path; I'd take an educated guess of somewhere in South Armagh.'

'What makes you think they're going to South Armagh?' Brett asked him.

'They're former Royal Marines, aren't they? They probably served in Northern Ireland at some point in their careers. They'll know the terrain there very well. Bloody-hell,' Dave exclaimed, clapping his hands together. It's the perfect place to hide the cash from the robbery. Mind you, I still don't understand why they've stolen another chopper when they've still got the Chinook. Unless my hunch is right and they've destroyed it so that it can't be found. They evidently needed another helicopter in a hurry. Those illegal immigrants must be involved with this, somewhere along the line!'

'Are there any other helicopters here that someone could fly to allow us to pursue them?' Dave asked the commanding officer, who was now present.

'Yes we have a Lynx helicopter available. I'll gladly fly it myself if it gives us a chance of recovering the Sea King,' he said with compulsion.

Another group of men entered the room. They were dressed in smart civilian suits and had a look of high importance about them. One of them flashed an I.D. card. He was a lean looking middle-aged man with short grey hair.

'Could you tell me where I can find Detective Sergeant Watson?' he asked one of the soldiers.

'Yes sir. He's the gentleman over there in plain clothes.'

'Could you ask him if I could speak to him in private?

The two men were brought together and went into an unoccupied room, where they sat around a table. Dave had no idea who this man was or even what he wanted to talk about. Nonetheless, he felt at ease and gladly accepted the hot cup of coffee that an orderly offered to him.

'Detective Sergeant Watson, my name is Major John Drummond. I work for MI6,' the strange man politely introduced himself.

'Military Intelligence,' Dave retorted, raising his eyebrows.

'Yes,' the Major smirked.

'But what's your interest in this case? Is there something specific about one of the choppers that's been stolen or have one of these men committed some sort of military crime against the government?'

'No, nothing like that,' the Major laughed. 'We've been passed a lot of classified information on this renegade, specialist group. We probably know more about them than what you think. All of them, like your good self, are former Royal Marine Commandos. Elite soldiers. The leader of their operation is a former Physical Training Instructor called Ron Jennings. He's been working as a debt collector since he left the marines and can be a very dangerous and violent man.'

Dave listened with interest, without interrupting or asking questions to clarify anything.

'Another of the group is a guy called Barry Broadhurst,' the Major continued. 'He's a former covert operations car driver, who also trained as a helicopter pilot. He's apparently had a lot of problems adapting to civvy-street since he was demobbed and has been employed as a shift manager in a steel mill. We are fairly certain that these two served together during their military careers. Next, there's Paul Williams. He trained as a Mountain Leader and was a renowned sniper, possibly one of the very best in his field of specialization during his service. He is also a small arms weapons specialist. Apparently, he somehow ended up living rough on the streets some time after leaving the marines. Both him and the fourth member of the team, Christopher Millard, worked together as doormen in a nightclub in Liverpool.'

'Yes, I know Christopher,' Dave sighed deeply, almost wishing that the major hadn't confirmed Spike's involvement. He was an Assault Engineer, an explosives expert that is. He too was trained as a helicopter pilot during his service. He suffered a serious head injury a couple of years ago, after being involved in a road traffic accident. The unfortunate incident caused him to suffer some form of memory loss. He too ended up living rough on the streets. Maybe that's where he met up with Williams.'

'You served with him didn't you?' the Major said, sitting back in his chair. .

'Yes I did. He once saved my life during the gulf war. So what is M.I.6's interest here, Major? Is it because the money was stolen from the military or is it because they've stolen the choppers?'

Initially the major did not respond. He just sat there and patiently sipped his coffee. Dave waited eagerly for him to answer.

'Our interest in this situation, Mr. Watson, has nothing to do with either the money or the theft of the helicopters. Believe it or not, we want to tap into the specialist skills and many years of experience that these men have. We want to utilize them in the interests of the country.'

'I'm sorry Major, but you've completely lost me,' Dave shrugged his shoulders. 'I don't understand what you mean. These men are thieves who will spend a long time behind bars when we catch up with them.'

'Possibly, and then again possibly not.'

'You're talking in riddles, Major. Please can you explain yourself clearly to me?'

'Okay. I'll enlighten you by sharing some information with you, but please remember it is classified information. The government have been talking about setting up a specialist group within M.I.6 to work on counter-terrorist operations. The group will also be used in the fight against organized crime, including drug trafficking and racketeering. To set up such a group and train them from scratch would cost an absolute fortune. It would probably take four or five years to build up their experience. Since this robbery and the theft of the two helicopters, it has become apparent that the skills and experience we need already exists and have been staring us in the face for years. All we really need to do to set this up; is to tap into the former servicemen who already have the required skills and experience.'

'It sounds good, Major. I suppose their skills and experience do go to waste when they leave the military.'

'That's right and we are keenly interested in recruiting our four friends, but only if they allow us to recover the stolen money. Otherwise they will be labelled as thieves and like you said, locked up for a very long time. On the positive side of things, we don't believe they have actually killed anybody yet.'

'Why don't you just recruit some other group of former servicemen with similar skills and experience?' Dave queried.

'You're missing the point,' the Major sighed. 'These men will work covertly for us, but as far as anybody else is concerned they won't officially exist.'

'Okay. So what are we going to do to try to make this happen? What are you going to do if they don't accept your proposal? They have a lot of money in their possession. They may even get clean away with it.'

The Major's eyebrows rose. 'Forgive me if I don't answer all your questions, Detective Sergeant. Yes, there is a strong possibility that they may get away with it. That's why we need your help to help track them down. These men crave the excitement of active service. They are a perfect match for our requirements. We're even willing to bargain with them.'

Dave sat back in his chair. He breathed in deeply and looked up at the ceiling, before focusing on the Major.

'The team have the news headlines at the moment,' the Major continued. 'If we can recover the money and recruit them for

251

our new group, we'll cover the robbery up and allow them to disappear amongst our ranks.'

'Listen to me, Major,' Dave grimaced. 'Several people have been killed so far. These men might have somehow been responsible for their deaths. It is possible you know.'

The Major's face twisted with disappointment. He glared at Dave. 'We're aware of the two murders, but also certain that these men haven't actually killed anybody. There are two illegal immigrants involved in this too, Mikel Yorskov and Lukic Misky. Both are dangerous and violent men, who are wanted for drug trafficking and murder in Kurdistan, where they came from. We've acquired video footage of them, which we took from motorway cameras during the attempted robbery of the decoy van. The guards were murdered in cold blood. We also have CCTV footage of them in the White Horse public-house. They were seen talking to Frank Cotterill prior to his death. We're certain that they also killed Kenneth Ferill, because DNA tests have shown traces of Frank Cotterill's blood on his clothing. It must have been on the knife used to kill him. We've even got footage of them illegally entering the country via the channel tunnel. Two other men were killed there too, but we're unsure if they killed them, because their bodies were torn to pieces and devoured by rats. I know you have already had exposure to some of this information, but not all of it.'

'Bloody hell, Major,' Dave said aloud. 'I'm the one who is meant to be the detective here! I am aware of most of these facts, but you guys seem to have your fingers in all the pies.'

'We also have CCTV footage of the two Kurds abducting your friend, Millard.'

'They've got Spike!' Dave gasped, expressing his concern. 'Is he okay?'

'I assume Spike is Christopher Millard?'

'Yes he is,' Dave confirmed.

'We don't know for sure, but one would guess that they need to keep him alive if he's going to lead them to the money.'

'Of course, of course,' Dave repeated, waving his hands out in front. 'That's why they've stolen the Sea King. The Kurds must have kidnapped Spike and are using him to lead them to the place where the money has been hidden. It looks like both groups are heading for South Armagh to get to the money. Oh, sorry, Major, I haven't told you. That's where the stolen Sea King helicopter is heading.'

The major finished his coffee and stood up. He put his thumb up and waved to his colleagues through the adjacent office window, before turning his attention back towards Dave.

'I heard the duty officer mention the availability of a Lynx helicopter to you,' he said. 'I'm coming with you. Don't worry I know my stuff. I'm a weapons specialist.' He raised a briefcase off the floor and tapped it with his free hand, probably to let Dave know he had weapons contained inside it. 'Also; believe it or not I'm a former soldier too. I served with the Special Air Service prior to joining MI6.'

'It's a pleasure to make your acquaintance, sir,' Dave said, shaking the major's hand without reservation. 'Let's get a move on. We've got a bit of catching up to do.'

The Major grabbed his briefcase and headed for the aircraft-hanger accompanied by Dave. A pilot was patiently waiting there, ready to fly the Lynx helicopter.

Brett was told that he would have to remain behind. There was limited space available in the helicopter, due to its onboard cargo and too little time to unload it. Dave instructed him to stand down and to return to the police station until he contacted him.

Soon after, the Lynx was airborne and the pilot set a course bound for South Armagh.

Chapter Twenty-Two

'South Armagh dead ahead,' Baz announced to his two very quiet colleagues.

Nobody stirred. Instead, they remained locked in deep thought, pondering about the fate of their friend Spike. Is he okay? Have those bastards tortured him or even killed him?

'I said, South Armagh dead ahead,' Baz repeated, raising his tone. 'We're on the home stretch now and will arrive at the weapons cache location in five minutes time. Come on lads, let's get organized.'

'Yes of course,' Beast piped up, breaking the silence. 'Sorry, I was just wondering if Spike was okay.'

'Yes, me too,' Bungy added, pulling something from his pocket. 'I'll guide us in with my map of the area.'

'He won't need guiding in,' Beast beamed. 'I told you the last time we came over here. We both know this territory like the back of our hands.'

Bungy nodded to confirm his recollection as the men busied themselves with checking their weapons in preparation for what lay ahead.

Beast pulled a pair of binoculars from his bergen and raised them up to his eyes. He rubbed some moisture away from the windscreen and looked out ahead. He searched carefully on the ground below, looking for anything that moved or stood out from the natural surroundings. As expected, he saw nothing out of the ordinary.

'There's no sign of anything unusual down there,' he said. 'I can see the wooded area near the weapons cache. It looks deserted. I think we've arrived here ahead of them. They are probably travelling by sea, because these choppers don't grow on trees, do they?' he tittered.

'You're right,' Baz agreed. He reduced height and hovered over the weapons cache area, clear of the trees beneath them. 'The cache is still hidden and seems intact, as far as I can see,' he continued. 'The grass sods that cover it appear to be undisturbed. We do have a small problem though.'

'What problem?' Bungy asked.

'I can fly clear of the tree line below, but the terrain doesn't look flat enough to land the helicopter on.

'That won't pose too much of a problem,' Beast said. 'There's a forty-foot rope in a box back here. We can hook it up to the chopper. There's also some leather gloves, so I'll volunteer myself to rope down to carry out some visual checks.'

Baz gave a nod of approval. His own climbing skills were not up to scratch these years on, so he was very pleased that he did not have to do it. Even so, he knew his assignment to this task was not really an option, because he was the only person who could fly the helicopter! He remained contently seated at the controls, keeping watch.

Meanwhile, Beast hooked the rope up to a shackle near the doorway. Once it was secure, he shuffled a pair of leather gloves on and slid the side-door open. An outside downdraft blew around in their faces and the nearby treetops swayed from side-to-side. He cast the rope out and watched it drop down until it freely dangled beneath them. Next, he peered outside at the ground below, slinging his fully automatic weapon over his shoulder. He grabbed a firm hold on the rope with both hands and gripped it between his knees and feet, swinging out and beginning a nervous decent. Close behind him, Bungy poked his head out of the open door, providing cover with his rifle. Beast landed comfortably on the grass below, in a clearing away from the trees. He stood contently in the downdraft, feeling pleased with himself. It had been a long time since he had used a fast roping technique from a helicopter. It was something he had always enjoyed, even though it always gave him butterflies. He moved away from the rope, remaining vigilant and speedily cocked his weapon ready to fire. After a minute or so, he was confident that they were unopposed and proceeded to check the integrity of the grassy sods that covered the weapons cache. They were undisturbed. He pulled his binoculars from inside his jacket and scoured the area in the middle and far distance. He saw nothing but trees and fields of grass, which ran off into the distance. Their blades swayed around gently in a mild breeze. When he was satisfied, he looked up at Bungy and gave him the thumbs up to signal all was clear. Bungy waved at him and used hand signals to tell him to climb back up the rope. Beast did this by using a roping-up technique. He removed his leather gloves and stuffed then inside his jacket pocket, before slinging his weapon over his shoulder. Then he ascended the rope, gripping with his knees and feet and pulling with his arms. He was confident about his climbing ability and made the climb seem effortless. Eventually, he clambered back inside the chopper, assisted by Bungy who slid the door shut behind them.

'There's nothing moving down there,' Beast informed the men. 'They can't be here yet. Let's find somewhere to put the chopper down. We'll hide it from view and set up an O.P. (Observation Post) to lie in wait for our hostile friends.'

Baz flew the Sea King about a mile away and touched it down on a suitable familiar plateau. Once the rotor blades stopped spinning, he switched the engines off. The three men climbed out and dragged a large camouflage net over it, breaking up its outline. They collected their weapons and bergens and yomped (hiked) the short distance back towards the weapons cache. They chose not to stop when they got there. Instead, they travelled about a kilometre further, along the approach route that they expected the Kurds and Spike to use.

Once there, they occupied a rocky area, covered with dense foliage. It was on high ground, giving them excellent cover and good observation advantages. It allowed them to see clearly through and around the valleys, without any possible obstructions. Bungy vigilantly scanned the area in the far distance, whilst his two colleagues collected as much foliage as necessary to enhance the natural camouflage. When this was complete they blackened their hands, necks and faces with camouflage cream and fastened pieces of cam scarf around their weapons. They patiently laid in wait, making them selves as comfortable as possible. Several hours went by. They were beginning to wonder if anybody was actually coming at all, or whether they would use a less likely approach route. Logically, they believed this to be most obvious way to reach the weapons cache.

'Bungy, is there any sign of them yet?' Baz asked, breaking a prolonged silence.

'No, nothing is moving down there,' he replied, temporarily breaking focus from his weapon sight.

Generally, they stayed alert and continuously scanned the ground below. Their thoughts occasionally drifted, thinking about other things. That was until Bungy detracted from his weapon sight without being prompted.

'Here they come,' he said excitedly. 'I can see three of them walking into a re-entrant in the far distance. Look down there at two 0'clock, at the foot of the valley.'

Beast and Baz stared into the distance, but it was too far to see anything clearly without binoculars.

'Is it definitely them and is Spike with them?' Beast anxiously asked.

'Yes, it's them alright,' Bungy verified. 'I can clearly see their faces. Spike's face is badly cut and bruised. He looks like he's been dragged through a thorn-bush backwards. Those bastards must have tortured him, like we suspected!'

'How far away are they?' Baz wanted to know.

'They're about fifteen-hundred metres away. You'll be able to see them soon. They'll be silhouetted against the skyline when they come further up the hill.'

'How are we going to implement our attack?' Baz asked Beast, hoping they could avoid a full on fire-fight. 'Spike might get killed in an exchange of gunfire.'

'Yes, you're right. We'll need to be very careful,' Beast nodded, thinking along the same lines. 'I'm not willing to take the risk of Spike getting killed in a shoot out. Bungy can take them out, with a single shot at each of the two Kurds.'

'No, I can't,' Bungy replied. 'They're walking in single file. Spike is walking in front of them, with the guy directly behind him pointing an Uzi machine gun at his back. Which means.........' he

257

paused with raised eyebrows. 'I can't risk taking the shot. Spike might be killed before I can get the second round off.'

'Come on, Bungy,' Baz sighed deeply. 'You're one of the best snipers that's ever walked this earth. Surely you can take the guy with the Uzi out and then shoot the other one, before the first guy's corpse hits the ground?'

'That's very flattering,' Beast said. 'He probably could, but there is a big risk involved here. We need to be sure Spike isn't going to get shot when we make the hit.'

'What do you suggest then?' Baz grunted.

'I suggest we let them pass here and allow them to make their way to the weapons cache. They'll be heavily focused on getting their hands on the money, rather than pointing a gun at Spike.'

Bungy looked up from his sight and waved towards Baz, agreeing with Beast. They watched tentatively as Spike and his two captors cautiously walked passed them - about fifty metres below their position.

'How much further is it?' Lukic asked, wiping his brow. 'My feet are bloody killing me.'

Spike stopped walking and rolled his eyes. He wiped the sweat from his brow with his sleeve and turned around. 'We're about one kilometre away,' he answered. 'We'll be there in a matter of minutes. I'm going to lead you to the money, just like you want me to. However, I need to know if you are planning to kill me afterwards. I have a family back home. I have a wife and two little boys.'

The Kurds smiled at each other and looked back towards Spike. 'No, we're not planning to kill you, my friend,' Lukic lied convincingly. 'We just want the money.'

'Yes, and we'll need you to help us to carry it back to the van,' Mikel added, logically thinking about the need to make multiple journeys with bags full of money.

Shit! He is right, Lukic thought. We will simply kill him after we have finished loading the van. No problem.

They continued to walk towards the weapons cache, completely unawares that they were being watched. As they moved along the valley, the team carefully followed them. On the way, they made good use of the natural foliage, being careful not to give away their near presence.

'Is it located amongst these trees?' Lukic asked Spike, when they reached the trees opposite the weapons cache.

'Are you going to set me free once you have what you want?' Spike nervously repeated his earlier question.

Yes of course we will,' Lukic assured him again. 'We've already told you that.'

Spike got the answer he was hoping for, but deep down he knew they would still probably kill him anyway. His usefulness would expire once all the money had been loaded into the van. Briefly, he stopped walking. Maybe I could make a break for it, he thought. Maybe I could get them to open the weapon's cache door. It's booby-trapped and the explosion would kill both of them. They might ask me to open it! His mind raced with uncertainty.

'So, where is it?' Mikel asked, disturbing Spike's thoughts.

'You're standing on it,' he replied submissively. 'You need to clear the clumps of grass sods away. The door leading to the money is concealed below it.'

Lukic and Mikel both smirked excitedly at each other. Lukic pulled a knife out of one of his pockets and used it to cut Spike's hands free. Without a second thought, Spike bolted and ran deep inside the adjacent tree line. He sprinted hard and fast, zigzagging and making himself a difficult target to hit with machine gun fire. The two disgruntled Kurds had not anticipated this break for freedom. They both cocked their weapons and moved with haste into the trees together, in pursuit of their fleeing captive. They didn't care about trying to uncover the weapons-cache door. They wanted him to do that; just in case it had been rigged with explosives!

Spike kept running through the dense woods. The going was tough, but mainly because of the excruciating pain radiating from his injuries. He felt certain they were chasing him and closing fast. He was sweating profusely and panting heavily when he reached the other side of the woods. He looked out onto a long green valley that ran off into the distance. The grass there was short and offered little cover from view. If he ran out, they would surely spot him and would shoot him dead. He was certain of that. As he stood contemplating his next move, a man stepped out from behind a tree trunk and pointed a rifle at him. Spike's heart sunk and a fearful shiver ran down his spine. He had moments to live. There was nowhere to run to escape. This is the end for me, he thought.

The rifleman was dressed in disruptive pattern material (DPM) and wore camouflage cream that broke up the outline of his face. Spike sighed, mentally preparing himself for the impending bullet, which would smash mercilessly into his body at any second. Contrary to this, the rifleman smiled and Spike could see the whites of his teeth.

'Bloody hell, Spike,' he exclaimed in a calm voice, lowering his weapon. 'You look like you've just seen a ghost!'

'Bungy!' Spike gasped with relief, recognising his friend's voice. 'How did you get here? Are the rest of the team with you? Wait, no don't answer. I'm being pursued by the two Kurds who kidnapped me and they're armed. They're after the money.'

'Yes, we know,' Bungy nodded, more concerned that his friend was still alive. You look like shit. Did they torture you?'

'Yes they did,' Spike told him. 'But more importantly I can remember my wife and children now, Bungy. I want to go home to be with them.'

Bungy smiled warmly; a moment before a hail of bullets smashed deep into Spike's body, ripping through his vital organs. The burst of rounds were fired from Lukic's Uzi machine gun. He was standing poised, ready to fire another burst from twenty metres away. The force of the rounds made Spike helplessly stumble backwards and he slumped down onto the floor. He was dead before he hit the ground.

Lukic heard a click at the end of the burst. The contents of his loaded magazine were spent. Instantly, he tore the empty magazine away and motioned to change it, quickly snapping another in its place. He turned the muzzle towards Bungy, who was already diving behind some trees. Bullets bounced around him, but were absorbed by a tree-trunk. Bungy's stomach was turning. It wasn't out of fear. He was grief stricken after watching his close friend dyeing so mercilessly in front of him.

Suddenly, Bungy saw somebody else racing towards him from another direction. It was Mikel. He was closing fast and was just a short distance away. He held a handgun out in front of him. Brushwood cracked distinctively under his feet as he drew closer. He pointed his weapon towards Bungy and squeezed on the trigger a couple of times. The successive rounds only just missed their target. Bungy was already in motion, diving into a forward roll towards this second attacker. The momentum allowed him to roll up onto his feet. Without hesitation, he fired his weapon. THWACK, THWACK. Two rapid shots rang out in succession and simultaneously smashed into the front of Mikel's skull. Their entry and exit wounds blew it apart. Blood and pieces of smashed fragments of bone scattered around in the air. The pursuing Kurd died instantly and his corpse hit the ground with a loud thud.

Lukic still did not have visibility of Bungy, but had helplessly witnessed his friend being shot dead by him. Mikel's merciless death incensed him with anger. He moved intently, looking to take instant revenge and end this situation quickly. He detected movement in another direction about thirty metres away. He rushed behind cover. He wanted to make sure Bungy couldn't shoot him and also that nobody else could either.

Beast and Baz had clear visibility of Lukic and began launching an attack on him. In turn, they began to fire and manoeuvre, moving forward one at a time in a zigzag motion, making themselves difficult targets for opposing fire.

'Move,' Baz yelled. He fired a couple of shots at the tree trunk that Lukic was now cowering behind, whilst Beast sprung up from the ground and zigzagged forward. He dived onto the ground, firing several shots and crawling to a flank.

'Move,' he screamed, signalling Baz to start his advance towards the target.

Lukic tried unsuccessfully to peer around the tree trunk to return fire. He was kept firmly pinned down.

Beast's weapon clicked when he squeezed the trigger. His magazine was spent! 'No ammo,' he bellowed towards Baz, frantically running his hand over his empty pockets. He speedily pulled a bayonet from a pouch attached to his belt and fixed it on to the front of his rifle.

Lukic had heard the click too. He broke from cover, firing a small burst of rounds towards his pursuers who were continuing towards him. He was aware that his own magazine was low or empty; so he ducked back behind the tree trunk to change it. Within seconds, his empty magazine was on the floor and he clicked the fresh one into place. He cocked the weapon and prepared himself to break from cover again, intending to fire another burst. Just then, he heard a fearsome, almighty scream. It was coming from Beast, who was running hard and fast towards him with his bayonet poised to strike. Lukic raised his weapon and squeezed on the trigger.

BANG, went Bungy's rifle as it propelled a bullet that smashed into Lukic's shoulder. The wounded Kurd dropped his machine gun and writhed in pain, only an instant before Beast thrust his bayonet into him. The jagged weapon repeatedly tore at his flesh and internal organs. Beast kept withdrawing it and mercilessly ramming it back in again.

'He's dead, Beast,' Baz shouted. 'He's fucking dead.'

Beast stopped still and panted heavily for breath. His heart was beating fast and his pulse was racing out of control. He looked at his hands; his clothes and then his rifle and saw that they were smattered in blood. He tugged on the rifle one last time and pulled the bayonet out of Lukic's lifeless body. Then he watched it flop down onto the brushwood floor, where it lay motionless.

Bungy raced over towards Spike's corpse. He was certain he was dead when he fell to the floor, but he wanted to be sure. His heart pounded heavily as he neared. He held a glimmering hope that he was wrong.

The three fatigued men stood over their colleague's body, whilst Bungy closed his eyelids. There was a deep sadness amongst them. They had lost one of their own. He was a brother in arms.

'Let's take his body back to the helicopter,' Beast said. 'We'll make sure he gets a proper burial with full military honours.'

Tears filled Bungy's eyes and dripped down his sunken cheekbones. He rubbed them away as Beast patted him on the back, trying to comfort him.

Just then, they could hear the sound of a helicopter flying nearby. They looked up and saw the Lynx helicopter approaching. It had been following the tracking device, heading towards the Sea King. That was until it changed course, circling the area after its occupants observed the fire-fight. Soon it was hovering above them, inches above the treetops. Its occupants were peering down into the small clearing, where the remaining members of the team could be seen in the open.

Chapter Twenty-Three

The side-door of the lynx helicopter slid open and Major Drummond's head peered out. He cautiously looked down towards the men on the ground, half-ready to duck back inside in the event that somebody fired a shot at him.

The group acted on impulse and immediately dived into cover, amongst the trees and bushes that swayed around wildly in the down draft. Both Bungy and Baz cocked their weapons and focused through their sights in readiness to fend off an attack from above.

Previously, Beast had only been armed with an empty rifle. He remedied this by ditching it and grabbing Lukic's Uzi before taking cover. Once he was hidden, he unclipped the weapon's magazine and checked that there were still plenty of rounds inside. It was full, so he carried out a further check to ensure that there were no rounds in the chamber. It was empty, so he cocked it and flicked off the safety catch.

Up above, the Major held a tannoy speaker up against his lips and spoke into it.

'Gentlemen our intentions here are peaceful. I say again, our intentions here are peaceful. Please do not open fire. Please do not open fire,' he repeated nervously, hoping nobody would deem him hostile. He scoured the ground below, wanting to see who had survived the fire-fight. Nothing stirred, which puzzled him. He was certain he had seen at least two men standing there, prior to reaching for the tannoy. He could see two blood stained bodies, which were laying face up and close to each other. Their presence gave him the impression that the hostilities had been fully concluded. Yet the lack of movement and continuing silence below, still made him feel vulnerable. Maybe the Kurds are waiting down there, he thought. Are those dead bodies two of our former marines or are they the Kurds? His vulnerability gripped him with anxiety and he strongly wanted to signal the pilot to fly away. Nevertheless, his gut feeling persuaded him to try again.

'Please signal me if you are willing to talk to me. I am unarmed and will come down alone.'

Again, nothing stirred apart from the blown greenery below and the sound of the helicopter blades rotating. The Major had one last look before turning away, fully intending to signal the helicopter pilot to leave and continue to fly towards the Sea King. At that point, he saw something move as one lone man stepped out into the clearing. It was Beast.

The team knew they could easily bring the helicopter down if they wanted to. It was a close and easy target. They were overly curious as to why someone wanted to talk with them. Maybe it was the police wanting to plea bargain for the stolen money or even the RAF wanting their helicopters back. There was only one way to find out, so Beast decided to give the stranger in the helicopter an opportunity to say his piece. He waved at the Major, keeping his rifle held down by his side. Close-by, his two colleagues kept their weapons poised in readiness.

The Major eagerly looked on, waiting briefly to see if anybody else joined him, but nobody did.

'Are you willing to talk to me?' he asked again through the tannoy. He observed Beast beckoning him to come and join him on the ground.

The Major passed the tannoy back inside the chopper to Dave, before throwing a climbing rope down from the helicopter. The bottom of it landed on the ground, with the top still attached to a metal frame inside the aircraft. He stepped into some straps, which he secured around his waist and attached a caribina to the dangling rope. Steadily, he began abseiling down to the ground. Once there, he established a firm footing and pulled the remainder of the rope free from the caribina, leaving it dangling loosely.

'What about your back-up?' Beast asked, glancing up at Dave, who was covering the Major with his weapon.

'What about him?' the Major grinned confidently. 'He won't shoot you unless you shoot me. Where are your colleagues?'

'They're close-by, but don't worry. They won't shoot unless your back-up guy shoots first. Your attire looks a little unsuitable for this terrain!' Beast smirked, referring to the Major's three-piece suit.

'They are my work clothes,' the Major smiled and looked around the clearing. His grin slowly faded when he noticed that there were actually three dead bodies on the floor nearby. He detracted his attention from Beast and walked over to them, viewing their fatal wounds. He scrutinised their lifeless faces and recognized Spike from a photograph, previously viewed back at his headquarters.

'This is one of your guys isn't it?' he said, sounding disappointed.

'Unfortunately yes,' Beast sorrowfully replied. 'He was a first class marine, whom we all respected. He was one of the best.'

'Yes I'm sure he was. I'm sorry that it ended this way for him. I'm aware of his skills and experience and even his courage during his military service. Do you want us to take his body back to the UK mainland so that he gets a proper burial? It will be with full military honours, of course.'

'No thank you. We'll deal with that.' Beast pointed to the other two corpses. 'Those two weren't my men,' he told the Major. 'You can take those pieces of shit away if you want to. Personally, I'd rather they were just left here to rot like they deserve.'

'I'm not here for the dead bodies, Ron. I'm here for more than that?'

'You know my name?' Beast grinned, looking a little surprised.

'Yes I do. I know all about all of you. I'm employed by Military Intelligence. MI6 My interest here; is in you guys.'

'Your interest is in the money you mean?' Beast sighed, hinting that he knew the Major was feeding him a cock and bull story.

The Major looked down at the ground. He closed his eyes and held them shut for a short while. Then he opened them and gazed around at the bullet-ridden bodies, before looking up at the hovering helicopter. He saw Dave Watson sitting patiently in the doorway with his weapon pointing unassumingly towards them.

'Okay, we've spoken long enough,' Beast said, breaking the silence. 'If you came here to oppose us, you would have chosen a more tactical approach. 'So......' he started, hoping to get a clearer response.

'Hold on a moment,' the Major insisted, cutting Beast off in mid sentence. 'I'll be brief with you. You are all former elite soldiers with specialist skills that you've used to successfully steal two helicopters and a vast amount of money.'

'Yes and....,' Beast prompted.

'My name is Major John Drummond. I'm a former S.A.S. Trooper, now working for M.I.6. When soldiers leave the armed forces, they have specialist skills that go to waste. Invariably they are a wasted resource.'

'Just cut the shit Major and come to the point, without stating the bleeding obvious,' Beast snapped, cradling his weapon with the muzzle pointing towards the Major.

'Okay, okay. Like I said, I'll be brief,' he answered nervously. 'I've been tasked with forming a team consisting of former elite servicemen. The initial team will already have specialist military skills and years of relevant experience. These assets will prove invaluable to the missions that they will be assigned to. This elite group will be the first of several teams that may be formed into an organization. However, this depends on the initial team formation and their subsequent deployment proving successful and worthwhile. The initiative is to use them to fight against terrorism, organized crime and drug trafficking, amongst other things. It will mean that some of the best may have an opportunity to put their skills and experience to good use after they leave the armed forces.'

'You mean you want to turn them into mercenaries,' Beast grunted.

The Major grinned broadly and took a reassuring look up towards the helicopter. 'You could say that, except they'll be working covertly for our government.'

'Why us?' Beast questioned, suddenly expressing a captured enthusiasm in what the Major had to say.

'Because you've already proven your capabilities, which truly highlights the potential of the skills and experience you hold. However, because of the robbery, your military skills and ability are in full focus of the media. You're currently on the wrong side of the law. At this moment in time, everybody in the country may well know who you are!' the Major exaggerated, knowing quite well that this information hadn't been released to the press yet.

'What makes you think we don't want to just keep the money and that we won't shoot you and blow your chopper out of the sky?'

'I don't think your operation was about financial gain. That's more than obvious,' the Major retorted - staring into Beast's eyes without blinking. 'I'm assuming I'm right.'

Beast held the gaze, studying the Major carefully. 'We'll think about it,' he smirked after Bungy and Baz broke from cover with their weapons pointing up towards the helicopter.

'I understand your situation,' the Major said. He raised his hands to remind the men he was unarmed. 'Will you allow me to leave and give you some time to think about my proposition?'

Beast looked up at Dave in the helicopter doorway and then back at the Major. He had mixed feelings about the proposal. It was a great idea that would allow them to work together in a role they all enjoyed. It would undoubtedly be fraught with danger, excitement and the adventure that each of them craved. On the other hand, the major might be trying to trick him to get his hands on the stolen money. That would save him a great deal of hassle. He stared at him coldly, assessing him. Then he cleared his dry throat to give his answer.

'We'll think about it,' he repeated, remaining cautious.

'Okay, good,' the Major said, pleased with the response. 'There is a condition attached to this.'

'A condition!'

'Yes. You'll have to return the stolen money before we can make any form of agreement with you.'

'We'll let you know,' Beast said, prompting the Major to leave by intently raising his weapon a little higher.

The Major glanced down at the muzzle of the gun and then back at Beast.

'Here are my contact details,' he said, brushing his hands over his jacket pockets and eventually handing a card over to Beast. 'I'll give you one week to make a decision. After this, I'll outlaw you to the world. Okay?' he finished.

'We'll let you know,' Beast reiterated, just as Dave pulled the loosely hanging abseil rope upwards and dropped a thick heavy climbing rope down.

The Major had nothing further to say, so he turned towards the rope and used it to ascend back up into the waiting aircraft. He felt optimistic with the response and hoped he would be able to cement an agreement within the dead line.

Once inside the chopper, he looked back and waved. The pilot set a new course for mainland UK and flew off out of sight.

'What was all that bollocks about?' Baz asked, applying the safety catch and unloading his weapon. 'Is he offering us an opportunity to work together as some sort of covert operations team?'

'Yes he is,' Beast answered.

'I'll have some of that,' Bungy chirped up enthusiastically. 'It'll be like being a boot neck again.'

'That's true,' Baz concurred. 'But what about the money? Can we trust this guy, and what are we going to do with Spike's body?'

'I don't know if we can trust this guy, Beast frowned. The risks are high. More importantly, we'll need to ensure Spike gets a decent burial. We'll also need to dissect some of this cash for his widow and their two children. Are we all in favour of this?'

The men gave their approval of the benevolent suggestion. It was the logical thing to do. Following this, nobody asked questions about what they were going to do with the rest of the money. It was almost as if it was immaterial to them. They reorganised themselves and worked together, carrying Spike's body back to the location where they had hid their helicopter. This proved to be a very challenging and cumbersome task. Initially they tried carrying the corpse between two of them, but struggled after covering a short distance. Then they agreed on taking turns to carry it using a fireman's carry technique. The idea proved fruitful, as the going became much easier from then on.

Once onboard the Sea King, Baz pulled a Tesla GPU Portable Unit (Dry Cell Battery) from inside and hooked it up to the nozzle on the outside of the aircraft. They needed this external power source so that they could restart the engines. Bungy assisted him with setting it up and with the powering up process. Before long, they met with success, were airborne and bound for Plymouth.

The journey back was uneventful. The men sat subdued in total silence, reflecting on the loss of their dead colleague.

Chapter Twenty-Four

Baz eventually landed the helicopter on a remote part of Dartmoor, a few miles south of Ryders Hill and not too far from their intended destination of Plymouth. They were familiar with this location and had purposely chosen it because they knew that the terrain's natural features would help to conceal the aircraft from view. In addition to this, they used sizeable camouflage nets, which they drew over it to break up its outline.

Spike's body was placed inside a body bag, found during a search of a wooden crate within the helicopter. The men felt more at ease after this, as it meant that they did not have to continually look at their dead colleague's corpse.

Baz busied himself unhooking a stretcher from one of the chopper's sidewalls to help them to carry it.

Outside, it was starting to get dark and a shower of rain came pouring down around them. Beast summed up the situation and sensibly made a decision to spend the night inside the helicopter, with a plan to head for Plymouth first thing the following morning. This would be weather permitting, because they knew the Dartmoor elements could often be treacherous and unpredictable.

Inside the Sea King, the men rummaged through the contents of a number of fixed steel storage-boxes. Their search proved rewarding when they managed to find an adequate supply of sleeping bags, ration packs and even a small gas cooker. They took full advantage of this, flashing up the gas cooker and brewing a hot drink in a large metal mug. Once it was ready, they passed it around whilst one of them cooked some food with the ration packs. There was no fear of burning their lips on the mug as it had a strip of thick masking tape over the end that they drank from.

'We're a bunch of lucky bastards,' Bungy said contently, looking out of one of the side-windows at the fog and driving rain. 'We've got shelter, food, drinks and sleeping bags.'

'Yes and its all down to the courtesy of the RAF,' Baz laughed aloud. 'It's a pity Spike wasn't still alive to share it with us.'

'Yes and may god rest his soul,' Beast added, briefly glancing at the zipped up body-bag. 'He'll have crossed over to the Royal Marine Corps in heaven now.'

'Why aren't we going to destroy the Sea King after we leave here?' Bungy asked, purposely changing the subject from the death of his valued friend.

'I thought about it,' Beast answered. 'But somehow it now seems more appropriate to keep it for future use.'

'Yes, you're right,' Baz concurred. 'It's just as well isn't it, because we could have been outside in the elements now, piss wet through, pissed off and bloody starving.'

'That's true,' Beast grinned. 'We've all been there many times.'

Soon afterwards, the conversation ceased between them and the men bedded down for the night. They chose not to post any sentries to keep watch, because they were confident that nobody would be scouring Dartmoor for them. At least, not in the current weather conditions!

The next morning, the team awoke early, soon after daylight had broken. The previous night's inclement weather had ceased and the sun came shining through gaps in the clouded sky. Initially, they spent a little time washing and eating breakfast, prior to getting organized and plotting a route across the moors. Beast led the way through the long steep valleys, following his compass bearing and occasionally reading his waterproofed map. Baz and Bungy worked together carrying the stretcher that supported Spike's body. The going was rough and tiresome for them, especially on the steep hills.

'Oh shit,' Beast sighed disappointingly. 'It looks like we're heading into a thick fog bank.'

The oncoming dense fog engulfed them in minutes and dramatically reduced their visibility. The men grouped more closely together and Beast checked his compass, ensuring they did not deviate from the plotted bearing. They kept walking for a while, but the fog became so thick that they were unsure what they were walking into or even if they were going up or down hill.

Beast stopped briefly, scrutinizing his map and holding it close to his face. He gazed at his compass and then back at the map again.

'Isn't that a bit pointless?' Baz frowned. 'Why are you looking at the map? We can't see a thing. It's like pea soup out here.'

'Yes I know,' Beast acknowledged. 'As silly as it sounds, I am trying to put map to ground in the fog to work out exactly where we are.'

'That's not possible in this weather,' Baz said.

'Normally I would agree with you, but I can hear a double trickle of running water close-by. I think it may be a fork in a stream that I've located on the map. If I'm right, I'll know exactly where we are. And if my memory serves me right, I believe there's a small wooden-hut on the other side of the stream. Civvy walkers generally used it. If it's still there, that is!'

The men stayed close together and walked towards the sound of the running water. Eventually, they came across a shallow stream junction that ran off in two directions.

'This is it,' Beast grinned as he stepped over the flowing water, feeling pleased with his navigation ability. 'The hut should be somewhere in front of us.'

Baz and Bungy held tightly onto the stretcher and walked close behind Beast, trying not to lose sight of him. Minutes later, they entered what appeared to be a poorly maintained wooden-hut that had evidently seen better days. It was dark inside so Beast shone a beam from a small pocket torch, allowing them to look around. The roof was in a poor state of repair and pools of water from the previous night's rain had formed on the muddy floor. There was a bench at the far end, which thankfully was dry and roomy enough for the three of them to sit on for a while. Beneath it and by pure chance, Beast found a wooden box containing two candles. He lit one with a waterproof match, pulled from a small survival tin that he kept inside the lining of his coat.

'Let's rest here and wait for a while,' he said. 'Hopefully the fog will clear soon and we can complete the rest of our journey.'

'Is there much further to go?' Bungy sighed, after they placed the stretcher down on a dry patch on the floor. 'My arms are bloody killing me.'

'No. There's only a couple of kilometres,' Beast said. 'I'll take a turn with the stretcher to give you a break. No problem. You can take a turn with navigating.'

About one hour or so later, the fog started to clear and daylight shone through the dispersing clouds. The men had waited patiently for this and didn't hang around once the opportunity to press on had presented itself. They moved with haste across the moors, until they reached a small place called Prince Town on the outskirts of Plymouth. This was close to the notorious Dartmoor Prison and not too far from some military shooting ranges that all the men had used at some point during their previous careers.

Once there, Bungy stayed under cover amongst some trees, along with Spike's corpse. The other two men searched for a van or a lorry to steal to transport Spike's body to a funeral parlour, which Beast had arranged via his mobile telephone. Their luck was in, as their search almost immediately met with success.

'This will do nicely,' Beast said; pointing at an aged, shabby looking transit-van and looking around to make sure that nobody was watching them.

'It's a bloody banger, mate,' Baz moaned. 'Can't we try and find something a bit more up market?'

'Do you know what your problem is, Baz?' Beast asked. 'You're too fussy. Look at it this way, whoever owns it will probably be ecstatic that someone has stolen it. They will be able to claim on the insurance money. Also, the police won't be too keen to waste resources searching for it.'

'Okay. I see your point,' Baz conceded. 'It's just like having sex with an ugly woman. Any port in a storm, I guess!'

Beast pulled some skeleton keys from his pocket and opened the doors without resistance. Both of them jumped inside, whilst he hotwired it. The engine burst into life, allowing them to drive back to where Bungy was waiting. The three of them loaded Spike's corpse into the rear of the van and secured it, before starting their journey towards Plymouth. They drove for sixteen miles or so, travelling along a minor road and then joining the A386 heading straight for the funeral parlour. It was located close to the city centre. A former Royal Navy officer, who knew Beast during his military service days, ran this business. He greeted the men on arrival and allowed them entry into a courtyard, through heavy wrought iron gates at the rear of the premises. The receptive Undertaker was a tall middle-aged man. His short-cropped black hair was neatly combed and shaved around the back and sides.

'Good to see you again, Ron,' he gestured, shaking Beast's hand. 'It's been a long time.'

'Yes I know it has,' Beast replied. 'It's a pity about the circumstances. Our friend's body is wrapped inside a bag in the van. We need to arrange a funeral for him, without any fuss.'

'Yes no fuss. That won't be a problem. I told you that on the telephone.'

'Yes I know. I just wanted to be sure. I also need you to dump this van. We had to hotwire it to get here.'

'Okay. Do you need anything else?'

'Yes, I need to hire a car. Can you arrange that too?'

'Of course I can,' he smirked. 'I'll arrange this quickly for you. Do you have any preference on model?'

'No. Please get me something ordinary that won't attract any attention.'

Baz and Bungy opened the van doors and the Undertaker assisted them. They unloaded the corpse and placed it straight into a waiting coffin, which they carried indoors.

Beast went into an adjacent room with the Undertaker, wanting to talk in detail about their requirements over a cup of coffee.

'I want Spike to have a decent burial with all the trimmings,' he said and sipped his drink. 'Can you also arrange for the provision of a Royal Marines' Bugler? You can hire one from the Royal Marines' Band Service.'

'I can provide anything you want, as long as I get paid for it,' the Undertaker told him.

'Good, money is not a problem. However, please remember that you and I have been good friends for a long time. So I will be expecting a respectable discount.'

'Yes as always,' he laughed. 'Seems it's you, I'll knock a few quid off.'

Beast nodded and shook his hand again. He reached into his pocket and passed him a bundle of fifty-pound notes, which he counted.

'Yes that will cover it. No problem,' the Undertaker said. 'I'll set it all up for you.'

Beast left the room and used the parlours' washing facilities along with the other two men. They cleaned up, put on fresh clothes, ate some food and organized them selves once again. Afterwards, they climbed into a hire car and headed off to Lindsay's house to share the sad news with her.

'This isn't going to be easy,' Bungy frowned, when they reached her house. 'She isn't going to take this lightly.'

'Yes I know,' Baz sighed. 'We'll just have to try our best to explain this without making a mess of things. What are you going to tell her?' he asked Beast.

'I don't know,' he shrugged, knocking on the door to her home. 'We'll have to see what comes out when I see her face to face.'

The door eased open and Lindsay peered out at her unexpected and vaguely familiar visitors. Initially, she thought they were more police officers looking for her husband, but the sullen appearance about them, made her feel that they weren't. Somehow, she sensed that they were still connected with Christopher.

'Yes,' she said, waiting for some sort of explanation for the unannounced visit. 'It's my husband you're looking for, isn't it?'

'Can we come in please?' Beast asked, not answering her question.

'Is it my husband you're looking for?'

'Can we come in and discuss it with you please?' he asked politely, indicating with open palms that his intentions were honourable.

'Yes,' she frowned and pushed the door open wider, allowing the men to enter. 'You're not Police-Officers are you? Wait a minute; I recognize you now. You are the men who were with Christopher when I found him in that pub near Union-Street, aren't you?

'Yes we are,' Beast affirmed, disappointed that he wasn't more reluctant about acknowledging her positive identification of them. 'Do you mind if we sit down, please?'

Lindsay shook her head and casually walked over to the window. She pulled the net-curtain back and looked out at her two young children, who were playing merrily in the garden. Then she turned and sat down. She did not know why, but for some unknown reason she felt a deep dread in her stomach.

'I know it isn't good news,' she said. 'I can tell.'

There was an instant silence between them, during which time they exchanged dull glances of uncertainty. Beast looked unsure of how he was going to break the bad news to her. It just wouldn't sound right if he told her that Spike had been killed by a foreign gunman, who was trying to locate the money her husband had helped to steal from a security van.

He swallowed to clear his throat. 'I'm afraid we have some tragic news for you, Mrs Millard. We're all part of a specialist operations group that work on covert operations on behalf of the government,' he lied sympathetically. 'Our work is extremely important and highly confidential. We fight against terrorism, drugs and organized crime, endeavouring to try to make this world a much safer place.'

Baz and Bungy sat listening in amazement. Their eyebrows had risen upwards and their jaws dropped open slightly. They were evidently gob smacked with Beast's comments, but also impressed with the constructive explanation that he gave to Lindsay.

Beast continued earnestly. 'Unfortunately during our last operation, Christopher was caught in a fire-fight with some dangerous terrorists who shot and killed him. I am sorry to be the one to break this sad news to you, Mrs. Millard.'

Lindsay's heart wrenched as she came over grief stricken for her husband. The news she had heard had always been her worst fears, especially when Spike had served in the marines. Even now, these years on with the current set of circumstances, she still knew it was an ongoing possibility. She cupped her hands over her face and sobbed heavily. Nobody uttered a word whilst she cried. Instead, they waited for her to say something to them. After several tearful minutes, she took a deep breath and slid her hands down her face, brushing away the tears. She looked towards each of the men in turn and lastly at Beast.

'I'll put the kettle on and make you lot a cup of tea,' she sniffled, getting up from her chair and going into the kitchen.

The men sat in silence whilst Lindsay poured the tea. She passed them a cup each and offered a plate full of biscuits to share. Then she sat down, appearing to be calm again and more subdued.

'The police came here a short while ago,' she told them. 'They had strong suspicions that Christopher may have been involved in some sort of robbery.' She turned her head towards Beast and waited for an answer.

'No, Mrs Millard. It wasn't a robbery he'd been involved in,' he tactfully fibbed again. 'It was one of our covert operations. The police are rarely informed about them. It's imperative that we operate this way.'

Lindsay listened carefully to what Beast had to say and gave him a look of acceptance. 'I can bring myself to live with Christopher's death you know,' she said, accepting her husband's fate. 'I actually lost my husband a couple of years ago after he got involved in that terrible car crash. He went missing for a long time after that and was never really the same person after I found him again.'

'Please don't take this the wrong way, Mrs Millard. Would you mind if we gave you some financial compensation?' Beast asked, hoping he was not being too blunt and that she would interpret the offer in the context that he meant. We know it won't replace your husband, Mrs Millard, but it will hopefully help you to manage better and to cope with your loss.'

'Yes of course. Any help will be greatly appreciated,' she sniffed, facing up to reality. Intermittent tears began dripping down her flushed cheeks.

Beast reached inside his jacket and pulled a bulky, brown-paper package out of it. He placed it on the table in front of her and opened it to reveal several thick bundles of fifty-pound notes.

'There's fifty-thousand pounds there,' he said softly. 'Thank you for accepting it. It's what Christopher would have wanted.'

Lindsay looked at the sum of money for a fleeting second only. She did not seem the least bit interested in it. The disappearance of her husband, his memory loss and now the news of his premature death, had taken their toll on her. Inside, she felt torn apart and her pounding heart was truly broken. Even so, she was able to draw strength from being married to a soldier for many years. The continuous high-risk and possibility of death or serious injury always remained in the back of her mind.

'Can I see Christopher's body, please?' she requested.

'Yes, we can arrange that,' Beast said warmly. 'He's lying in rest at a funeral-parlour near the city centre. We're hoping to hold his funeral in a couple of day's time, providing that's okay with you.'

'Yes, but please can we bury him in Prince Town at the same church that we made our wedding vows together?'

'Yes that's no problem. I can arrange that too.'

Lindsay briefly thought about her wedding day. Spike was still in the marines then and was smartly dressed in his blues uniform. He looked very handsome and complimented her on how beautiful she was, lifting her veil and kissing her. Tears started streaming down her face again, whilst her visitors looked on. Beast hugged her gently to console her and sat with her for a short while, before telling her they would be leaving. She walked to the front door with them and said goodbye, closing the door behind them and locking it. She called her two children in from the garden. She thought it best to tell them the truth about the death of their father. The sadness and emotion that followed was overwhelming, but the natural mourning process needed to take its course.

Chapter Twenty-Five

The day before the funeral, Beast left the other two men at the hotel they were staying at and travelled alone to collect Lindsay from her home. He drove there in a short space of time, but as he neared her house, he found that his nerves were getting the better of him. Because of this he chose to circle the block a couple of times, hoping to calm them. He was unsure what he was going to say to Lindsay when he saw her again. He had never really had a problem with this kind of thing in the past, but this occasion was undoubtedly a difficult one. Eventually, he pulled up outside her house, sucked in a few sizeable breaths and parked the car. His seatbelt whizzed back on its mechanism as he released it and stepped outside. He looked up and down the street without really paying any attention to what was going on around him and then ambled up the garden path.

The door rattled when he knocked on it a couple of times and again when he repeated the action. He stood nervously fidgeting with his hands, waiting for an answer. Fortunately, Lindsay made things easy for him when he was greeted him with an amiable smile.

The two of them did not really exchange many words on the way to the funeral parlour. Beast couldn't think of any subject that he could talk about, apart from the weather and that just wasn't appropriate. On the other hand, Lindsay didn't want to talk. Her mind was on other, more important things. No matter how preposterous it may seem to anybody, she just wanted to be sure that Christopher really was dead. Deep inside she had a glimmering hope that mistaken identity remained a possibility. She gulped anxiously as they drove beyond the heavy wrought iron gates into the grounds of the funeral home. Beast brought the car to a halt and pulled on the handbrake, before switching the engine off. He did not look towards Lindsay, which she expected. Instead, he jumped out of the car and rushed around to the other side, opening the door for her like a chauffeur.

Lindsay paused for a short duration. She stepped outside into the deserted yard, opposite the entrance to the grim looking building. Even though she was standing next to Beast, she felt very much alone. It was almost as if she didn't have a single friend in the whole world. She stared emptily at the closed entrance door and could feel her whole body starting to tremble. Thoughts began to race around erratically in her mind. Maybe they've got it wrong, she hoped. Maybe it wasn't Christopher who had been killed. Maybe it was somebody else who looked like him. The uncontrollable trembling spread to her lips. They quivered as she tried unsuccessfully to find the words to tell Beast she was ready to go inside.

Beast stood vigilantly close-by and was keeping a watchful eye on her in case she fainted or allowed her emotions to get the better of her. He knew what she was trying to tell him and put his arm around her shoulders to give her some support. Then they walked in through the parlour entrance doorway. The inside was dark and gloomy with a number of small rooms that were accessible via a long narrow corridor. A tall middle-aged man, dressed immaculately in a black suit, came to greet them.

'Good morning, Mrs Millard. My name is Paul. I'm the Funeral Director. Please accept my sincere condolences about the sad loss of your dear husband.'

Lindsay looked at him with tearful eyes, her face taut with sorrow. She motioned to speak but couldn't find the words.

Paul was used to it. He ushered them into one of the adjacent rooms. The door creaked open to expose interior, with a limited offering of light coming from a single table-lamp. They cast their eyes on an open coffin. It was supported on trestles, situated in the centre of the carpeted floor. At this point, the funeral director stepped away into the background and respectfully went about his business. Beast held on firmly to Lindsay, who was struggling to walk towards the casket.

Lindsay's eyes focused on Christopher's dead face and her mouth dropped open. She did not want to believe it was her husband. She really wanted to be able to stand back and say, that's not Christopher. Yet sadly, she knew without any doubt that it was. She stepped closer with tears dripping down her cheeks, gently raising her arm to tell Beast to let go of her. She leaned over the coffin and paused, before gently running the back of her hand down Christopher's cold cheek. She smiled warmly. He looked like he was merely taking a nap and could possibly wake up at any moment.

'He's asleep,' she whispered to Beast. 'He's just asleep.'

Beast's heart sunk with empathy, as he walked up to Lindsay and placed his arm around her shoulders again. 'He's not going to wake up, Mrs Millard. I'm really sorry,' he said softly.

The reality of the situation struck home with an overpowering feeling of loss and emptiness in her life. Lindsay's emotions engulfed her and she broke down in his arms sobbing inconsolably.

'No, no, no,' she cried, taut with heartbreak. 'No, no.'

Beast knew better than to say anything to try to ease her sorrow at this time. He sensibly chose to let her emotions pour out without interruption.

Once she had calmed down, she stepped away from Beast. He looked to make sure she was okay and passed her a handkerchief, which she used to wipe her eyes. She breathed in a couple of deep breaths and made her way outside towards a waiting taxi that Beast had arranged to take her home. He assisted her as she climbed inside and sat down on the back seat.

'Here's my mobile number,' he said, passing her a card with his credentials on it. 'Please give me a call if you need anything this evening, including somebody to talk to. Don't hesitate to call me.'

'I'll be okay. Thank you,' she sniffed.

'Okay, but please don't hesitate if the need arises,' he insisted. 'A car will come to collect you tomorrow morning, around a quarter to ten. It will take you to the church for the funeral service. Will you need somebody to look after the children or will they be accompanying you?'

'Yes they will be coming with me. It's their father's funeral. I think the least I can do is to let them pay their last respects to him.'

He acknowledged her wishes and gently pushed the door shut, tapping on the roof a couple of times to signal the driver to pull away.

That evening the team headed into the city centre with the intention of drowning their sorrows in copious amounts of beer. Baz had suggested that they all get dressed up in Santa Claus outfits, complete with toys in a sack. It wasn't Christmas time or anywhere near it, nor was there any reason for such a party or celebratory mood. It was quite-frankly the opposite. Nonetheless, they weren't looking to mourn the death of their colleague, but more so to celebrate his life and to give his memory a good send off. This was the commando way of keeping their spirits up. They called it showing cheerfulness in the face of adversity.

'Hey babe, I'd love to empty my sack over you,' Bungy called out bluntly to an attractive woman in the pub they had just walked into.

'You're full of seasonal spirit,' she retorted in a surprisingly humoured tone. 'I'll bet your Santa sack is full of shit like you are.'

Beast laughed aloud, passing a cool pint of beer to Bungy who was already in full flow with his reply to the woman's witty response.

'So you're a betting woman are you?' he grinned broadly. 'I'll bet you wear small white ankle socks and that you have piss stains in your knickers.'

The young woman's eyebrows rose up high and her eyes opened wide, glaring at him with disgust. She believed his vulgar words to be lewd, uncouth and degrading. She had taken his initial comments in a light-hearted way and had even felt quite pleased with her fitting reply. However, this was becoming too much and had offended her. Even though normally, she was not easily offended!

'I wouldn't want anything from you for Christmas,' she sneered. 'You've got a foul mouth that needs washing out with soap and water.'

'Don't you worry, darling!' Bungy replied incisively. 'Santa Clause only comes once a year because there's a Clause in his contract.'

Her disjointed frown returned to a receptive grin, just as her friend tugged on her coat sleeve and led her out of the pub into the street.

'You're such a charmer!' Baz remarked. 'I'll bet all the women love the sweet-nothings you whisper in their ears,' he jested.

'Sounds about right,' Bungy scoffed, before drinking a mouthful of beer and gargling with it. 'Hey, Babe,' he called out to the next attractive female who caught his attention. 'Did you get what you wanted for Christmas?'

The woman winked cheerfully and looked him up and down, admiring his seasonal attire. She appeared interested in him. 'Yes I got everything I wanted for Christmas, thank you. You couldn't possibly give me anything that I didn't get off my boyfriend.'

'I think you're absolutely gorgeous,' Bungy called out, hoping to flatter her. 'I bet butter melts in your mouth.'

'It does, but only when my boyfriend spreads it on my toast. Nice try, darling,' she smirked.

Bungy didn't want to get the cold shoulder. He'd been slapped more times than he could remember by females, who didn't like his approach. Yet, he always managed to pull a women somewhere during the evening. 'I've seen this body with no clothes on and you don't know what you're missing,' he told her.

The winked again to acknowledge she liked his comments, finishing her drink and leaving through the exit-door with her friend. She waved goodbye to him as she went.

'Wait a minute,' Beast said to Bungy, who was making short work of finishing his drink to chase after the woman. 'No women tonight, mate. We've got a busy day ahead of us tomorrow. Let's just drink beer and retire early. We need to give our friend, Spike, a bloody good send-off like he deserves.'

Bungy's face scrunched up and he instantly stopped in his tracks. His mouth dropped open he let out a deep sigh. He briefly looked at the exit, before turning back towards the bar and ordering another round of drinks.

285

'Do you believe in an afterlife?' he asked Beast in a serious tone.

'Yes I do.'

'Do you really?'

'Yes I do, mate,' Beast assured him. 'I believe we are spiritual beings living in a physical world. I also believe that when you die, it's your time to leave this world. Nobody stays here forever. It's the way of the ancient Samurai Warriors and my belief too.'

'What about you?' Bungy said, glancing towards Baz. 'Do you believe in that type of stuff?'

'Me!' Baz grinned. 'I believe in this life. I'm in no rush to find out about any other. Anyway, there's plenty of ale and women in this life. It looks pretty cool to me.'

Suddenly, Bungy became over-come with emotion and burst into tears. He cupped both of his hands over his face and sobbed inconsolably. His colleagues knew what was wrong and moved in to try to comfort their grief stricken friend. The anguish of Spike's death had overpowered him.

Mutually, they believed it as being natural for them to let their feelings pour out when they mourned the death of a colleague. It was something that was ingrained into them when they had served as marines. They readily accepted death, but at the same-time, they hated it too.

'Let it come out, mate,' Baz said, pulling Bungy close and hugging him. 'Let it all come out. It's the best way.'

Bungy's emotion changed the atmosphere amongst them. They became dismal with a severely dampened appetite for enjoying themselves. Consequently, they decided to finish their drinks, hire a cab and head back to their hotel.

Chapter Twenty-Six

The following morning, the team rose early as usual and showered before eating breakfast. The mood between them was jovial, as they pressed their suits, polished their shoes and shared a few jokes together. Their banter included reminiscing about fond military memories.

'Hey, Baz,' Beast grinned, briefly stopping his shoe polishing motion. 'Do you remember the time when we tried to run off to join the French-Foreign-Legion?'

'Yes I do,' Baz chirped up. 'The Sergeant-Major got wind of it and impounded our passports.'

'Yes he did. Bloody spoilsport, wasn't he? I wonder if he would have confiscated them if we had planned to join the Salvation Army.'

'Probably not!' Beast laughed aloud. 'But then again I couldn't play a trumpet.'

'Neither could I,' Bungy scoffed. 'But I would have been fine if I was playing the triangle. Ting, ting, ting.'

The men laughed amongst themselves for a while, periodically checking the time. Eventually, there was a loud knock at the door.

'It's the funeral car,' Baz said. 'Come on lads, its time to go.'

They pulled their coats on and made their way outside, climbing into a long black limousine. The driver of the vehicle closed the door gently behind them and jumped behind the steering wheel, pulling away. After a short journey, the car arrived outside the funeral-parlour. It joined a small precession, including the hearse that carried Spike's coffin. The convoy of vehicles then drove off slowly towards the church.

'Look,' said Beast, pointing behind them with his thumb. 'I'd recognize one of those cars anywhere.'

'Yes me too,' Bungy piped up. Why do they always use grey cars for covert operations? They look blatantly obvious. If it was a mere Ford Mondeo with a couple of dents in the bodywork, we'd never have known. Who do think is in it?'

'It'll be Spot Watson and the Major,' Baz said. 'They may have come to pay their last respects. Spot was a big friend of Spike's during their time in the Corps together, wasn't he?'

'Yes that's true,' Beast agreed. He tapped his hand against the underside of his jacket, indicating that he had something concealed there. 'It's just as well I decided to bring a side-arm.'

'Yes me too,' Baz added.

'And me,' Bungy grinned. 'Wait a minute,' he frowned, unintentionally changing the subject. 'Why are we driving down Union-Street?'

'Oh, that was my idea,' Beast told him. 'Spike drank so much beer down here and pulled so many loose-women when he served, that I thought it would be a most respectful gesture to pass this way to the church.'

'Good idea,' Bungy said, highly amused with the idea. 'I bet there's a few of his former conquests lying in the graveyard too.'

'Yes,' Baz smirked. 'I'd heard he'd bedded his fair share of zombies during his time. He was never fussy. If they had a pulse, they were game!'

'Hey, I used to love drinking in The Two Trees and Noah's Ark,' Bungy said, pointing out old haunts. 'I remember seeing a marine in the Two Trees who once pinched a whole set of road works, including the traffic lights and cones.'

'He was a mate of mine,' Baz chuckled. The last time I saw him, he was dressed up as a Buddhist monk with a begging bowl. I think he was calling himself Buffalo Two Horns.'

288

'Those were great days,' Beast said. 'We had friends who were second to none and the laughs were hilarious. He reached inside his jacket and pulled a shiny metal hipflask from it. It was full of whiskey, which he selflessly shared with his two grateful friends.

Half an hour later, the hearse and accompanying cars completed their journey along the A386 and arrived at a small church in Prince Town. Once the cars came to a halt, the team stepped out and vigilantly looked all around. They were checking to see if the major had brought in reinforcements to capture them once the funeral was over. They looked through the windows of the other cars and then scanned the roof of the church, the extensive graveyard and the adjacent fields, where possible. The mass of gravestones scattered around the area could have been the perfect hiding place for snipers or undercover operatives. It was more than possible that they were lying in wait. Unfortunately, a more thorough search down to this level was unrealistic and probably impossible under the current circumstances. Nevertheless, nobody apart from the expected mourners were visible, except for the Major and Spot who were now standing conversing together outside of their car. They observed the men watching them and waved to acknowledge their presence.

The team walked with the pallbearers who made their way to the back of the hearse, where they helped them to remove the few bouquets of flowers. They slid Spike's light brown coffin out of the vehicle and Beast took charge with coordinating the lifting onto their shoulders. One of the pallbearers assisted them.

'Ready, slowly march,' he said.

Lindsey ambled behind them, entering through the church entrance. She was dressed in black with a black face-veil covering her sorrow stricken face. One of her close friends accompanied her and walked with her arm around her waist. Her two children walked beside her. They were holding hands and had their heads sorrowfully bowed down. There were also a couple of other people present, who walked with Lindsay. They were old-age pensioners, so everybody assumed they were part of the family.

The inside of the church was dull, apart from the alter which was well lit by candles. They flickered gently as people moved around inside. The parish vicar was waiting to greet them.

289

He stood tall at the end of the aisle, holding a prayer book between his hands. He assisted the men, giving guidance and helping them to place the coffin onto some supporting trestles.

The people who were present seated themselves and waited in silence, apart from the odd whisper. The vicar's footsteps echoed as he stepped out at the front, moving to start his service with a brief welcoming speech. When he had finished, he waved his hand for the congregation to stand up. 'Please could you all turn to page ninety-seven and sing a hymn called Onward Christian Soldiers.'

Not everybody was confidently vocal, but most people made an effort to sing anyway. Once the hymn had concluded, the vicar cleared his throat to address the attendees once again. Unfortunately, everything had been arranged at short notice; leaving him a little unsure of what he could possibly say about Christopher's life. He had received practically no information about him at all. Nevertheless, he was a man of experience with these situations, so he invited those present to assist him.

'Is there anybody here today, who would like to say a few words in respect of Christopher's life?' he called out sincerely, hoping someone would accept the invitation.

For a brief time, the church fell silent. The mourners were standing, holding onto their hymnbooks and looking around at each other to see who would step forward. There appeared to be a level of uncertainty amongst them, until eventually all eyes settled on Beast.

'Err, yes me,' he said, raising his hand into the air. He walked out into the isle and towards the front of the church. His footsteps echoed in the background and up into the rafters above them. Once he reached the alter he turned around to face the congregation. He fleetingly gazed at the coffin and inhaled a deep breath, preparing himself to make his unrehearsed speech. All eyes were focused on him. 'We are gathered here today to mourn the tragic passing of Christopher, or Spike as he was known to those of us who served with him in the Marines. He was a dedicated marine, a loving husband to Lindsay and a dear father of their two children.'

Lindsay sat with tears dripping down her face, trying to stay composed. She managed to raise a smile to express her pleasure with the words that Beast had used in his introduction.

'Spike had a decent upbringing,' Beast continued. 'Although I didn't grow up with him I feel I am correct in saying this. He often spoke of fond memories of his parents and his sister with whom he has now been reunited. When he turned eighteen years old, he joined the Royal Marines. It was his childhood ambition. During his military service, he had specialized as an Assault Engineer, an explosives expert that is. He also trained as a helicopter pilot and saw active service during the gulf war in Iraq. And, quite recently he had served with us as part of a covert operations team.'

Dave Watson's eyebrows rose up sharply. He looked eager, with a sudden keenness to address the congregation. This alarmed Beast, as he believed he was about to tell everybody that the covert operations statement was untrue. This would inevitably nullify the white lie that he had previously told Lindsay, about the cause of Spike's death.

'Excuse me,' Dave called out from a nearby bench, next to the Major. 'Please could I add something?'

'Yes of course, please do,' Beast said nervously.

Dave stood up, immediately becoming aware that all eyes were focusing on him. 'My name is Dave Watson. I too am a former Royal Marine Commando and a former Assault Engineer like Spike was. We served together for a number of years and were very good friends. Once during the gulf war, we were caught up in a fire-fight with the enemy. I got shot in the shoulder and fell to the ground. Spike broke from cover with total disregard for his own safety. He ran to my aid, lifting me up onto his shoulder and carrying me out of harms way. I owe him my life. He truly was a fearless, heroic marine whom I shall never ever forget.'

The Major patted Dave gently on the back, after he had finished saying his piece and sat back down. He smiled at him, showing his approval of the gratitude he had expressed for his former friend and colleague.

'Thank you,' Beast said to Dave. 'Your kind words are very much appreciated. Sadly, at this time, Christopher is leaving behind his loving wife Lindsay and their two lovely young boys, Paul and David. He was very proud of them and always talked about how much he loved them at practically every opportunity he got.'

Beast was exaggerating about this. He knew that Spike never mentioned his family to him, because he could not recall his life with them. Nor could he remember his sister or his parents for that matter. Some how, it just seemed the best thing to say.

'Please could I ask you all to put your hands together and join me in saying a prayer?' he requested.

On conclusion, Beast nodded towards the vicar, signalling that he was ready to let him take over again. The vicar stepped forward and invited everybody to make their best efforts to sing the last couple of hymns. Once they were finished, the vicar waved to Beast and to the lone pallbearer to collect the coffin. They needed to carry it outside into the graveyard. The men assembled in a group of four, lifting the casket up onto their shoulders.

'Right men, prepare to move off with your left foot first,' Beast instructed. 'By the left, slowly march.'

They marched off in step and carefully made their way down the aisle and out through the exit door.

Outside, the weather remained cool and fresh and the sky was blissfully clear of clouds. The men halted opposite the hearse and lifted the coffin back inside. The driver of the vehicle was standing by it. He closed the rear door shut and climbed back into the driver's seat. The engine started and purred quietly until he lightly pressed the accelerator, driving deeper into the extensive graveyard. He led the way to the place where they would lay Spike's body to rest. The small gathering of people gradually ambled along the path behind the hearse in separate groups. Beast and the other two men constantly looked around, checking for the presence of unwanted and uninvited guests! Eventually, after walking for a couple of hundred metres, the disjointed groups stopped close behind the stationary hearse. This was adjacent to the area where a freshly dug grave was waiting. They unloaded the coffin for the last time and placed it down onto the muddied turf, opposite the grave. There was a pair of straps underneath it, which they used to lower it down into the deep, dark hole below. It made a dull thudding sound as it completed its downward journey and made contact with the bottom. The straps were released and dropped down on top of it.

The crowd gathered around the grave and the vicar began to read a sermon from the holy-bible. Nobody spoke whilst he did this and everyone used the time for reflection.

A car pulled up and parked behind the hearse. Heads turned and everybody's eyes lit up when a tall, fit looking man stepped out. He was dressed in a military blues uniform, reflecting membership of the Royal Marines Band Service. He was holding a brass bugle in one hand and his pith helmet in the other. He placed the helmet on to his head and smartly marched to the side of the grave, where he stood to attention. Lindsey looked on with tears still streaming down her cheeks. She guessed that Beast must have organized this as he had a satisfying beam on his face. Dave and the Major looked on avidly too. They stood to attention, along with the rest of the team, when the Bandsman placed his bugle between his lips and started playing The Last Post. They all remained silent and their thoughts drifted back to the loss of their respected friend and colleague. Beast, Baz and Bungy reached inside their coats for something. The Major and Dave saw this and were a little nervous about it, believing them to be reaching for weapons. However, the men each pulled a green beret out into the open and placed it neatly on their heads. It was their military berets, complete with Royal Marines insignia. Beast pulled another green beret from his pocket and casually dropped it inside the grave on top of Spike's coffin. It was their way of showing their respect. They stood to attention and raised a salute. They held this pose until the bugler had completed the last note of the piece of music he was playing. Once he had finished, he paused momentarily and then saluted the grave himself. Then he smartly did an about turn and marched off towards his car. People looked on as he removed his helmet, climbed inside and steadily drove off out of sight. At this point, another two cars arrived and collected Lindsey, her friend and the children. The old age pensioners and the vicar climbed into another of the cars and all of the vehicles, including the hearse drove away. This left the team, the Major and Dave, who all remained behind. The two groups of men cautiously studied each other and the former marines removed their berets, stowing them away inside their pockets. Each of them took it in turn to reach down to pick up a piece of earth, which they threw down into the grave. This made a dull thudding noise as it splayed across the polished surface of the coffin. When they had finished, they looked up and stood back facing the Major and Dave.

'Do we talk now or later?' the Major asked Beast.

He ignored the question. Instead, his two colleagues and him self began scanning the vast areas of the churchyard. They half suspected that the Major might have taken advantage of the time they had spent inside the church. Placing marks men who may be lying in wait to attack them. Nevertheless, nothing threatening could be seen. The only noticeable movement came from the branches of nearby trees, swinging gently in the cool and easy breeze that blew around them.

'Gentlemen, I can assure you that there's nobody else here apart from you three and us,' the Major said. 'Are we going to put this Special Operations team together or not?'

'We can't give you all the money back,' Beast frowned and shrugged his shoulders. 'We gave Spike's widow fifty-thousand pounds to help her cope with her loss. It's the least we could do for her.'

'That's not a problem,' the Major said. 'If I was in your position I would have done the same thing. We can make allowances for that. Its small potatoes compared to the main haul.'

'We didn't pull the robbery just for the money, Major. We did if for the excitement, the rush of adrenalin and also to rekindle our comradeship. We didn't kill anyone, apart from the two foreigners who kidnapped Spike and attacked us.'

'Yes I know that,' the Major affirmed. 'Things won't be much different if you form as the team of specialists we talked about. That is, apart from the killing of the enemy of course!' he scoffed.

Beast casually slipped his hand inside his jacket without detracting his gaze from the Major. Dave and the Major became twitchy, believing he was reaching for a gun. To counteract this, both of them reached for their own handguns. Easing off them after Beast pulled out a piece of folded paper and offered it to the Major.

'These are details that explain where the money is hidden and how to recover it. They include the instructions of how to defuse the booby-trapped explosives too.'

The Major and Dave looked at each other and then back at Beast. The Major raised a smile and took the piece of paper from Beast. He shook his hand and nervously pushed the note deep inside one of his pockets without reading it.

'Are you in?' he asked.

'We'll need a replacement for Spike,' Beast answered positively. 'He was an Assault Engineer and could fly helicopters too.'

'Dave Watson was Spike's colleague during their time in the Corps,' the Major said. 'He would be the ideal choice of replacement. He can't fly helicopters but I was told he was an exceptional Assault Engineer.'

Beast turned his attention towards Dave, who was nervously smiling at him and nodding his head to confirm that he would gladly take Spike's place, if the team formed.

'Are you in?' the Major repeated.

'Yes we are,' Beast beamed, looking at his colleagues and then towards the Major.

The Major stepped back several paces and raised his right arm into the air. He appeared to be signalling somebody. Suddenly, three gunshots rang out in quick succession. The rounds ricocheted off the gravestones on either side of Beast and his team, who looked completely startled.

'Sorry gentlemen, but I'm afraid I'm going to have to take you in,' the Major frowned. 'Please don't go for your handguns or you'll be killed by our marksmen. They've only fired warning shots and have good visibility of you in this area.'

'But...., but what about the formation of the team?' Bungy asked; feeling totally deflated. 'Was it all lies?'

'I'm afraid so gentlemen. It was the best way to end this without unnecessary bloodshed. Dave and I made a personal bet that I could convince you to join us. I never ever thought I'd also get to recover the stolen money, but I guess that's an added bonus.'

'Run now,' Beast screamed towards Baz, who instantly started running in the opposite direction from where the shots came.

He zigzagged as he ran, making himself a difficult target to hit.

The rest of the men all drew their handguns and dived for cover. The Major and Dave hid behind a couple of gravestones, whilst Beast and Bungy jumped down into Spike's grave, on top of his coffin. Several loosely aimed shots were being intermittently exchanged. A series of them ricocheted off the gravestones and made loud pinging noises as they zipped inches away from their intended target.

Baz continued to run hard and fast into the far distance and remained unopposed, weaving in and out between the gravestones. The distant snipers' repeatedly tried to shoot him down, but their efforts proved futile. He reached a perimeter fence and frantically searched for a hole to climb through it. He knew climbing over it would silhouette his outline to the shooters. His search met with success and he was soon squeezing himself underneath the fence and out the other side. He kept zigzagging across the open moors, panting heavily as he went. Ryders Hill was only a mile or so away, so he kept running towards the location where they had hidden the helicopter. No further shots rang out from behind him. He was out of sight. His healthy level of physical fitness allowed him to maintain a steady pace and he made good progress. Before long, he reached the landing-zone and busied himself with removing the camouflage netting. He rolled it up and threw it into Sea King. Next, he pulled out the Ground Power Unit (GPU), struggling with it immensely until he got it down onto the ground. He dragged it towards the front of the chopper and hooked it up to the A/C receptacle. This was on the front right-hand side of the aircraft, below the pilot's window. Normally this would be a two-man operation between the pilot and one other, but unfortunately, he was on his own with this. Once the equipment had been securely hooked up, he started the GPU.

It fired up without too much hassle, so he turned all the dials on full, causing it to buzz and rattle. He then ran back to the helicopter and climbed inside. He was unsure if this was going to work, but under the circumstances, there was no other way. The pilot's seat creaked under his weight as he leaned forward and pressed the starter button for engine one. He made the micro switches (micros) in the correct order and released the button with a flick of his wrist. He turned the generators on and pulled power from the external power source. He smiled to himself with the progress he was making, there were no problems so far. He flicked three switches on the overhead console and engaged the rotor blades, which spread hydraulically. Once the blades had locked in flight position, he started engine two, increasing the power and releasing the rotor-brake to engage the rotor. Soon the rotor was spinning at maximum capacity, so he set the first engine to idle and excitedly made the switch from accessory drive to flight drive. He made a couple of more micro switches to switch the operation and brought engine one backup to match engine two. Both engines turned the rotor, making the helicopter ready to take off. Bungy left the engines ticking over. He climbed out of the aircraft and turned off the Ground Power Unit, unhooking it. It banged gently against the framework as he operated the winch to lift it up and in through the side-door. Minutes later, he was sitting in the pilot's seat and the helicopter became airborne.

Back in the graveyard, the heated stand off between the two groups of men continued. The snipers' had moved in closer to join the Major, whereas Beast and Bungy remained inside Spike's grave. The two men took it in turns, raising their head up and looking towards the area where the opposite group had taken cover. They continued to exchange the odd shot here and there, but neither side had foolishly tried to storm the other.

'Give your selves up, men,' the Major shouted. 'You've got no chance of getting away. There is no point in sacrificing your lives for nothing.'

'You've betrayed us, Major,' Beast replied despondently. 'There is no chance of us giving our selves up to you.'

'Yes I have betrayed you and I'm sorry about that. Truthfully, I was initially tasked with forming the special operations team. However, for a reason unknown to me at this time, my orders were changed a couple of days ago. I was ordered to bring you in. Give yourselves up before the rest of our men arrive, otherwise you will both be killed and that will be pointless.'

Bungy fired a shot off. It zipped passed the Major's head, clipping the outer edge of one of his ears. He ducked back behind a gravestone, cupping his ear with his hand and looking at the blood on his palm.

'Have you been hit, Major?' Dave called out, hugging a nearby gravestone. 'Are you okay?'

'Yes I'm okay. It's only a flesh wound.'

The sound of a helicopter's rotor blades filled the air, whooshing in the near distance. Baz was flying the Sea King over the perimeter fence and into the graveyard. He was purposely flying low, a mere few feet above the highest gravestones.

The Major defocused from his minor injury and grinned excitedly towards Dave. He nodded several times as the chopper neared. 'Our reinforcements are here,' he shouted above the sound of the nearing helicopter. 'Give your selves up, men. It's pointless. You can't possibly get away. It will be suicide.'

Baz slowed the helicopter until eventually it was hovering directly above Spike's grave, when he put the aircraft into autopilot mode. Bungy and Beast looked up at it, unsure if it was Major's reinforcements or against the odds, Baz. The side door slid open and Baz peered out with a rifle in his hand. He could see Dave and the Major and two marks-men, hiding behind gravestones a short distance away. They were looking up at him, but did not fire their weapons like he'd expected. Of course, he thought. They don't know whose flying the helicopter. They must think its one of their own men.

'Come out with your hands up,' the Major hollered. 'We've got you surrounded. There is no possibility of escape'

'Shit!' Bungy gasped towards Beast. 'I thought that might have been Baz up there in the chopper.'

'So did I!' Beast retorted. 'I haven't got any rounds left, mate. We've had it now.'

The Major and his group felt confident with the position of the helicopter and kept a trained eye on the grave. They grinned contently at one another, cautiously breaking from cover to approach and arrest the two helpless men.

Baz cocked his weapon and took aim, purposely winging several shots of gravestones, forcing the Major and his confused team to dive for cover. He fired several more shots keeping them pinned down. This gave him the opportunity to drop a rope ladder over the side and down into the grave. He fired one more shot and then threw a number of smoke grenades. Each of them made a loud banging noise and began to omit thick black smoke. The lack of wind allowed the smoke to smother the area and linger, providing the ideal cover for Bungy and Beast to make a break for it.

'It is Baz,' Beast said excitedly. 'Let's go.' He grabbed a hold of the rope ladder and started to climb it, followed closely by Bungy.

Baz fired a couple of more shots, aimlessly into the smoke screen and then scrambled back into the Pilots seat, taking control.

The Major and his men were flabbergasted with the unexpected turn of events, now realising that the helicopter was hostile.

'Shoot the chopper down,' the Major screamed, realising that they too were able to use the smoke screen.

Volleys of shots were fired blindly into the smoke. Two of them struck the chopper, but failed to hit anything critical. Another struck Bungy in the heel of his shoe, almost forcing him off the dangling ladder.

Beast saw him struggling to hang on and grabbed a hold of one of his wrists. 'Got you,' he called out.

Baz began to fly the helicopter away, gaining height so that the rope ladder didn't tangle on any of the gravestones.

'I'm okay,' Bungy said. 'Let's climb on board and get the hell out of here.'

Before long, they were sitting next to Baz and flying off into the distance unopposed.

The Major and his men stepped out from behind the cover of the gravestones. They looked on powerless, through the dissipating smokescreen. Dave moved with urgency and reached inside his pocket for his mobile phone. He pressed a speed dial button to dial an emergency contact number. Nothing happened!

'It's not going to work,' the Major informed him, relaxed about it. 'My phone is exactly the same. There's no mobile phone signal coverage here.'

'But we need to call HQ. That helicopter is fitted with a tracking device isn't it?' Dave reminded the Major, who smirked at him.

'It had a tracking device fitted!' he said, rolling his eyes. 'These men are sheer professionals. I'll bet my next month's salary that it's no longer in action!'

'What about the directions to the location where the money is hidden? You have got that haven't you?'

The Major pulled the folded note from his pocket and opened it. 'Bastards,' he sneered, scrunching it up and casting it away. 'Chances are; we may never find them now!'

Several miles away inside the chopper, the former marines made themselves comfortable and Baz set a course for Beast's remote farmhouse. The plan was for them to hold up there for a day or two, allowing them time to plan their imminent exit from the UK.

'It's a shame we lost all that money,' Bungy moaned, looking at Beast who was sitting in the co-pilot's seat. 'It was an awful amount of money, wasn't it?'

The seat creaked as Beast slouched back with his hands clasped behind his head. He didn't reply and appeared to be pondering and staring aimlessly out of the window.

Maybe he can't hear me over the sound of the rotor blades, Bungy thought. 'It almost feels as if Spike has died for nothing,' he blurted, raising his voice.

300

Beast still didn't acknowledge him, nor did Baz!

'Oh well, not to worry. At least his wife got something out of it. I'm pleased about that,' he finished.

'Should I tell him or do you want to do it?' Beast laughed, patting Baz on the back.

'Tell me what?' Bungy squinted, looking perplexed.

Beast grinned at him with a look of glee in his eyes. He began to laugh out loud. So much that tears ran down his face.

'What are you laughing at?' Bungy asked. 'What does he find so funny?' He turned to Baz for an answer.

'The note that Beast passed to the Major earlier didn't contain directions to the weapons' cache,' he grinned. 'It was his bloody shopping list!'

'Say that again, please,' Bungy requested, breaking into a beaming smile.

'You heard loud and clear,' Beast chortled. 'And you're absolutely right! It is an awful lot of money, isn't it?'

'Wow!' he gasped, throwing his arms around his colleagues. I guess the cool beers are on me.....................'

Lightning Source UK Ltd.
Milton Keynes UK
UKOW032201130312

188923UK00010B/64/P